The Terrible Tehran

Morteza Moshfeq Kazemi

Firouz Media
www.firouzmedia.com
contact@firouzmedia.com
IG: @firouzmedia

Author:
Morteza Moshfeq Kazemi

Cover Illustration:
Usto Mumin (Nikolaev, Alexander) 1897 - 1957
Illustration for Tehran-e Makhuf (The Terrible Tehran)
Ink on Paper, 25.5 by 16 cm

Laleh-Zar Street, Tehran

Chapter One
Chaleh Maidan Coffee House

On the Monday evening of the 17th of Sha'ban al-Mu'azzam in 1330 Lunar Hijri, a strong wind blew in Tehran, the capital of Iran. The same country that is proud of having an ancient civilization, and great and famous poets in the world. The dust that had risen from the storm made it difficult for people to cross the streets. Only a few were seen as if they had been forced out of their homes in this stormy and dusty weather, and each was heading in a different direction. Although Tehran is a big city, you can't pass by carriages and wagons except in its northern parts. And the southern part has very narrow, winding alleys which have houses belonging to the poor. In the south part of the city, there is a neighborhood called Chaleh Maidan, which is very similar to the neighborhood of the Court of Miracles in Paris a few hundred years ago. In this neighborhood of Chale Maidan, like that neighborhood in Paris, in the old days, there were some people who, due to illiteracy and ignorance, had strange customs and morals, so they would fight over insignificant matters. They would argue over a small amount of money or trivial events such as the falling of a sign or palm tree, or a group of people fighting against another group trying to kill and destroy each other, especially in the Baba Nowruz Ali alley, and the events that took place there in the past confirm my statement.

The people of this neighborhood are completely far from politics and continue their particular carefree life. They are often unaware of the important events that take place in the northern part of Tehran that the whole world becomes aware of it, such as a change of government that goes unheard and unsaid in this area of town for a long time.

Whenever a thief or a criminal escapes from Nazmieh prison, the police often search for the fugitives in this neighborhood and usually succeed in arresting them. There are many coffee houses in this neighborhood, each of which is a hangout for groups of such troublesome people.

On the day our story begins, in one of these coffee houses, a group of people was sitting and talking. They had to close the doors because of the strong wind. It was getting dark. Inside the coffee house, behind the hazy, there are small top windows, which were open while the rest of the bottom windows were covered with newspaper papers, a lot of dust had risen in the alley due to the wind. The air in the coffee house was so full of plumes of smoke that if someone not used to the kind of conditions entered, he would become disgusted and nauseous.

The crowd present in this coffee house was composed of a group of different people, and everyone with a keen social knowledge would easily grasp that the lowest class of every guild were gathered on a corner to take a sip of tea or a whiff of an opium pipe.

There was only one person alone, smoking his cigarette unhappily without talking to anyone. The young man, who appeared to be about twenty-five years old, had a wheaten-pink skin color, a Greek-shaped nose, and a very receptive eye. His lips were thin and between those two rows, his white teeth were visible, compared with his poor appearance. He wore a very tangled and mended dress, and his posture showed that the person was tight-lipped and trapped, as if he had many thoughts at the time. He occasionally raised his head and looked around and sank back into the sea of sorrow and grief.

He wanted to smoke the last cigarette he had in his faded can when a man approached. This person was the owner of the coffee house and he wore a large felt hat, and his outfit was Murad Beigi attire made from Fastoni fabric with several large patches and other color fabrics. He wore a thick apron around his waist. His big eyes, which were slightly bulging from his eye sockets, and his big nose add a strange look to his face, and as soon as he reached the young man, he put his hand on his shoulder and said

"Javad, why are you so upset today?"
The young man replied as if he had just woken up from deep thinking
"No Amoo Jan, nothing. I had some fantasies, but thank God when I saw you, I dropped those thoughts."
The old man said: "No, it is not like that, Javad. It's been a while since you've been so sad. Don't you want to tell me the truth? It is very bad that you do not tell me about the pain in your heart."
"No, Amoo Jan, there is nothing, I simply don't feel well, maybe it's just one of those days," Javad replied.
But the old man was not convinced, "what you said doesn't narrate the whole truth, do not be shy with me. At least tell me why you have not been going to work for the last few days."
Javad said sadly "Yes, Amoo Jan, I had an argument with my master a couple of days ago and quit working for him."
A waiter, Baba Hassan, who was closeby laughed when he heard this answer, then moved closer to Javad, tapping his shoulder several times and saying "no worries then! I'll quench him with a couple of teas and reconcile you too if you want!?
Javad said hurriedly "No, no, do not do any of that!"

The old man, who turned out to have made his decision, said:
"So all of your bitterness was for this?" He asked.
"Yes, Amoo Jan, you know I have to provide for my mother, sister, and two nieces with the salary of four or five Rials I earn daily, but now, I have been going home empty-handed for the last three days. The situation is very difficult for me and I tried to find another job, but I have not got any results and I do not know what will happen next."

Baba Hassan, despite his tough appearance, had a heart of gold and the story of the young man made him genuinely upset.
- "Son! Wait! Do not despair…!" and then he put a hand in his pocket and took out two pieces of white money and left it in Javad's palm and said:
"Go and get some bread for your family with this dosh. Insha'Allah (God willing), I will find a suitable job that will relieve your grief for you soon."
"Baba Jan, how can I thank you enough? You made me blush with your kindness and generosity." Javad said with teary eyes.
Baba Jan Hassan smiled: "Oh dear Boy! It is not the time for these words, God willing, I will do something for you soon." He immediately headed to the counter where the Samovar (tea brewing apparatus), teacups, and sugar cubes were placed and gave some orders to his apprentice who was pouring tea.

Javad was left alone, although he had enough money to provide bread for his family for the night, he still could not free himself from the shackles of his thoughts, and again he sank into the sea of sorrow.

It would not hurt to put the past life of this young man in perspective to understand his current situation.

***

About six years before this incident, in one of the neighborhoods of Tehran called Sangeladje, there was a dwelling that seemingly belonged to a working-class family of three men, two women, and two children. The eldest man, who was the head of the family, was about forty-five years old. He was very fit and strong. The second man was about thirty years old. And the third one was almost twenty years old. One of the women was the spouse of the head of the family and the other was a young woman in her early thirties, and the two children were both small; one was three years old and the other was still an infant. The inner state of the household, although humble, appeared to be in a cozy and neat shape. The head of the family was one of the famous artisan cobblers/shoemakers of Tehran. The 30-year-old man named Reza was his son-in-law and the children both belonged to him. The third young man was Javad, the son of Master Ali, the Brother-in-Law of Reza. This family earned a respectable living and had a relatively prosperous generating income from Master Ali's shop and Reza's daily wage, all-in-all they had a happy and prosperous life.

Yet as if God does not want a prolonged period of happiness and prosperity for anyone, the pillars of this family suddenly crumbled and soon would lay in ruins.

Typhoid fever was rampant in Tehran back at that time and had taken the lives of the unfortunate population of the destitute and lower-class in hundreds. Master Ali suddenly contracted the disease and the efforts of doctors were futile. He passed away after a week of hospitalization and left his family in great pain and agony.

Yet as if Mother Nature didn't consider this calamity sufficing the devastated family, in a few days Reza also got infected. Although it is only imaginable how the women and Javad were living those hellish days in anguish and disarray. Yet the will of God was not to ameliorate their situation by sparing the life of Reza, the poor man succumbed to the disease after ten days.

It was obvious how the grief-stricken family was failing to make ends meet. Javad's wages were not enough to support them and soon they were forced to sell or pawn some of their furniture and belongings. After two years of debt, they were forced to sell their property and went out to rent two small rooms on very small premises. Javad also quit the shoemaking business and began laboring in the construction business barely feeding his mother, sister, and the kids. Three years passed like that, and no light appeared at the end of the tunnel of misery for the family until one day Javad argued with his master over a trivial matter and in the heat of the argument got insulted by his master. The young man who has been living a comfortable life in the past could not bear this condition anymore and rushed out of his workplace vowing never to return to such a job again.

Now that the readers have realized the cause of the sorrow of the poor young man, we return to the coffee house.

Javad's perplexing train of thoughts could not leave him, nor the bitterness and sorrow that crept all over his face. Despite having little money to buy bread in his hand, he still did not intend to go home or get the bread. His eyes were circling for a while but occasionally his gaze was cast downwards. Javad felt a hand on his shoulder and saw the familiar face of a twelve-year-old boy standing next to him. He was the page of the grocery shop in the Bazaar.

The boy told him that a man was expecting him in the bazaar passage. Javad stood up and without any hesitation left the coffee house and headed for the bazaar following the boy. When he got closer, he noticed a strange young man leaning on a wall.

Chapter Two
Destitute Is The Construct Of Everything

The stranger was a young man with fair skin, brown hair and prominent large eyes, and striking eyebrows, and wore a black coat and a black hat known as a "service hat". Everyone who cared to look at his appearance realized that he was not from that neighborhood and he came for a specific purpose. His fair-skinned hands were very obvious clues for his social class and placement.

As soon as Javad cast his eyes on the individuals' eye asked

"How can I help you, sir?"

"Yes." The young man replied and implied with a hand gesture to keep quiet.

"It appears you are not willing to speak here. If so, we can head to my place, which is 200 steps away from here." Javad whispered.

"Certainly we can't talk here but I can't come to your place either." The stranger answered.

He urge Javad to follow him at some distance and after passing through a couple of very narrow and short alleys they reached a grand square. The gusty weather has calmed down and a drizzle began as the dusk was approaching and the number of passersby started to dwindle. The stranger and Javad sat on a platform in the corner of the square.

After a few moments of silence, the stranger raised his head and faced Javad, and after a profound gaze indicative of building up trust he said

"Sir, your name is Javad, is that correct?"

"Correct sir! My name is Javad." He answered immediately without hesitation.

"Could I trust you, Javad?" The stranger asked again.

Javad was startled by his type of question and defiantly replied

"That's not up to me. It depends on what it is required of me to do."

The stranger hastily answered

"No! No! I felt that I could trust you from the first moment that we met!"

And following a slight hesitation added, "if you are interested let's discuss a bit more seriously!"

"As you wish," Javad replied nonchalantly.

The stranger started to examine his surrounding to make sure that there is enough privacy then laid his hand on his forehead and started pondering his thoughts for a few moments, while Javad remained silent. Suddenly the stranger raised his head and a few droplets of sweat started to appear on his forehead

"Do you want to make the kind of money that can set you free from a miserable life?"

Javad replied with a sigh of grief

"Sir, that's my ultimate wish."

The stranger said

"I'm fully aware of your status and even your past life and I know you are living a life of misery and hardship. I was passing near the coffee house and noticed from your appearance how miserable you are and so I thought that this makes you a suitable person for the forthcoming affairs of mine. Hence coming after you to give you my proposal."

Javad immediately interrupted the stranger. "Then Sir, you might also know how fed up I'm with this miserable life and surely know that I'd do anything to save myself from this hardship."

"Yes, this clearly shows that you are willing to partake in the affairs and willing to receive the compensation that follows." The stranger said confidently.

"Yes, Sir I'm ready for any job to get out of this hardship," Javad said.

The stranger pulled out four pieces of three Toman Banknotes and put them in his hand and said. "take this amount for the time being and God willing when the time comes you will have more…But be aware that the nature of the service I want from you is nothing regular and is of an extraordinary type that requires absolute obedience without any questions asked and to be prepared to do any task in this regard."

Javad nodded and the stranger once again looked around and once assured of their privacy said "Sometimes I might be want to take an individual and hold him in a specific location and similarly, there might be an obligation to kidnap other individuals for which I'd need the help of a sturdy young man like you so I can get the job done properly." "Unfortunately, there is no time to elaborate on the subject matter more and if you are determined to keep my company we will proceed to train you in some basics so that you adjust your traits accordingly." The stranger concluded.

Javad replied with a tone indicative of all his miseries. "Sir these past times of destitution have made me so much in absolute poverty that perhaps if someone asked me to take part in ill-natured or illegal activities I would have complied. However, as far as I can read on your face and my gut feeling says taking part in your activities might even be morally right."

"You have guessed right. I don't conduct these activities with any malicious intent. I only follow my heart in conducting these activities." The stranger replied.

"Sir, you don't need to explain yourself and I have figured out that you have some sort of plight."

"Yes Javad, you got it right! And in the advent of realizing this truth are you still willing to take part and help me?" The stranger replied after a short moment of silence.

Javad replied, "I will not hesitate to make any sacrifices in advancing your cause, sir."

"In this case, get up and go tell your mother you have found a job and your master is leaving the city and wants you to accompany him and give them some money."

"Really?! We must leave?" Startled Javad said hurriedly.

The stranger replied "Yes, occasionally going on a trip might be necessary and we might even leave tomorrow but it will be short. Telling your family will make them feel at peace during your absence and to know it's a full-time job."

Javad said:

-"Alright, but I must send them a stipend monthly."

"That would be on me! Now get going for the time being and return early in the morning to my place tomorrow." He said as he leaned and whispered the address of his home to Javad's ear and Javad nodded to show he got the address.

It became dark and Javad and the stranger separated and set off heading in separate directions. The stranger took to the north and after trespassing several narrow alleys, he reached the bazaar and continued passing through a few more crosses (CharSou) took a carriage in front of a coffee shop known as Ghanbar's coffee shop, and gave his address to the hackie. The carriage passed through Nasserieh Street, LalehZar, and a few more streets, and near the Dowlat gate stood in front of an ally and the stranger got off and entered the alley and knocked on a large door painted blue. Immediately after the door opened he quickly got in and slammed the door shut.

Who was this young man?

Chapter Three
Who Is The Unknown Young Man?

Ten years before this incident, on the evening of one of the first days of spring, the weather was clear and extremely gentle, there was an interesting view in a large and charming garden located in the north of Tehran. The rivals were competing. Two children, a boy, and a girl were playing in front of the garden residential mansion and did not pay attention to anything else. The girl was very beautiful, she had golden hair, blue eyes, a narrow nose, and thin red lips, and at this time she was happy and was playing with her teammate with excessive interest. The boy was no less handsome, with curly brown hair, large eyes, and eyebrows. At the same time, two women were standing next to each other on the porch of the garden mansion, talking. One of the two women who looked older was white, she had a medium body and a sullen and grim face. Superficial glances and motionless muscles on her face showed that she was very unaware of the world and can be easily deceived by the words and flattery of others. But the second lady was taller with a tanned-face, and black eyes. Her facial expression and deep gaze presented an experienced and worldly woman.

"Honestly, ma'am, do you notice how much these two children love each other?" The second lady said suddenly.

"Yes, ma'am, your son and my daughter are very familiar with each other, and Mahin does not rest for a minute from the time Farrokh comes here until he leaves." The first lady replied with a continuous nod.

"May this love and affection become the cause of their happiness one day." Mrs. Tanned-face added.

Mrs. F..., as if she did not like her word, said with complete arrogance

"Yes, to see what God wants." She said

The second lady seemed to regret what she had said and replied in a hurry: "Madam, do not worry unnecessarily. If our situation is like this, my son will never be a nuisance to you, and we will not make the same request for you."

"No, madam, I would very much like this to be done on time, but what can I do about my husband, who you know cares a lot about some things and I am afraid he will not accompany me this time."

"Now is not the time for these words, if our situation remains the same later, we will never have these thoughts." Farrokh's mother added hopelessly.

How this sentence was uttered was real to Mrs. F... and she immediately said to appease the other party,

"As you said, the time for these talks has not come, God willing, if it's God's will, it will be done at the proper time."

"See how much these two kids are playing, I think nothing can stop them from playing." She softened the tone of her voice while pointing to the children.

The second lady, who was deep in thought and did not pay attention to what her friend had said, nodded and said slowly

"Yes, yes, it is."

***

For readers to better understand our story, it is necessary to be aware of the living conditions of these two women, and especially the degree of their relationship and acquaintance.

These women are close, Mrs. Tanned-face is the wife of Mrs. White's brother. Mrs. White's husband had gained a huge fortune, he had earned more than a twenty-thousand Tomans a year. And usually, people who are fascinated by wealth and status are willing to do anything to achieve their goal, and when they achieve their goal after enduring thousands of hardships, they completely forget their past situation.

Mr. F... Al-Saltaneh gained a lot of wealth by flattering and paying a lot of bribes in various enterprises, and also occupied an important position in one of the ministries. He was an exploiter and he humiliated his poor relatives with complete impunity and arrogance. His wife was an illiterate woman, when she was twelve years old and living in her brother's house, several women entered their house one day, and after a short stop and drank cherry juice. Three days later, their maid said to her with a meaningful smile.

"Miss, Thank God, a suitor has been found for you. You will get married soon."

Mrs. F... who at that time was called Malek Taj, did not understand much when she heard this sentence from their maid.

A few days later, the wedding party was held and without the Malek Taj knowing what it was like to get married, the word "yes" was forced on her at the wedding and they took her to the groom's house.

The Malek Taj's luck was that she was her husband's taste both physically and spiritually, and a kind of agreement was made between them on the way of life, and after a while, she gave birth to a beautiful daughter.

Of course, it is known that such a poor woman, who, due to illiteracy and ignorance, did not cross the wall of a residential house, and in this strange way, without knowing and understanding what marriage is, became the wife of Mr. F... Al-Saltaneh. Her husband did not believe in love, vivacity, and love-making. He did not believe that sometimes in the world, two beings can have special feelings for each other and have great interest in each other, and want to meet each other with great enthusiasm and desire.

The reason for this is obviously because when a person knows what another person enjoys from a blessing that he has benefited from, he also feels pain when he suffers from it, and for this reason, he is a rich and happy person who always rides in his carriage or luxury car, he can hardly feel for a poor man on foot, who has not eaten for two days and nights, wanders along the alley!

Malek Taj like her husband, had completely forgotten her brother and sister today, and she has no recollection of what a monotonous and limited life she had in her brother's house after her father's death. Now that the passage of time had prospered their situation, he left his brother and only occasionally uttered his name with complete arrogance and restraint. As it was said, she was a very suitable woman for her husband, and as they say, God had knocked on their door and boarded well. (Every Jack has his Jill)

***

That day, Mrs. Tanned-face had come to visit Malek Taj and her husband; she brought along her son.

Now that the readers have learned about the two women's relationship, it is time to see what the two children are doing.

The girl's name was Mahin and the boy was called Farrokh. Two children ran after each other, sometimes the boy ran after the girl, and sometimes the girl ran after the boy. They were so busy playing that it was as if nothing, not even lightning and calamity, could stop them from playing, and perhaps only fatigue could keep them calm, but children usually do not notice how tired they are during the game. Although these two children were playing, if someone paid attention to their movements and behavior, especially to Farrokh's face, one would see how sometimes the effects of happiness appear on his face and how he is sometimes depressed and taken, what was all this for?

If we want to say that Farrokh fell in love with Mahin at that young age, the readers may not believe and should criticize whether a boy at the age of eleven or twelve might fall in love with a girl of the same age! But yes Farrokh had a special feeling for Mahin in his heart. Farrokh was happy with Mahin's happiness and sad with her cousin's sadness. What should this state be called? What should this boundless kindness, that is far from filth, call? Could we call it anything except pure love?

Farrokh, during the game, like a butterfly around a candle, was constantly moving around Mahin, and every time the girl's turquoise eyes coincided with his brown eyes, it was as if an electric spark came out of Mahin's eyes and entered his eyes and hit deep into his heart. The poor child has been in love since he was a child, and although he did not know anything about it yet, he wanted to be with Mahin always. Mahin did not view Farrokh's behavior with coldness or apathy, but she also enjoyed meeting his uncle's son and playing with him.

Mahin was tired from running too much and went to a wooden bench that was placed next to one of the garden roads. Farrokh supported her and he slowly brought Mahin to the bench. He helped her sit slowly and she was now leaning on the back of the bench, taking a deep breath and gasping from the gentle air of the garden to rejuvenate herself.

Farrokh, who was sitting next to him, could not get enough of watching Mahin's beautiful face. Speedily, he felt a special state in himself and his heart was pounding. He instinctively leaned towards Mahin's moonlike face, and without knowing what he was doing, he kissed her on the corner of her two crimson lips.

"Oh, how I love you!" he said softly.

Chapter Four
The Ladder

Seven years have passed since this incident.

The air was extremely clear. There were not many stars in the beautiful sky of Tehran, the moon disk dominated the blue scene and did not give its small rivals a chance to show off. The heart of every despairing lover was getting darker at that time, and tears flowed from his eyes involuntarily and flowed on his cheeks. Why is he so depressed and heartbroken in this good weather? Shouldn't the poor lover who has no hope of connecting with his mistress be depressed?

He wants the world for his mistress and knows the pleasures he will get from the world being with his beloved. But the lover could not smile at the slightest smile of the mistress and could not be disappointed by her slightest depression.

The lover of misery who is far from the beloved, whether he benefits from the moonlit night or the gentle and fragrant breeze of the flowerland. On the contrary, he wants the earth and time to sympathize with him, to become dark, and cry like him.

On a late spring night like this, a young man was standing in front of a wall behind the branches of the trees showing that he belonged to a garden. He turned and listened carefully each time, and it was clear that he expected to hear a voice from inside the garden. Although it was early in the night and not more than two hours after sunset, the place was very secluded and there was no sound around it. The west end of the street was open, most of the land around the street was not yet built, and houses and gardens were far apart.

It took a quarter of an hour for the young man to hear a voice. He listened carefully to the wall, but after a few moments of despair, he returned to his original place and whispered slowly to himself:
"I do not know why she is not here yet. Mahin couldn't have forgotten her promise. Half an hour had passed, and she is not here. What should I do?"
"I can't go inside and see things for myself." He thought to himself.

Then he approached the wall again and listened. When he did not hear a sound, he said to himself impatiently, "Mahin is not coming, there must have been an accident!"

The young man's anxiety and discouragement increased moment by moment. Suddenly, he touched his heart and said:

"Oh God, why is my heart like this, why has something so disturbing happened to my dear beloved?"

At that moment, a footstep was heard in the distance, which became clearer as it moved closer, it was clear that someone was passing through the trees. The young man, who had a hard time understanding the direction of the sound, said to himself slowly.

"Oh, oh, let me see, this is the sound of footsteps," he was so sure.

"Farrokh, Farrokh, my dear, you must forgive me for keeping you waiting for you so long, wait for me to climb the ladder, and then I will tell you what happened." He heard a voice from the other side and was relieved.

Then the first two tips of the ladder sticks appeared on the wall, and then the beautiful head of the immensely beautiful girl appeared on the wall. Gradually, half of her body leaning against the wall, appeared and immediately said apologetically.

"My dear, did you think for sure that I had forgotten you or that I had forgotten the promise, you know from my heart and know well that it completely belongs to you and only your love will reign in my heart."

The moonlight, which had fallen beautifully on Mahin, had greatly enhanced the girl's image. Mahin was now eighteen years old, and it is known that girls at this age reach their peak of beauty.

His eyes were filled with love and desire.

Farrokh was now twenty years old, and if in the past he was not convinced to be with Mahin, now he was eager to be with her.

Readers may want to know what happened between the two lovers during these few years and why they arrange a date on this wall.

***

Farrokh used to come to his aunt's house most of the time after playing and running with Mahin in the garden, but because he entered high school a year or two later and his lessons and homework became more frequent, he had less time to play and have fun with his mate and his lover, but he used the opportunities as much as possible and was protected from the important encounter. Four years passed and nothing new happened except that the love and affection of the two for each other was increasing day by day and little by little their feelings took on a different form, that is, if in the past they were happy with simple kisses, but even the juicy ones did not put out the fire that was burning in their hearts.

Once, as a result of Farrokh's final exams, he could not meet Mahin for three weeks but was surprised when he came to his aunt's house at the end of the exams. Mahin refused to see him and instead, sent a greeting from their maid. Farrokh was surprised but soon came to his senses to show his indifference and answered calmly:

- Thank you very much and please give my greeting.

At the same time, he noticed his aunt's serious face, she gave him a dissatisfied look as if she is not in support of their relationship and doesn't want them together and Farrokh was forced to leave. His heart was not ready to endure such a blow. How could he continue his life without seeing Mahin? Farrokh knew his aunt was uneducated and Mahin was the one who was reading her letters, so he wrote the following letter to Mahin:

My Beloved,

I am holding the pen with the world of depression and sorrow, and I am writing these few lines. I want to see you as much as you can so that I can explain my inner feelings after this bitter and unforgettable incident, which is funny at the same time. Let's get together and find the ways and means for our future meetings.

He who worships you,
Farrokh Daqiq

Meanwhile, Farrokh prepared another piece of paper for his aunt, from another aunt who lived in Qazvin and filled it with prayers and greetings — written boldly and clearly, that he wrote the second letter to deceive Mahin's aunt.

On the same day, one of Farrokh's close friends was on his way to Anzali. Farrokh gave the letter to him to post on his way. Of course, this way was very practical, after two or three days, the postman stood at F... Al-Saltaneh's house and handed over the letter to the maid and finally, Mahin received it. After lunch, she went to her room and thought about sending a letter.

After half an hour of thinking, she thought of a way. They had a gardener, a fifty-year-old man who was very good-natured and well-mannered. But he was, unfortunately, suffering from weak eye sight that did just see a shadow of people or objects. He also had a daughter, she was sixteen and not very beautiful. She was his only child, and was very close to her dear father. This girl also got sick for a while and made her father very depressed. During that time, Mahin spent most days comforting his daughter, and occasionally giving her money or clothes. Mahin's love and kindness paid off, and both father and daughter became her true devotees and wished to serve her, but Mahin had never needed them until now.

The gardener's daughter was happy she could confide in her and promised her she will do whatever Mahin wanted. Mahin also asked told her to see her father before doing anything and to narrate the case to her father and ask the gardener to help her find a way to meet Farrokh.

Shokoofeh, the gardener's daughter went to her father and some minutes later, she returned to Mahin and informed her it was done properly. "My father had found a good way," she said as Mahin's heart began to beat as she hurriedly asked how.

Shokoofeh replied, "After thinking for a while, my father said that the best way is to put a ladder next to the western wall of the garden to the other side of the empty ground, and you can go up and meet Farrokh, who will come behind the wall, once or twice a week." Mahin liked this arrangement and without hesitation took the pen in her hand and wrote the letter to Farrokh.

Farrokh, my dear,

I received your letter. If you want to visit me, go behind the western wall of the garden for about two hours after the sunset. You will see me there and we will be able to talk it all through.

She who only loves you,
Mahin

Mahin handed the paper to Shokoofeh and asked her to let Farrokh know their meeting place. That night Farrokh came and met Mahin, thousands of secrets were exchanged between them and it was often done with a lot of fear as they were not able to meet each other with ease.

They used to do this for two years until that night.

A few minutes passed between the two lovers and the young lover, Mahin opened her mouth and said.
"Oh Farrokh, I do not know what will happen to us in the end, do you want to know why I kept you waiting for so long? Although I wanted to hide the reason from you, I see that hiding it might be more harmful to us."
"Of course, my dear, I want to know. Tell me from your sweet voice, which

is more musical and soulful to me than any other instrument." He hurriedly said eagerly anticipating an answer.

"Farrokh, I am not very happy with what I heard and I am afraid it will bother you. I see that I have no choice but to say it because our future depends on it," Mahin said with sadness.

Farrokh move swiftly to the wall and said. "Dear Mahin, you are confusing me a lot with these words. Please, my dear, tell me what happened and what has been bothering you."

"Farrokh, come a little closer so I can tell you what happened. No one must hear us." Mahin said softly.

Farrokh moved closer as he could to the wall, grabbed Mahin's hands, which she had stretched from the top of the wall, and closer to his heart as if trying to calm her nerve down.

Mahin turned her head towards Farrokh and said softly.

"About an hour ago, my father summoned me and told me things in detail which will sadden you."

"No, my dear, it is not like that, on the contrary, I would like to know about it as soon as possible," Farrokh said.

"My father said that he heard some rumors that I'm saying inappropriate things about you, and I must not talk about my cousin, the way I compliment you."

Farrokh, who was very curious, asked.

"How did your father find out about these? Maybe he also knows about our meetings, so what was your response?"

Mahin wanted to answer Farrokh, who had turned his face towards the garden as she suddenly said softly, "Do you hear Farrokh?" She asked. It was as if someone was coming in their direction. "no, no, what would I do if they find us here?" He said as they move to the middle of the garden, and as soon as they reach the wall fifty steps from the part of the garden which was known to be used for sitting in the evening and moonlit nights, with wooden benches and tables placed there, with colorful and fragrant flowers. They sat next to each other.

As she noticed those coming, Mahin lowered her head and said softly to Farrokh.

"They are my parents, it seems something has happened, they wouldn't come out at this time of the night. If you also want to see them and hear them talk, come slowly to the wall and sit next to me."

Farrokh moved closer to the top of the wall with caution so that no sound could be heard and was next to Mahin. Mahin's mum was hiding. Farrokh took Mahin's hand and raised it so close to his head that his breath mixed with Mahin's warm breath. A conversation started between Mahin's parents and the two lovers listened carefully to everything they said.

The weather at this hour of the night was extremely gentle, a cool breeze was blowing and the moon was at the end of its ascent in the blue sky, the scent of beautiful flowers caressed the nose, and complete silence filled the garden as if all the inhabitants had slept.

The wife and husband were sitting opposite each other, their faces gloomy as they waited to hear what they wanted to say.

"Madam, do you know why I deprived you of sweet sleep this time and brought you here?" Mahin's father said.

Malek Taj answered. "No, sir, I must say that I did not understand anything about your move and I am especially waiting to understand the reasons you brought me here at this time."

"Listen very well, lady."

Chapter Five
The Father And The Daughter

Before informing the readers about the wife and husband's conversations, and before know-ing what happened to the two young lovers on that moonlit night on that wall, it is neces-sary to go back a little, to know what happened hours ago ... The conversations between Mr F... Al-Saltaneh and his daughter Mahin.

Earlier that night, before Mahin came to the wall, Mr F... Al-Saltaneh was sitting in front of a desk in one of the rooms of his giant mansion. The room had two garden windows, and although it seemed Mahin's father was writing, getting closer and looking at the movement of his hand and pen, he was angrily scribbling lines on a notebook.

Why this behavior, what was disturbing him?

F... Al-Saltaneh had heard a rumor that his daughter was saying things that she shouldn't. He saw those words as contrary to his thoughts and es-pecially as an obstacle to carrying out his plans, he got angrier that night. People like F... Al-Saltaneh, who has achieved wealth and status, is commit-ted to maintaining it.

F... Al-Saltaneh remained angry in this state for almost half an hour. He finally got up and thought to himself. 'This girl is stupid. She wants to jeop-ardize the good plans I have for her.' He was devastated. 'Her love for her cousin will waste all my efforts and destroy her future, but as long as I am alive this will not happen. She does not understand that only through her marriage to Prince K's son, I get to be their family property lawyer, and If one does not become a lawyer, will not become a minister.'

After this thought, he shook his head with both hands. His face became frightened as if the traces of all the heinous plans that he had committed during his lifetime appeared on his face. He shook the bell ringer and after a few moments of silence, a plump woman entered and bowed in front of him.

Mr F... Al-Saltaneh asked:

"Firoozeh, is the lady back?"

"No sir, she has not come back yet since she left in the evening, but Mahin is in her room and reading a book." Firoozeh replied.

F .. Al-Saltanah, hearing the word book, said sharply:

"She reads books! do you know what books?"

Firoozeh who was trying to hide her ankles with her Chador, and said: "Sir, I am not literate, but I only saw books that talk about love and romance and stories about how a boy fell in love with a girl! They say that reading them improves literacy"

"Maybe she is reading a novel?"

"Yes, sir, that is what she is reading." Firoozeh replied.

"Well, go and tell Mahin to come here."

Firoozeh bowed and left the room while Al-Saltanah thought to himself: 'Now, I understand why this girl is so ignorant. She has read enough love stories.'

Then he followed his chain of thoughts: 'During our time there were no books except Amir Arsalan, Iskandarnameh, and Hussein Kurd. There were no talks of love. It is all my fault that Mahin went to those new schools...I never read a novel and I do not have the correct literacy. I do not know anything about arithmetic except addition and subtraction, and in a matter of time, I will become a top lawyer for the nation and I will even become a leader of lawyers. If my daughter wants to have my blessing and not be excluded from my inheritance, she must obey me and accept the husband I choose!'

The sound of footsteps got closer, and Mahin appeared at the entrance. She was looking pale. where she stood at the corner of the room. A few moments passed in silence and it was as if F... Al-Saltaneh was practicing what he wanted to say, and finally, he raised his head and turned to the girl and said kindly. "My darling, why don't you sit down?"

Without answering, Mahin immediately sat down in a nearby chair in front of his father.

"My daughter Mahin, do you know why I asked you to come? I want to talk to you about an important matter"

'Certainly, an important issue has occurred so I have to be calm.' She thought.

"Yes." Mahin calmly replied.

"There are many things I want to tell you. First, I heard you are reading some misguided books, which is nothing but a waste of time and it also weakens human belief and disturbs one's thoughts, and I heard you read constantly. Your father is not satisfied with that at all."

"Father, if you want to give orders or control me in this regard, I am not willing to listen at all, and please let me take my leave." Mahin, who listened carefully to all his father's words, said rudely.

F... Al-Saltaneh, hearing this answer like a bomb exploded and shouted.
"Girl, you seem to have forgotten that you are talking to your father or that you have forgotten who you are!"
"No, Father, I will never forget the respect I should have for you, but when I see that you want to spend your time discussing things that are contrary to my opinion, of course, I will not listen." She said calmly.

Al-Saltaneh thought a little and after a few moments, in a clear tone, he said. "Yes, daughter, you are right, this issue is not very important and I realized that shouldn't have come first, but what do you say about the other issues?"
"Father, I don't understand you. Please clarify."
F... Al-Saltaneh stood up from where he was sitting and took Mahin's hand and said calmly "My beautiful daughter, you know I want the best for you. In this case, it is not good for you to be so ignorant and not admit to things that I know are constantly going through your head."

Mahin replied calmly "Father, I told you I do not understand anything from these words. If they have told you anything about me, please let me know." F... Al-Saltaneh again took a serious look and said with a sigh:
"Girl, you do not need to be so ignorant. Now that you do not want to say, very well, what is this rumor I'm hearing about Farrokh, your cousin, I mean?"

Hearing Farrokh's name, she blushed and her heartbeat intensified, but soon the feeling disappeared and the paleness of her face increased, and then, after a little reflection, she strengthened herself like someone who wants to confess before a judge.
"Father, I did not want to make a statement and explain my inner thoughts to you, and I thought you would finally find out about it, but now that you have heard, I have to say yes, I love Farrokh and he loves me too. Is anything wrong with us loving each other?"

Hearing the clear expression, he got angrier. "Mahin, I thought these words were not true, but now that it turns out to be true and you want to darken your bright and good future and disrupt my plans. I will also plainly tell you that this is not possible."
"Father, you do not need to tell me what to do if you don't give me reasons not to do it, so please let me know the reason."

F...Al-Saltaneh knew she was afraid to go against his will, 'of course, this girl can not go against my will, and if I explain the reason for my opposition to her, she will understand my perspective, and also my plan. What I will tell her will surely put aside these imaginary fantasies.' Then he said loudly: "My darling, you know no father has a bad intention for his daughter, and I'm saying this because I love you, of course, you know that in this period and time everything relies on money and property. I am a firm believer that It is my responsibility to make you happy." He paused before he continued, "Although Farrokh is your cousin you know that he has nothing, my daughter I want you to forget the relationship between you two, it is impossible. Do not ask me to give you more reasons. I hope now that you understand the reason for my opposition. You must know the father must get rid of these absurd thoughts in their daughters."

Mahin, who had listened quietly to his father's words, said.
"Dear father, Farrokh's little wealth would not change my heart's choice, if you have other reasons, let me know."
"Well, wealth does not matter to you?" He said while mockingly laughing. Then he softened the tone of his voice like someone who commands.
"Daughter, most people use their children and relatives as a ladder to achieve high positions, especially in our country, where dependence and communication are the best means of progress. I could be the deputy of one of the ministries. Hope you understand me, daughter?"
"No, father, I don't understand anything yet."

F... Al-Saltaneh said angrily: "It is strange, how can you not understand me, Mahin. Every parent wants their children to have a wedding, to have a grandchild, so they could take care of them once they get old. I have considered a good husband for you and secondly, with your marriage, I will become their property lawyer. Wouldn't you help your father for the sake of all of the things I have done for you?"

Mahin listened carefully to his father's statements and said sarcastically: "Father, now I understand what you mean. You want me to fall victim to your greed and status."
F... Al-Saltaneh hastily stated:
"No, my daughter, this is not the case, as I said, I am on your side and I have chosen a rich husband for you."

Mahin said indifferently: "I will not give up Farrokh for these reasons."
F... Al-Saltaneh, hearing this word, became very angry as he raised his hand with all its intensity and hit her.

Mahin screamed in pain, but immediately got hold of herself and stared at his father without saying anything.
F... Al-Saltaneh lands more fists on her daughter.
"Now you dare to go against me. Very well, I will deprive you of my wealth."

Mahin shook his head and seemed to be ashamed of his father's savagery instead of his pain. The girl's composure and calmness affected her father's hard heart, as the F... Al-Saltaneh's anger subsided a little, he artificially laughed and said:
"Girl, as this is what you want, you can leave my room, but be aware that

your wedding with Farrokh will never take place."

Mahin slowly walked away without saying anything else. She opened the door and left the room. She made her way down the corridor to her room and went straight to her bed, exhausted like someone traveling. She crashed hard on the bed and slowly thought to herself.

'Oh no, how can I ignore Farrokh with all his love and intimacy, no, no, such a thing is not possible, I just want him and no one will be my husband except him!'

Mahin's eyes turned red and a great deal of sadness was visible. As tears flowed from her eyes through her cheeks like a flower leaf, she whispered helplessly,

"God, why are women's lives miserable in this world?"

Chapter Six
What Happened To Those Two Lovers On The Wall?

After Mahin left, his father remained angry for about half an hour, until he calmed down and then spoke to himself slowly:
'No, no, this girl should not cultivate these imaginary fantasies in her brain. She should prevent it as soon as possible. I can not consent to this. Although Prince K has not yet made an official statement, and I did not promise. It was just a few days ago that he mentioned that my power of attorney depends on this marriage. How can I reject this opportunity and make Farrokh my son-in-law? This girl does not want to listen to me and stubbornly stands against my will. Well, tonight she refused to listen to me, which is only for her good's sake. But she will certainly listen to her mother. Her mother will be able to guide this girl to the right way.'

He shook the bell ringer again. A few moments later the door opened and Firoozeh entered. She bowed and stood in the corner. She was surprised to see that F... Al-Saltaneh asked gently:
"Did the lady come or not?"
Firoozeh replied, "Yes sir, she has just arrived and is praying right now."
"Very well, in this case, tell her to come here immediately for an important matter."

Firoozeh bowed and left. Mr. F... Al-Saltaneh walked up to the room and looked at the various paintings that hung on the wall, and the carpet that covered the room's floor. He heard the footsteps. It was clear that someone was moving with the utmost arrogance and confidence. A few seconds later the door opened and the Malek Taj entered. She wore a sky-blue silk dress and her hair was center parting style. As soon as he saw her, took his wife's hand, kissed her kindly, and sat down together.

Malek Taj started talking with coquettishness and asked: "Well, sir, you ordered to see me."
"My dear, what can I say? I wanted to ignore and not listen to what I hear, but I see that it has become extremely important and it is about to ruin the basis of my plans. I'm sure you get what I mean!" He said.
Then, as his eyes fell on the moon through the window, which shone in the courtyard of the sky, he added. "You don't know how much I have been distracted by these happenings. Let's go to the garden in this pleasant weather

so we could benefit from the scent of flowers and in a better secluded place, I can express my meaning to you."

They got up as F... Al-Saltaneh took his wife by the arm and descended the stairs of the mansion. They went to the part of the garden which had a wooden bench. Farrokh and Mahin, who were sitting on the wall, listened carefully to their discussions.

***

Mahin was lying on her bed crying, and tears running down her cheeks. This young girl, whose whole heart was full of Farrokh's love and affection, was deeply moved and saddened by her father's words. Mahin saw that his father cared more about money and properties. He wanted to make her a victim of his greed and ambition. The poor girl could not find a way to save herself, no matter how hard she thought about it.

'Oh, it is half past eight, two hours have passed for the sunset. Oh, my dear Farrokh is waiting for me.'

She got up and hurriedly combed her golden hair, put on a thin white scarf on her shoulder, and left the room. She slowly descended the stairs of the mansion and went to the end of the garden. As soon as she approached the wall, she went a few steps to the right and leaned against the wall at the promised point.

***

F... Al-Saltaneh said. "My daughter has disturbed me a lot, I do not know what way I can take to get rid of her."

The lady said in surprise "I do not understand what you mean, I'm sure our daughter is fine."

"It seems you are completely unaware of everything. She loves her cousin Farrokh and wants to ruin her life and ours with these raw fantasies."

Malek Taj aggressively said: "Who are those people feeding you with lies? They are bad people!"

F... Al-Saltaneh gently stated: "My lady, you are wrong. There is no such thing as lying and mischief. Mahin herself has confessed her love and affection."

"Mahin said she loves Farrokh?" She asked.

"Yes, yes, Mahin told me personally."

"So what did you say?"

F... Al-Saltanah slowly lowered her head near Malek Taj's ear so no one could hear him.

"My dear lady, I have nothing to hide from you. My position in the ministry is shaky and they will fire me soon. I have to think about my future job, so I think I have to become a lawyer during this period to keep my job. And of course, that is not possible without the help of Prince K, who wants to propose to Mahin for his son Siavash Mirza. You now get my point and I just could not find another way."

Malek Taj asked, "what can I do?"

F... Al-Saltaneh replied. "These thoughts must be removed from Mahin's head.'

"How?" She asked immediately.

"It is very easy to cure love."

"Do you mean we help Mahin to marry Farrokh?"

F... Al-Saltaneh laughed devilishly and said: "No, but the means of their separation must be poured out and these thoughts must be removed from Mahin's head."

Malek Taj, who was convinced by her husband's statements, said:

"But it is not very easy."

F... Al-Saltaneh thought for a while and said a few words in his wife's ear.

"Will you come too?" Malek Taj asked.

"This issue needs some thought, but I do not think my presence is necessary."

The couple stood up and went to the mansion, their footsteps could still be heard in the distance when Farrokh said to Mahin: "Well, darling, you understand what your parents think of us."

"Unfortunately, I could not hear all of their words and I think what they whispered was very important which is difficult to guess correctly."

Farrokh hold Mahin's hand tightly and said:

"Darling, you don't need to guess. I'm sure your father has a big plan for our separation."

Mahin looked at his cousin with the endless love and desire and said:

"Do not be distressed, I will keep my word and no one will have me except you!"

Farrokh kissed Mahin's hands passionately and whispered to her:

"My darling you have to forgive me, I don't know what to do. Unfortunately, I don't believe in my luck, but could I hope you can keep your promise to go against your father."

Mahin said in a reproachful tone: Farrokh, you want me to repeat what I told you thousands of times, you still do not trust me, I will renew my oath to you tonight.

"Yes, darling, I love you and you will be my only beloved spouse!"

This clear expression left no doubt for Farrokh to embrace Mahin, and the lips of the two young men clung to each other, and the intense kissing sound resonated in the silence of the night in the garden as they hugged for a few seconds. Farrokh was getting closer to Mahin every moment. The souls of the two young lovers were getting more mixed up. At that time, it was as if two kingdoms had descended from the sky and were sitting on that wall.

Suddenly, Mahin pulled herself away from Farrokh's arms and said: "Darling, it seems that it is too late, maybe they have noticed my absence. Wait for me here tomorrow night exactly this time."

Farrokh was still anxious. He did not want to leave Mahin at all.
"Stay a little longer. The weather is very good. Baby stay, I want to hold you while I watch you, Mahin, I do not want you to go. I do not want you to go"

Mahin gently comforted his beloved, "Farrokh, why are you so upset? What happened? I will be here at this time tomorrow night, maybe by that time I will be able to find out what my parents said and tell you, now baby let me go I'm afraid it's too late."

Mahin slowly descended the ladder, and as soon as she reached the ground, she turned his head towards Farrokh, and send him kisses. She hurried away from that place.

Farrokh looked at Mahin from behind for a while, and as soon as her stature disappeared from his sight in the maze of the garden, he suddenly felt a strange revolution in him. He felt that he wanted to jump out of the wall into the garden and run back to Mahin and look at her beautiful face and fiery eyes again. But he did not and whispered to himself:
'I do not know how these fantasies have taken me. Why is my heart pounding, she swore not to accept anyone other than me as a husband, her father will finally be ready, why worry?' He stayed on top of the wall for a few more minutes, and then, without making a sound, he climbed down the wall and left the area with a word of hope that he would meet his beloved again soon.

Chapter Seven
The Rival

On the same night that these events took place in the garden of F... Al-Saltaneh, a series of other events took place in another part of the city, in the southwestern neighborhood of Tehran, which is called the Qazvin Gate.

In one of the rooms of a mansion in the neighborhood, two people were talking. From the way they talked, it was clear that their conversations were very interesting and especially fun. One of the men was younger and was sitting in a leather armchair and the other was standing in front of him.

The mansion was massive and luxurious, and its numerous rooms were all covered with expensive carpets and rugs. Each room had its distinguished furniture. Two people were talking in the room, there was an oak desk and several chairs of the same color and two leather armchairs, and selected pieces from famous calligraphers were mounted on the walls.

The young man was about twenty-two years old. He was sitting on an armchair very freely and vulgarly, with a small part of his body resting on the chair, with his legs straight without a slight deviation. He had very small dimpled eyes and a sloping nose, a black line behind his lips, a sign of his mustache, and the size of his outstretched legs showed that he must have a tall body. This young man, Siavash Mirza, was the son of Prince K ... who was one of the famous princes of Tehran, but in fact he had nothing left and all his properties were pledged and he owed a lot of money.

The person standing in front of Siavash Mirza was a waiter, with a well-proportioned body, dark eyes, and a look that made him look smart and intelligent. His name was Mohammad Taqi and he was about thirty-five years old. There was a very hot conversation between them at that time. There was a small bowl of yogurt and cucumber. During the conversation, every few minutes, Prince would drink the white drink called Arak.

Siavash Mirza was smiling while having a cigarette in the corner of his mouth, he was staring at Mohammad Taqi with his round and shining eyes and asked: "Would you say that some notable pieces can be found there?"

Mohammad Taqi lowered his head and said: "Yes, sir, I said after the night that His Highness was there almost a month ago and expressed his dissatisfaction. The landlord thought he would make fundamental changes in the situation there to satisfy him. I'm told to go there yesterday to see the new situation. Honestly, sir, you do not know what beautiful women they brought, especially one of them who is very beautiful and spectacular."

Siavash Mirza laughed and listened to Mohammad Taqi's words with full concentration while drinking another glass,

"Mohammad Taqi, you captured my heart with these words, now tell me when we should go to them?"

Mohammad Taqi, who saw his desire, said: "Whenever the Almighty desires, I am ready to serve."

"Very well, we are going right now. But before that, Mohammad Taqi, I wanted to talk to you, who is the confidant of my secrets, about another subject. Do you know what my father's plan is for me? Yesterday, when he summoned me, he told me that now is the time for him to choose a wife for me. As much as I said that this was too early, he did not accept it and stated that he had considered me a woman who is very beautiful and wealthy, and if I take her, a lot of wealth will fall into our hands, and father's work, which has been ruined recently, will be restored and take shape. I also said to myself, what is wrong with taking the girl in this case and hitting not only two but three marks with one arrow. That means I can quench the fire of my lust with the beautiful wife he chose for me, and with her wealth and properties, I can enjoy other beautiful women. I also can be superior to my father who has become very penniless and destitute due to his great extravagance lately. So that's why I accepted my father's offer, well do you think I counted it badly?

Mohammad Taqi politely replied: "Your Excellency, your thoughts are very excellent and your calculations are extremely correct. Of course, there is nothing wrong with being married in this way, but did you not understand who the girl is and how much she is worth?"

Mohammad Taqi had a special intention in asking this kind of question because he was a diligent servant. He was skilled in establishing relations between men and women, and since he entered the house of the prince, he has helped Siavash Mirza a lot in this way, often taking him to certain places, and Mirza's father calls him a son. When he heard about the marriage, he immediately tried to find out who it was intended for, so that he might be able to provide the means of this connection to his master or by disturbing others who had an opposite opinion of the marriage.

Siavash, while smoking a cigar and spewing thick smoke through his teeth, replied:

"My father did not say her name and no matter how much I insisted, he refused to tell me, but of course, he will soon inform me of the details." He stood up after drinking a few more glasses of Arak in a row, then he said,

"Well, let's go," then he puts on a shawl made of black broadcloth and puts on a small hat made of leather, and a short stick in the shape of a whip and went straight ahead. Mohammad Taqi also moved behind and both of them walked down the stairs of the mansion into the courtyard.

The moonlight illuminated the whole space at that hour. Siavash Mirza and Mohammad Taqi crossed a small street between two gardens full of various flowers. The lust had taken over Siavash Mirza, and Arak had done its job. Mohammad Taqi was happy too that he would earn money that night. Near the mansion an old man was sleeping in a room, he got up and opened the door for them and slowly left.

It was about two and a half hours into the night. Inside the house, Mirza said to Mohammad Taqi, "Well, does that mean we have to walk this way?" "His Highness has told me that whenever we go there, we will see for our-selves. But the later the better it is. It is half past two. If we walk happily in this good weather, we will arrive on time." Mohammad Taqi replied.

Siavash did not insist anymore and they walked towards Hassanabad crossroads in that good weather. At the crossroads, Siavash saw a woman walking towards the gate of Baghe-shah and her beautiful body and espe-cially her attractive black eyes attracted his attention. So he said to Moham-mad Taqi. "How about we follow her and talk to her and if yielded a good result we will not go there tonight."

Mohammad Taqi did not say anything, even though he was saddened by this incident. Siavash also fell behind the woman and started joking and flirting with her near Istakhr Street, but to his surprise, he noticed that the woman did not answer. Suddenly the woman said loudly:
"Sir, it seems you want to spend your five Tomans and two Qirans in your pocket for violation of the vows of the head of the court!"

Siavash realized from the serious tone of the woman that his pursuit was fruitless. He was not happy that the woman didn't give in, so he nodded to Mohammad Taqi, and they both went to the end of the road and turned right to the northeast.

***

We left Farrokh in that situation where he came down from the wall of the garden of F... Al-Saltaneh, and left for his mansion.

Farrokh was very distressed. So many different thoughts had occupied his mind and if someone was shoving him at that time, he might not have no-ticed. He gradually calmed down and tried to comfort himself, saying: 'Why should I be so anxious, I will surely have Mahin loves me and I don't need to worry. She said she is going to figure out about her parents' plans and will let me know soon.' Still immersed in his thoughts, he noticed that two people were walking in the same direction in front of him. So, without paying any attention, he made his way to the side of the street, sad and thoughtful, and went straight to his house.

The British embassy clock rang at ten o'clock and announced three hours had passed from the night. Naderi Street was gradually deserted at that time of night and pedestrians were rarely seen. The solitude of Tehran's streets was nothing new because the people of the city were not interested in staying up at night except during Ramadan. Some young people stayed in the streets until late at night, otherwise, most married men would have to go home at sunset and put their heads next to the mothers of the children!

As soon as Farrokh approached them and wanted to pass by, one of them, who was moving a little ahead of the other, shouted and stammered: "Well, we must see that this man, like us, goes there at this time of night!!" The second said: "Sir, what are you doing?"

It was Siavash Mirza, who raised his voice on his servant and said: "Mohammad Taqi stop, curiosity killed the cat." He laughed out loud and because his gait was irregular, he hastened his steps and as soon as he reached Farrokh, he put his hand on his shoulder and said sarcastically: "Well, sir, you do not want to tell me what time of night it is. Do you have a plan and where are you going?"

Farrokh raised his head in surprise and after overthrowing Siavash Mirza, he replied: "Sir, it turns out that you are very intruder and self-satisfied and you still do not know that no one has to explain his life to you."

Siavash Mirza was staggering from drinking a lot of alcohol during the previous hours, stuttered: "Oh, now you're not going anymore!"

Farrokh, who had realized that he was dealing with a stupid young man, did not answer as did not want to deal with a drunk man. He went on his way. Mohammad Taqhi, who considered this dispute an obstacle to his plan, reached out to Siavash Mirza and repeatedly whispered in his ear: "Sir, now is not the time for this talk, let's go, it may be too late and they will not let us in."But neither Farrokh's negligence nor the mediation of Mohammad Taqi calmed him down, so he reached to Farrokh again, who was a little farther away, and while holding his small stick in front of Farrokh's chest, he said: "I will not let you go until you tell me, I will not let you go!"

Farrokh realized that the young man is ignorant and would not get rid of him without any trouble. So he thought of a cure and decided that if Siavash persisted again, he would punch him in the brain and free himself from him, but once again he took control of himself, gently removed Siavash's stick from his chest, and said gently.

"Sir, if you have nothing to do, I have a lot to do."

Siavash, who was now completely entertained, took Farrokh by the collar and wanted to throw Farrokh on the ground, but Farrokh did not give him a chance and shook Siavash with one hand. He removed his hand from his collar and clenched his fist with the other hand to land Siavash Mirza a blow as tightly as possible. Suddenly, his hand was caught in the air and when he turned his head, he saw Mohammad Taqhi holding his sleeve with one hand and the other holding Siavash's arm.

Siavash left Farrokh's collar and while he was still talking nonsense, Mohammad Taqi dragged him to the other side of the street, and Farrokh, who did not want to quarrel with this drunken young man and start a riot, took the opportunity and followed his way.

In the distance between the sidewalk and the street, there was a narrow stream which, the reflection of the moon and the shadow of the trees on it, had created a natural and beautiful landscape. Mohammad Taqi took Siavash close to the stream without any resistance and sat next to him and poured a few handfuls of water on his face after two or three minutes the cold water had its effect and the drunken effects left Siavash's head to some extent and as soon as he came to his senses he asked.

"What did I do? Who was it?"

"No, there was nothing. You just feel a little dizzy. Praise be to God that it was resolved. I think we can go now." Mohammad Taqi said with flattery.

Siavash got up from the ground and said while his legs were still slipping. "Yes, yes, Let's go, it does not matter, I will even come to the top of the mountain!"

Chapter Eight
The Unwell Neighborhood 1

At the northeastern end of Tehran, between the Darvazeh Dowlat and Shemiran, there is a street, most of which is now known as Sepahsalar Street. If we take this street from the west to the east and go about two thousand steps away from Masoudieh Zell-e-Sultan Park, we will reach to a neighborhood with the small houses were been built far from each other, and except for a few groceries and liquor stores, there are no other shops.

The east-west street was known as Atashkadeh (the fire temple), while the other street perpendicular to the east side of Atashkadeh Street, is called Sheni (sandy) Street. Narrow alleys can be found between these two streets. Above some of the houses on both streets and alleys, small lanterns were seen, often with tinted glass. Constables were always walking in this area, paying attention to the behavior of passers-by, one would see that some of them sneak into houses in the maze of alleys after looking around for a moment, and others seemed to be knocking on one of the houses. The sound of strings, violin, and the songs was often heard by passers-by on these streets, and it was only during the months of Ramadan, Muharram, and Safar (Islamic sacred months) that anyone passing by would be deprived of hearing these sounds.

The men who were passing through those streets and alleys, no matter how young or old, ugly or beautiful, intellectual or mullah, will be targeted by the inhabitants of those houses. Some of the women who lived in these houses often sat near the door and as soon as they heard any footsteps, got their heads out of the house and shamelessly invited passers-by inside.

The neighborhood is so ignorant because it was as if neither their eyes could see the situation nor their ears could hear. They would go silent even when hearing an argument between a man with one of the women living in these houses and they did not interfere.

The same night that Farrokh met Siavash on Naderi Street was the same night that Mahin swore to Farrokh on the wall of her father's garden that she would remain faithful to him, and that same night F... Al-Saltaneh and his wife plotted to separate Mahin and Farrokh. One of the houses in this neighborhood, located in Atashkadeh Street, had four women sitting in the middle of the yard, next to the pond on a rug - an oil lamp with a blue crystal base was in the middle, and it's broken pipe was so dirty, it seemed that it wasn't cleaned for a long time. There were couples of large cucumbers, dried leftover bread and a small bowl of porcelain filled with water. This house looked like a new one. There were buildings on its three sides, the east, west, and north, which the floor was more than one meter above the ground, and the lower part of which consisted of several basements reservoirs, storage room, and a kitchen. In front of the northern building, a small porch with a round pond was built, which was connected by two staircases, each of which had about four steps, to the courtyard on both sides.

Most of the rooms were empty and there was no proper furniture. Only one of them had a few chairs and there was a bench and two wooden tables, a large mirror with a red wooden frame was mounted on the wall above the heater, and torn and old wooden beds were placed in the corner of the rooms.

The four women were talking. One of them was sitting behind the pond facing north, she is tall and fair-skinned. Her hair was packed in a ponytail, but it was clear that her hair color was not natural, she had changed it. She wore a lemon-colored decollete dress. She was called Ashraf.

The second woman, named Aqdas, was short compared to her other friends. She had black hair and thick eyebrows. Her eyes were small and slightly sunken. Her white teeth showed off more because of her bronze skin color. She wore a sky blue silky dress adorned with many white beads. At that moment, she had a cigarette in the corner of her mouth.

The third was called Effat who looked sad. She seemed like a stranger and wasn't laughing like others. She was the prettiest among them all. She wore a silk garment with a very loose sleeve.

The fourth, whose name was Akhtar, looked bulky and plump. It was clear from her appearance that she was older than the other three women. Her nose was short and large, and her lips were thick, but she had white and tidy teeth with a large chin. She wore yellow clothes with open collar, her breasts were protruding.

No one had visited them yet that night. Ms. Boss had gone to the streets to buy some necessities for trapping the young men, these four women took advantage of her absence and sat together. They all had extreme make-up on, which masked their mental state.

One of the women expressed her disgust with the filth of her client that had happened a few nights ago, and the other complained of Ms. Boss's obscenity and injustice. She explained that a young man had spent the night in extreme depravity with her and had run away early in the morning without paying. But It was her reprimanded, and Ms. Boss accused her of allegedly being an accomplice with the young man, and finally fined her.

The third woman complained about the arrest she recently had on the street, telling how she had been unjustifiably taken to the commissariat and detained for twenty-four hours.

From all their statements, it was clear that they had a hard time with their life and wished to be saved from this miserable situation.

"Let's tell each other our stories tonight, now that there is no guest," Ashraf said. Everyone except Effat liked the suggestion, but she was reluctant to do so, and her gesture showed that she did not want to tell her life story because she was not comfortable, to tell the truth. However, the other three insisted so much until she finally gave in, she had no choice but to accept and promised to tell the story of her life.

It was in the evening, and the moon was slowly rising in the sky. Suddenly, due to a strong wind, the light of the lamp went out, but because the moonlight had illuminated the space enough, they didn't need the lamp anymore.

In addition to these four women, two other people were living in that house. An old woman who was a cook, but occasionally was a deal-maker, and the other was a boy who was a footman. They were sitting by the stove, busy with their work.

Ashraf, who was supposed to narrate her life story first, took a cigarette, lighten it, and after taking a puff, said:

My story is not very long. My father was a butcher, and my mother is Ms. Boss's sister. My mother was busy spinning cotton at home. We had a small house with two rooms in Khaniabad Street.

Although my father was a crook butcher and used to sell cat and dog meat to people to gain more money, but he did not earn much profit and only got five or six Qirans a day.

I was extremely jealous and spoiled. Every time I saw our neighbor's girl in new clothes, I cried all day and night and I was so annoyed that my parents had to provide me with those clothes.

In our neighborhood, there were some noble houses, in one of which there was a wealthy man. I liked the young man very much, and most of the time when we played in the alley with the children next door, I would push myself in front of his house anyway, and so to speak, without realizing it, I would show off. The young man who was eighteen or nineteen yeras old, sometimes smiled when he saw me. When I was twelve years old I always dreamed of beautiful and stylish clothes and dreamed of a luxurious life.

One day, while we were playing with a group of boys and girls, I suddenly fell to the ground. My knee hurt a lot. I limped and stood by the wall. I fainted at sunset, when I opened my eyes, "what do you think I saw?" Ashraf asked before she continued.

I noticed I was in a beautiful little room, lying on a bed I had never seen before, and that young man was beside me smoking.
I hurriedly asked him, "Where am I? Why am I here? Where is my mother? What happened to my father?"
He laughed out loud and then brought his head close to mine and kissed me. "Do not worry, your mother and father are at home and safe. Stay here tonight."
"Why will the hand of a beautiful girl like you be so dirty!" He concluded.
It was getting darker and that young man pressed the white button mounted on the wall, and a few seconds later the door opened and a man who turned out to be a servant entered the room.
The young man smiled and said:
"Is the bathroom heated?"
The servant replied as he bowed and make his way out of the room "Yes sir, it is warm."
"Very well, go to Hamideh, tell her to go to the bathroom and wash this girl's head and body very well."
And then he turned to me and said: "Please go and have your bath, God willing, I will be back after your bath."
Unfamiliar with such words, I got out of bed and, as my leg was still a little sore, I carefully placed it on the floor.
The young man immediately took me in his arms and said, "The hot water will also eliminate this slight bruise." Then, with the help of a servant holding my arm, we passed a very large yard with several gardens and entered a small bathroom, the entire part of which was decorated with photo tiles. Hamideh, who was a young lady, was waiting for me there. She immediately took off my clothes and took me to the bathroom. And for me, who had never seen anything but public baths in Tehran, it was spectacular.
First of all, Hamideh rubbed my feet with her hands to treat the bruises, then she washed me thoroughly. They presented me with beautiful clothes, it was a bit loose though. After Hamideh put them on me and combed my hair, I looked in the mirror, I couldn't recognize myself in a new look with that dress and that makeup.
A few minutes later, with the guidance of a servant who was waiting outside the bathroom, I entered the young man's room again. He was waiting for me with foods I had not seen until that hour, he

drank with me under the pretext that it will completely relieve my pain. After dinner, I saw that he did not leave the room and started to take off his clothes. And then he approached me and without resisting, he also undressed me and hugged me ...

When I woke up in the morning, I couldn't find the young man next to me, so I cautiously got out of bed and looked at the large mirror that was installed on the wall. Suddenly Hamideh entered and said:

"Mr. Shemiran came and told me to give you this envelope and send you to your house."

Without realizing that my situation had changed from yesterday, I took the envelope from the door and went to our house. As soon as my mother saw me, she hugged me tightly and while tears of joy flowed from her eyes, she called the neighbors, "Come, come, my daughter has been found." My daughter was found. And they informed the commissioner, then he asked me:

"Tell me, what happened, where did you go?"

Neighbors, who were informed of my discovery by my mother's voice, came around me one by one and wanted to know about where I was and what happened. I let my mother open the envelope in a hurry, and as soon as she saw that a five-toman banknote had been put in it, without understanding why, she sat down and stroked her chest with both hands, pulled her hair, and cried:

"They have dishonored my innocent daughter."

Women around my mom started comforting her to stop crying while the ones near asked me for the address of the young man's house, and as soon as he found out where it was, she said,

"Oh, those people!"

And thus I found out that the young man last night was one of the leaders of Hamedan.

Finally, when my mother calmed down a bit, she took my hand to the commissar and told him what happened. Chief Commissioner immediately sent an agent to the young man, but after ten minutes, the policeman returned and said:

"Sir, they did not come, but they had entrusted their servant that he would come to the commissar later." At that moment, the servant entered and went straight to the head of the commissioner and talked to him briefly."

Then the chief commissioner turned to my mum and said,

"Well, Madame, what do you want?"

My mother said:

"No, sir, it is not possible, if he wants to consent and compensate for his mistake, he must at least temporarily marry my daughter."

I liked my mother very much because it was so sweet to know that she was adamant. But I had the shock of my life when I heard the head of the commissioner say to my mother in a loud voice:
"You idiot woman, what did you just say, how can they take a butcher girl, even as a concubine, if you want, I will ask them to give you 30 tomans to compensate for this, and if you insist I will send you out of here right now."

My poor mother was terrified and realized that the threat of the chief commissioner might come true. Mr. Haidar Qoli Khan is used to bribing, so she had no choice but to give in. She accepted the money.

My mother cried for a long time until she seemed to calm down, but despite my young age, I felt that she was very sad. Because my mother was a good woman and everyone knew that I did not do it on purpose, finally a young man who lived in our neighborhood came to marry me if my mother paid 30 tomans for her grocery store's debts. My mother had asked God for this, so she immediately consented, and on the same day, in the evening, A mullah issued the marriage contract, and Ahmad and I got married.

Six months later, my mother died, which made me extremely sad because I was the reason for her a lot of pain. My father also became more addicted to opium use, so much so that he became impoverished and lived at home, and after a year and a half, he died.

Their death was very hard for me and I cried for a long time. Four years had passed since my father's death. One evening, my aunt, Nahid, came to our house. I did not know what she was like. We have long cut ties with each other because I could not travel, and Ahmad did not allow me to leave the house. Anyways, I promised to visit her soon as she had also invited me. One day, Ahmad was not around so I asked around about where I could board to get to my aunt. I went to LalehZar and asked from there. Luckily for me, I saw my aunt and she welcomed me warmly as she collected the tea and syrup I bought for her before she said:
"I do not want my nieces and nephews to wear these badly sewn clothes. Go to that room. My safe is full of beautiful clothes."

I was seventeen years old at the time. Out of curiosity, I immediately went and put on a beautiful dress from the trunk and adorned myself with white, and magenta. As soon as I came out, my aunt said: "Look at how beautiful you are, let's go to the room, someone is waiting for you."

I entered the hall with my aunt without asking who the person was, and I saw an official sitting on a chair. He was a young man who had just shaved his face and traces of powder were still visible on it, and his mustache, which was swinging up from both sides, was very pleasing to me. I was embarrassed to see him and wanted to leave the room, but my aunt would not let me.
"Where do you want to go, this gentleman is your people and is here only to meet you!"

I was not interested in what she said, and after a few seconds my aunt got up and said: "I will leave you two alone to talk!"

I was a little worried and did not understand the purpose, but the beautiful and smiling face of the young man made me forget all my anxiety and worry! A few minutes after my aunt left, the young man approached me and reached for my breasts without introduction.

I was so embarrassed that while I was holding my head down, I pulled back his hand and said to me: "Why is he treating me in such a way that he suddenly grabbed my head with both hands, kissed my hair, and whispered in my ear:
"What your aunts said was a lie, I do not have a relationship with you, but I want you!"

I saw that if my aunt had lied, she would have lied well because in this case, it was preferable to hang out with such a young man thousands of times than to sleep with Ahmed, so I said nothing more and did not refuse and flirted with him for almost an hour. And he stayed in the room ...

After we are done he stood up and kissed me again and said goodbye and left. Two minutes later, my aunt came in and said to me in a serious tone
"You are welcome here, your husband who does not know where I live. If you like this place and this young man, come here tomorrow without saying anything to your husband, so that you will be regularly happy and associate with such young people, and you will wear great and stylish clothes and eat good food."
Then she gave me some money and said:
"Find a carriage tomorrow and come."

I got up and went home. I couldn't forget the man's face all night, and every time I saw Ahmed in front of me and thought that I had to stay with him all the time, I became more disgusted with my life.

Finally, I made my decision, in the morning after Ahmad left, I took some of my belongings, put them in a bag, and came to my aunt's house.

I have been in this house for three years now, and I have been seriously ill several times, and with the accounts that my aunt has prepared for me, I owe sixty tomans, which I do not think I will ever be able to pay!

Chapter Nine
The Unwell Neighborhood 2

There was a few minutes of silence after Ashraf's speech. Then Aqdas raised her head and said, "Now, I am going to tell you my story."

I'm a mercer's daughter. My father did not do much business in the Abbasabad neighborhood. My father had two daughters and I was the youngest. My older sister did not have a beautiful face, and she had a lot of smallpox pimples on her face that made her look ugly, but my parents like their first child. They thought God was very cruel to her so they loved her immensely but I did not like her very much. Most of the suitors who came to our house did not like her and wanted me, but my parents refused them all and said that our eldest daughter should get married first.

In this way, my destiny depended on my sister's destiny. And I knew that only the day she finds a husband, I too could hope to get married. Finally, my sister used magic or some sort of prayer from Mullah Ibrahim Yahudi, to seduce a young cigarette seller. I was relieved from that day and found hope. Three months after my sister got married, I reached my goal of getting married, but what husband?

One day, two women came into our house and liked me and said that the groom was a wealthy businessman who is a tobacco trader and that he was young. But my parents, who were not very interested in me and my future, did not try to investigate and without hesitation gave their consent to the marriage. On the day of the wedding, I thought I would get married to a beautiful young man but what I saw shocked me. I saw a tall man with smallpox with a red beard, shaved head, with large yellow and black teeth, some of which he had lost. He wore a robe and a long woolen cloak, a wide white scarf, and a large leather hat. I turned my head and an old man kissed me on the left cheek.

Seeing such an ugly presence, all my people and relatives were startled and lost in thoughts.

"If you want a good handsel, you must also kiss the groom." One of

them said it in my ear slowly.

I said in my heart that he should take handsel to his father's grave, how could I be willing to kiss this ugly bearded face old man, but I could no longer express my opinion, it was too late. I had already said yes, because I thought I was going to marry a young handsome prince. I did not have a choice. He was my husband. Haji Agha also took a ring made of ruby, which was not very expensive, from his big pocket.

Fortunately, he did not torment me more than twice with his kisses and left. Later, I was taken away at night and thrown into the arms of the ugly old man. However, Haji Agha was not a bad person morally and he treated me with love and kindness. He was a man of God and he always prayed days and nights, or for any new business he wanted to venture into, he would first practice divination. He resorted to chickpeas, rosaries, and Hafiz's book. He has complete belief in these three things.

After a few months, Haji Agha did not come home by chance for three days and nights. I became very worried and said to myself that he is a man of God and that he is not like a naughty young man who has gone dumb in some places. And when at this time one of the neighbors came in and I told him about Haji Agha's absence, he said without surprise.
"Certainly, he has gone to the house of the other wife, do not be afraid!"

I was very surprised to hear this and asked her how she knew and it turned out that Haji Agha is a real Muslim and besides me, he has two other wives and two concubines (Sigheh), and even the woman next door said that Haji Agha's fortune-telling, which he recites with Hafiz and Tasbih, are not only for business.

I thought to myself that it would not be easy to live with a man who looks like that, if Haji Agha was for me alone, I could bear the ugliness and his old age. But now that he wants to marry another woman because of a fortune-teller, I will be unhappy in this marriage.

The next morning I went to the market to buy some sewing necessary items such as spools and threads. I saw a large crowd in the market, unemployed men moving behind women in groups. I stood near a shop and asked people about the prices of some goods and watched. Suddenly, a 20-year-old man wearing a funnel hat with a black frock-coat and a green satin tie in the middle of which had a picture of Ahmad Shah emblazoned passed by me and said:

"Madam, do you not want to glorify me for an hour?"

I was not familiar with such words, but I liked the young man. I said jokingly:

"Sir, what do you want?"

As the young man repeated the invitation, I asked:

"Is your house nearby?"

"Yes, my house is very close and if you want, we can go there and smoke a cigarette together?"

Not knowing what he meant by smoking, I accepted his offer and left with the young man. After passing a few more narrow alleys, he stood in front of a very humble house as knocked on the door.

The young man complimented me as I entered the house which got me flattered, and although my heart was trembling at that moment, I entered the house and thought to myself:

'I don't care if thousands of men are here, no one will blame me if they see what my husband looks like!'

As soon as we entered the yard, the young man turned his face to an old woman and instructed her to do something. Then he took me into an old small room. There were several niches around the room and a ledge was made on top of the niches, but the old white plaster dust on the walls made me sick. The young man invited me to sit down and he sat next to me on the carpet. He immediately pulled my Chador back from my head and offered me a cigarette.

I took a cigarette and we talked for a while before he asked me who I was. I answered without consideration: "Haji Agha's wife ... tobacco seller." Some minutes later the tea was ready, and after we both drank the tea, the young man came closer to me, hugged and kissed me. I was very embarrassed, but the young man's face was shaved and was clean unlike Haji Agha's beard. Little by little, I noticed he was not satisfied with the kiss and wanted other things. I thought to myself, whatever it is, he is better than Haji Agha ...

He gave me some money before I said my goodbyes. When I came out, I saw a golden five thousand and also he told me to come back there twice a week. When I returned home, I thought about what had happened and I was very happy. I did not know that the young man had taken me on a disrespectful journey.

I went there twice a week for a few weeks and I was delighted with the young man. Then one day I realized I had gonorrhea. A few days later, Haji Agha also contracted the disease. But poor Haji Agha, because he had many wives, did not know which of us was guilty and traitorous.

Then I realized if Haji Agha found out that he had gotten the disease from me, he would expel me from the house with disgrace and will marry another wife. So I behaved badly to that extent until he divorced me and returned me to my father's house.

I lived in my father's house for two months and whenever the opportunity arose I would visit the young man and his friend who he had introduced to me. As far as I understand, both were members of the Ministry of Public Works. But unfortunately, the money I was taking from them was not even enough for my treatment for the diseases I got from them ... The doctor also made the matter worse as he diagnosed a minor and mild disease and promised to treat me like a fortune teller at the ransom saffron market in less than six months. One day, when I complained about the length of my treatment because I haven't been visiting due to lack of money, he seemed to be disappointed and told me he would not be able to treat me if I skip treatment:

"Your symptoms have become chronic and your treatment is very difficult and will take time!"

Hearing his words, I changed immensely and said in a loud voice:

"Doctor, what do you say, why do you treat people like this? After that I have spent a lot of money. Now you said my disease has become chronic." But the doctor calmly answered me: "Calm down, madam, or I will have you thrown out," I screamed angrily and he called his servant and they kicked me out of the room.

When I returned home, I promised myself not to go to that doctor anymore and change the doctor, then I met another doctor who had a house on Cheragh-e-Gaz Street but was not better than the other one, neither in terms of the information nor in terms of morals, so I left.

In the meantime my parents went to visit the holy shrines and pilgrimage to Karbala, and I was left alone at home. I was constantly having fun with the youth of the bazaar and Lalehzar Street. One day one of the neighbors who had a very holy appearance and prayed on time, and never a miss a fasting day during Ramadan, came to me and said:

"Ms. Shaukat, I know you are busy!"

I blushed but did not say a word.

"But let me take you to a place where you will meet young and rich people!"

He was fully aware of my situation and it was useless to deny it because my parents had also put me in a difficult situation, I accepted his offer. She brought me here and changed my name to Aqdas. It has been two years and I am owing forty Tomans to Nahid. I have not received any news from my parents since then. It is not clear whether they were caught by thieves or suffered in Karbala and Baghdad.

Aqdas finished her story here, she took a cucumber from the tray and cut it into four slices. She divided the three slices among her comrades and put the fourth one in her mouth.

It was Effat's turn to talk.

At first, she did not want to tell her story, but at the urging of three other women, she reluctantly told her life story:

I was neither a butcher's daughter nor a mercer's daughter, I came from one of the well-known families in Tehran.

Hearing the well-known family of Tehran, three other women pricked up their ears and listened carefully to her story.

Our house was in the northwestern neighborhood of Tehran. My father was wealthy and my mother, who loved me very much, was a noble and chaste woman. I was very dear to my parents. They made sure I'm always satisfied, even when I was thirteen or fourteen. Instead of sending me to school, they only encouraged me to play with my peers. Of course, it was clear how ignorant and blindfolded I was as a girl who spends all day playing instead of studying. The only thing that I knew well was to be obedient to my parents, which my nanny often reminded me of, and she had said it to me so much that I no longer made any exceptions, and blind obedience to my parents was mandatory at any time.
Believe me completely in the power of that ball.
Due to my family's reputation in the city, everyone knew that they would give me a large dowry. Every day a group of suitors came to our house and they were often well-educated and well-groomed, but never understood why my parents rejected them all.
Until one day two women entered our house and I knew from their behavior they were suitors. I hurried to my room and hid. After a quarter of an hour, our maid came and announced that my mother told me to go to her room.
I went to my mother's room after putting on a little make-up, but

as soon as my eyes fell on the two women, my heart trembled as if an esoteric voice was telling me that connecting with their family will be bad and unpleasant for me.

Half an hour passed, those women left but unlike me, my mum was happy and she was ready to go with the marriage. After a week we set the date and time for our wedding. On the day of the engagement ceremony, more than two hundred respectable women from Tehran were invited into our house. A magnificent wedding ceremony took place.

The groom was handsome and polite. Seeing him, I said to myself, 'I think I was unnecessarily worried. My mother was right.' His job also turned out to be in the ministry... deputy director of the accounting department, and everyone was told that someone who is a deputy director at this young age, certainly, when he reaches the age of thirty-five or forty years old, he will be a minister.

A month later, after a detailed dowry was prepared for me, my parents allowed me to get married, and my wedding took place on a winter night.

Coincidentally, the weather was very cold that night, and it had been snowing heavily since that evening. In my husband's luxurious mansion, which was located on ... Abad Street, a lot of lights and lamps lit up the ballroom and a glorious wedding party was held.

As soon as I entered, they took me to a small room, and immediately one of the ladies touched up my makeup, which was a little messy, and then they brought me a glass of syrup. I drank it. They sat down beautifully in the middle of the hall at the top, and after a quarter of an hour, one of the women approached and said in my ear that it was time, and the groom was coming.

A few minutes later, the door opened, and I was surprised to see that instead of the groom, who had to come with his sister, a short, young man with gold-chain glasses and a brown robe on his shoulder came in. The groom was behind him, and was heard saying loudly:

"Please, your excellency! Please, the house belongs to you, your excellency. We are nothing but caretakers!"

This was where my misery began. A group of women, seeing this terrible scene, got up and left. I also wanted to get up and go out the other hall in protest, but a soft voice said in my ear:

'Don't you know that your husband is the owner and has authority over you and he has the right to do whatever he wants!'

When I turned my head, I saw that the words were from my nan-

ny, so I stayed in my place with the certainty that my nanny wanted me the best. I didn't pay attention to my inner feelings.

The short young man, whom my husband called him your excellency, approached me and without hesitation lifted the net veil that was on my face and said:

'Wow! such a beautiful bride!"

Then coughed and said to my smiling husband:

"Very well, it seems you should hold hands now."

Then he took the groom's hand and brought it to me, and when he felt my hand gently squeeze it, he put my hand in the groom's hand and immediately put his head close to my husband's ear and said something slowly. I saw that my husband's color suddenly turned very red, but he came to his senses immediately and said in a flattering tone:

"Of course, the orders of his excellency are obeyed!"

He was emphasizing to my husband again, not to forget, that He will be waiting. Then after a small bow to me and the others, I left the hall.

My husband hurried behind him and shouted:

"Get a lamp. Get a lamp for his excellency."

A few minutes later, the groom returned to the hall and stood next to me. The guests who were still standing stood in groups and each one made an excuse and said goodbye. Finally, the groom took me by the hand and led me through several rooms until we got to a small room decorated for us to sleep in. The bronze bed with a mosquito net on the back of a colored flower was in the corner, with two comfortable chairs and a dressing table. The walls were also decorated with various colorful postcards.

I sat down in a comfortable chair, tired, and my husband sat down next to me in another chair, and after a few moments of reflection, he said to me:

"I want to talk to you about something very important!"

I thought to myself, what is important about the groom on the wedding night? In any case, I said slowly.

"Please. Go on"

"Dear lady, this person you saw is my Chairman, I got to where I am today only with his help... He has helped me enormously for a long time and has never hesitated to help me, he promoted me to this position... Tonight he asked me something and I could not reject it. I was also afraid that bad things will happen to me if I say no to him. It means that not only I will lose my job, which of course does *not matter, but there may be a risk of some charges or even going to Nazmieh prison, and you know as a result, I will be deprived of seeing you!"*

Without realizing it, I said impatiently when I heard the name of Nazmieh prison:

"Sir, I do not understand you, are you worried about what he told you? What help can I render?"

He also said recklessly:

"Yes, my lady, well, you guessed it correctly. I need your help because he ordered me to give up my groom right tonight and leave it for him, and as I said, I am afraid if I refuse to obey him, tomorrow I will find many troubles!"

I was shocked, but I did not understand exactly what he meant. I was sorry for my husband and was also remembering my nanny's advice. I was not aware that 'yes' that I told, will make me miserable and will ruin my life, I said:

"Sir, I do not understand its meaning correctly, but if this will help your work, act as you see fit."

My husband, as if waiting to hear such an answer, took a deep breath and said:

"You are satisfied my darling, Praise be to God that I was saved!!"

Then he called a maid:

"The lady and I want to go out for some fresh air. Give the lady a Chador. Do not tell anyone about this, tell them that the bride and groom have slept for dinner, and if anyone wants to get close to our bedroom, stop them and tell them. I do not like it!"

Then he turned to me and said: Hurry up. I still did not understand his intention and got up and put on my Chador.

It was almost five o'clock in the morning. It was snowing heavily. My husband took me by the hand and we left the room. He took me to a small yard that was covered with orange trees, then we passed through a long corridor and entered the alley next to the mansion. He hurriedly ran to call the carriage, which was standing near the big yard, to come to the alley, and when we got on, he said to the carriage:

- Go to the park ...

Chapter Ten
The Unwell Neighborhood 3

The carriage was moving towards the western part of Tehran near Darvazeh Bagh-e-Shah Street. Although the weather was very cold, I was so distraught that I could not feel the cold. Instead of resting in a warm bed, I had to sit in that carriage and go back and forth around the city.

Finally the carriage stopped at the iron door of a large garden. Immediately two doors opened as if they were waiting for it to enter. My husband, who was silent all the time, immediately opened the carriage door and said, "Lady, please," so I gathered myself up and came down from the carriage with his help. We went up the marble stairs while he was holding my hand.

The mansion looked very luxurious. The windows on both sides of the building were symmetrical. There was a roof on the upper stairs at the entrance to the roofed mansion that could protect the staircase from snow and rain in winter. A porcelain lamp hung under the ceiling, and a slight light arose from it.

My husband and I entered the foyer and a waiter came forward and led us to a large hall. The short young man was near the fireplace where a beautiful fire was burning. He returned and smiled when heard our footsteps,

"Oh, Ali Ashraf, you came, I was about to lose my patience!"

My husband bowed and said:

"There was a slight delay, of course, your excellency ...forgive me, it was not my fault, I had to prepare according to your wish.

The short man no longer paid attention to my husband's explanations, he approached me, took my hand and kissed it, and then went to my husband and put his hand on his back and said:

"good job, well done, hurry up and leave us alone, God willing, we will see each other tomorrow."

My husband bowed again and stepped out the back door as he looked me in the eye. As soon as we were alone, His excellency put his hand under my arm and said: "Madam, wouldn't you like to take off your Chador and go check out my house, which of course belongs to you, and then rest."

I took off my Chador and put it aside. He first showed me the various rooms in his mansion, and every time he came across the expensive paintings and rugs of Kashan and Kerman that hung on the walls, he explained them with pomp. Without realizing any of my actions, I blindly followed wherever he took me, according to the promise I had made to my husband.

Finally, he took me to a relatively small room with a window overlooking the large pool of the mansion. He offered to sit on a chair. He brought two glasses full of yellowish liquor and said it was cognac. He handed one to me and took the other to his lips and said: "It is very useful for relieving colds. Please drink it."

I was still shaking, I drank cognac and after a few moments I felt a little warm and my anxiety was reduced. Two or three minutes later, a maid arrived and announced that dinner was ready.
His excellency took me under his arm to the dining room.

On the dining table, there were all kinds of dishes made of fish, chicken, and turkey, and the pleasant smell of them irritated my hungry stomach. He opened a large bottle and poured the yellow liquor that was full of foam into the tall glass in front of me:
"Madam, this bottle is one of the best champagnes found in Tehran and you should drink it to your satisfaction!" He said with a laugh. Then he clink his glasses to mine and made me drink champagne.

Little by little, the effect of alcohol appeared in me and I did not understand what happened anymore. I remember that I laughed over and over again. An hour later, he and I were sleeping together on a large bronze bed in the bedroom ...

I woke up when the wall clock in the mansion rang at five, I saw that no one was in bed except me. But my husband is standing at the bottom of the bed and says:
"Lady, lady, get up, let's go, it's too late!"
I was so tired that I did not want to leave that comfortable and soft bed, but because my husband was very demanding, I jumped out of bed as quickly as I could, then my husband took me to the bathroom in a hurry and washed my face with a handful of water. He turned my head and immediately helped me and put on my Chador, and we went down the hall and other rooms with him without noise, we passed the stairs of the mansion. We entered our back yard and from there we slowly entered our bedroom.
My husband immediately helped me take off my Chador and slept naked next to me.

Two days after this incident, my husband came home in the evening and I saw that he was very happy. He kissed me and said with a smile:
"Darling, did you see that night's efforts were not in vain?"
Then he took an envelope out of his pocket and handed it to me:
"See my darling, read what he wrote!"
I took it like I was literate, but how sorry I was that I could not understand except for a few black lines and a stamp and signature. Embarrassed, I passed the paper to my husband so that he could read it to me.

Mr. Mirza Jalaluddin Khan resigned due to an illness.
It is necessary to appoint a worthy person to head the Ministry of Accounts and according to proposal No. 8950 of the Masharalieh Employment Office,... Mr. Ali Ashraf Khan, the deputy of the said office, is appointed to the above-mentioned position, May he rise and take action with full care and diligence in performing his duties. Mr. Ali Ashraf Khan's salary is estimated at two hundred tomans a month, and also fifty tomans monthly allowance and this will be spent at the expense of ...

After reading this sentence, he hugged me again and kissed me hard, and said with great joy: "I have reached this rank and position because of your charm."
I said in my heart that all these should be over because if that were the case, we would no longer have to go to His Excellency's house on that cold night with that fear and trembling, and then return secretly in the morning.
My husband interrupted my thoughts and said the following statements:
"Do you know for sure who did this?"
I said embarrassedly:
"I guess, yes!"
"Very well, my dear, in this case, you know that in Iran, for every job, you have to compliment first, and after the job is done, you have to offer something like cardamom and flower. The complement of this promotion was the night you went there. His Excellency has expressed a great desire to see you again, and especially this matter was told to me discreetly yesterday evening in front of a closed group, tonight we have to go to his house again.
I saw that my husband has strange expectations of me and wants everything to reach the highest positions only through me. Although my understanding at the time did not allow me to fully understand

that the majority of women became notoriously bad and infamous as a result of such incidents. But since I did not like that night or that short man very much, I told him:

"Sir, I am not ready to go there at all and I will not go."

Hearing this answer, my husband fell to his knees in front of me and while he was looking like a poor and miserable person, he kissed my hands and feet one after another and said repeatedly:

"My lady, do you want me to be destroyed, do you want me to be disgraced, do you want to destroy me, do you want two agents to come to our house tomorrow and accuse me of participating in the theft of Kashan tax fund or the fire at the ministry ... They will take me to prison and imprison me. If you love your husband, if you want his reputation, you will not be satisfied with what could happen. Please accept my request and go there tonight. This time will be the last and I know that His Excellency will no longer hold interest in you since he is a variety seeker!"

I thought he was deeply sad and I might cause him misery and trouble. I reluctantly accepted his request, and that night we went there the same way as the night before. At dinner, he gave me a diamond ring that cost more than two hundred tomans.

My life with my husband seemed to be calm and pleasant for a while, and a few nights later he took me to His Excellency again and begged me not to say anything about it to my mother and even my maid.

One day, my husband came home, he sighed and said:

"Do you know what is going on, His Excellency will travel to Europe tomorrow!" When I saw that he was contemplating, I asked him why he was upset, and he replied:

"If His Excellency leaves, I won't have his support. I will be helpless and I am afraid of being demoted and even becoming unemployed and homeless!"

He did not say anything else that day, but at night he left me again and I met His Excellency for the last time.

About ten days had passed since His Excellency left, and one evening my husband came home happy and said:

"Praise is to God, we were saved, praise is to God, my work is done!" I asked what happened? He replied:

"Didn't you hear that the cabinet fell, the new minister ... is familiar with me and is very friendly with His Excellency."

The next week, my husband announced in the morning that he had a guest for the night and that we should make sure that the

guests were taken care of. He had suggested that we go to the room. I followed him into the room without thinking and I felt that my husband had something to say, so I said kindly why he did not say what he wanted to say. He took on a poor and important look and said:
"Lady, tonight you must receive and welcome my esteemed guest!"

And this time I could not take it, and while I was very upset I shouted:
"You are not ashamed, you once made me do those ugly things. I did not say anything to protect your reputation and myself, as if it is not enough now you want to repeat it, I am no longer interested and if you insist, I will go to my father's house right now and I will quote everything you have done."

But without being afraid of my threat, he blocked my way and said sarcastically:
"Hey lady, calm down, now I understand how much I was wrong that first day I treated you with kindness and respect, if I was like other Iranian husbands, I would forcefully put everything I needed on your neck and give it to you. So you understood how much authority a husband has over his wife!"
Then he raised his voice and said in a threatening tone:
"Madam, if you do not accept my offer, you will kick your luck, because before you complain about me, I will announce your adultery, unchastity, and immorality to all my acquaintances and explain it to the whole city through the newspapers."

If lightning had struck me at that minute, it would not have affected me more than this sentence. My eyes went black, the world became dark in my eyes. I saw the things that he had made me put on my neck with complete arrogance and indecency, and at the same time, I could read well in his countenance that he did not turn away from anything and did not mind. As a result of his ugly ways, such as forcing me to have sex with other people, he finally got out of the way and forced them on me, and threaten to later be announced in the newspapers, and further tarnished my reputation.

My husband took advantage of my silence and approached me and said in my ear following his threats:
"If you utter any word to any one of the guests, I will embarrass you!"

I was completely miserable, I was afraid that his threats would come true. I knew very well that I would not be able to easily prove in any court that he was the real culprit. Because I am a woman, and in this environment, there is no right for me and my type.

In a country where women do not have the right to express their opinion about their husband for a lifetime, in an environment where husbands can treat their wives anyhow, where women are considered as furniture and if they are old and Burnout can easily be changed. In a country where a man can point out the slightest flaw in a woman. But the poor woman does not even have the right to object to the filth of the man. What could I do? The depth of the abyss that he had opened in front of me was embodied in me. I did not see a way out for myself. Immediately tears flowed from my eyes and I cried loudly, but unless these tears broke the barrier of his greed and these waters quenched the fire of his greed.
Instead, he said softly with all his might:
"Crying is useless, it is not the time for this, you must go for it."

Out of necessity and misery, I once again accepted his offer. That night, the minister, who was thirty-five years old and had black, curly hair, came to our house in his car. Due to my husband's order, I went to welcome him and received him at the mansion. It was an elaborate party, and we prepared everything from food and drink, and talks came from everywhere. Even though I was very upset and homesick inside, I was looking happy and artificially laughing. Two or three hours passed and they finally brought dinner for Mr. Minister ... My husband got up and left, and Mr. Minister and I were left alone in the room ...

That morning my husband came to me very happy and with an innocent look and it was clear that he wanted to console me:
"What I said yesterday was only for expediency, how can I lose a woman like you and disgrace her in front of the people." And he repeated these words so much that he calmed me down and I was deceived by his words again and I gave up my intention to go to my mother the same day to narrate all the events.

When Effat got to this point of her story, the bell rang at the Sepahsalar Mosque and announced that it was two o'clock in the morning. It's been an hour now that these women have been recounting their life history.
It was two o'clock and Effat had arrived. It's been an hour now that these women have been recounting their life story.
Effat continued her stories:

A few days later, my husband came home in the evening and said happily:
"Darling, we are traveling to Isfahan."

I asked him the reason for this sudden trip and he replied:
"This morning, the minister summoned me and said that I deserved
a more important position. That the head of … Isfahan, due to em-
bezzlement the ministry has parted ways with him and planned to
send me there with sufficient salary. Of course, I thanked the Minis-
ter for his kindness and expressed my readiness to accept this mis-
sion."

Three days later, my husband announced that the necessary ver-
dicts had been issued and the carriage will arrive and we would
have to leave in two days. I went to my parents' house and informed
them about my husband's trip and mission. Everyone congratulat-
ed me. Then we hurriedly gathered the things. My maid was very
willing to come with us, but my husband did not agree to take her. I
cried a lot on the day of the move and no matter what others said, I
should be happy that my husband had progressed so soon, my heart
was not happy and I felt that I would not enjoy that trip.

Finally, we started our journey and after five days of passing
through the cities of Qom and Kashan, we arrived in Isfahan. On
the way, my husband treated me differently. He did not tell me, my
lady or darling anymore. He was harsh and even uttered some rude
words. I was very shocked, but I did not say anything thinking that
he was joking. He was the husband after all and he was right.

In Isfahan, we did not associate with anyone. Two months after
we arrived in that city, little by little, my husband changed his mor-
als and gave up all the respect he had for me in public. He drank a
lot every night and got drunk, cursed, and often beat me. One night,
when he opened his mouth again and started slandering me, I asked
him why he was saying such things if he did not want me, divorce
me and send me to Tehran. In response, he said with a strange laugh:
"It turns out that you are very distracted and you still think that you
are my wife. I have divorced you since the first night you went to
His Excellency, and during this time you were nothing but a tool to
carry out my purposes."

I was extremely angry to hear him say this. I wanted to kill him
so that his disgraceful life might end at that moment, but unfortu-
nately, I could not muster the courage to do so. I said softly:
"Very well, in this case, now that you are no longer benefiting from
me, why don't you send me to Tehran to at least go to my parents."
In response, he said sarcastically again:
"It seems that you have imagined me very simply, you think I do
not know that if you go to Tehran, you will immediately complain

to your parents. But I have also thought about this part, I wrote to your father and mother about how scandalous you became. This is the answer your mother wrote to me. Then he took a piece of paper from his pocket and read it to me:

My dear son-in-law,
I am aware of the misfortunes that this unfaithful girl has brought upon you. I am writing to say that her father is overwhelmed by the intensity of grief and sadness. Maybe you can stop her from this ugly behavior and put an end to the disgrace that has gripped us all.
your mother

As soon as he finished reading the letter, it was as if the world had collapsed on me. Each sentence of that letter was pounding on my brain like a big stone. My legs began to tremble. I later found out that I had a high fever for about twelve days and I was delusional. Finally, when I came to my senses, I saw an old woman sitting beside my bed, holding a bowl and saying:
"Drink this, my child, God willing, you will be fine soon."
I looked around and saw that it did not look like our house. It was a very small room with thatched walls, its doors and windows were made of colorless white wood, and the mat was a piece of carpet. I was lying on a dirty torn red quilt with cotton out, and a hard quilt made of the same red cloth was placed under my head. Surprised, I asked the old woman, "Why am I here? Where has my husband gone? What happened to our servants?"
She laughed and replied:
"My daughter, your husband, and servants are not here, God wills, you will find a husband, and God willing, you will have a servant and maids!"
Then she said in a more serious tone,
"A young man brought you here eight days ago. He suggested to me that If I want to make money, he can bring a sick woman to me so I can take care of her. Then he put ten tomans in my hand. The young man also promised that if you did not feel well after seven or eight days, he would come again and pay again. I was grateful and excited for such a thing and I immediately accepted his offer and forgot to ask for his address. Now, nine days have passed. He gave me a piece of paper and ordered me to give it to you when you are well."

"Where is it? Bring it now. Let me see what he wrote." I asked, but I was illiterate, so I told her that she should find someone to read

the letter. Then a twelve-year-old boy entered the room in disheveled clothes. The old woman called him Hassan Ali. She said to him if he read this paper well, she would give him a pomegranate and immediately took a pomegranate from behind the bed and gave it to Hassan Ali.

The boy, who had studied in the school of one of the Mullabajis of Isfahan and it was clear that his eyes were only familiar with the prayer book of his mullah, took the paper and after reviewing it several times, finally read the words with great difficulty. I understood what he read.

Madam, do not think of coming back, no one will accept you. If you go to Tehran, do not go to your parents' house, because I have written to them that you have run away from my house and you are in one of Isfahan's brothels, and they have replied to me, that they have disowned you!

Chapter Eleven
The Unwell Neighborhood 4

As soon as Hassan Ali finished reading the letter, I fainted again, and this time I was in a fever and delirium for six days. When I finally woke up, I had nothing to do but cry. My husband himself had forced me to do these things, and now he called me all those names and even wrote those lies to my parents. Now I understand that it was him to bring His Excellency on our wedding night. He had brought him to show me to him. And the night that he had invited the minister, especially to our house, to get a better and higher job again through me, and now that he had reached a high position and was a worthy and important person in Isfahan. He didn't need me anymore.

That old woman named Shahbaji. She had a pure heart and a good nature, and during this period she showed me love and affection for two weeks. After my fever subsided, she asked me about my history. I narrated all the events to her. I even said who my parents were and what my husband is like in Isfahan.

Shahbaji was very surprised and cursed all the men and comforted me for a while and finally said that I should go back to Tehran. She said whatever it is, it is better to return to my parents, because of the morals of my fellow citizens. She knew Isfahan and told me that I could not do anything there and that my husband would bother me, especially since he is the head of the department ... and he is very influential and all departments and people consider him.

Shahbaji was right, but money was needed to return to Tehran, and I had nothing. My unjust husband even had taken our wedding ring from my finger when I was sick, but I remembered that the gold watch and its chain was still with me, which my evil husband had not seen.

I talked to Shahbaji that if I wanted to go to Tehran, I would have to pay for the trip and that I had nothing but the gold watch and chain. If she can sell it, maybe I could return to Tehran. Shahbaji immediately got up, put on her Chador, and went to the bazaar. She returned around noon and announced that she had sold the watch and chain for ten tomans, she was not lying, It was bought thirty tomans in Tehran.

I took the next commercial carriage going to Tehran. Shahbaji gave me a box of meatballs and bread. She kissed me very lovingly and said goodbye. I promised her that I would never forget her kindness. Finally, we left Isfahan at about three o'clock in the afternoon. I sat on the flat furniture. Besides me, there were three women and two other men travelling.

The single woman started talking to me. I wanted to tell her all of my sorrow and grief, It was a long way to Tehran. Because these carriages did not travel more than forty kilometres a day and would stop to sleep between the roads at night, I knew we would not reach Tehran until fifteen or twenty days.

The woman was from Tehran. She was a medium-sized person with a brown complexion, sharp but small eyes, and a thick lip. She looked forty-five years old. Of course, I did not think she could harm me. I told her briefly how misfortunate. I was hoping that she would help me intellectually and put a solution in front of my feet, as soon as she was informed of my sufferings that had befallen me, said kindly:
"Oh dear daughter, I was in Tehran a month ago and I happened to work in a house near your house, and I heard something that, of course, may not be good to say, but I'm afraid if I hide more it will not be good for you."
I asked her anxiously what she knew and what she had heard!
"When I was in Tehran, near Azizkhan crossroads, I was at the house of one of the nobles. And I heard how your parents are angry. They have sworn that they will not allow you in their house." She replied.

It is obvious how sad and affected I was by what she said. I did not know what to do and I kept telling myself where to go and where to turn. I had no relatives to mediate with so maybe my parents could forgive me. I was so disturbed by these events, and especially this recent news, that every minute I thought I would soon go crazy, and I became so suspicious that I sometimes said to myself that maybe all these slanders were true, and I have done this myself!
She noticed my extraordinary anxiety and uneasiness and she tried to appease me with kindness and gentleness:

"Why are you so sad? I know men and I know that you are not to blame and without causing so much harm and suffering, I have a sister in Tehran who has a decent home. I will take you to her and after a few days, I will go to your mother. I will tell her the truth and prove your innocence and I am sure they will be willing to accept you again."

I was so happy to hear this offer that tears welled up in my eyes. I thought God had opened the door for me.

We arrived in Tehran, near the car station in the ChaparKhaneh (courier-house). We walked to ToopKhaneh Square, and from there we went to Alaodoleh. In the middle of the road, we entered Borj-e-Noush and finally got to a crossroads, then turned to the right side alley. We stood at the green house.

"Did she take you to the major bride's house?"
Ashraf and Aqdas said together when they heard the address.

"Yes, the major bride's house, but I did not know where it was then."
Effat said with shyness.

She knocked on the door and as soon as it opened she told me: "It is a safe place." I entered the yard behind her without thinking, then pointed to a room near the door and said:
"Please sit here so that I can inform my sister to come to you."
I went to the room she had shown and saw that it was a relatively clean room. There were chairs and velvet benches, I sat on one of those and thought about my life; from my father's house, the events of the wedding night, and the unforgettable tragic events of Isfahan flashed in front of my eyes. The misfortunes that befell me were really much more than the endurance of a poor woman. My eyes and ears were closed. At that moment, I was consoling myself that salvation had been found.

Unfortunately, this was not the case and it turned out that God has not ended my suffering yet. Suddenly footsteps tore my thoughts. A tall woman, who I later found out was the landlady entered.
"Her face and shape are not bad! She may be useful"
I stood up and my eyes were fixed on that lady's mouth, I was shocked to hear this phrase, so I immediately turned my face towards my fellow traveler and said with all my might:

"You brought me here to a safe place and promised that you would go and talk to my parents so that I could go home as soon as possible, and now we are talking about immoralities. What do these words mean!"

A fellow traveler approached me and said softly:

"Darring lady, I told you that your parents swore not to let you in the house. This lady's house, and as I said, it is a very safe place. Sometimes some young people come here. If you like it, you may use it. If it doesn't work I will go to your mother tomorrow as promised to prepare the ground for reconciliation, maybe you will not stay here for more than two or three days."

I was not convinced by her words and I protested, and finally, after she swore thousands of words that she would go see my parents tomorrow, I calmed down a bit. I had nowhere to go for the night so I stayed.

That night, a twenty-five-year-old man wearing a leather hat and electric shoes came there. His face looked more like a monkey than a human. The lady of the house threatened me that if I refused him, I would have to leave the house at that time, and finally, I reluctantly entered the room with him.

In the morning, I immediately asked my fellow traveler to go to my parents. I cried and begged her to leave sooner. She promised me and put on her Chador and left the house.

It was noon when she got back. She told me that my parents had gone to Mashhad and would not return for another few months. I was so saddened by this news that I knew that if I stayed there, there would be talk every night of a newcomer coming. It was like that for the two or three months that I stayed there, I spent most of the night embracing a new man, and it seems that I needed to be thankful because one day a woman who was like me said that before It was busier!

During that time, whenever I asked about my parents, they always told me to be patient. Apart from me, there were four other women in that house, but we did not talk much, and whenever there was no party, I stayed in my room.

About a month later, one day there were three or four women, including Nahid, our boss. They came and I asked one of the women what was going on and who were they?

She said softly in my ear.

"Have you not heard that work and business are sluggish these days because the major bride's house is no longer open. She has seen the

right time to repent and wants to go to Mashhad. So the rest came to pay our debts and take us to their house."
I simply asked, "Do you have a loan?"
She laughed: "You are still talking as if you are not in debt!
I said, "What do you mean, I do not understand anything? How can I owe when I have never taken money from anyone?"
She said sarcastically: "These clothes that are worn at work and the dinners and lunches are taken into account, and without a doubt, your pampering bills are now in the major bride's box."

I thought to myself that this girl had gone crazy talking about these things. At the same time, those three or four women came together in the room where the girl and I were sitting. . Then the major bride came from outside and pointed at us and said: "If you want any of these ladies, you can have them." Then she pointed a finger at each of us and set a price. When she reached me and said: "she owes me seventy tomans."

I became very angry. I wanted to throw out everything I had in my heart and tell those women that I was brought there cunningly and shamefully. But I realized it was useless. These women will not believe me. I got up and left the room with a headache. A few minutes later, Ms. Nahid, who liked me, came to me and said calmly: "I understand you have a very bad past here, but my house will not be like this. All amenities will be provided."

I hoped I will be satisfied with this arrangement until my parent are back. I accepted and she brought me here and as you know, I have been in this house for almost a month now ...

The last word had not yet come out of Effat's mouth when she had a bad cough and coughed for a while, and then, in a state of tears that flowed from her eyes, she said following her remarks:

Unfortunately, to protect the honor of my parents, I can not say a word to any of the men who come to me.

Now it was the turn of Akhtar, the plump lady:

I was neither the daughter of a butcher, nor the daughter of a mercer, nor the daughter of nobles, I do not know any parents for myself. As far as I remember we had a house in a small house near the barracks of the viceroy. My living conditions there were very bad, during the day I was expected to sweep the yard and the room, at night I slept in a corner on a torn quilt.

At that age, I did not understand what kind of life was going on in the house, so much that I sometimes saw that some people, such as tripe sellers, perfumers, grocers, and cossacks, came to our house at night and stayed in the same room with two very ugly women who were in the house.

In those days, no one in the house paid much attention to me, and it was clear that Ms. Baji, the landlady, had kept me for later. Sometimes she was giving me yellow and plaid cucumbers or a bunch of grapes, most of which were raisins. In the winters, she would let me sleep at the bottom of the heater chair a few nights a week, and the rest of the nights I had to stay in the hallway under my torn quilt, shivering from the cold until morning.

And ironically, I was a light sleeper. So many nights there were fights and quarrels in our house which sometimes led Ms. Baji and some guests to the commissariat. But because I was not very curious, I did not throw myself into the fight.

Years passed like this, I grew up well with all the misfortunes, and since I was a little fat and needed money, I often turned my attention to the people who came into the house, and as soon as they saw me, they called me, and I went to them recklessly. Sometimes they would flirt with me by touching my chin or kissing my face. Sometimes they put white money in my hand, but the money always went to Ms. Baji.

When I was thirteen or fourteen, one day I asked Ms. Baji:

"Did I have parents?"

"Of course, you have parents, but the truth is that they have neglected you. Your father was a wealthy and noble person who did not want to have a daughter and had ordered your mother that if she gave birth to a child, especially a girl, he would divorce her. Your mother gave birth to you while your father was traveling. She feared her life, so she left you and told your father that a dead child had been born."

I was very affected sadly by hearing that. But what was the result of grief, from a young age I understood what the power of money is and the lust of the rich on earth is unlimited, and I knew well that as long as money is at stake, unjust sentences will be issued at any time by any court.

By the time that I knew myself and I was a relatively good-looking girl. I was checking those coming to the house more carefully. One day I saw a young man come in, he was different. He was a shoe-

maker. The young man with a medium-sized body, large black eyes, a black elongated eyebrow, a well-shaven beard, and a black mustache. His black hair was turned upwards at the back of his neck. It was called duck style. He had tidy teeth, although they looked a little yellow from the smoking and carelessness.

Ms. Baji and the two women were extremely happy to see him because it was a great blessing for them to have such a person with this posture instead of the other clients. But how sorry they were when the young man did not pay attention to either of the two women after a quarter of an hour of stopping by.

"I don't like what I'm seeing, if you have others let me see," he said.

Ms. Baji jumped, she did not know what to say, and because she did not want to lose this young rich manat no cost. She had no one other than the two women, but suddenly a thought came to her. She showed me:

"f you want, I have a girl here!"

I was standing in the corner of the yard, and the young shoemaker told her, "This is not bad!"

I did not understand the rest of the negotiations between the two. I just remember that the young man left and Ms. Baji immediately took me to the bathroom and gave me a new dress, and made up my face. That night, the young shoemaker came there and I spent the night with him until the morning without knowing what was going on ...

Nothing new happened later in my life and I have been doing this for almost thirteen years now I have been to Qazvin several times and I have changed my house almost ten times.

Akhtar had not finished talking when they knocked on the door. Nahid was swearing about why they did not open the door quickly. She was upset because she could not deceive the young men and bring them to the house. So-called fishing had not fallen into her trap!

Chapter Twelve
The Second Accident

Ms. Boss, Nahid, who owned the house, was a plump woman with short stature, a large nose, and thick lips. Her face was very red, and there were many black and brown spots on her face. The muscles of her face, especially those around her eyes, were so large and prominent that had narrowed her eyes' under circles. Although she was about fifty years old, she had not yet fallen out of favor, especially from the point of view of some people who knew of her cash register!

As soon as she entered the courtyard, the sound of her growling and shouting was heard:

"I do not know what happened to the young people. Where have they gone? It seems as if every man in this city has melted and sunk to the ground at once. If young people had money, how could this house of mine, which is famous and privileged in every way, be left without guests!

Hearing her footsteps and grunts, four women got up and stood next to Nahid. They greeted her with full respect.

"No one came here during my absence?"

"No, no one came." Ashraf said.

"How is it that no one came here and there was no news about Mohammad Taqi?"

"No Ma'am, I said no," Ashraf replied.

Ashraf's polite response was a spark that fell on Nahid's gunpowder bag.

"You are also telling me with this attitude and you are answering with sweetness and cuteness! Since when have you become so dear?"

Ashraf, who was familiar with Nahid's morals and had a history, knew that arguing with her was useless, and remained silent. Then Nahid wanted to turn her face towards Effat.

"How are you? Did you finish sewing the dress you started?"

Effat, whose voice was muffled by a large cough, replied calmly:

"No, ma'am, it is not over yet, God willing, it will end tomorrow."

Nahid seems to have run out of patience and started shouting: "I do not know who has given you so much courage that you do whatever you want."

Then she made a mocking tone and said:

"Ms. Lady, you should know you are not with your family here. You should obey me here. Dry and empty expressions do not work for me. Lunch, dinner, and clothes are not free. We are ... and we are eating w... bread!

The unrelenting violence, and especially the ugly words that Nahid uttered, severely upset Effat, so she angrily grabbed the handkerchief she was holding and hurried to the room on the north side of the courtyard. But during the hot disagreement with Nahid, she did not sit down and continued to grumble and talk to herself:

"I do not understand the house ... why is the house always empty."

At this point, the chef's grandmother took her head out of the kitchen and greeted her.

Ms. Nahid also asked: "What did you make for dinner?"

Abji replied in a hushed voice: "We have nothing, I just had a little spinach, I made a Nargessi because Reza did not have money, there is no egg."

Nahid said sarcastically: "What do they expect from me? She says we only have Nargessi, you made it seem that Nargessi is the small thing and claiming eggs. No, Grandma, tonight we do not have guests, with this expensive firewood, why did you even set the stove on fire?"

Nahid's words had not yet come out of her mouth and grandmother had not yet returned to the kitchen when they knocked on the door. Nahid was hoping that the party had finally come, first of all, she informed Abji not to turn off the stove. Those poor women, who had prepared themselves for no-shows, took a deep breath when they heard this second order. Nahid ran to the new clients. Minutes later, the voice of Ms. Boss was raised, and Siavash Mirza and Mohammad Taqi, who came behind him, flattered him,"

"Come on, come on, very welcome!"

As soon as the guests entered the courtyard, Mohammad Taqi turned to Nahid and said:

"His Excellency wanted to come much earlier, but you know how much trouble they have."

Nahid acknowledged him with a laugh and said: "God willing, the troubles will be resolved."

Siavash Mirza shook his head and then said.

"But I must say you did not treat us well that night!"

Nahid became anxious but immediately use a kind tone:

"Then there will be retaliation tonight."

Mohammad Taqi also added to the conversation

"Yes, my lord, I already told your Majesty what a beautiful piece you have found for them."

Nahid took the guests to the guest room and invited them to sit down. She hurriedly turned on the light of the heater and turned them on.

They are yet to have dinner so she quickly gets rice to cook pilaf.

Then she returned to the room, with a smiling face and asked Siavash Mirza: "What would you want?"

Siavash had drunk a lot of alcohol from the beginning of the night and as we know, was completely unconscious in the street and came to his senses with the help of his servant.

"If you have Arak and wine, you can bring them."

Nahid, contrary to what she used to do with other guests, that is, will not prepare until she received money, immediately called Reza and ordered him to take the empty bottles and buy a bottle of Arak and a bottle of wine from Shamoon Yahudi, who had a shop on the same street. Then she said to Siavash Mirza:

"Well, tonight, His Highness will surely make us proud and stay here."

Mohammad Taqi, who was standing in the corner of the room, answered instead of Siavash Mirza, "Yes, yes. His Highness got a little disorder on the way here and can no longer go home, of course, prepare a good dinner."

Siavash, who had been half drunk all this time, confirmed his servant's saying. Nahid suggested that in this case, let me know if you need girls. Siavash stammered and said, "Yes, yes. Let them come to see how they are." Nahid turned her head towards the yard, called the women one by one, and invited them to the inn.

A few minutes later, Aqdas, the short-haired lady, and behind her, Ashraf, the tall, dark-eyed woman, and then, Akhtar, the plump woman, entered and each of them sat on a chair.

It was clear from the prince's face that none of them satisfied him, and for this reason, he looked at Muhammad with a disapproving look. Mohammad Taqi, who had promised his master a new woman, noticed his disapproval and immediately looked at Nahid reprimandingly. She also pointed out to him to have a little patience.

Then Effat hurriedly put on make-up. Her countenance at that moment was exceedingly sad, and her motionless eyes and cold gazes gave a special effect to the matte-colored face at that time.

Siavash was surprised to see the newcomer and held her hand for a while when she shook his hand. The women, who, as usual, asked every newcomer for a cigarette, asked Siavash Mirza for a cigarette. He opened his silver cigarette case and offered a golden lip cigarette to each of them. A few ordinary words were exchanged between the ladies, then everyone got up and said goodbye. Then Mohammad Taqi, who was close to Siavash, flattered him and said: "Did you see I wasn't lying?"

Siavash smiled at Mohammad Taqi and hit his back with a short stick and said: "The last one was good, very good, go get her."

Nahid entered and placed a tray on the table in front of Siavash, between which was a crystal jar of Arak, a bottle of wine, a bowl of nuts, a plate full of cucumbers, and a bowl of yogurt.

Siavash immediately filled his glass with Arak and drank it. While Siavash was enjoying himself, Mohammad Taqi, left the room with Nahid, "His Highness like the fourth one, what should we offer you for the night?"

Nahid, who flirted like a young girl, replied, "With the respect that I have for His Highness, of course, I will not charge too much, you know that whatever you give, they have not given less and will not go away!"

Mohammad Taqi was not satisfied with this answer: "Leaving aside the compliments. How much does he need to pay?"

Nahid thought for a moment: "Have mercy and pay fifteen tomans including dinner and alcohol."

Mohammad Taqi frowned:

"Fifteen tomans, it is too much, I will pay you ten tomans, but of course, I will take something extra for myself from the gentleman. But you should not say a word."

Nahid did not say anything else, Mohammad Taqi also returned to the room and informed his young master that he had finished the deal for fifteen Tomans for tonight. And only because he is a former client that Nahid was satisfied with this amount, otherwise It was much more and it cost from forty to fifty tomans.

Siavash, who was constantly drinking Arak, seemed to believe his words, while drunk said:

"You wanted to tell her that this gentleman is getting married one of these days and will get rich so that she should not be so hard on us now."

Mohammad Taqi said with flattery: "I said it all sir, she was very happy and with the hope that there will be retaliation in the future, she agreed to a discount."

Ten minutes later, Effat came to the guest room again and sat next to Siavash Mirza. An hour later, an uncooked dinner was brought for them. It was something bad that could not be eaten at all, but Siavash was drunk and ate it with joy. After half an hour, they went to the room which had a bed ...

Mohammad Taqi, because he promised Nahid to bring His Highness there, more in the future, had persuaded her to leave plump Akhtar to him for that night.

It was after midnight, all the people in the house had fallen asleep, when they suddenly knocked hard on the door, but none of the people in the house was willing to move. Then it was slammed hard for the second time; This time, Nahid got up and while grumbling, asked from behind the door, "Who is it?"

A loud, abnormal voice, which turned out to be utterly intoxicating, arose and stammered:

"Why don't you open the door? You don't want our money!"

"Dear sir, everyone pays, but I asked what is your name?" Nahid said softly.

The voice rose again and said: "I do not care what it is, open the door now." And immediately he kicked the door again.

Nahid was frightened and at the same time very shocked that someone could break into their street in the presence of security. But her surprise did not last long, because the stranger did not stop kicking. He constantly threatened that if she did not open the door, he would break it and kill everyone. Frightened, she opened the door and when she saw his stature in the moonlight, she understood why the security agent didn't interfere! The man looks scary. He was a young Cossack, about thirty years old, with short stature and a slender body.

As soon as Nahid opened the door and saw the Cossack, she hid behind one of the door hinges that turned towards the wall. Cossack entered the yard and shouted:

"Who did not open the door, and who asked for my name, in case you don't know my name is Hasan Rizeh, everyone in Tehran knows me."

Nahid stood for a moment behind the door handle, then dared to walk behind the Cossack, and as soon as she saw Hassan Rizeh going to the west of the yard, she went to the opposite side, to the east, then returned once and as if coming from there.

"Reza, bastard, why did you not open the door? You should know that Naib Hassan Khan can come to our house whenever he wants, the house belongs to him and we are his caretaker."

Nahid's flattery that was out of fear had its effect. Cossack turned his face towards her, laughed, and said:

"Hello, ma'am, I'm sorry for troubling you at this time of night, but this Rez of yours kept me behind the door for a while."

Nahid, who knew that she was dealing with a drunken Cossack, thought to herself that he had drunk more than he should, and if he was given a little more time, he would surely pass out. Then happily said: "Accept my apologies, forgive him for the sake of my gray hair. I will cut off his ear tomorrow. please go to the guest room and have some rest."

Hassan Rizeh, who was struggling to stand up due to the intensity of his drunkenness, went behind Nahid and to the guest room. Nahid also turned on the light, the room was very messy, cucumber skins and nuts were spilled around the table and on the carpet due to Siavash's carelessness, and empty Arak and wine bottles were still there on the table. Nahid thought that Cossack was so drunk that he would not notice the mess in the room. But this did not happen, because as soon as he saw the small, half drunken Arak and a bottle of wine on the table and the skin of cucumbers, he mocked:

"Well, now I understand why you did not want to open the door for me. It turns out that you have guests and apparently the good ones. Tell me who they are."

Nahid, who was afraid of Cossack's eyes and saw the situation as dangerous, said: "No, I swear to you we did not have a guest tonight, this is last night's mess, they haven't cleaned it."

At the same time, Siavash, who was sleeping in the other room, fell off his pillow and his snoring voice rose. Nahid jumped in fear. No matter how much she tried to prevent his snoring from being heard, she could not, and every second Siavash Mirza snorted louder.

Hassan Rizeh, noticing the snoring sound while drinking from the Arak bottle, said to Nahid: "Madam, why are you lying to me?" Then he turned his face towards Siavash and Effat's bedroom, and said to Nahid with all his might: "I swear to God if I found anyone in the room, they will not survive." Then he got up and headed toward the room.

Nahid was very scared and realized that now there will be a quarrel. She was not afraid that Siavash would be killed, but mostly afraid that he would be taken to the commissariat tomorrow and then to court, that she would be arrested for a while and finally fined, and, worst of all, that her house would be closed. So she placed herself between Hassan Rizeh and the bedroom so that he might prevent the Cossack from entering the room. But Hassan Rizeh pushed her hard and opened the bedroom door and entered it.

Siavash and Effat are in the room together. Siavash was asleep so deep due to the amount of Arak he drank, and despite the loud noise, he did not wake up. But poor Effat, who could not sleep, heard the footsteps of Cossack, and in the moonlight, she saw the person who, like a clock dancer, entered the room.

Hassan Rizeh was three steps away from the bed and saw the white collar and tie of Siavash Mirza hanging on the bed, so he said in a harsh voice: "Dandy, dandy, I knew he must be a dandy!"

It was dark, Hassan imagined that Siavash was trying to defend herself, deftly took his machete from the cover and threw it at them. But the machete landed right between the feet of Effat and Siavash and scratched her thighs.

Effat whined from the pain and fainted. Siavash woke up in a hurry and saw Hassan Rizeh in front of him. Nahid was constantly calling for help in the middle of the yard. Siavash got out of bed without hesitation and attacked Hassan Rizeh. Hassan no longer had a machete. As soon as he saw Siavash coming, he reached for the pistol he had in his waist, but Siavash hurriedly threw himself on him and did not let him take the pistol out of his waist. Siavash was awakened, but on the contrary, Hassan was completely drunk and constantly cursing and shouting..

The two of them wrestled together for a few minutes. Suddenly, Siavash lost his balance, slipped, and fell to the ground. Cossack was so drunk that he did not realize the consequences of his actions. Nothing could save Siavash at that moment. A second or two later, maybe the prince would be gone... Hassan Rizeh put his fingers close to the heel of the pistol and pulled it back, shooting, but Siavash survived!

Chapter Thirteen
How Siavash Survived

Farrokh was walking along Naderi Street. The incident between him and Siavash Mirza was not so important to keep his mind busy. Instead, He did not give up thinking about what F... Al-Saltaneh could have said in his wife's ear. He knew him well that F... Al-Saltaneh believed in nothing but money. He also knew that the words merit, grace, and perfection did not make sense in her aunt's husband's dictionary. This hard-hearted person considered everything, even the love of his homeland and fellowman as empty words, and does not use such words except in cases where his benefits were involved.

Farrokh's familiarity with the state and spirits of F... Al-Saltaneh, made him more aware of his hopeless situation. He despaired that he could easily embrace his beloved Mahin one day.

But could he give up Mahin?

Farrokh did not want Mahin just to relieve his intense desire and extinguish his instinct. Farrokh saw his life without Mahin as empty and soulless. He nurtured every goal and desire in his brain. He knew that he would not enjoy any success without Mahin. Mahin was everything to him and without Mahin he had nothing. He was constantly thinking about what to do, what path to take, what plan to devise to soften the hard heart of the F... Al-Saltaneh. He had become religious, visited holy places, and made vows, He prayed to God to remove all obstacles.

He was so engrossed in these thoughts that he did not pay any attention to himself as he walked slowly towards his house. And at that time, there were no electric lights on the street of Tehran, but fortunately, on that night, those who remained in the streets like him until that hour did not bother by the high and innumerable pits and potholes of the streets because the moon appeared in full view in the sky and The floor of the street was lit.

Eventually, Farrokh came close to home, but he was still so upset and confused that he thought to himself that it might be better to make more use of that moonlit night and the mild weather, and he thought himself that he might find peace with the beautiful nature.

When he got to his house, which was near the Darvazeh Dowlat, he turned right in front of the gate and went over the mounds of dirt that existed next to the ditches of Tehran.

For a while, Farrokh looked at the city of Tehran from the top of the mound of ditches, which was gradually becoming completely silent; he wished he could have Mahin there with him. The young man's gait was irregular. Sometimes he would stop and think deeply, and it was so obvious that he would find a means and study its practicality, and then at once, he would take a sharp breath as if it were a sign that he was on his way. He will be as fast and steady as he is, and with such agility, he will carry out his plans, and then he would stop again and take a long, deep look at the blue sky, realizing that he has again encountered an obstacle, and He wants to use that infinite atmosphere to find his way to success.

Farrokh did not notice the time, did not know how long it had been and did not feel the desire to sleep. Anyone who saw him in the middle of the night on the mound of the ditch thought he was crazy, and anyone who came across him did not think of him as a rational person, he seemed like someone who escaped from the shackles of a mental hospital. He pounded his foot on the ground or threw his fists to the sky. He would sent his inner fire on the earth and time.

The lights of the houses went out one by one, and with every moment Tehran sinks deeper into darkness.

Suddenly, a voice was heard and cut off his chain of thoughts. He did not pay attention to it at first, but when it was repeated, he listened more carefully and knew that it was the voice of a crying woman, asking for help: "Somebody help. My house has been destroyed. People are being killed in my house!"

Farrokh came down from the top of the ditch at full speed and ran in the direction of the sound, and after a distance of two hundred steps, arrived in front of Nahid's house. He immediately shook the door and entered the yard. Nahid's voice was getting weaker and tired. She saw Farrokh, pointed to the room with her hand, then suddenly fell to the ground and passed out.

Farrokh ran to the room without hesitation and entered when Hassan Rizeh threw Siavash to the ground and placed his pistol on the prince's forehead. Farrokh realized that if he moved late and had the slightest doubt, someone's life would be lost, so he immediately reached for Hassan Rizeh's head with a jump and hit the arm of Cossack with a fist. Hassan Rizeh's hand slipped and the pistol went off. But because the tube was far from Siavash Mirza's forehead, the bullet passed under the bed and hit the wall.

Hassan Rizeh came back to see who had dared to do so, and at the same time, the drunkard Cossack was plotting severe punishment for the newcomer, but Farrokh did not give him a chance, another hard punch landed on Rizeh. This severe blow did its job and the pistol fell out of Cossack's hand and Hassan Rizeh fell to the ground.

Siavash, who was lifeless on the floor, immediately got up as he saw Hassan was unconscious and turned his head towards his savior, who he thought was a security guy, and wanted to promise him a reward in which the moonlight shone once. He saw a young man who he had met on the street a few hours earlier. Then he said in a hushed and trembling voice:
"You! You saved me! I am Siavash Mirza, the son of Prince K ... and I will never forget your help!"

Farrokh interrupted and said: "Now is not the time for this talk, we should get away from this place as soon as possible. They may take us all for investigation, and although we are not guilty, in this city, the innocent and the oppressed will be caught and condemned!"

Siavash acknowledged what he had said and tried to get up, but he could not, because he felt a burning sensation in his left thigh. Then he realized that the machete that Hassan Rizeh had thrown at him had injured his leg and that he had lost a lot of blood. Farrokh realized that he would not be able to walk alone with that injury. Mohammad Taqi appeared on the doorstep half-naked, and while trying to show he had just woken up by the sound of a pistol bullet, he ran towards Siavash Mirza and asked with artificial worries and anxiety:
"Sir, sir, are you harmed?"

Farrokh, who was well aware of the servant's fraud and hypocrisy, did not want to reprimand him at this time and waste his time in vain, so he commanded: "Your master is injured. If you do not want to discredit him anymore, get him out of here as soon as possible."

Mohammad Taqi did not dare to oppose Farrokh's order, so he immediately went to his bedroom and hurriedly put on his clothes and turned around and took Siavash Mirza, who was very weak due to his injury, and brought him to the courtyard. They left without paying attention to Nahid, who was unconscious in the middle of the yard.

Farrokh approached the room, where the horrible incident took place. Hassan Rizeh was completely unconscious. But there was a moaning, So he took another step forward, this time he heard a woman say:
"Save me too, save me too!"

Farrokh looked carefully around, and he suddenly saw a foot under the bed, and it belonged to a woman who had fallen between the wall and the side of the bed, and there was a lot of blood on her white sleeping shirt. He saw a beautiful woman who looked at him with her half-open eyes and said in a charming voice:

"Sir! Sir, save me from here."

Farrokh made his decision in a few seconds. An esoteric feeling was that this woman should not be one of those who came to this place on her own and willingly lived a disgraceful life, and he was sure that she had been deceived and forced to do so. He immediately took her both hands and lifted her off the ground. And when he realized that she, too, was weak from injury and could not move very well, he had no choice but to throw her on his back, and hurry out the door.

Farrokh was afraid that he would encounter the security guy on the way and cause him trouble. And as far as possible, he passed through the alleys, and went at full speed towards his house. Although the woman was very thin and light, Farrokh had to spend a few minutes catching his breaths.

There was complete silence in Tehran at that time of the night. The color of Effat's face on that moonlit was so pale. Every time Farrokh laid her on the ground, she looked innocent, miserable, and at the same time beautiful.

The voice of Effat, "Save me, save me," kept repeating in his ears, as if the reflection of that voice strengthened him so that he could easily bear the weight of the woman on his shoulders and save her as soon as possible.

Meanwhile, Mahin's face did not go unnoticed and he wondered what she would think if she saw him in this state, then he thought to himself: 'Mahin knows me, Mahin is aware that only her love what strengthens me.' Fortunately, there was no passerby on the street at the time to see Farrokh.

Half an hour later, Farrokh reached his house, knocked on the door, and immediately an old man opened the door. Farrokh entered the house with Effat on his shoulder.

***

After Mohammad Taqi grabbed Siavash Mirza by the armpit and they left the house, and after Farrokh threw Effat on his shoulder and went to the house, there was silence in Nahid's house.

Nahid, who had been shouting for a while and asking the locals for help, She got exhausted and could not stand in the middle of the yard. Reza, who was lying on the roof, had heard the sound of Hassan Rizeh's car and even a bullet but did not interfere. The elderly chef, who had age-related hearing loss, was asleep hard and her snoring was loud. Akhtar, who was sleeping next to Mohammad Taqi, heard a gunshot but thought that it was in the neighbor's house or it was a dream, so went back to sleep, even when Mohammad Taqi went to Siavash's room, but she did not notice.

Ashraf and Aqdas slept together that night and talked to each other for a while before going to sleep, complaining about their bad times and unhappy life, so they were still awake when the incident happened. They saw Nahid walking towards the door and then taking the drunken Cossack to the hall. The two women were very familiar with such events, they did not panic, but each promised in their hearts and waited to see which of them would be called to sleep with a drunken Cossack. So even though they had put their heads on the pillow, in fact, they were waiting to hear the voice of Nahid to invite one of them to the inn. But after a while no one called them, instead, they heard Nahid shouting and a few minutes later, they heard a gunshot. So they hurriedly got up and sat on their bed, but they were so frightened by the sound of gunfire that they did not dare to move from their place. Even after Mohammad Taqi and Siavash and Farrokh left the house with Effat, they were in complete silence.

Two men finally came to Nahid's house, which had four rooms left open. One of them said to the other: "The deputy chief is here."
He stepped forward, and the police, whose gun and baton showed entered the yard behind him and immediately reported it to his superior:
"Sir, half an hour ago, I was walking down this street and saw someone beating people severely in this house, and because I recognized from a distance that he was a Cossack, and I knew that I could not do anything with him, I thought it would be better for me to go to the nearby station to report. As I was walking away, I heard someone shouting for help, but I did not pay attention, thinking that I would be back soon."
The deputy said: "Very well then, now we have to see what happened here and why it is left open and no sound is heard."

They both headed to the bedroom where Siavash and Effat had been an hour ago and the doors were left open. The policeman saw a body on the ground! "It turns out that a person was killed!"
He approached the deputy and said:
"oh no, She Nahid, the owner of this house, she is not feeling okay!

There were no signs of wounds or injuries anywhere and it was clear that she was just weak, so he immediately went to the tank and brought some water and splash it on Nahid's face, then rubbed her arms and shoulder. And after a few minutes, she opened her eyes and asked, "Where am I, what happened, where did he go?"
And when her eyes met the police officer, she asked:
"You caught him, did you catch him?"
The incumbent also replied gently:
"We have not arrested anyone yet, but be rest assured, we will definitely

arrest him, get up now and tell us what happened."
Nahid got up with the help of the policeman and they all went to the guest room but was surprised when she didn't find them in the room except Hassan Rizeh. The official, as if in a hurry and wanted to go to the commissariat or his house as soon as possible, aggressively said:
"Tell us what you know."

Nahid explained in detail the arrival of Siavash Mirza and his interest in Effat, adding that after everyone had fallen asleep, Hassan Rizeh had entered the house threatening to kill her or anyone, that she tried to stop him from entering the room but he forced his way in...

Ashraf and Aqdas, came out of their bedroom and while trying to pretend that they had just woken up, they approached Nahid and the men.
As soon as Nahid saw them, asked anxiously:
"Where is Effat, isn't she with you?"
Ashraf and Aqdas answered together: "No, madam, we just woke up now and we have not seen Effat since nightfall.

Nahid called on Effat several times, and when she did not hear any answer, she started shouting and screaming and kept saying:
"They came to my house, and they kidnapped her. If my Effat is gone, my house will not prosper anymore. I paid seventy Tomans for her!"

The ignorant official, without paying attention to Nahid's sighs and moans, leaned on Hassan Rizeh, who had fallen into a deep sleep due to drinking a lot of Arak. He wrote the details in a book in his hand and then turn to Nahid. He promised that the commissariat would take action tomorrow morning and the damage caused will be taken care of by Hassan Rizeh, and then gave orders to the policeman, and they both left the house.

Hassan Rizeh woke up in the morning and after looking around, cursed Nahid a lot and complained about the way he was received. He threatened them that if he was treated like this again, he would cut off the ears of everyone in the house!

Nahid did not say anything and thought that Cossack would soon be caught and would be punished... But months passed and her repeated visits to the commissariat did not yield any results, and in the end, he did not know whether the head of the official had dared to report about Cossack that night? However, if he had given a report, it was not clear where.

Chapter Fourteen
Mahin's letter

As we said, Farrokh had a house near the Darvazeh Dowlat and lived in that house with his old father. Farrokh's mother had said goodbye to life almost three years ago.

The house had a courtyard and an area of about five hundred square meters, the other building was a new building facing north, which was a mixture of east and west style, and had two floors with a basement. In the middle of the foyer, wide and beautiful stairs were built and there were three windows facing the courtyard.

Farrokh's father kept the upper part of the mansion and the rooms on the east side and gave the rest to his son. On the night of the incident, someone was anxious and worried, even though it was past her usual bedtime, she could not sleep while leaning her head on the pillow, and apparently, she fell asleep, all her attention was on the house, and every time there was a sound in the street, she would get up and listen, and as the sound faded away, she would rest her head on the pillow again in despair.

She was fifty years old with gray hair and a smiling face. If one looked carefully at the lines of her face, one would realize that in her youth she enjoyed the beauty and her heart was drawn to the men of her time. This woman was Farrokh's nanny and the reason for her worry and anxiety was that he had not come home that night, contrary to his habit. Her period of anxiety and worry lasted for several hours, and finally, after midnight, she heard a knock on the door of the house, and immediately the old servant, who was sleeping in the nearby yard that summer night, got up and opened the door.

As soon as she saw Farrokh's shadow, she took a deep breath as if a burden had been lifted from her shoulders, and then hurriedly got up to make sure it was Farrokh, she walked quietly and suddenly, to her surprise, saw that Farrokh was not alone. She noticed another person at his back. The poor woman wanted to ask him but Farrokh ordered her to be quiet.

Farrokh, without lowering Effat from his shoulders, climbed the stairs of the foyer slowly and entered a small room on the west side of the upper building, and placed Effat on the bed. His nanny was more disturbed by the sight of large blood stains on his clothes, but he told her to bring a container of hot water as soon as possible. She placed the lamp on the stove and went out to look for hot water, and a few minutes later she brought thatch, rose water, and a container full of hot water. Farrokh and the nanny began to wash the wound and then covered it with a white and clean cloth. Fortunately, the wound was not deep but only scratched. Little by little, the thatch and rose water that Farrokh's nanny had brought near the woman's nose helped her regain her consciousness and opened her eyes. But even at that moment she couldn't believe her eyes but hoped that her dream had come true and that she had been saved from that disgraceful and painful life. A smile appeared on the corner of her mouth.

Farrokh did not take the time to talk and ask about anything, so he kindly advised her to rest and after reassuring her several times that she was in a safe place and that no one would be able to hurt her, and she could go anywhere the day after if she wants to. Farrokh asked her nanny to stay with her as he left the room and went downstairs to the bed that the nanny had prepared for him, after a short moment he fell asleep.

At about seven in the morning, Farrokh woke up as usual and was surprised to see his nanny sitting beside him with a smiling face and looking at him with a meaningful look, she said with love:

"Well done my son, good job, it turns out you have good taste!"

Farrokh realized that the poor woman thought that he was attracted to Effat. She said that Effat had spent the night easily and was awake. But she is still on the bed.

Half an hour later, Farrokh went to where Effat was and entered after knocking on the door, then, with all gentleness and kindness, first asked about her:

"Madam, I guessed from your look and behavior, you are not a resident of that house and I think you were taken there without your consent. Certainly, someone had deceived you. In any case, I am ready to help you. If you have relatives and you want to go to them, I assure you that as soon as your minor injury heals, I will send you home."

Poor Effat, who had not seen this kind of kindness for a long time, and had not heard this kind of words other than vulgar words, was fascinated by the charming and warm voice of the young man and said with embarrassment:

"Sir, as I see you are very different from those who have dealt with me lately. I am really happy. Thank you for your help and support. I will let you know in time."

Farrokh wanted to know about her story as soon as possible out of curiosity, so Effat briefly described her misfortunes without hesitation... Farrokh listened with interest to Effat's life story and was fully informed that she had suffered due to the collective lust of the lowly and miserable men, and she had endured hardships and humiliations as a result of the greed and ambition of her vile husband.

The unimaginable and bitter events of Effat's life had affected him immensely and at the same time made him very angry, and when Effat finished telling her story, Farrokh thought for a while. He cursed at humanity and wondered how such lowly people could exist on earth. He wondered why people always give their destiny to a few and why a strong person can easily trample on a weak right and honor, life, and ethnic property are subjected to the whims and desires of a few people every day!

Finally, Farrokh raised his head and said with full sympathy:
"Sorry, I am extremely moved and sorry for what happened to you, of course, these unfortunate events were partly the result of your ignorance, the guilt of which is more on your parents. Because if you were a little literate, you would not have been deceived by such a vile person and you would not have succumbed to his filthy intentions. But I promise you I will take your revenge on him in no time. But first of all, you have to make your parents aware of the events and make them ready to accept you, because your stay here will not be good enough."

Effat nodded at him and then remembered her parents' letter: "But sir, my parents said in a letter that they have disowned me. In this case, how can I apologize to them for my mistakes?"
Farrokh replied:
"You said you are illiterate, so how can you be sure that they wrote such a paper!"
She shook her head embarrassingly as Farrokh continued:
"In any case, I will personally go to your family and explain everything you've been through to them as soon as possible. But unfortunately, today, due to some things that I have to do, I can not, and God willing, I will do this before noon tomorrow. In the meantime, you should focus on getting better."

As she heard the word tomorrow she was shaken, she remembered that her fellow traveler also promised her a tomorrow. But Farrokh's kindness erased this bad thought from her head, so she said nothing more, and Farrokh got up and went to his room and started writing letters.

Effat was once again immersed in a sea of thought, and all that had happened to her seemed like a dream. She feared that what she was seeing now was just a happy dream, each of which would end, and again she will start seeing the ugly bodies and strange guests. And strangers will come to her in no time. Suddenly the door was knocked softly, and her thoughts were interrupted by a new voice. Effat was frightened, but soon her panic disappeared as soon as she knew the newcomer was a doctor whom Farrokh had brought to examine and treat her injury.

The doctor examined Effat's injury and did not diagnose anything major, stating she could get up at any time she wanted, but since she was still weak, rest can be important. At that time Effat had a severe cough that lasted for a while and was forced to cover her mouth with a handkerchief. The doctor soon noticed her coughs. Then he examined her heartbeat and lung movements, then turned his face to Effat and said:
"You should be very careful and take your health seriously."

Farrokh, who was absent during the diagnosis asked about her condition the doctor and the doctor replied: "This woman is infected with tuberculous but fortunately the first stage of the disease can be treated with good food and healthy air."

* * *

An hour later, the door was knocked. Farrokh's servant who had gone to open the door, saw a young girl asking if Farrokh was at home.
The servant wanted to stop the young girl, but Farrokh, who had seen the gardener's daughter Shokoofeh from behind the glass of the room, hurried out of the mansion to the courtyard. After greeting, Farrokh realized she was carrying a message but did not want to say anything in front of others, noticing her gesture, took Shokofeh with him to the basement of the mansion and asked her anxiously:
"What is the matter? Why are you here at this time of the day?"
Shokoofeh answered gently:
"There is no accident, Mahin instructed me to give you this letter."

Farrokh hurriedly took the letter from her and kissed it before he put it on his heart, as if he was putting his lover's handwriting as an ointment on his wounded heart, then he opened the paper and read:

Dear Farrokh,

Last night your thought did not leave me for a minute, I am sure you trust me, your face was stuck with me all night and I was making thousands of plans for our future, what can I say, this morning my mother summoned me and explicitly stated that I should get rid of your thoughts and emphasized that she and my father will not be satisfied and accept you as my husband. She mentioned a prince's son and insisted that I should accept him as my husband and have to agree to this as soon as possible.
They are taking me to Qom, it is not for pilgrimage, but because they have heard that you

and I have meetings without knowing the place and time, thinking that the distance will stop our love, they want to take me away from you. We will be gone by tomorrow, or the day after. Besides my mother, a maid and a servant will come with us. They are going to force me to accept the prince as my husband. Of course, my mother said a lot about my wedding to the prince. Time is short and I am afraid about the whole thing, and they notice that I am always writing a letter in my room. I refuse to explain it.

My dear Farrokh, our meeting tomorrow night will not be possible. I wanted to see you tonight but I think they are suspicious and watching my movements and I am afraid that it will cause trouble. Fortunately, Shokoofeh came here this morning. I was only able to write this letter to you.

My darling, be sure of one thing, I only love you and no force can take your love and affection away from my heart.

Mahin.

After reading the letter, Farrokh became deeply thoughtful. The young man saw that his quarrel and struggle with the F... Al Saltaneh had reached a narrow stage. Mahin's father wanted to separate them at all costs and make his daughter a victim of his sinister and shameful ideas. Farrokh reads the last sentences of Mahin's letter over and over again as if asking for strength to fight Mahin's father from the confession he made to his lover. Then he got up and walked in the room for a while, he was heard to say to himself that Mahin loves me and Mahin has not forgotten me, if God helps me, she will surely be mine. Then he hesitated and asked himself:
'But does God always help lovers?'
Finally he turned to Shokoofeh who had been silent all the time and said: "I will reply to her letter soon, but by the way, do you know when they plan to leave."
Shokoofeh replied: "There was some talk that they would leave at three o'clock."
Farrokh asked Shokofeh to come early tomorrow morning so he can give her the letter to deliver for Mahin.

As soon as she left, Farrokh took his head between his hands and thought deeply...

What was he thinking about?

Chapter Fifteen
The Mother and The Daughter

That night, when Mahin came down from the wall, she went straight to the mansion without making any noise, slowly opened the door, went to her room with the tip of her foot, took off her clothes, put on her nightwear and lay on her small bed. The sound of her breath was heard constantly, and everyone who passed by was sure that she had slept well, but in reality, this was not the case because sleep was not in her eyes and the girl was having a hard time with her disturbing thoughts.

Mahin loved Farrokh very much and she knew for sure that his life would be bitter and unbearable without Farrokh. Mahin's misfortune was that he had read more than those around her and had become more acquainted with the mysteries of life than them, and therefore she could, unlike her ignorant and uneducated people, look at the world and its events and appreciate everything.

Mahin knew and believed that it is obligatory to respect and be obedient to one parent. But at the same time, Mahin believed in obedience to her parents, but she could not leave her future decision in her parent's hands especially when she knew that her father wanted to use her as a ladder to achieve his material goals and make his only daughter a victim of his greed.

Mahin knew that she had to live with her future husband, and she would be the man's permanent partner. So if her husband is one of those men who legitimately beat their wife, she has to endure that rudeness and indecency, or if her husband is an opium addict or a drunk who has thousands of other social disadvantages, or if her husband is incompetent and malicious, she knows she will be the one to bear the consequences. In this case, why should the opinion and will of the parents be decisive in such an important matter, and why should the parents be the ones to choose? Such as making their daughters miserable and trapped.

Mahin knew her mother well and loved her too much and did not want to lose her respect and obedience in any way. But at the same time, knowing how ignorant she was and how ignorant of social affairs she was, it was clear to Mahin that her mother was just an instrument in his father's hand. That is, her poor mother had no thought of herself and was therefore captivated by another thought.

Mahin knew that if her mother was involved she could fight for her, and she could easily soften her mother's heart. 'If you want me to become a princess, I will be miserable and you will regret it.'

But she could not talk like that with her father. Because he knew and understood what his decision would be. F... Al-Saltaneh knew in his heart that her daughter was right, but his greed and longing to be a lawyer had prevented him from paying attention to her daughter's happiness.

Mahin was subject to these thoughts for hours. Finally, sleep and fatigue overcame her eyes and she slept off. When she woke up, the sun had risen. She still wanted to know what her father had said in her mother's ear, got up, washed her face and put on a little make-up, and then asked for her breakfast, as usual, she ate a bite with reluctance and anorexia. Suddenly Firouzeh entered her room and said:

"Miss, please come to your mum's room, your attention is needed."

She was worried that her mother had summoned her prematurely, and thought to herself that certainty was related to last night's talks: 'I will seize the opportunity and inform them of my final decision sooner and more recklessly!' She thought to herself.

Mahin greeted her mother and asked her how she was, and her mother told her her father had to visit someone early in the morning. She invited her to sit down. The girl sat down in front of her mother, then Malek Taj said with a smiling face and a half-reprimanding tone:

"Well, Mahin, what happened last night between you and your father? I did not want to say anything to you about this. But I honestly noticed my silence might be worse. I'm sure you know you should not be so bold and aggressive towards your father. A father who cares about the comfort of his children and always tries to make them stand out among all friends and their peers."

Mahin felt that these words were not the words of his mother and that she had learned them that night. Because she knew her mother well and saw his father's soul through these sentences, she said slowly:

"What should I have done?"

Her mother also said in a joking tone:

"So it turns out that the rumors are true. Well, my daughter, if your father chose a husband who is suitable and worthy in every way for his daughter, you shouldn't mock or take it for granted. Worst of all, you, not ashamed, stood up to your father and said that you love someone else. But you do not know how ugly these words are and it is not at all desirable for a modest girl who has a family."

Mahin remained silent as her mother continued.

"Do you think your parents want to throw you in the fire or do they want to make you miserable? If you have thought so, that is very wrong. We do

not mean anything except your goodness and your happiness. If your father does not want Farrokh, it is only because he does not consider him worthy to be your husband. Of course, you claim you love Farrokh, but the young man is not smooth and clean. We know many things that you do not know, Farrokh spends most of his time doing nothing, and although he has been able to work a hundred times and earn a living, he is still unemployed, he only cares about inheritance and that is not good enough for you."
Mahin hates the way her mother is slandering Farrokh.
"Mother, at least do not forget that Farrokh is your nephew."
Malek Taj, who was not hard-hearted, was impressed by Mahin's statement and hurriedly tried to correct it.
"Of course, I know that he is my nephew, and since he does not have a mother, I have to be his mother too, but he does not want to be educated and become successful!"

Mahin, realizing that the argument with her mother about Farrokh was fruitless, asked her to shorten the conversation: "Well, mom, why do you call me here, and why are you saying all these things about Farrokh!"
"My dear daughter, this is the truth. I realized that you were so aggressive towards your father, and I hoped that you would put aside these thoughts and would no longer be fascinated and seduced by immoral young people like Farrokh. It's bad for us, and you have to accept whoever your father chooses. My daughter, have you not heard that a father has the right to throw his daughter in the fire? After all, you do not know the dignity of a father. If a father like your father is considered a young and educated prince, a man like Siavash Mirza who has no blemishes, unlike others who are proud of drinking and gambling."
Mahin said softly again: "Was this all your orders?"
"Yes, my daughter, you know I am your mother and I love you more than you think, and I have worked hard for you, and therefore I expect you to trust me. Listen to what your father wants."

Mahin shrugged and raised her head in disapproval, but her mother did not despair and followed up:
"Very well, this is what I have to tell you today, I see that you are not in a good mood and it is as if you do not understand what I am saying. Inshallah, after returning from the trip, you will understand completely and listen to your parents' words better and more carefully, and you will accept our advice."

Mahin, hearing the word "travel" came as a surprise: "Travel! Where are we going?"
"Don't you remember? For a long time, you wanted to go to Qom. Your father last night approved our travel to Qom for a month."

Mahin realized the intention of his parents on this trip and thought to herself that they wanted to prevent her from meeting Farrokh she said loudly to his mother:

"Mum, I wanted to go to Qom during the season of Nowruz, not summer and most especially not a time like this."

"My dear, we are on pilgrimage, God willing, we will return from the pilgrimage with more good health."

Mahin, who knew that there was no point in resisting, said to herself: 'Why should I object to the trip? So she got up and asked her mother'

"Very well, when are we going?"

"Tomorrow or the day after tomorrow, we will go by carriage, but the day and time of departure are still unknown."

Mahin left the room without saying anything and was deep in thought talking to herself, 'Although my mother's face did not show anything, I am sure she knew about my meetings with Farrokh. And it's okay anyway I accepted this trip because on the way I will have more opportunities to talk to my mother and maybe I can finally tame her and convince her to take my side.'

When Mahin did not see anyone near her room, she took a pen and wrote the letter to Farrokh, and when Shokoofeh came, she asked her to take the letter to Farrokh. Mahin spent the rest of the day gathering her things for her trip. But at the same time, all her thoughts were on Farrokh. The more she thought about it, the more she realized how difficult the situation is, and with such parents and the way she knew they think, it would be difficult to meet Farrokh in the future. She spent the night thinking and worrying.

She woke up a little late in the morning. As soon as she opened her eyes, she saw Shokoofeh standing there holding a small piece of paper. It was Farrokh's letter, her lover, whom her parents were trying to defile Mahin's heart towards him and to fill her heart full of love with greed, ambition, and money. And ignore pain and resentment.

She hurriedly read the letter, shook it once, as if she had read the wrong letter, she was shocked! Shokoofeh, who was standing silently, was astonished and did not know what to say and wondered in her heart what was written in that letter that she read several times!

Finally, Mahin read the letter again and this time Shokoofeh heard her reading it loud:

"With such a parent, there is no other choice!"

Shokoofeh, who saw Mahin's reaction, did not want to tear up her thoughts with a misplaced question. So she left the room without saying anything. Mahin was walking like a mad prisoner, she walked near the window of the room facing the garden, and after looking at the space of the garden and the sky, she turned to the other side of the room. Suddenly Mahin changed her direction and went to the other room and called Shokoofeh, and when the gardener's daughter came, she said:

"Go to Farrokh and tell him that our trip has been delayed for a day, but I will act according to his wishes."

Chapter Sixteen
Another Parents

Around noon, the same day that Mahin's letter reached Farrokh, the rental carriage stopped in front of the renovation mansion on the Street in the northwest of Tehran.

A young man, wearing thin yellow silk clothes known as čučunče wearing a dark tie around, got out of the carriage and asked the waiter who was standing near the door:

"Is Mr. R... Al-Dawlah's house here?"

The waiter bowed and answered politely:

"Yes, sir, this is it, did you have a request?"

"If he is in, give this card to him and let him know I should talk to him."

The servent took the card and entered the garden, climbed the stairs of the mansion at the end of the garden, and after two or three minutes he returned and said to the young man:

"Please, sir, he is waiting."

The servent went forward as a guide, and the unknown young man passed behind the garden full of colorful flowers, around which short walls lined with half-red bricks, went up the stairs through the corridor, and entered a large room. The chairs and benches in the room were beautifully placed and following the latest fashion in Tehran, and its living room was covered with Qashqai rugs. On a tall, narrow table with porcelain in the middle of the upper surface, in a wooden frame, was a large green vase with beautiful patterns, and in it was a small vase of a Japanese lemon tree.

An old man was sitting in a chair in the corner of the room, so the young man greeted him politely, but to his surprise, he noticed that the owner of the house did not move or complimented him with a movement instead.

The young man was surprised by this kind of reception and said in his heart: 'Why is this man so arrogant?' But the old man himself tried to explain and said that if he did not show the necessary respect, he was sorry because he had been paralyzed for a while due to severe rheumatism and could not move without help.

The servent immediately entered and held two cups of tea in a crystal cup, on the Isfahan silver tray.

Then the old man said to the guest:

"The truth is that no matter how much I looked at you, I did not remember anything and I do not know where we met. In the era of the martyred Shah and Muzaffar Shah, may God have mercy on them and let the light fall on their graves. We would be rewarded with four hundred and five hundred tomans for a hunt that someone else had caught before. Now thousands of these greengrocers and grocers are sitting at the table."

The young man who listened carefully to the old man's words in his heart acknowledged how those who had received such funds just as a reward had amassed enormous wealth by receiving compliments and squandering the funds of the government.

The old man, under his white and convex glasses, looked at Farrokh all over again, then shook his head in despair and said:

"I do not remember seeing you anywhere."

Then he took the anonymous card he had placed on the table and look closely:

"Nothing is clear from these new names."

Then he shouted the name written on the card:

"Farrokh Daqiq."

***

Farrokh thought about Mahin's trip for a while after Shokofeh left, especially the part of her lover's letter that said they wanted to force her to marry on their return, which had saddened the young man. He now understands the plan of F... Al Saltaneh, the greedy man, has devised to separate them. He could not tolerate Mahin's distance, and besides, he was also worried that if Mahin was left alone with her mother, she might be influenced by her mother's words. Because he, like all lovers, was not sure of his luck and considered his building of happiness to be subject to the whirlwind of events at any moment.

He decided to go to Qom, so they could at least meet each other. Then He tried to prepare the ground for the implementation of his plan, and first of all, he wanted to hire a young and smart servant who he could trust and who would be a good help to him.

Farrokh believed very much in the simple people who lived in the south of the city, and he considered most of them to have a good heart, unselfish feelings, and pure intentions. He also believed that if they were treated fairly and with zeal, they would be willing to make any sacrifice. And as it is known, they go through everything in time to die with you and even sacrifice their lives.

Farrokh was sure that the people in the south of the city are much less hypocritical and these gentlemen are not like those who are just after money and material benefits. He knew that these people avoid lies. And they rely on their capable arms to make a living, unlike some of the unemployed and leeches of society, who spend all their time flattering and pettiness from one place to another.

Coincidentally, the day before this incident, Farrokh, who had gone to the southern neighborhood of Tehran to see one of his schoolmates, passed by a coffee shop described in the first chapter of this story and saw a young man sitting next to a thoughtful and important man. His face had a strange effect on Farrokh and a heartfelt cry said that this man would play an important role in his life. Under the pretext of buying some raisins, he asked the shop owner the name of the young man. He had said:
"Do you mean Javad?"

Then he explained and described Javad to Farrokh, and because the grocer was aware of Javad's predicament, he thought to himself that maybe God had opened a door for that unfortunate family. When Farrokh asked if Javad came to the coffee house every day? the grocer had answered;" Yes, he comes here often, which means that this coffee house is the hangout of all the people of this neighborhood, and if you have anything to do with any of them, you will find them in this coffee house."

Farrokh, who was impressed by hearing Javad's biography, thought to himself that maybe he could do something for Javad or hire him one day. Without saying a word, he paid for the raisins and gave most of them to a boy who was standing next to the shop and looking at them.

When Farrokh was thinking of going to Qom, remembered that young man, Javad. He decided to go to that coffee house in the evening to see him. In the meantime, he needed to clarify the situation with Effat as soon as possible, so he had no choice but to meet with Effat's father and bring this unfortunate woman to his parents. He got up and called his nanny and asked about Effat, asked to take good care of her and provide what she needed. Then called out the first carriage and gave the address of Mr. R... Al-Dawlah.

***

Effat's father called Farrokh's name on the card in front of him again, but as he was more careful, nothing sounded familiar, so he waited for Farrokh to start talking and explain what he want. Farrokh, who understood his expectation, said to the old man:

"My family is close to His Excellency, I am the son of Mr. H... Al-Sultan."

Hearing the title of Farrokh's father, the man shook as if he could see clearly now, he was very happy to know where Farrokh came from: "Oh, now I know, my dear son, why did you not say this from the beginning? Mashallah, God Bless, such a nice lad. Your father is a good man. We worked together. I remember especially well that one day the late Shah ordered us to put our feet up and beat them for fun." Then the old man remembered those days and sighed!

Farrokh, who laughed about the old man's simplicity in his heart, did not lose his serious face with the words of R... Al-Dawlah, who all complained about the people's disregard for religion and criticism of the new era, cursed the constitutionalists and the libertarian's song with him, assuring the old man that his father had the same opinion, and often told him about the merits of the past.

The old man was more than happy with the young man's statement, asked him to get closer, and finally asked after a while:
"Well, dear son, now tell me why are you here, of course, I will do whatever he asks of me."
Farrokh did not let R... Al-Dawlah finish his speech and said in a hurry:
"No, sir, my father did not send me to you!"
The old man was more surprised. Farrokh was also silent and did not know how to raise the issue. Finally, he dared to bring his head close to the old man's ear and said slowly: "My visit is related to a family member and about your son-in-law!"
The old man shook his head again and asked anxiously: "What happened, did my son-in-law hurt my daughter ... my daughter ... is the husband dead? Tell me what happened."
Farrokh was silent for a while and the old man said angrily:
"Did you come here to give such ominous news?"
But Farrokh's face was calmed and he says:
"Sir, you have not heard me, why are you getting unnecessarily anxious? Your son-in-law is not dead, and your daughter is also alive and well, but strange things have happened to them."
The old man asked in a trembling voice:
"What happened? Did she have a dispute with her husband?"
Poor father, out of extreme interest in his daughter, could not take it anymore.

Farrokh saw how difficult and unfortunate it would be for such a person to know the sad story of his daughter, but there was no way out. So he said gently to Mr. R... Al-Dawlah, "If you are willing to listen to all the events calmly, I will tell you what I know."

The old man realized that something serious must have happened, so in a state of anxiety, he became somewhat overwhelmed but promised to listen to everything calmly. Farrokh told him more or less what he had heard from Effat, and when he reached the case of the house of the major bride, he paused and wanted to end the story, but R... Al-Dawlah, was listening with great sobriety and attention until then, drops of cold sweat appeared on his forehead as he said commandingly:

"Please do not hide anything from me and tell me the truth."

Farrokh reads in the depths of his eyes the effects of severe anger that melted the heart of any evil, so he could not turn away from him and told him all that happened and even said how and in what situation he saved Effat from the house.

The old man's face was intense at that moment. His eyes were shining despite the weakness of old age and he was staring at Farrokh so firmly and deeply that he thought he would rush him at any moment. He had asked his beloved to submit to such dishonesty and how could he have imagined a man from Ali Ashraf Khan's class to make his wife so miserable and not only make her fall into the arms of others but also let her spend some time in brothels and hear thousands of words from the mouths of wicked women and endure all the sufferings and shame.

In the meantime, the old man asked Farrokh, "Did you say that a letter from us disowned Effat?"

Farrokh replied: "Of course, the letter was not from you and your lady. He had written it himself, but since, unfortunately, your daughter was illiterate, how could she have understood that you had not written it."

R... Al-Dawlah noticed Farrokh's sarcasm and thought for a moment, and in his mind, he acknowledged his negligence in educating his daughter, and the effects of regret and remorse appeared on his face.

After a moment, he called the servant and told him to go inside and call his wife. He also ordered a hookah. Al-Dawlah pointed to Farrokh and said: "You are a good man, thank you, my son."

Farrokh bowed a little and thanked the old man for his kindness and said with politeness, respect, and sincerity: "What I have done is the duty of every person with a conscience."

A few minutes later, Effat's mother's footsteps rose and she asked her husband from behind the door, "You called me?"

The old man, who had now put the hookah under his lips and was constantly spewing thick smoke said:

" He is our good son, come inside. He is not a stranger"

Ms. R. Al-Dawlah did not think anymore and entered with anger.

Effat's mother was tall, wearing a white veil with black dots, and half of her white face was covered with a Chador.

Al-Dawlah could not bear seeing his wife anymore and suddenly burst into anger as tears roll down his cheeks as he kept saying:

"Do you know what happened? Do you know how our daughter became miserable? Do you know where this gentleman saw our dear child!"

The woman, who was unaware of everything, was very upset to see her husband's condition, and hurried to her husband and asked:

"What happened?"

She was told about what happened, she couldn't stop crying, she begged Farrokh: "Sir, please tell me it's not true."

He was silent and showed Al-Dawlah with his hand, and finally said to the poor mother: "He will explain." He asked for permission to leave and gave his home address:

"This is the house address and you can come there at any time and see your daughter, and then he turned to Effat's mother, who was still standing in astonishment and looking at them:

"Madam, I would like to say that there have been incidents that, of course, should not have happened, now it is useless to dwell on the grief of the past".

Then he hurried out of the room!

Chapter Seventeen
On The Way To Qom

It was near sunset when Venus appeared in the west of the sky and with its successive twinkles, promised a beautiful night with a blue sky, which was decorated with the light of the stars.

The road led to Qom and the point where the carriage was passing at that time was near the Shoor River, near one of courier-house. Half an hour later, a carriage stood in front of the house. The mansion of the courier-house, like most of them, consisted of a series of rooms of the same shape and size, which were built at a height of one and a half meters from the ground and had a wide width in front of the rooms.

Malek Taj and Mahin, who were very tired and exhausted from the constant movement of the carriage on those rugged roads, got out of the carriage without protesting, and behind them, Firouzeh, their maid disembarked. The women entered one of the entrance hall rooms and sat on the small carpet that Hassan Qoli had brought from the carriage.

They all were very tired and hungry, so immediately opened the pots and started eating chicken, kookoo, and kebab with bread.

Malek Taj was satisfied with the impromptu trip. She was happy, however, anyone could look at Mahin's face and realize she is not happy.
"Mahin, hope this is not about The Prince or Farrokh? Why are you frowning? why don't you enjoy yourself while we are traveling." Malek Taj said.

Mahin did not respond to her mother, and it was clear that her mother's loving words did not calm her disturbed mind at all, and it seemed that with each passing minute of that night, her anxiety intensified. But it was the letter she had received from Farrokh before the trip that had left her with anxiety.

After couple of hours later, they had to go back to the carriage to continue their journey. Malek Taj and Firoozeh fell into a deep sleep, but Mahin had fixed her eyes on the ceiling beams of that house, in a sea of thought.

***

Malek Taj, who was not hard-hearted, became anxious about her daughter's continuous silence. She was thinking to make a vow of a candle in the

Saqakhaneh or reciting prayers for four Friday nights so that Mahin would forget her lover.

Mahin suddenly broke her silence,

"Mother, Don't you want to tell me what you have in mind about my future?"

Malek Taj was happy and thought to herself that Mahin had finally come to her right senses and realized that obedience to her parents was more important than anything, so she turned her face and said:

" My dear daughter, concerning this matter, we do not need to repeat that anymore, my only request to you is to accept the prince as a husband and to comfort your father and me."

Hearing his mother's words, Mahin shrugged her shoulders and said in a delicate voice:

"Mother, I knew your opinion and that of my father. There was no need to repeat it. You are not willing to consider your daughter's happiness after? I have not changed my mind and I will not accept anyone except Farrokh as my husband!"

Malek Taj, who realized that arguing with her daughter at that time would cause more arrogance, remained silent and said to herself, 'Why should I bleed her heart now? God willing she will be calmed soon,' so she said kindly: "Very well, Mahin, there is no time for these words now as we are going to Qom, so there will be no other conversation aside from pilgrimage."

At this point, Firoozeh, who had remained silent throughout the mother and daughter conversation, said: "Ma'am, this is my fifth trip to Qom." She started talking about her late husband. "One day a woman came and threw black magic into our house. From that day on, my husband's behavior and morals changed with me, and three days later he married and the following week divorced me." Firoozeh narrated her whole story with pomp and circumstance and Malek Taj, who had a complete belief in all kinds of superstitions, listened to her words with all interest, but Mahin could not refrain from hearing this story with a smile. She was sorry for her ignorance.

The coachman constantly whips the horses' necks, and in that silence of the night, they all hear the sound of the horses, which arose from their regular movement. For another three hours, the carriage continued to move, until finally stopped in front of Nusrat Palace.

The condition of this house on the way to Tehran and Qom seemed very interesting compared to other courier-house. It was located next to a beautiful hill and there was a lake called Hoz-e-Sultan on the southeast of it. It was the early hours of the morning and the surface of the lake was gaining momentum at that moment due to the brightness of the sun.

Hassan Qoli immediately opened the carriage door and invited the women to disembark.

Malek Taj told him, "I want to get to Qom as soon as possible. Tell the deputy of the house not to delay us here for more than an hour."

Hassan Qoli bowed and at the same time, the deputy of the house approached the carriage and asked for the tariff. Hassan Qoli gave the tariff and said:

"The lady wants to get to Qom as early as possible. Please tell them to give us a horse as soon as possible.:"

Khan Nayeb , the deputy, who understood the passengers, and especially Hassan Qoli's way of talking, attends to the noble family, hoping for a good gratuity, and immediately said with flattery:

"Please take a short break and the horses will be ready."

But at the same time, the coachman, who had brought the horses to the stable and was returning, approached the deputy and said: "This letter came from Tehran for you." He took the letter and wondered what had happened. He was worried about complaints, opened the letter, read it, and felt relieved. Then took a deep breath.

Malak Taj, Mahin, and Firoozeh went to one of the rooms and sat on a rug, they decided to have a rest until the horses were ready...

Two hours later, the sun had risen and the sun's disk was slowly rising from the surface of the lake, and at the same time, the reverse was constantly falling into the water, creating a very interesting view in front of them.

Malek Taj and her companions woke up and drank some tea.

Hassan Qoli ran to the stable to get the horses, "Please bring our horses. The ladies are ready. We want to move."

But to his surprise, the deputy moved his head with despair and said:

"Unfortunately, the knees of two horses have been cut and it is not possible to move them. We have to wait for another carriage to arrive from Qom so that we can move you."

"You said they were available two hours ago and we could move at any time and now you say that the horses' knees were cut!" Hassan Qoli said angrily. "I am not responsible for horses' injury, wait a while and the carriage will arrive from Qom, then you will leave."

Hassan Qoli thought that the argument was fruitless, hurried to the room, and quoted the deputy's remarks to Malek Taj. She thought that the deputy was one of those who would change his words with a gratuity, so she told Hassan Qoli: "Go to the deputy and tell him that we know you have more than one horse in the stable and so we are ready to pay more."

Hassan Qoli went to the stable but returned five minutes later and reported that the deputy swore he had no other horse and that we should wait until noon."

Mahin, who had not made any comment from the beginning and had ignored all this incident, said: "Mother, why the hurry, be sure that we will reach Qom at the end and you will make a pilgrimage."

Since there was no other choice but to surrender, Malek Taj did not say anything more, so they decided to wait until noon. Each of them sank into a corner to relax.

At around noon, Malek Taj asked her servant, "Go and see if the deputy has words to say about the horses." But he returned disappointed and said: "Ma'am, he says that the carriage has not arrived and the horses' feet have not healed yet, in which case we should wait for a little longer."

Malek Taj was so bitter, "Go and tell him not to treat us like this, it will not be good for him. He will be punished, let him understand who my husband is, let him know he is a parliamentary candidate, especially in this period and he will become a lawyer soon and of course, he should know as soon as he becomes a lawyer, he becomes a minister, and his first ministry will be the courier-houses and the telegram offices, which are with this ministry. Let him understand the consequences"

Hassan Qoli went to the deputy again and simply conveyed all the imaginary threats of the lady to the deputy, but he did not pay any attention to those words and said softly:

"Tell them not to get angry unnecessarily, and shouting is useless, we can not do anything until another carriage comes from Qom."

Hassan Qoli narrated the deputy's answer exactly to the lady. She thought that maybe she could tame him better, "Ask him on my behalf to come here, I want to talk to him myself."

The deputy obeyed and came to the nearby porch in the passenger room, he greeted warmly and softly.

"Khan Nayeb, why are you treating us like this? We have been waiting for a horse here since last night. Give us a horse as soon as possible so that we can go to Qom for our prayers."

He replied gently:

"Ma'am, I swear to you and Hazrat Masoumeh, who you are going for her pilgrimage. I swear it is not my fault, we do not have a horse, I will not keep passengers waiting longer than they have to."

Malek Taj was satisfied with his remarks and the deputy's oath. In this way, it was clear that the horses would not be available until a carriage arrived. But what could be done, she did not benefit from offering the money, nor her husband's name. There was no choice but to wait.

Chapter Eighteen
Strange Incident

The day was getting dark, and a black cloud appeared in the sky. Due to the hot wind that had started to blow, dust rose in the desert that summer night. It was difficult to breathe, intense heat and heavy air were unbearable. Malek Taj, who had not been able to tame Khan Nayeb and get a carriage, sat on the rug of the room and read the prayer book. She cried out loud like a child and hoped that these prayers would finally soften the heart of Nayeb and free them from this predicament. Mahin, on the contrary, disregards everything that was happening. She was far away from the world and her thoughts were not there. Occasionally she would get up and leave the room of the guest house, and walk around. It seemed that she was expecting to hear a voice, and after a while, she returned to her mother in despair and anger. Firoozeh approached Malek Taj and asked her to recite the prayer slower so that she could listen and repeat it with her. The illiterate Malek Taj could hardly recite a few prayers, she could only recite the ones she learned as a child.

About two hours after nightfall, the sound of a carriage wheel was heard from a distance. After a few minutes, it turned out that the carriage was from Tehran, and a quarter of an hour later, the carriage stopped in front of the courier-house. Immediately the carriage door was opened and a young man with a large leather hat, who had pulled it down close to his eyebrows, got out of the carriage. Someone else in the carriage said to him: "Go find the deputy and tell him to come here."

The young man in the leather hat, who seemed a servant, went to the house and a minute later returned with the deputy.
The passenger in the carriage said: "Did you get the order? The message was delivered yesterday. Are the passengers still here?
The deputy bowed: "Yes, sir. It's been eighteen hours that I have kept them here"
"Very well, thank you for your service, take this letter and read it now."
The deputy took the paper while reading it and went towards the coffee house.

Then the person sitting in the carriage was heard saying to himself: "God's willing everything will go according to plan and we will be on schedule."

The deputy came back after reading the letter. "I have been instructed to follow your orders so I am ready to carry out your orders."
The carriage passenger said:
"Go and inform the ladies that the horse will be ready in half an hour to gather their belongings and be ready to move."

The deputy announced that the horse would be ready in half an hour, Malek Taj was extremely happy and turned her face to Firoozeh and said: "Did you see how prayers work!" This news had another effect on Mahin, it added to her inner anxiety, and she was constantly thinking without making a statement.

The deputy went back to the carriage, and said in response to the young passenger who asked him how many carriages had passed since yesterday: "Except for one carriage that went to Tehran in the evening, no other carriage has passed."
The passenger then turned to another person sitting in the corner of the carriage and said:
"Did you hear that? So if you had to say something, you would say that you were riding in a carriage going to Tehran. You got off the pavilion because the carriage was standing in front of the coffee house. Then by mistake, you took another carriage. You are supposed to act deaf and mute first, and as soon as you reach the next house in Qom, go to the head of the courier-house and show the paper that you have with you. They will send you to Tehran as soon as possible."

It was a very dark night. Firoozeh and Hassan Qoli were gathering their belongings at night. They were getting ready to leave. Mahin got up and said to his mother, who was still sitting on the ground praying, "It's too hot here. until you get ready, I'm going to sit in a carriage. Whatever it is, the wind blows and the air is cooler here."

A few minutes later, Malek Taj and Firoozeh went to the carriage. The black clouds now completely covered the sky. The darkness was so great that it was impossible to distinguish an object or a person in two steps. Four strong horses were tied to the carriage.

A quarter of an hour later, the carriage to which the young passenger had come was ready to leave, and after the passenger had expressed his satisfaction to the deputy with the gift of money, his carriage moved in the opposite direction, towards Tehran.

The carriage of Malek Taj and her companions was moving as fast as it could. Four hours later, they reached Manzarieh. Malek Taj, who was in a hurry to get to Qom, did not want to stop there for a short time. She ordered the coachman to go ahead..

The carriage was two or three miles away from Manzarieh, the air was slowly clearing, the clouds were scattering and the last stars were disappearing one by one, the dome of Qom had appeared in the distance.

Malek Taj noticed Mahin's shoes, she was expecting good shoes but surprisingly Mahin wore bad shoes instead, she was surprised, and when she paid a little more attention and looked up from her shoes, she also noticed the color of the socks. Mahin's chador also changed, and when she finally raised her head completely, she looked at the girl and was astonished.

Malek Taj and Firoozeh were stunned. Because instead of Mahin, a beautiful tanned young woman with big black eyes was sitting in a carriage and without paying any attention to the surprise and astonishment of her companions, she looked at them with a fixed gaze as if nothing had happened!

The state of astonishment of Malek Taj and Firouzeh only lasted for a few seconds or minutes. Finally, Firoozeh dared to ask the lady sitting with them in the carriage:

"Who are you? What are you doing here? What happened to Mahin?

But every time she asked this question, there was no answer, and the woman was constantly looking at them with a fixed gaze. Then Malek Taj, whose astonishment had diminished somewhat, took the girl by the arm, shook her hard, and shouted:

"Why don't you answer? You are not my daughter. What happened to my daughter? Where is my daughter? Answer me!"

Hassan Qoli, who heard the sound, stopped the coachman and jumped down from the top of the carriage, opened the door to see what had happened. He was surprised. He couldn't believe his eyes. There was a lady who had not been taken to Mahin's place. Malek Taj did not stop and kept asking the woman who she was and what she had done. And since the girl could not open her mouth at all, Firoozeh had discovered her disability and said:

"Maybe she is deaf and mute!"

It was as if the unknown woman was pleased with this statement.

Firoozeh, without thinking if the woman is deaf:

"See, yes she is."

Meanwhile the coachman who had come down from his place got close to the carriage door, said with shock that he hasn't come across such an incident in his entire existence. He questioned and threaten that woman, but did not work and the woman kept her silence with all perseverance.

Malek Taj who was disappointed and couldn't hold back tears cry out loudly:

"What should I do, who should I turn to, what happened to my daughter, what happened to her, where was she abducted, who did this, what should I tell her father?"

Firoozeh and Hassan Qoli tried to calm the queen down and reassure her that Mahin would soon be found safe and sound, but their effort did not yield anything as the queen continued to cry.

Finally Hassan Qoli thought of something. He turned his face to the coachman and said: "Take us back to Manzarieh, I'll ask the lady to give you whatever you want."

The coachman raised his head as a sign of rejection and said: " It is not possible because the horses are tired. We are close to the city. If I return with the tired horses, they will be injured and I will be held responsible."

All this time, the unknown woman was sitting in the carriage in silence, staring at the desert without paying attention to the negotiations. Malek Taj would hit the girl so hard so she could get a confession from her, but Firoozeh stopped her every time and said:
"What is the use of beating her, we have to get back to Qom and take her to Nazmieh to interrogate her and find out the truth of the matter."

Hearing the words of order and interrogation, the girl made a move and thus showed that she was scared, but this change of state did not last long, and her face soon returned to its original state and remained silent.

Eventually, Malek Taj was convinced and agreed to go to Qom. She thought she would immediately inform the Gendarmerie department of the incident and ask them for help in finding Mahin.

The carriage moved and about an hour after the last toll gate, it entered the street that led to the Qom River Bridge, and after a few hundred steps, the carriage entered a large space on the right side of the street that was the way to the house. Malek Taj was not feeling well, she was shaking and thought she was going to pass out. Firouzeh holds her and massages her arms.

The tanned face girl, who was still sitting in the carriage saw the situation, and as Hassan Qoli was walking away, she hid under her Chador and hurried to the room that seemed to be the courier-house chief's office.

It was sunny, about four o'clock in the afternoon. The chief was sitting in his room when he saw a girl who was coming toward him in a hurry. He was surprised and the girl immediately handed him the paper. After reading it, he looked a look on girl and said:
"Very well, a carriage is going now, you can go to Tehran with it."
Then the girl put her head close to his ear and said a few more words. The chief also showed her the door behind him:
"Go there, no one will come." The girl entered the room and left an hour later, changing the color of her face and clothes.
His black chador had now been transformed into a colored chador made of chenille, similar to what was worn by Qomi women, and she wore a wide

shawl and her high-heeled shoes had turned into flat ones and loads of make-up on her face. As soon as she came out of the Charpar's room, she saw the Malek Taj and looked away, and went straight to the checkpoint. Malek Taj had now calmed down a little as a result of Firoozeh's massage.

A few minutes later, Hossein Qoli came and reported that he had met one of his old acquaintances who had a good house. Suddenly, Firoozeh remembered the girl and said to Hassan Qoli, "Look, where is she??"

Hassan Qoli looked everywhere, but he did not see any trace of the woman and did not find her. They were all very puzzled and did not know how to interpret all this incident, as if they were dreaming, they concluded something is fishy they searched all over the place and were disappointed they couldn't find the girl.

Firouzeh saw a woman with a wide shawl and a Qomi-style chador, near the courier-house. She was suspicious. Asked her
"What's day is today sister?"
The woman raised her mask a little and turned her face halfway towards the Firouzeh and answered gently:
"Today is the twentieth of Sha'ban."
Firoozeh, who was convinced she is the one by the sight of her teeth and gazes, shouted that this is the same girl who was sitting in a carriage:
"Woman, do you think that you can hide from me? You are the one who was sitting in our carriage instead of Mahin."
"Keep this woman and do not let her run away. This is the same girl who was sitting in the carriage, the bastard went and put make-up on, changed her chador, and thinks she can deceive me!" Firoozeh said to Hassan Qoli. But that girl said quietly without paying attention:
"You are wrong, I do not understand what you are saying. I am a traveler to Tehran, I got a ticket yesterday, I came to see if the carriage is going to Tehran today or not."

Firoozeh was not convinced, she was holding her Chador ad would not leave her. As a result of the noise, people gathered around them. Firoozeh saw the chief, "Sir, this girl came to our carriage instead of our little lady, now we have to give her to the Gendarmerie to find our little lady."

The chief seemed to see these words as more like delusions and the words of lunatics, laughed and said:
"Sister, you must be wrong. I know this woman. She came yesterday to get a ticket and she wants to go to Tehran, I don't think you have ever seen her."

The crowd that had gathered around them dispersed when they heard him, Firoozeh shouted for a while, but no one paid attention anymore.The chief went back to his room and the girl was waiting for a carriage in the corner.

Malek Taj's eyes were very red from crying so much and her legs could not move, but with the help of Firoozeh and Hassan Qoli, they slowly went to the bridge and after crossing the bridge, they entered the alley on the right, which leads to Dar al-Shafa alley. They entered the house on the right.

Ms. F... Al-Saltaneh remained silent for a while due to the advice of Firoozeh and Hassan Gholli, but resumed her crying as soon as she entered the courtyard:

"My daughter was abducted, what happened to my daughter? What should I tell her father?"

But was her daughter abducted?

Chapter Nineteen
Friend

We left Farrokh in a situation where he got in the carriage and gave an address to the coachman.

Ten minutes later, the carriage stopped in front of a large wooden door at the beginning of Burj Noush Street near Ala Al-Dawlah Street. Behind this door was a wide corridor and at the end of the corridor was a military space with several carriages in the middle of it. Above the large door, a long board was installed with a large letter written on the courier-house of Qom, Iraq, and Isfahan.

Farrokh got out of the carriage and after asking the carriage to wait for him, he entered the corridor of the house and went straight to the middle of the corridor, and followed a small sign showing the office of the chief.

After Farrokh received Mahin's letter and information about their trip to Qom, he decided to go to that city and meet her, He didn't mind if it was for a few minutes, he would tell the secret of his heart to Mahin.

As soon as Farrokh entered the office of the chief, he saw a young man behind who was deeply into reading papers. The chief raised his head to footsteps and suddenly both sighed in surprise. Farrokh was expecting to see a different person but saw his friend, Ahmad Ali Khan. They had met each other during their first year in high school, and from the very first minute, a sincere relationship was established between them.

Fortunately, in the school environment, where young people learn new information every hour and find new thoughts every minute, some of the destructive factors of human morality, such as greed, money, prestige, influence, and lust, have not yet found their way. Knowledge is not blurred by these toys of life, and the school environment is the only arena for the display of intelligence and ingenuity. And it is easier for them to find an opinion, Farrokh and Ahmad Ali Khan sat together on the classroom bench and spent hours of fun talking together, and every year they took their exams together and passed with flying colors, on holidays and other times, the two young men were often together. The friendship between these two people was proverbial among the other classmates, and their fathers considered this interest and relationship as a pleasure, and when they saw the two of them as sincere and united people, they were so happy that each of them thought that in Instead of one child, they have two sons.

There was nothing in Farrokh's life that his friend did not know about, nor was there the slightest incident in Ahmad Ali's life that was hidden from Farrokh. Finally, at the end of the sixth year of school, the two comrades received high school diplomas. Farrokh was not agreed to take governmental jobs due to his independent opinion and also to make a small salary of 15 Tomans, but Ahmad Ali Khan was forced to take any job because his father died and he had a family to provide for. He got a job as soon as he received his diploma and was constantly moving forward. After three years, he was transferred to the courier house.

Farrokh often visits his dear friend, but in the last weeks, due to personal problems, he did not visit Ahmad Ali Khan and therefore did not know about his friend's recent promotion. He was recently appointed as Qom-Iraq road administrator.

Ahmad Ali Khan was happy to see Farrokh and immediately put aside the papers and hugged his dear friend.

"How did you know I was here?"

Farrokh responded to his friend with a smile and said:

"I am also surprised I met you here. I came here to get a travel ticket."

Ahmad Ali Khan asked with surprise:

"Where are you traveling to? How come you did not inform me before?"

"No, no. I have not bought the ticket, I only want to go to Qom for pilgrimage." Farrokh replied.

Ahmad Ali Khan knew Farrokh better than himself, smiled meaningfully, and said:

"But my friend, I tell you that there is no pilgrimage, who are you looking for?"

Farrokh soon realized that Ahmad Ali Khan had seen Malek Taj and Mahin carriage so he asked:

"Did they come here to get a ticket?"

Ahmad Ali Khan also replied:

"Yes, about an hour ago, F .. Al-Saltaneh's servant came and bought the ticket for Qom.

Farrokh, who did not hide anything from his friend, handed the letter Mahin wrote, which was brought to him that morning,"Read to understand."

Ahmad Ali Khan took the paper, but before reading it, he called and ordered the waiter to bring some tea, then read the letter carefully, and at the end, he frowned:

"So what did you think and what do you want to do?"

"I am going to follow them and not let her mother separate us, but at the same time, I have to think of a fundamental plan. I have to finish this nonsense with those ignorant people." Farrokh replied.

At this time, the waiter brought tea and Ahmad Ali Khan immediately took a cup of tea from the tray and placed it in front of Farrokh and picked up the other cup for himself, and said:

"Something came to my mind right now, if you dare to do it, it may bring you closer to your goal."

Farrokh asked curiously how.

Ahmad Ali Khan replied: "If you want to follow them now, you can arrange a means to kidnap Mahin from their carriage without them knowing and the two of you will get married."

Farrokh, who asked God for such a thing, asked his friend to explain the plan he had in mind. Ahmad Ali Khan added:

"The plan is not a big problem, in my opinion, the best way is to exchange Mahin with another woman on the way between Tehran and Qom at night."

Farrokh, who wanted nothing more than Mahin and was willing to make sacrifices to have his love by his side, accepted his friend's offer without hesitation and asked him to explain the implementation of this plan to him.

Ahmad Ali Khan, seeing the commitment of Farrokh and how he was eager, wanted to know what had come to his friend's mind, first urging him to calm down and then saying: "But you should know that this plan requires Mahin's consent and support so that when necessary, she can do her part well."

Then he followed his statements:

"In my opinion, the best way is in one of the houses on the way, which, of course, the farther it is from Tehran, the better it will be to arrange your carriage twenty-four hours after their departure, to the carriage. Then when it's dark, instead of their carriage, she will ride in your carriage and be replaced by another woman and you will leave with her. This plan will not be as easy as it was said and it needs plan B. If Mahin is satisfied, you will inform me so that I can provide the means to do it.

Farrokh could no longer contain his excitement. He knew that this plan will work, and it was as if he felt Mahin by his side at that moment, and it seemed to him that he could put his hand around his beloved's neck and whisper in her ear. 'My dear Mahin, do not be depressed, do not be sad, your parents will not hurt you, there will be nothing but a small reprimand,

and I will always be ready to serve you and I will defend you against any danger, even at the cost of my life. I am your servant and slave, I am your devoted lover. I am …'

Once he realized the situation and calm himself, he freed himself from those sweet thoughts and said to his friend:

"What if Mahin accepts or rejects my offer, arrange the carriage please, I will go to Qom anyway, and of course, if she is satisfied, I will execute the plan."

Then he shook hands warmly with his friend, went out the door and got into the carriage that was waiting for him, and asked the carriage driver to go home as fast as possible. Farrokh wished the horses had wings at that moment to take him home in no time so he could write it all for Mahin and inform her of the decision to abduct her, but he suddenly remembered that Shokoofeh had said that she would come tomorrow to get the letter.

Ten minutes later, Farrokh arrived home, he rushed into the house and saw his maid in the yard. He first asked about Effat, although at that time all his thoughts and attention were focused on Mahin and the plan to kidnap her but he could not ignore Effat.

His maid replied with a smiling face that Effat was much better, and she asked to let her know when you are back home. Farrokh went upstairs and greeted Effat with kindness and told her that he had guessed it right, all her husband was a lie and based on his coward's dishonesty and unconscionability and he added that her parents thought that she was in Isfahan and that she was living a happy and comfortable life with her husband. And they have not disowned her.

Hearing this good news from Farrokh, Effat was very happy, as if every word that Farrokh said made the blood flow faster in her weak body, then she said in a subtle voice that expressed her gratitude:

"How can I thank you enough for your brotherly kindness?"

"I did not do anything, it is the duty of every person with a conscience to help his fellow human beings. Anyway, I think your parents will come here by this evening. When you see them, please stay calm and restrain yourself and do not hurt their hearts by explaining the details of the events."

Effat nodded and Farrokh added:

"I am deeply moved and saddened by these events that happened to you, and I seriously promise that I will find this coward as soon as possible and take revenge on him." Farrokh's voice trembled when he said this, and the veins in his forehead and neck were enlarged, and everyone who saw him in that state realized the extent of his anger and could read in the young man's eyes an unbreakable decision.

Then Farrokh suggested Effat to rest as he went down the mansion and sat behind a small table, took a pen in his hand, and wrote a letter to Mahin:

Dear Mahin,

If you will, this series of fantasies that your father has woven in his brain, and in fact the result of which is nothing but a chain for your future captivity, will be easily broken. If you are still in your decision and you are not willing to accept the husband who wants to impose on you, and if you still accept and prefer my unbridled love to the deceptive appearance and absurd statements of those who wanted your hand not for love but other purposes, and finally if inwardly You call me with a clear heart and you are sure that there is no one there except me, believe that this journey is a good opportunity to be separated from your mother for a while. Come to me and how welcome your steps are, I will embrace your whole existence. Do you know how we could arrange this?

When you arrive at Nusrat Palace, the deputy of the courier-house will suspend the movement of your carriage for the pretext of the horse injury. Then at night, I will arrive with another carriage and they will give you horses immediately. This is the best opportunity my dear Mahin if you are willing to show courage and if you consider me worthy of your servitude, please allow me to give you my soul and a heart full of love. Come to my carriage so that we can return to Tehran together... Of course, instead of you, the other woman I bring will go to your mother's carriage in the dark of night and an arrangement will be made so that no one will notice for several hours.

Mahin, you know better than anyone that your father does not believe in love and you know well that he will not be willing to put your hand in mine, and with his way of thinking and spirit, hopes for a happy and sweet future are very weak. Dear Mahin, your father is so greedy and ambitious, he counts your happiness as nothing. My darling Mahin, your mother has no idea about herself, do not rely on her, do not hope that she could do anything. Mahin, just refer to your heart and make your decision at this critical time.

The one who loves and worships you - Farrokh

Farrokh put the letter in the envelope, and it was a while since they had been brought lunch, he ate a few bites in a hurry. Then sat in a chair, held his head between his hands, and continued to think about the difficult task he had decided on. He wanted to declare war on those who do not believe in anything other than wealth and position. His beloved did not know of the great sacrifice he was willing to do.

This love and affection gave him a special strength and prepared the young man for any eventuality, so he talked to himself frequently:

'God is with me, it was God who gifted me Ahmad Ali Khan at this time so that my dear friend would set such a path for me.'

The poor young man, like most hard-core lovers, had been deceived by the good side of nature and had a definite hope of his full success, but he was not aware of what frustrations the universe had hidden beneath this seductive appearance!

Chapter Twenty
Seeking Revenge

At about two o'clock in the afternoon of the same day, a black carriage tied to a strong white horse stood in front of Farrokh's house. The servant sitting next to the coachman deftly got down and opened the carriage's shiny black door, grabbed the old man sitting in the carriage by the arm, and lowered him gently. A tall lady, who seemed to be old, got out of the carriage, and behind her was their maid. The servant knocked on the door of Farrokh's house, and minutes later the old man and the lady entered the house.

Farrokh came out to greet them and sincerely bowed to Effat's Parents. Then he reached out to R... Al-Dawlah and took him in his arms. They were exhausted and in a state of distress at that time, with traces of grief. They were all looking sad as they make their way to the room where Effat was. Effat has heard some noise and knew her parents are there. She was impatient. The poor woman wanted her parents to come as soon as possible and hear from their mouths that they had forgiven her. It was as if she still was not sure if she had left the disgraceful lifestyle behind, even in Farrokh's house, she imagined a happy dream that would lead to tragic events. And so she believed that this long nightmare would end only by seeing her parents, and only when she returned to her parent's home, her birthplace.

Suddenly the door opened, and Effat saw her father on the doorstep, leaning on her mother's arm, who was standing next to him, she wanted to get up from the bed and go under her parents' feet and pay homage by kissing their hands and feet, but she was still weak to do that. She could not quantify the joy in her heart and passed out. But it did not take long until she opened her eyes again.

Soon enough, they were sitting beside her on the bed holding each other's hands and kissing them, with hot tears on their faces. They were crying softly without saying a word. None of them dared to open their mouths and talk about those horrible events, and only used their tears to lift a heavy burden from their hearts.

Effat's parents cried over their faults and mistakes and how their negligence had blackened the lives of their only child, and how, as a result of their negligence and lack of further research on their future son-in-law, they had made their only daughter miserable. Effat was reviewing all the events from her wedding day up until now, and now after waiting for a long time, she saw her parents again, she was caught between two opposite feelings of sadness and happiness, and tears flowed.

Farrokh entered the room and said,
"Now is not the time to cry, the past can not be repaired, one must think of the future and revenge, and without such, a dishonest and unscrupulous man will not understand that the status of a noble family should not be a toy of his lust."

Little by little, the tears stopped and they begin to talk. Effat's mother kept asking her daughter about the details of the unfortunate incident, which she heard a hint of and thought she was dreaming as if she still could not believe it. She hoped that their daughter would deny it all, unfortunately, Effat had to narrate a few ominous events, her mother stood up and cursed and angrily took the silk handkerchief she was holding in her hand to chew it.

While R... Al-Dawlah holding his head down asked about Ali Ashraf Khan's behavior in Isfahan and his address. Farrokh, who was standing in the corner, interrupted their conversation again and said:
"Regret does not work on the past, one should think about the future. He has to pay for it."

Effat also confirmed Farrokh's advice and stated: "You are right, the past is past, and what should not have happened, happened. He and his peers can no longer hurt anyone else, just to find a way to prevent such incidents."

But what could those parents do and what did Effat expect from them, because her father was accustomed to idolatry in the court of tyrannical kings, and it was obligatory to bow and honor the immortal being, and to disobey the orders of the bloodthirsty king. He considered it contrary to God's command and endured every misfortune in the name of destiny. R...Al-Dawlah, who saw himself walking to the end of the world, now considered other events as cold-blooded and looked at life from his humble point of view, and for whatever happened, he was content to say that this was God's will!

And her mother, who was raised in the arms of a simple and uninformed maid and attended the school of Mullah Baji, was illiterate and fanatical, and instead found superstitions in everything, believed in Jinn, bogeyman, and put her trust in imposters, and resorted to the purpose of prayers from Mullah Ibrahim Yahudi, and practiced their rituals. What they could come up with and what Effat might have expected from them?

And it was their negligence in choosing a husband for their only daughter, and that well showed their ignorance. Their careless acts led to misery and a dark age for their daughter, Effat.

Farrokh realized Effat's thoughts, and became her consolation,

"Do not grieve, ma'am, revenge will be taken on that coward, I am aware of your misfortunes. I will not succumb until I bring him the punishment he deserves."

Effat read determination from Farrokh's eyes, so she smiled and said in a pleasant voice: "You are my only supporter!..."

The voice of Effat said this sentence had a strange effect on Farrokh. The young man's heart pounded. Effat felt feelings for Farrokh. 'Could Farrokh consider her more than a sister?'

Half an hour later, R... Al-Dawlah shook his head and said: "We have to go, we will take Effat with us, we would announce at home that she came to Tehran with one of her friends to see a doctor for treatment."

Effat liked his father's idea, and since her injury was minor and the doctor allowed her to move, she agreed to leave with the help of her mother. Then R... Al-Dawlah asked Farrokh to visit them anytime and thanked him for his kind gesture. Farrokh led him to his father's room, and the two old friends stayed together for a few minutes, recalling the days of the past.

Eventually, it was time to leave. R... Al-Dawlah and his wife and daughter each thanked Farrokh. The three of them looked at him again and thanked him. Effat's father thought what a blessing if only God would give him a son like Farrokh. Effat's mother desired the happiness of her daughter and wished for a groom like Farrokh, but Effat could not discern how she felt about the young man at that moment. She was sad about leaving Farrokh since she had a very sweet and pleasant memory of her. Farrokh promised not to forget them and visit them often.

***

Farrokh had to hurry to go to the south of the city, to the neighborhood of Chaleh Maidan to see Javad and inform him of the travel. Farrokh wore ordinary clothes to not attract the attention of the locals, especially the addicts. So he changed his western countries style clothes to an old Sardari waistcoat and a traditional wool felt hat.

As we know, Farrokh found Javad in the coffee house and asked a small boy to call him. When Javad agreed to help him, he gave him 4 notes from three Tomans, which made him happy and promised a better future.

Farrokh returned home early in the night and was surprised to see Ahmad Ali Khan sitting in the lower room of the mansion waiting for him.

The young man trembled and thought that there was something wrong with the plan and now his friend has come to disappoint him, but as soon as Ahmad Ali Khan opened his mouth, Farrokh's anxiety disappeared because he heard him say:

"I came to hear if Mahin was satisfied with the arrangement and willing to act accordingly so that I could explain the other details of the plan for you."

Farrokh replied that he would send the letter he had written to Mahin tomorrow morning, but he was eager to know what his dear friend had planned.

Ahmad Ali Khan also explained:

"As I said this morning, you will leave Tehran twenty-four hours after they leave. I will give you an official letter so that when you arrive at the courier-house, you can show yourself to the deputy. You will arrive in the evening or early at night and you have to use the darkness as a shield and go with the lady you want to exchange for Mahin. But of course, you have to teach the lady not to let the Gendarmerie interfere because it will cause trouble and if possible she should run away at the first opportunity and for this purpose, she needs to have another Chador with her."

Farrokh listened carefully to all his friend's words and promised to follow his lead. After Ahmad Ali Khan left, he ate a little food and went to bed and thought about this bold plan for a while, and finally fell asleep.

Early in the morning, when he got up, he heard that Shokoofeh had arrived, so he picked up the letter and asked her to get that to Mahin as soon as possible.

When Mahin read the letter several times, called Shokoofeh and asked her to tell Farrokh that she would act according to the instructions.

Shokoofeh immediately returned to Farrokh's house and informed the young lover about the decision of his cousin. Farrokh was extremely happy. He immediately sent his servant to Ahmad Ali Khan and informed him that Mahin agreed, therefore they could go ahead with the plan.

Javad had long been waiting in Farrokh's house and asked the servant to inform him.

"Since early morning, a young man has been waiting downstairs." The maid said.

Farrokh was surprised that Javad had arrived on time, he did not expect such punctuality from someone who lives in the infamous suburbs. He asked Javad if he had informed his people about his new job. Javad replied that he had given the money to his mother and informed them about his new job and was going on a trip, although they had insisted on coming with him to the house but did not accept.

"But you should know that we have a trip ahead and we will go to Qom tomorrow or the day after tomorrow morning, but the trip may not last more than two or three days," Farrokh replied.

Then Farrokh tried to find a suitable woman who could follow him, and after a while, he called his maid and asked her if she could find her niece, whom Farrokh knew well and they were playmates as a child.

The maid hurried to bring her niece. Her niece was called Batool and had a strange life story. At the age of nine, a young carpenter who was not more than eighteen years old got married to her and after a short time, they separated due to young incompatibility. Until today, before the age of twenty-five, she had had several other husbands. After her first husband, Batool spent some time with an Akhund and then spent the nights with the group of revelers in the southern neighborhoods of Tehran. And she was concubine to one of the famous princes of Tehran for two or three months. She was a woman who has had several husbands in thirteen or fourteen years and has experience with different morals and natures, her eyes and ears were open, and as they say, she has seen the world.

Farrokh was sure he would not find anyone better than Batool for this purpose, and she was the only one who could, if necessary, fight with a male army to carry on with the job. An hour later, his maid came back with Batool. Farrokh, who knew her from a young age and had a special respect for her as she was trustworthy in every way, shared the matter with Batool without fear.

"I need you today, I hope you accompany me and take this fearful task, no matter how difficult, needs to be done skillfully, and first of all, you must know that we will go to Qom tomorrow."

Hearing the Qom, the girl's face showed great joy as she replied: "What a bliss is higher than going to Qom with a gentleman like you!"

Farrokh replied, "I mean, we may not reach Qom but our trajectory will be Qom anyway, and when we might reach the Nusrat Palace at night, you should go and sit in another carriage. Of course, those who are in that carriage will notice you after a while and will scare you, and maybe they will hand you over to my Gendarme, and maybe there will be an interrogation, but first, you have to keep quiet as much as you can, and finally if they push and force you to speak. Tell them you were going in a carriage in Tehran and in the darkness of the night you mistakenly switched carriage in the courier-house, don't worry, you will get help because all the courier-house officials have orders to help you. In Qom, tell one of them and show them the paper that I will give you, they will assist you in all kinds of ways. On the way, if the situation becomes difficult, whatever it is, you will be disguised so you can leave without being noticed."

Batool listened carefully to all of Farrokh's words, without any surprise, acknowledged the details of the young man's plan one by one, and confirmed that she was well aware of the dangerous task, however, she is confident even though she may have spent a few nights in the Nazmieh detention center. Doing these things did not seem to be a problem at all, so she promised with courage and boldness that she would execute his plan.

Farrokh promised Batool that he would arrange her life when he returned and would give her enough money to help her get a new husband. Hearing the word new husband, Batool's other doubt disappeared and she was ready to carry out Farrokh's order with all interest.

Two hours later, they brought the letters that Ahmad Ali Khan had written to the deputy of the Nusrat Palace and the chief of Qom courier-house Farrokh opened and read the letter,

My dear friend,
After dedicating my devotion and inquiring about your noble temperament, I wish to ask you to provide the means of movement for the petitioner who must return to Tehran as soon as possible, and if she needs any help and support, do not hesitate to render assistance. I will be grateful. The bearer of the letter will give the necessary explanations to you.
Sincerely - Ahmad Ali

Farrokh gave this letter and two gold coins to Batool: "When you get to Qom, go to the chief immediately and show this letter to arrange your return to Tehran. He will help you.

Farrokh spent the rest of the day anxious. The young man knew that he had a difficult and dangerous task ahead of him, and although he was not afraid of its drawbacks and dangers, he was worried that he would not be able to overcome them all and thus achieve his goal.

Two days later, Farrokh, accompanied by Javad and Batool, traveled to Qom.

Chapter Twenty-one
Two Tricksters

In the northern part of Tehran, along Lalehzar Street, there is a cross-roads called Kent. In the northwestern corner of this crossroads, a large two-story mansion has been built, which had a backyard garden. This house is on the street front. On its second floor, there is a long and wide porch in front of all the rooms, looking to the east. This porch is located on a series of stone pillars from the floor of the street, which make a good refuge for passersby in the scorching summer sun or the snow of the winter. The main entrance of this house, the southern end of the mansion, is located almost at the corner of the crossroads.

If enter through this large door, at the very beginning of the corridor, on the right side, there are wide stairs that lead to the first floor. Going up those stairs, there is a small space on both sides of which wooden sticks have been installed for hanging clothes of the guests on the walls so that the entrants can hang their coats or cloaks depending on the season, and sometimes Persian hats there. It can be seen that passing through this part, there are a series of connected rooms, each of which has special furniture, including a large rectangular table covered with green mahogany, as well as a few other small square tables, which also have green mahogany in every corner, these rooms are playground and there are chairs with handles and several bench-es in other room, all covered with thick plain or flowery fabrics. There are several Iranian and French newspapers scattered on the round table in the middle. This mansion is an imperial club and the center of entertainment, gambling, and leisure for certain groups of rich, modern, and western peo-ple in Tehran.

Often many famous political and wealthy men from Tehran come there, and some members of embassies and other non-Muslim Iranians are also members of this club, and these people occasionally bring their wives with them, and most of them spend their time in that club until late at night.

In the evening of the same morning, when Malek Taj found out that her daughter was missing on their way to Qom, two members of the club, who had their thin Naini robes in the corridor and gave them to the servants, sat opposite of each other while wore coat and ties, and the only thing that set them apart from European members was the long black hat they wore.

One of them was fat and had a dark face, a thick mustache, and large eyes.

He wore a military hat, the upper part of which seemed wider than the lower part. His friend, who was a little thinner, was white, with his slender mustache twisted upwards on both sides. They looked older and spoke hotly, and occasionally when a European or non-Muslim member entered with their wife and left her near them, they will both look lustfully at them.

Meanwhile, Mr. fat, who had a dark face, turned his face to his friend and said: "Well, continue, you said that you sent your family to Qom for pilgrimage, but you preferred the pilgrimage of some people who come here?"
F... Al-Saltaneh, laughed out loud at this statement and said:
"What can I do, you know you have to go through the world, and my Mrs is a mother and of course, she must think of the afterlife but you know me I can not close my eyes to hot ladies until the last hours of my life."
He was talking to Prince K ... Siavash Mirza's father,
"Of course, the world should have days of fun. I have the same opinion and I often tell my son the same thing, but is he willing to listen? This young man has made life bitter for himself, he is constantly sitting in the corner of the room, reading scientific books, and recently he has forced me to set up a chemistry laboratory for him at home. I do not know what to say about this boy's morals, and sometimes I think the morality and this degree of interest in education are not from me. After all, it is not hidden from you, and you know well that I have never thought about lessons and books, and I am always having fun, but on the contrary, Siavash, despite being young, does not go around doing fun things. I can boldly say that his eyes and ears are still completely closed. Books will weaken his mood, man should be interested in his health first. But whenever I talk to him, you know what he told me in response, father, do not bother yourself in vain, I will not give up books and I can not, like other young people, make drinking and going to some places the motto of my life. I do not want that and all my efforts are to save my compatriots from misery and humiliation, and to get rid of greedy and unfair drug dealers! Notice how great this boy's thoughts are and how far he will go.

Then Prince K ... took a cigarette out of a case, lit it and took a puff, and added: "There is a big difference between me and my boy! I'm into drinking and women and he is into science and humanity"
F... Al-Saltanah, who listened carefully to all the words of the prince and seemed to believe completely, said with concern:
"God forbid, their health and well-being should not be harmed and I should not be deprived of the honor of having such a groom!"
Prince K ... acknowledged him:
"I am also afraid of this, the poor man has had severe swelling since three nights ago and his right thigh has been completely injured. Due to his many

intellectual pursuits, the doctor said his blood flowed too fast due to too much work, and he was told to rest for a while.

F... Al-Saltanah, who was worried about the news of his future son-in-law's and was afraid that the plans he had made would fall apart at once, heard that Siavash Mirza's illness is minor said with a sigh of relief:

"I also think that rest is the best treatment for him and be sure to take the prince out for some fresh air."

Prince K ... said:

"I had the same thought, and maybe by the weekend we will go to the property up-country, it is the best time to go due to the weather condition."

F... Al-Saltaneh picked up a large glass of whiskey in front of him and sip as he said:

"Anyway, you have made me worried. Please do not leave me unaware of the health of Siavash Mirza and give me the good news of his full recovery as soon as possible."

At this point, the wife of one of the members of the club entered. It seemed that she was looking for her husband, one of the Cossack officials. She was adorned with a pleasant red lipstick, and her white and tidy teeth and delicate style, and most of all, her brown hair, captivated every viewer. Immediately after F... Al-Saltaneh saw her, he said slowly to his friend:

"This is the lady I was talking about, the one I met last night."

Then he stood up, bowed a little, kissed her hand with great interest, and immediately introduced her to his friend.

"Let me introduce His Highness Prince K ... my esteemed friend."

The smiling woman extended her hand to the prince, and the prince, who was fascinated by her beauty, took the lady's hand in both hands and brought it close to her lips with complete interest.

Immediately, the lady asked F... Al-Saltaneh in broken Persian, "Is her husband in the club, and have they seen him?"

F... Al-Saltanah replied that he had only been in the club for half an hour and had been in the same room all the time, and was not aware if her husband was there. Then she went to the game room.

Prince K ..., who was still immersed in watching the beauty of the lady.

"She is good!"

F... Al-Saltaneh enjoyed praising her as if she belongs to him, he proudly said:

"Last night, a European friend of mine introduced her to me. It turns out that she is one of the Russian cossack officials who has been in Rasht for some time and was recently transferred to Tehran. I fell in love with her since I laid my eyes on her. Well, I hid it from you to not show off, even though I reduce my gambling, I banked the big banks several times but also

lost about fifteen hundred tomans, but what does it matter, because I could see that the money had its effect and I am sure she did not hate me!"
And the prince, who is interested in the lady, had found himself in a rivalry with F... Al-Saltaneh, but laughed inside and thought to himself:
'What a selfish poor little thing, why would such a beautiful lady fall in love with someone like you with this posture.'

A few seconds passed in silence between the two friends, F... Al-Saltanah had left all his whiskey and took a cigarette out of his pocket, complimented to prince too, and said:
Indeed, I can be sure that with God's help, success in that matter is inevitable!
The prince answered,
"Of course. I already assured you that you will have 4,000 votes from my party, my western neighbor has also promised to help, and with his 2,000 votes you will get a total of 6,000 votes, and in this way, you will have a complete majority and you will certainly be a proud lawyer. You will have the true representation of the nation, and if necessary, we have other means that we can use, we may change the ballot box or delay the election by burning the ballot box and in the meantime agree with the opposition, but fortunately, we do not imagine any of this to be necessary, because my villagers are so illiterate and ignorant that they can not do anything about representing the parliament, let alone comment on the personalities of the candidates and the good and bad of the candidates, although fortunately this part is taken care of, I fully believe that they will not find a better lawyer than you, because, you are an honest and flawless person and you have declared yourself a supporter of the working class."

F... Al-Saltaneh had listened carefully to Prince K..., hearing the recent sentences, he was confident and said in the right tone,
"Your Excellency, you know better than anyone and I have no material opinion in this matter, thank God, God has given me a piece of bread that I do not need for others, my purpose is only to serve this land. It is my homeland and the citizens that have made me think of occupying the position of a lawyer so that I serve them to the best of my ability, and I imagine that because I have a slight political interest in this country more than others I am aware of the peasants and I know better what laws are necessary and useful to correct and improve their situation.
Then he pondered a little and added:
"Your Excellency, you have a good record. You know that most of these gentlemen who supported the peasants have not had the slightest contact with them and there is no way the real needs of the working people could be realized in such a manner, and because they have no familiarity with

the subject, words will come out of their mouths that will shake the status quo, and as a result, will cause rebellion of others. The peasants should have nothing but the work in agriculture, and whatever the Lord gives, they should be satisfied and grateful and suffice with it, and in my opinion, if it is possible, like Russia, to give them millet instead of wheat."

By lowering his head, the prince confirmed his statements. And F... Al-Saltaneh continued.

"I forgot to tell you a few days ago, I was in the parliament where some young educated people from Europe were present and having the scientific discussions, I don't understand them because of my little knowledge. I was silent and listened intently to the conversation. I heard one of them explain an interesting opinion, an English scholar named Darwin."

Prince K ... asked more curiously:

"Who was Darwin and what is his opinion?"

F... Al-Saltaneh further explain, as if he was like a teacher who tries to clarify a problem or issue well for his students, "According to the belief of this English world, if a person sees one of his fellow human beings in misery lying next to a wall and has lost his will to live, he should not have mercy on him, because that miserable person is certainly not worthy and has not had more than this fate."

Then he paused and explained after his speech:

"As much as I understood, according to the theory of this great world, whoever reaches any position or suffers humiliation is only due to his merit, and what should I hide from you? I agree with Darwin and have the same opinion."

"Eventually the wolf will be born a wolf."

"In my opinion, mercy and compassion are not permissible for any human being at all, and when people like us help the helpless people often cause trouble, so why should a human being interfere in the work and situation of others for whom God has so willed. For example, God observed how it is useful to have a graceful physique in all stages of life, and being well-dressed, opens all the doors for human beings. After all, it can not be denied that Mirza Hussein, will always be the son of the mercer, Mirza Ali Akbar, even if he goes to school for a few days, he still does not act like the son of a respectable and noble family, and he should sit next to his father and drops an abacus."

This was a series of reverse logics that F... Al-Saltaneh expressed with all his heart for his comrade and tried with these sophistries and these strange reasons for the rights of the majority of his compatriots except for one rich and illiterate person. In his opinion, because according to him people are often not noble, they do not have the right to progress and achieve high positions, and some of them open the way to their progress due to hardship and suffering. Because they do not have the necessary factors.

The club clock struck six o'clock in the afternoon, at that time a waiter arrived and went straight to F... Al-Saltaneh, and presented an envelope on a tray. Mahin's father was surprised to find out the paper was written for him and the club's address was hastily removed from the envelope, and when he saw that it was a telegram and that it was urgent, he was convinced that it was the news of the lady's arrival.
He smiled and said to the prince:
"Let me see what the telegram says. Certainly, she thought I was worried about her being away." Then he laughed, opened the envelope and held it in front of his eyes. Suddenly a lot of redness appeared on Mahin's father's cheeks and the veins of his neck rose as he throw away the telegram and said to the prince with a complete stutter:
"You know what happened, you know what happened, my daughter was kidnapped!"
The prince, who was shocked to hear this news, hurriedly lifted the telegram from the ground and read:

Tehran Street ... very urgent.

Your Excellency Mr. F... Al-Saltaneh, an unfortunate incident occurred. Mahin was missing at Nusrat Palace. Instead of her, there was another woman in the carriage. That woman also escaped when we were in the Qom courier-house. We have informed the Gendarmerie.
Your maid, Firoozeh

The prince thought for a moment and did not know what to say. He was affected by this news. He was afraid of the marriage of Mahin and his son would not take place, he would not be able to use the wealth and properties of F... Al-Saltaneh to pay for his large debts.

But the news of Mahin's abduction had aroused a sense of anger and sadness in F... Al-Saltaneh, because on the one hand, the father's heart had been wounded, and at the same time, his selfish sense had caused great damage! F... Al-Saltaneh loved her daughter so much that he could not remain indifferent to such incidents, especially since with this incident, all the plans he had made for her advocacy collapsed and fell apart. He was afraid that the prince would no longer be willing to help him in his work as a lawyer and provide him with the means to advance his ambitious goals, and therefore he could not consider this incident insignificant and careless.

A moment passed, and little by little drops of sweat appeared on the forehead of F... Al-Saltaneh was pensive and puzzled. Mahin's father kept asking himself who was involved in this work, who was involved in this work?! Suddenly a name came to his tongue and he said softly:
"Farrokh!"

Chapter Twenty Two
Conquest Of Love

We left Mahin in Nusrat palace when the news came that the horses were ready. She stood up and told her mother that she will be waiting in the carriage until they get ready. At that moment, the clouds covered the entire sky and were so dark that it was not easy to detect an object from a few steps away.

As soon as Mahin left the room and came to the porch of the courier-house, she stood for a moment and thought to herself:
'If I accidentally go to our carriage, all the plans will be destroyed. I have to identify the carriages from each other, then I only need to go to Farrokh's carriage without making any sound.'

The poor girl's heart was pounding hard at that moment, Mahin knew what she was doing, that she was standing against her father's arrogance and stubbornness. She was hoping this will make clear to her father that she is willing to pay the price by damaging her dignity, but will not accept the husband her father chose for her.

Mahin knew Farrokh well and was aware of his cousin's heartfelt feelings. She was only worried and upset about her mother because Mahin loved her very much and knew well that in this case her mother is not guilty but a tool in her husband's hand, and when her mother notices that she is not in the carriage, she will be very sad and heartbroken, her heart beat faster as she thought to herself: 'My poor mother will surely be hurt a lot and she will be very worried about my absence, but what can I do?'

At that very moment, one of the coachmen lit a match for his pipe, a short light came on, and as a result, Mahin was able to see the carriage a few steps away. And she saw Hassan Qoli standing next to the first carriage in the direction of Qom. She stopped thinking and slowly, without making a sound, went straight to the second carriage, and as soon as she approached it, she felt two strong hands coming out of the carriage lifting her from the ground and pulling her into the carriage. Then Mahin, who seemed to have completely lost her mind in fear, recognized Farrokh's warm voice, which whispered in her ear with all kindness:
"Mahin ... My dear Mahin, the truth is I did not expect this level of courage

from you and I couldn't be happier that you are willing to do this, Mahin, how can I thank you."

Mahin, whose heart was still pounding and the sound of its beating could be heard saying in a hushed voice that expressed her anxiety and worries: "Farrokh, now is not the time for these words. Let's get out of here as soon as possible."

"Moving before them is not good and may attract attention,"Farrokh, who was holding her hand, tried to calm his lover.

Mahin said nothing more and thought deeply. A few minutes later, which was like a few months for Mahin, Malak Taj and Firoozeh got into their carriage and headed for Qom. Then Javad, who was standing next to Farrokh's carriage, jumped up agilely and stood next to the coachman. This carriage also went in the opposite direction, that is, towards Tehran.

The carriage was not even a few hundred steps away from Nusrat Palace when Farrokh felt the tears of Mahin on his hand. Her escape showed the extent of her interest, and she could no longer bear thinking about her mother's worry and anxiety.

Farrokh's heart was pressed to see Mahin's tears, so he took Mahin's delicate hands and hugged her: "Mahin, my dear, what are you crying about and what are you worried about? Why do you want to hurt my heart, don't cry I can not bear to see it. If you are worried about your mother, I will inform her of your health at the earliest opportunity, and she will soon be informed of your safety, and she will also know that if she asks your father for permission to marry me, she will be able to visit her daughter immediately."

Although Farrokh's statements were made with complete honesty and ultimately intimacy, they did not eliminate Mahin's worries and anxieties and did not alleviate the girl's inner pain.

"My poor mom is ignorant, she is not to blame."

Then she turned to Farrokh and said:

"Let's go back together to Qom, we will see my mother there, we will both fall on our hands and feet together and we will ask her to give us consent and then she will convince my father in some way."

Farrokh was caught between two feelings, he knew his aunt well and he was familiar with Mahin's mother's morals and spirits and he was sure that this plan was not practical. But what if he loved Mahin very much and wanted her satisfaction more than anything, she will do what she wants. Mahin's tears flowed regularly like raindrops, which had put Farrokh's nerves to a severe test. Mahin did not stop and Farrokh's consolations did not work, and the girl kept insisting on returning to Qom. With the sound and shaking of this severe blow, the coachman and Javad jumped down as they heard Farrokh's voice, which ordered them to stop. The next moment, the carriage

stopped, then Farrokh turned his face to Mahin and said in a disappointing tone:
"Mahin, do not cry, I don't like to see you cry. If you do not stop crying and do not calm down, I am ready to free myself from the shackles of life here so that you too can return to your parents with peace of mind and marry the rich man intended for you!"

Mahin's crying became more intense with Farrokh's words and squeezed her beloved hand angrily, Farrokh said with all his might:
"Mahin, do not cry, whatever your desire is, it will be the same, we will return at this hour and soon you will be in your mother's arms. I will stay far away and I will not disturb your peace and comfort for even a minute under any pretext."

This commanding expression and sincere words had their effect. The girl stopped crying. But such harsh and reproachful words of Farrokh disturbed Mahin's soul and made her unconscious so that she could no longer utter a word. Farrokh also considered Mahin's silence as the reason for his desire to return, he opened the carriage door and went down to the coachman, who was waiting for an order, and told him to return to Nusrat palace. Farrokh's order surprised them, but without delay, he turned the horses' in the direction of Qom.
Mahin said in a delicate voice:
"Farrokh, what are you doing, where are you going, I promise I will not cry anymore, we will go wherever you want."

Farrokh, who was extremely affected and angry at the same time, did not pay attention to Mahin at first, and they were not given any order to stop or change the course of the carriage.
"Farrokh, you do not listen to me, so it turns out that you do not love me anymore!"
Mahin's sweet voice did its job this time, Farrokh's anger subsided, but he was still confused. It was very difficult to blame and doubt Mahin about her love, and because Mahin was still silent and waiting for his decision.

Mahin, like all lovers, had chosen love. She loved her mother, but she could not give up Farrokh at any cost. She filled her heart with her mother's great affection, but her strings of interest seemed stronger to Farrokh. It was a natural relationship and the love of mother and child, and this burning love and natural force embodied sexual desire. Of course, if forced, she could stay with her mother for years and enjoy her unrequited love, but living with Farrokh, who promised to fulfill thousands of sweet dreams, was something else. She knew her mother's heart would be hurt by her distance, but she was sure that Farrokh's heart would be more broken and burned by the separation.

Time passed quickly, the carriage was moving in the direction of Qom. So the girl made her decision and, despite the weakness because of her tears and all other emotions. It was as if she had concentrated all her energy and announced her decision to Farrokh:

"Farrokh, what are you doing, where are you going, be rest assured, I will not cry anymore and we will go wherever you want."

Farrokh gradually calmed down and his heartache subsided and now he was sitting next to her. Farrokh respected her silence and drowned in the sea of his various thoughts and thoughts about what happened and their future. Finally, after half an hour, Mahin asked in silence:

"You promised to inform my mother about my health as soon as possible, I wanted to know where we are heading and how you want to tell her."

Farrokh noticed Mahin's calmness, turned his face towards her, and while holding Mahin's hands on his lips and kissing her repeatedly, he said:

"Mahin, you do not know how happy I am to see you next to me, I can't believe my eyes."

Then he added:

"Of course, my dear, as I promised, when we arrive home, you will write a letter to your mother in your handwriting, and they will understand that you had to do so. It is their fault because they did not want to consent to our marriage. If they assure you that they will not give us any more problems in our marriage, they will meet you soon. I will give the letter to the deputy of the courier-house and ask him to deliver it to her as soon as possible."

Mahin did not say anything more and immersed herself in thoughts again, Farrokh was still holding her hands as she remained silent, he kissed her hands.

About two o'clock in the morning, they arrived at the fort of Mohammad Ali Khan. First, Farrokh jumped out of the carriage, then took Mahin under his arm as they got off the carriage. Upon entering the room, she remembered having dinner with her mother the night before. Tears welled up in her eyes. But she did not want to offend Farrokh, she smiled. A few minutes later, Javad brought a pen and paper, she took the pen and wrote a letter to her mom.

Dear mother,

I hope this letter meets you well. I am miles away from you, mother. I don't know where I am at the moment but be rest assured, my heart is not far from you and I remember you at every moment.

Mother, I know very well that I have hurt you badly with this behavior, but unfortunately there was no other way and I had no choice but to do so. Although I have expressed my dissatisfaction with the husband whom you and my father had chosen for me, not of my own free will, but your own free will. Also, you did not support me, I wanted you to consider my opinion and desire about my future, but rather you insist on choosing a man with whom I do not feel the slightest bit of affection in my heart. Of course, if I was a thoughtless girl and did not take the importance of marriage seriously and, like many of my friends, would accept your proposed marriage and not consider my happiness, I would live a miserable life.

I did not want to disobey your will and accepted anyone you recommended, but, I do only the formalities of marriage and the celebration of marriage. I consider marriage to be the prelude to a new life and a long period of a happy life with a husband of my choice. You may say that I am very difficult. What can I do? It's not my fault you brought me up this way. In any case, because it was beyond my power to blindly obey your orders in this serious matter with this intellectual structure, I had to formally go against my father. Now you may have realized the disadvantages of being too dictatorial to your only child and whose future happiness should mean more than anything else.
Farrokh lives in a free environment. He loves me and all his efforts are to make me happy. I am also interested in him and I intend to make him happy as well. He wants nothing but my consent and I have no other will than his will, he wants my happiness, and I want his happiness.

My dear mother, I know that my absence will have a great impact on you and you will suffer a lot from this incident, and I am sure that you will curse me a lot, but I have no complaints and I give you the right because I know you are innocent — I know father insists on giving me out and impose this on you, I know you would not have insisted so much on carrying out this sinister plan, so if you notice the mistake now and want to amend try to get father to agree to my marriage with Farrokh and you will be able to see me soon, and only if you agree with our wedding will you see me under your feet again.
Forget that Farrokh doesn't have more wealth and possessions, but think about other behaviors, deeds, and virtues, and know that he is my beloved, my soul, and finally my future husband.

She who always loves and respects you, Mahin

After Mahin read the paper again and put it in the envelope and asked Farrokh to send it to his mother, Farrokh immediately called the deputy of the courier-house and handed over the letter to him. Coincidentally, an hour later, a carriage arrived heading to Tehran. The coachman had been promised a good reward, explaining how to deliver the letter.

After writing this letter, Mahin found herself in a better situation, she felt

the lightweight in her heart and was smiling. Farrokh was overjoyed to see Mahin's smile. They hold each other's hands with great desire, and from time to time their faces came closer together, and in the small space of the carriage, the sound of their kisses resounded.
Farrokh couldn't hold the joy anymore. He had achieved his greatest dreams. His beloved Mahin, who had come for him, to the other side of the world just to be with him, was by his side, in that narrow space of the carriage, no one was bothering those two lovers.

Mahin said with her happy and smiling face:
"I am sure my mother will immediately inform my father about what's going on, she will ask him to agree to our wedding so she can come to see me. My father loves me and will certainly not bother me anymore and will give his consent... Farrokh, you and I are happy, we love each other and we have a bright future ahead of us."

Farrokh, meanwhile, was explaining his plans to Mahin:
"We are going to stay in one small village in Shemiran, which is far from the road and people's access, we will live in a village house that I know. The weather there is very pleasant this season, you and I will not only enjoy the mild weather but also for a while we will live with the people of the village who are very kind in terms of morality and good nature, and if you wish, you will write a letter to your father from there, and God willing, we will return to the city together as soon as the news of your parents' consent arrives."

It was a series of sweet thoughts, and the so-called golden dreams of lovers, but they did not know how much nature is powerful and skillful to disturb and overthrow happiness and prosperous life.

Chapter Twenty Three
Only One Night

Evin is a small village in Shemiran, located northwest of Tehran. This village is far from Tajrish and other villages of Shemiran. A small river flows from the north to the south and it's always raining until late summer. The houses of the residents of the village, like other summer houses in Iran, all have short walls and most of them are made up of two or three small thatched rooms. Most of the garden houses are overlooking the hill and river, located on both sides and look so beautiful.

Farrokh had chosen Evin because the village was remote and far from Tajrish, the center of Shemiran. In addition, he had an acquaintance in that village so they could stay in his house.

This garden house was located on the west side of the river. It was a small rural building that had three rooms. In front of this humble house, there was a narrow garden that led to another garden, which was located at a lower level, at a distance of ten or twelve meters. The various trees that rose among these gardens and the green wild grasses that covered the surface of the earth were particularly refreshing this season, and all the beauty and natural scenery of this humble country house were greatly enhanced.

About two hours after leaving the city, the carriages reached the beginning of Evin after passing through Yousefabad and Vanak. Farrokh paid the fare and gave a good gratuity. Farrokh asked Javad to take some of their belongings, and all three went to the village house at the northern end of the village. It was not a holiday season and no one from the city had come there. The streets of Evin were deserted and for this reason, they did not encounter many passersby on the way.

Fortunately, the owner of the house was at home, and as soon as he saw Farrokh, he greeted him warmly and invited the young man and his companions in.

They went straight to the house, and entered the first room. Javad put the things in the corner of the room and went out. Farrokh, after inviting Mahin to sit down to rest, told the landlord,

"Amoo Karim, we want to stay here for a while, but I want no one to know that we are here."

Amoo Karim smiled and said:

"Sir, this house belongs to you so that you can visit whenever you want, my wife and I are at your service and we will provide you with everything you need and you can be sure that we will not let anyone be informed as you wish."

Farrokh, who knew Amoo Karim for his morals and believed his words, said nothing more and asked him for some hot tea to relieve their tiredness. As soon as Amoo Karim left the room and went to the garden, Mahin, who had been wearing a mask, took off her mask and her beautiful face appeared in the middle of that black chador, a shining moon through the dark clouds. Farrokh was overwhelmed by the look on her charming face,

"Mahin, my darling, do not be upset. I have predicted everything, I will send your health news to your parents regularly and we will stay in this village until they consent to our marriage. Of course, on Fridays and Sundays when the people of the city come here, we will not leave the house, but on other days, especially on moonlit nights, we will go for a walk and enjoy the natural scenery of this village and its mild weather."

Mahin listened to Farrokh's words without saying a word, and although it seemed that she was paying full attention to the young man's statements, she had lost her inner peace again, and deep in her heart there was a heavy burden, Mahin was aware of their difficult situation, she knew that The status of a man can not be damaged in terms of association with a woman. Innocent Mahin knew that when acquaintances and people were informed of his daring action, they would not object, but could she also be sure that she would be saved from ridiculed and blamed by relatives and acquaintances, and finally by all her fellow citizens?

Every time Farrokh talked about how long they would stay in that house, Mahin's heart trembled and an inner feeling told her that they would not last long and that this situation would not last long! When Javad brought tea, both of them had been silent for some time and were immersed in a sea of thoughts.

Seeing Farrokh in front of her, the feeling of his presence creates peace and relieves her inner anxiety, and she repeatedly recuse herself in her heart, saying: 'Farrokh is with me, this is the person I wanted to be with, this is the same beloved that I had promised myself not to accept anyone other than him. I know him and I am aware of his degree of interest, I know that he will not give up on me until the last hour of his life, and I am sure that he will defend me against any danger and incident. Farrokh is my beloved, he is my lover, he is my soul.' The more Mahin strengthened these thoughts in her brain, the less her inner anxiety decreased, and because she could see how Farrokh had no other thought but her comfort.

Mahin smiled and acknowledged Farrokh's words about their future and sometimes even added her sweet ideas to it and quoted them to Farrokh, but

deep down Mahin felt, 'This life will be short!'
Mahin trembled at the thought and asked herself with all her heart:
'No one can separate us, no strong hand can separate me from Farrokh?'
Then a bitter thought came to her mind, 'If they take me away from Far-
rokh, I am sure our meeting will not be possible.'

At about five o'clock in the afternoon, when the intensity of the summer
sun had subsided, Farrokh suggested to Mahin that they should go for a
walk around the garden and the river. The two lovers put their arms under
each other's arms, passed through the room outside the house, in front of
which was a small pond, and descended the uneven and rugged stairs of the
gardens, which were made of small and large stones, and slowly descended
to the river. Due to the heavy rain that fell on the mountain the night before,
the water of the river had increased. The water collapsed around the head
of the rock.

Mahin and Farrokh each sat on a rock in front of each other and watched
each other silently for a while. Both of them were immersed in watching the
beautiful nature, and both of them seemed to enjoy watching each other.
The sun was slowly setting in the sky and was slowly disappearing behind
the hill. Farrokh, who was sitting on a rock in front of Mahin, did not take
his eyes off her. Mahin felt a strong magnet for the soul and body of her
lover. There was a boundless mystery in his gaze. Farrokh got up, went to
Mahin and took her hand gently, and kissed her lips.

It was dark and the stars appeared one by one in the blue sky, but the
two lovers did not rise or show interest in leaving the river, and it seemed
as if they were sitting together on a soft bench. In the meantime, they were
silent as both of them were deep in thought, but their thoughts went hand
in hand, and they were both worried about their unknown future, and yet
their souls were connected.

Javad call them out for dinner. He had set the white tablecloth in a large
room. Amoo Karim's wife had also prepared a very delicious dinner, broth
in ad with plums and pumpkin stew with rice. Farrokh ate with a full appetite and constantly encouraged Mahin who did not want to eat. Finally, the
girl ate a few bites to accompany Farrokh.

Half an hour later, Amoo Karim, who just had one extra single mattress
brought it for them, but Farrokh insisted on leaving it to Mahin and spending the night with the blanket he brought with him. But could Mahin accept
this arrangement and not worry about Farrokh's comfort? Eventually, they
decided to share the pillow and mattress together. Farrokh happily accepted
this arrangement and feeling the warm and pleasant breath of his lover was
magical.

The weather was cold that night. Farrokh, who had only a blanket, wrapped it tightly and planned to send Javad to the city tomorrow to get what they needed. The cold hit harder and he felt colder, he trembled and gnashed his teeth. Mahin, hearing this sound, became very anxious, as she could not bear Farrokh getting sick.

Suddenly, Farrokh heard Mahin crying and tried to comfort her;

"Mahin, my darling, why are you crying? I am here with you and you know I love you so much. You know I can sacrifice everything for you. Tonight is not a night of crying." Farrokh's lips touched hers. Her teardrops fell like dewdrops on her face, like dropping dewdrops on a flower leaf. After a while, finally, on a night when sleep did not enter Mahin's turquoise eyes, the goddess of love, with a smiling face that indicated her success, descended for an hour in that humble rural room and put her beautiful wings over their head so that they could spread their love ...

About five o'clock in the morning, the sun rose and penetrated through the window. Farrokh had fallen into a deep sleep. Mahin gently pushed the quilt away without making the slightest sound. She looked pale, opened the door, and was astonished by the beautiful view of nature. She tried to move back a little to observe what was going on, then a rifle was pointed at her. As she was about to scream. she noticed Farrokh was deep asleep. She was puzzled, turned to the river, and saw more people with riffles.

Mahin did not think anymore as she shout:

"Farrokh, Farrokh, wake up! The gendarmes have surrounded the garden!"

Farrokh got up when he heard Mahin's voice, and with a single leap he reached the window, and when he saw the gendarmes behind the wall and by the river, he shook his head in despair and said:

"It is not possible to escape, but in any case, we will resist."

Then he shouted Javad's name and asked him for help.

Chapter Twenty Four
How The Nest Of Love Was Discovered

F... Al-Saltaneh was thinking of a way to save Mahin from this dangerous young man, but how?

Prince K... respected the silence and did not say anything. After a few minutes, F...Al-Saltaneh finally got up and went to the other room to make a call. He called his close friend, who was the head of the gendarmerie and asked him to give immediate orders to the roads gendarme to arrest Farrokh and Mahin wherever they saw them. The head of the gendarmerie assured Mahin's father that he would give such an order and they would surely find them.

F... Al-Saltaneh returned to his chair and informed Prince K... that intended to go to Qom at that time. He could not believe that Mahin had abandoned his mother, and had been deceived by a young man, a hopeless adventurer. After saying goodbye to the prince, hurried out of the hall, got in the carriage, and went straight home. As soon as his arrival,, he summoned his servant, Reza Qoli, and ordered him to rent a car at any cost, and make it ready to travel to Qom in an hour. Reza Qoli, realizing his master's face was disturbed, left the mansion without asking for any further explanation.

There were not many cars in Tehran at that time, and cars were rented only in a few places, one of which was located at the beginning of Ala Al-Dawlah Street near Topkhaneh Square. Reza Qoli got in the carriage and gave the address of the place to the coachman. Fortunately, they got a car. The owner of the garage, who was Belgian, promised to provide him with a car immediately if he paid a hundred and fifty Tomans for a return trip. Reza Qoli, who had all kinds of authority on behalf of his master, promised that whatever he wanted would be paid. Although Reza Qoli considered the price very expensive, in order not to take responsibility, phoned his master. F... Al-Saltaneh, who was in a hurry to find his daughter, accepted the fare without hesitation.

There was a gendarme post in Hazrat Abdul Azim, the driver stopped and called the gendarme standing in front of the post and after introducing himself, asked him if any carriage had passed through there. The gendarme replied: "According to the order received from the center, if such passengers pass, we will definitely detain them, but no one has come yet."

F... Al-Saltaneh ordered the driver to go to Kahrizak. They also said that Farrokh and Mahin's carriage had not passed that point. The car passed Kahrizak and headed towards Hassanabad, the next courier house. Fortunately, the car engine was working well and had not caused them any trouble in the desert until then. After a quarter of an hour stop in Hassanabad, they went to Mohammad Ali Khan Castle. No information was obtained.

Little by little, despair overcame F... Al-Saltaneh. His knees weakened, he did not know which way to go, and to whom he turned. Most of the time, Mahin's father was angry, he was hesitant and could not make a decision, and he kept asking himself whether he should go to Kushk or return to Tehran and look for Mahin in that big city.

F... Al-Saltaneh was walking in front of the courier-house. It was midnight. The deputy had gone to his room and was resting. Suddenly someone put a hand on his shoulder and said in a very low voice:
"I know which way they went, those you are looking for, but I can not tell you anything here, because if the deputy understands, he will fall in with me and fire me."
F... Al-Saltaneh asked him happily:
"Who are you, who is your deputy, tell me soon which way they went?"
Anonymous replied:
"I am the coachman and I mean by the deputy, is the deputy of the courier-house that if he knew I told you this, will trouble me."
F... Al-Saltaneh took a gold lira from his pocket and put it in his hand.
"The people you are looking for came from Qom in a carriage last night. It was six hours into the night, and they moved to Tehran after a short stop."

F...Al-Saltaneh no longer doubted the truth of the anonymous statement, so he hurried inside the car and ordered to return to the city. Reza Qoli and the driver got on, but this time no matter how hard the driver tried to start the engine, it did not work. F... Al-Saltaneh, was in a hurry to return to Tehran, he became very angry and cursed the land and the time, cursed the Europeans and the Americans, and asked why they should make such an imperfect invention and why this car should be made. The driver, who was busy with the engine, consoled him with his broken Persian, saying that he was thankful that such a thing did not happen in the desert.

The car engine finally got fixed two hours after midnight. They left the castle of Mohammad Ali Khan and arrived in Hassanabad the next hour. The deputy who found out in F... Al-Saltaneh had learned about the incident and was also convinced that Farrokh and Mahin had gone too far and that they must have reached a safe place. He no longer insisted on hiding what he knew and pretended that they passed from there a few hours ago.
"Yes, yes, such a carriage passed through this morning."

There was no doubt left for F... Al-Saltaneh and he moved towards Hazrat Abdolazim and he stood in front of the gendarme post, but no one knew about the carriage and the passengers.
One of the gendarmes, who saw his distress, came forward and asked:
"Tell me what the young man look like."
F... Al-Saltaneh answered. The gendarme replied that he saw them going to Tehran, and confirmed a lady and a servant were accompanying him.
"Because it is not yet morning and I can not go to the gendarmerie office in the city, please give me two gendarmes if possible. Of course, I will pay whatever I have to." F... Al-Saltaneh said.

The head of the gendarmerie post, who had received a phone order from the general director that evening, agreed without hesitation. They all got into the car and moved quickly to the city.

It was dark, and a complete silence filled Tehran. Except for the roosters who started singing, no other sound could be heard. It was closed in the railway station and no one was walking in the street. Sixteen hours had passed since the arrival of Farrokh and Mahin in the city. Suddenly, F... Al-Saltaneh saw homeless man on the side of the street in front of the last station of the city wagon. He went to the poor man who had fallen into a deep sleep and shook his head hard. The poor man, lying on the dirty ground and having a good night's sleep, got up in a hurry and, to his surprise, saw a noble man in front of him who asked him:
"Uncle, are you always here?"
The poor man, who was so relieved by the gentle tone of F... Al-Saltaneh, wanted to say yes, I am always here when suddenly his eyes fell on the cars and the gendarmes, so he begged:
"Sir, what have I done? What do you want from me?"
F... Al-Saltaneh, who read the poor man's thoughts, looked at him with contempt, with a strange laugh that if they needed to arrest him, he would no longer have to act in person, and his lowest servant would be instructed to do so. He gently assured:
"Uncle, do not be afraid, we just want to know if you saw two young men and a woman who got out of a carriage and passed here yesterday morning, and can you tell which way they went?"
The poor man took a deep breath from this question and then said with a mysterious smile:
"Well, if I happened to see them and told you where they went, what would you give me?"
F... Al-Saltaneh reached into his pocket and took out a few five thousand silver and threw them into his lap. His poor eyes sparkled.
"Yes, I saw them. They were here yesterday around noon, and they got in

the carriage, and I especially heard the coachman saying they are going to Evin."

The car started moving again at full speed through Nezamieh, Shahabad, and Naderi, which were all quiete. After a few hours, the cars stopped. It was early morning now. The people of the village usually leave their houses one by one for going to their farms. A twelve-year-old child came out of a house.

"Did you see a young man and a woman from the city who came here yesterday afternoon?" F... Al-Saltaneh asked.

The child was very happy to see a car and was afraid of the gendarmes' answered without thinking:

"Yes sir, yesterday two men and a woman came from the city and went to Amoo Karim's house."

F... Al-Saltaneh asked him where Amoo Karim's house was and if he could show them.

"Of course, I know, let me take you." The boy replied. He went ahead and F... Al-Saltaneh and the gendarmes moved behind him and as soon as they reached Amoo Karim's house, he no longer needed the boy so he asked the boy to go back to the car. The boy ran away from them with the two Qiran coins in his palm.

Then F... Al-Saltaneh turned his face and ordered:

"We must do the work very quietly. Farrokh should not be harmed, but the other one who has dared to be his assistant and helper must be arrested and handed over to the authorities."

Immediately one of the gendarmes climbed the mud wall and looked inside the garden, then came down and informed them that since this garden is connected to the river house, one of them had to go there carefully so that they could not escape. F... Al-Saltanah liked this opinion, so one of the gendarmes was ordered to go down to the garden and block the way along the river, and the other stood by the garden wall in the alley and watched the door. Then F... Al-Saltaneh knocked on the door with all his might and a voice came at the very moment when Farrokh was telling Mahin that we would resist as much as we could.

Amoo Karim's wife, who was in the kitchen preparing fire for samovar, heard a noise and heard a gendarme standing by the river ordering Javad, who wanted to go to Farrokh, not to move.

Farrokh, who heard this threat, shouted:

"Do not move, they will kill you!"

Javad stood without moving, the door was pounded hard, but no one took the step to open it. Finally, the gendarme, who was by the river, slowly walked towards it and opened it.

F... Al-Saltanah hurried into the garden and went straight to the room, angry and frowning. Mahin realized her inner voice and was sure that she should expect her father's anger and wrath and she was afraid that she would not be able to see Farrokh.

Farrokh, who had lost the thought of quarreling, remained calm and firm steps toward F... Al-Saltaneh and said in a gentle tone:

"Sir, do not be heartless. Do not shout. Your daughter wants to come here willingly, because she and I love each other, and Mahin has preferred a humble life with me to a luxurious life with the princes you have chosen for her. I worship her and will take care of her."

"F... Al-Saltaneh was silent and did not answer Farrokh and looked at him with a fixed gaze with his eyes wide open. At this moment, a happy thought entered the young man's brain and Farrokh thought that his simple and pure expression had finally worked in the hard heart of Mahin's father and that hard-hearted person had regretted it. But his silence was only because he did not believe that Farrokh was so bold and after what he had done, he would stand in front of him again and talk to him. The fire of F... Al-Saltaneh's anger exploded and before Farrokh answered, he showed Javad to the guards and ordered them:

"Take that bastard first."

Then he turned to Farrokh and said bitterly:

"Get out of this place soon, I'm afraid I'm going to hurt you badly."

But could Farrokh have given up on Mahin and was he able to easily leave his beloved? Mahin looked at Farrokh as if she said, this is not the time to argue and stand up, that he should obey.

Farrokh walked towards the yard while looking at her with a heavy heart. He walked helplessly and felt that his soul was separated from his body. He was close to the door, turned back to take another look at Mahin's beautiful face, but at that moment his eyes fell on Javad and he saw that two gendarmes surrounded him and took his arms behind his back, and tied him with a rope. Farrokh was severely upset and, although he had no hope of success, he wanted to return and defend Javad, who himself had caused him trouble. But he could see that any action taken at that hour would have no effect other than drawing neighbors' attention to Mahin and his family. So think to yourself:

"What can they do with him who is not at fault and I will not let them harass him."

Farrokh left Amoo Karim's house, but could he go away?

Chapter Twenty Five
Stony-hearted

As soon as Farrokh left the garden, F... Al-Saltaneh said in a bitter tone:
"I do not know, after this, can I still call you my daughter?"
Mahin had kept her head down and did not answer his father... He continued his words:
"Did you ever think what harm you would do to your mother by doing this?"
Then he took his wife's telegraph out of his pocket and threw it at Mahin, adding:
"read and see how your mother is!"
Mahin leaned and picked up the paper that had fallen under her feet and read it, then said in a trembling voice:
"Father, I had predicted this and I knew that my mother would be hurt a lot by my absence, but it was not my fault, as I wrote to her, I know she is not guilty of this, she was not to blame, but only you are to blame for forcing me. These issues have caused me so much, if you had not insisted or wanted to force me to marry against my will, this will not happen. Farrokh is not to blame, I informed him of your proposal and we are both thinking about a way out."

F... Al-Saltaneh, who had listened to Mahin's words with a flushed face and an angry mood, and was constantly tapping his foot on the ground due to the intensity of his anger shouted:
"That was all you wanted to say at such a time. This is your apology. Now, after these ugly gestures, you have made it a point that you both blame me and insult your father. Just know that you and Farrokh's wedding, as I have said before, is one of the impossible things, and if you do not want me to disown you after this indecency and effrontery, you have no choice but to accept the prince's hand immediately and end this talk."
Mahin replied to her father in one sentence:
"It's impossible."

F... Al-Saltaneh became angrier because of her daughter's stubbornness and because she stood up for herself. He took a step toward Mahin, and it seemed that he wanted to hit her, but again at the last moment, he was calm. Then he remembers why he is doing this:
"Since when have you become a woman with intellectual abilities, found the

right to talk, and have an opinion. Who allowed you to say these things? It is not your fault. I sent you to those new schools. I made a big mistake by allowing you to go to school!"

F... Al-Saltanah expressed his true belief. He considered those schools harmful. Especially women should not have any legal rights. He thought the modern world inflicted severe blows based on false beliefs, opened people's eyes and ears, and introduced them to the mysteries of nature, which he considered a deadly poison. F... Al-Saltaneh, like his other selfish peers, uses the tactic of takfir to silence the voice of any literate man or woman. He considered a woman as a means of quenching the lust of a man, and for this reason, with his lustful heart, he wanted a frequent change of women, and he believed in sleeping with different women!

Mahin's father tired of the argument and decides to take her to her mother: "We are going."

Mahin said nothing more and went into the room, and while he looked at that humble village room, sighed, put her chador on, and after a few minutes, returned and got ready to go to the city.

Amoo Karim's wife, was standing in the middle of the yard and watching this in wonder, did not dare to make the slightest statement, then Mahin reminded her father before he left.

"Farrokh may not come to this house anymore!"

F... Al-Saltanah understood the purpose of the girl and took a three Tomans banknote from his bag and threw it at Amoo Karim's wife, then told the gendarmes who had treated poor Javad like a dangerous thief:

"Keep this bastard here so that I can go to the city and the car will come back and take you to the city." Then he gave a five Tomans banknote to them, and immediately took Mahin's hand, who was standing like a lifeless statue and in the possession of her father. They left the garden house.

Mahin looked around the alley so that he might see Farrokh again, but she did not see a trace of him, so she walked down in despair with her father, and they got in the car.

Mahin and his father arrived home, Mahin, no longer ready to continue talking to her father, went straight to her room. There was a lot of sadness all over her and every time she looked at the furniture and the bed, it seemed to her that she had been away from that room for many years. She thought about the happy promises that that letter gave to her. Then said Farrokh's name and asked herself: Where is he now? How will I see him again? and following these thoughts, she started crying and shed bloody tears.

But did these tears affect her father's heart, and could these supplications soften the hard heart of that man?

F... Al-Saltanah, who had gone to his office, took a pen and wrote the following telegram to his wife:

"I found Mahin in Evin with Farrokh after a long search. Your daughter is at home at this hour. She is alright. Do not worry, if the pilgrimage is over, return immediately."

The next hour, the car, which had gone to Evin for the second time, returned. Two armed men came to take Javad, and Mahin, who heard this news, despite her distress, hurried out of her room, went to her father, fell on his feet, and asked him with tears in her eyes. Do not put poor Javad in prison. Do not send this innocent person as a thief or criminal. His father, who at first thought that Mahin had come to apologize for her mistake, smiled, but as soon as he understood what Mahin meant, got up and went to the other side of the room, watching the garden through his window. Mahin begged and cried all the time. It was clear that he had directed the fire of anger and resentment that he had on Farrokh towards his helpless servant.

Eventually, Mahin was disappointed, and when she knew that this hard-hearted father was not the slightest hope, she returned to her room. This defeat had added to her distress, the girl's knees were shaking and she was about to fall in the corridor, reached her bed with great difficulty, and immediately lost consciousness.

The two agents treated Javad like a prisoner. They were walking to Nazmieh, they had crossed several streets, and threatened him that he would be shot if he thought of fleeing, and especially They pointed out that in the event of such an event, they would not be held liable under the law!

The young man, who lowered his head and was thinking about his strange destiny, was moved to hear the word law, he started laughing bitterly and thought to himself:

'Law! Which law! What abuses have not been beautified with this word. Is it the law that a person should be treated in this way because a leech rich said so?'

When they arrived, the agents reported the matter to the duty officer. After passing through several courtyards, hand Javad over to the prison guards. They threw the poor young man into a dark, damp dungeon.

***

We left Malek Taj when she was crying and saying repeatedly:
"They kidnapped my daughter, see how miserable she will be!"

And as much as Firoozeh comforted her or tried to give her hope, but did not satisfy the poor mother's heart. Inevitably, Firoozeh got up and went to the gendarmerie, which was next to the city and far from the village.

The head of the gendarmerie, who did not like unpaid requests and did not know F... Al-Saltanah and was unaware of the extent of his influence and the degree of his relations, warmly promised that immediate action would be taken. But his promises, like the majority of the ministers' statements, were nothing more than words because after Firoozeh left, he did not do anything about this missing report.

That evening, Malak Taj, was not feeling well but there wasn't any educated doctor in the small town of Qom, and the gendarmerie's doctor had left at that hour. Firoozeh inevitably sent Hasan Qoli after one of those authorized doctors. He came to the patient's bedside but he did not know about the disappearance of Malek Taj's daughter. He prescribed some medicine and food.

Firoozeh, who did not understand the doctor's medicine and was very worried, thought of sending a telegram to Tehran, to let F... Al-Saltanah knows about the situation. She put on a chador and went to the telegraph office and asked the telegraph operator to send a telegram to Tehran as soon as possible. The wire was not busy, so it was transmitted to Tehran immediately.

When Firoozeh returned home, Malek Taj's condition had improved a little and she was resting in bed, but whenever she mentioned Mahin's name, tears welled up in her eyes again. About three o'clock in the morning, someone knocked on the door. She felt that he should have news of Mahin, so she put it in her heart and then tried to find a literate person to read it.
Hasan Qoli went to the landlord and brought his son with him. And once Malek Taj heard that her daughter was with Farrokh and the coachman had not abducted her, she calmed down a bit and then shook her head and said:
"I knew this crazy girl would finally disgrace me. Now that it is too late, we must inform her father early in the morning. They can not escape from us. We will find them anyway."
Then she thought about it and kept asking herself:
"How did Farrokh find out about our trip? We did not mention it to our relatives."
Eventually, she realized that Mahin had informed her cousin, and in confirmation of her opinion, she said:
"Now I understand why Mahin was finishing her argument with me on the way and why she insisted on knowing my final decision, it was clear that she wanted to remove the blame from her neck."

The next morning, with the help of the landlord's son, Malek Taj prepared another telegram for her husband and gave it to Hassan Gholli to send it. Then she went to the shrine with Firoozeh to pray so that God would protect Mahin wherever she is and remove these evil fantasies from her head and guide the girl to the right path.

When they returned home around noon after a full pilgrimage, the telegraph house delivered a message and they were once again in need of the landlord's son's help.

Malek Taj was extremely happy with the good news about finding Mahin, and this time tears of joy flowed from her eyes. She gave the boy a golden five thousand money as gratuity. She immediately sent Hassan Qoli to arrange their return for the next day.

The poor mother spent the whole night imagining her beloved daughter. She wanted nothing but the girl's happiness. She knew Mahin's happiness was in marrying the prince. She saw it as the right path, and she believed that Mahin's brain had been damaged by reading errant books, and she repeatedly expressed this theory:

'The girl is young, my daughter is ignorant, she does not know the value of money and wealth, she will surely realize her mistake soon.'

Early in the morning, they went to the courier house and rode to Tehran in a carriage. They did not delay any more. Twenty-four hours later, they arrived in front of their house in Tehran.

F... Al-Saltanah was waiting to meet her. They kissed and immediately Malek Taj asked about Mahin.

"Nothing is wrong, she is a little unwell"

And because his wife was concerned more and wanted to be informed more about her daughter's illness, her husband explained:

"Mahin has been ill since yesterday and she is constantly delusional."

The poor mother, no longer recognizable, rushed to her daughter's room and saw Mahin wearing a white dress, lying in bed with a bag of ice on her head. As soon as Mahin saw his mother, she said in a mocking tone:

"You come soon, surely you drown his head."

And she laughed out loud after that.

Malak Taj was stunned. Poor Mahin became crazy!

Chapter Twenty-Six
Another Sick Place

There is an alley between Grand Bazaar and Shoemakers Bazaar, both of which are important markets in Tehran. At both ends of this long alley, there are several shops, including a grocery store, a small coffee house, and a small barber shop.

This alley is not straight and in the middle of it, in addition to one or two small turns, there is a large curvature. And within this curvature, there is an alley with a short entrance, that is, because the surface of the alley has risen over time due to the accumulation of mud and soil, and the lower part of the frame has gone under the ground.

Once you are in, there is a courtyard and an old building can be seen on the north side of the courtyard. This building consists of a large room in the middle and two small rooms on its sides, and its large room is in the form of an old hall, which is called a sash.

The sash differs from ordinary halls in that on its sides there are small rooms, plus in the middle of that part, which is called Alcove, and it faces to the courtyard or garden through a large door, which should be considered a tall and wide window. Because it is not used for entry and exit of people. Above the main frame of this large window, there is a semicircle, and at the bottom, there is a thick railing about a quarter of the height of the floor.

This large window is often divided into two sections by each of the three wooden beams. The piece goes up and down between the narrow railings and the upper diagonal part between the narrow walls of the frames. The entire surface of these three components, as well as the surface of the semicircle above the frame, is beautifully divided by narrow sticks according to the design, and between these divisions, small pieces of different colored glass are placed when one or all three parts which are rising to the sun. They are held in place by special fasteners that are next to the frames.

In front of each of the two small rooms on either side of the hall is a porch that leads to the courtyard with two or three steps, and each of these rooms does not have more than one porch.

It was early autumn, and it was cold and windy. Each time the wind intensified, it ended the shaky life of the leaves of a single tree in the middle of the yard.

At about four o'clock in the afternoon, a handsome young man stealthily entered the alley, his face was yellow, with black circles around his eyes, wearing a clean black Sardari waistcoat. It had some various stains on it, but it was obvious from the edge of the sleeve of his white silk shirt, which had a very tight wrist, and also from the cufflinks, which are made of two pieces of gold and occasionally come out of his sleeve was one of the "fashionable" youth of Tehran.

As soon as he reached the curve of the alley, he slowed down and looked around for a moment to avoid passersby and use the opportunity to enter the house without being seen.

Why was this person so scared and why did he try so hard to hide from others?

Human beings have restrictions, some of which are global, and some of which are specific to a nation or ethnicity, and sometimes the restrictions of one nation are the exact opposite of the restrictions of another nation. For Orientals, it is considered disrespectful to take off a hat, however, in Europe, it is rude to wear a hat in front of an important person.

The restrictions are common in the world and some nations are hard to adhere to, but the strange thing is that if someone has the necessary courage, and would turn their back on these restrictions and act against the will and habits of that nation. And if that person stands tall, there are always some followers out there. And as soon as people see that by ignoring the restrictions, and acting against them, the course of the world and things did not change and the so-called heaven did not come to earth, their sense of imitation is stimulated. After they follow that innovator, its disgustingness disappears and its ugliness is forgotten.

Entering those sorts of houses in those days was embarrassing. It was bad, because it was an opium den, and at that time going to such a place to smoke opium was unacceptable because it was such a place that a group of Iranians wasted their zeal and effort. But as governments later popularized poppy cultivation to fill their coffers with illicit proceeds, regardless of the serious harm, they made the dangerous opium available to the public on the street and in the market. They were forcing the Opium Restriction Office to collect more revenue for the government in any way they could, but the implementation of this order involved consuming more opium and increasing the number of opium dens.

The young man had recently suffered from this pain of addiction and had to go to such a place to take the deadly poison because it was not easy for him to prepare it at home, and because he knew the ugliness of his action, he tried not to make others aware of his arrival.

Fortunately for him and unfortunately for the health of the Iranian race, the alley was deserted for a moment, so he entered.

In one corner of the room was a platform with a large brass samovar and a blue teapot that had been broken and tied in several places, as well as a small brass sugar-cube bowl. People were lying on the floor around that large room, using opium. The newcomer told the coffee-house keeper who was standing by the platform,

" I do not want anyone to see me here, if you have a secluded room, show me."

the coffee-house keeper who was the manager of the Opium den, takes off his felt hat and scratches the middle of his shaved head, and replied:

"Of course, sir, it is not the first time one of you came here." Then he went ahead and walked the young man through the yard and then to the east porch, which was on the other side of the hall.

This room was similar to the other one, and on its walls, there were still blue pieces of plaster, and it was a sign that this house once had glory and elegance. There were niches around the room. The smell and smoke would bother the nose of any newcomer and would make non-addicts very dizzy.

There was a small lantern on one of the windowsills. As soon as the unidentified man entered the room, and sat on a rug, he ordered the coffee-house keeper to bring him two half-mithqal balls of opium as soon as possible and provide him with the tools.

The coffee-house keeper left the room, and the young man, who was constantly shaking. He really needed to smoke since It had been long overdue from the last time, and was talking to himself"

'How did the bad guys make me miserable, even though it was my own fault, if I had not gone so far in opium, I would not have had to deal with this one.'

A few minutes later, suddenly someone opened the door who was not the coffee-house keeper. He also wore a Sardari waistcoat with a Namadi felt hat. He wanted to tell the newcomer that it was his room and that no one else had the right to enter it, but that person did not give him a chance and said:

"Excuse me, Mr. Ali Ashraf Khan, I have important things to say and I did not know a more suitable place than this place for our conversation."

Ali Ashraf Khan, who had tried so hard that no one would recognize was shocked that the young man came with that courage and without permission and called his name, and he was about to vent his anger but remember where he was and said softly:

"Sir, you see me now and you know why I came here and I do not have the mind or patience to talk at the moment, please leave me alone, especially since I have not seen you before and I do not know what you are talking

about. You want to mess up with my head," but the newcomer ignored what
he said:

"Indeed, you have never seen me, but I know you, I just said your name and
if you allow me to share other information I have about you, you are the
former head of ... Isfahan and have been in Tehran for almost two months,
Well, you used to be the head of the Ministry of Accounts, I even know how
in a short time you became the head of the department...!"

Ali Ashraf Khan was astonished as he listened, his eyes bulged out, and
looked at the newcomer impatiently, wanting to know his ultimate purpose.
But the young man did not wait long and said:

"Of course, you would like to know who I am and where I got this information and how I found the details of your life. My name is Farrokh, although
this name does not tell you anything, you should know that I met a woman
with whom you make your ladder of progress, and her presence added to
your status and glory."
Then Farrokh took a restricted tone and said with all his might:
"Surely now you know who I'm talking about!"

Effat's husband's face which was already yellow, looked paler when he
heard Farrokh's words. A tremor shook his body. At that time, he did not see
the ability to argue but come to terms with Farrokh, so he said in a muffled
voice:
"Sir, I did not understand what you meant after all this talk, now you know
me, only opium cures my pain, please go and come again, we will talk about
this together.
But Farrokh, who was looking at him with disdain, did not give up:
"No, sir, you should spend some time listening to my words!"

***

The day that this conversation between Farrokh and Ali Ashraf Khan
took place in the corner of Chaharsoo alley, nearly ten months had passed
after the day that Ali Ashraf Khan abused Effat, and he reached the point
of his cruelty and unconscionability. And he had left his poor wife in the
house of an old woman in Isfahan.

Ali Ashraf Khan was one of those kitty and promiscuous young men
who preferred celibacy and complete freedom to live with a certain woman
over family life, and although Effat did not prevent his ugly deeds. She had
become illegitimate now that he had used her to get what he wants, he still
felt a kind of unhappiness because of Effat, and he was constantly thinking

about his premarital periods, and every hour he wished to meet again with a group of friends of the same class, so every night they could go to the garden and drink a bottles of Arak. Therefore, as soon as he sent Effat to Shahbaji's house, he immediately gathered with friends he had found in Isfahan for entertainment. They suggested that they finally go for a walk around the gardens outside the city, and then a servant was assigned to find some expert beautiful female companion.

That night passed happily and was repeated once or twice a week and every time Ali Ashraf Khan and his comrades drank various drinks and partied, they looked tired with yellow colors and felt reluctant to work in the morning.

For those who are prone to alcohol, opium is not a long way off. The comrades suggested opium to relieve the hangover and pain, and mentioned the intense and concentrated parts that would make his boredom go away, in the meantime, he explained the miracles of opium, and with full conviction explained how someone with a disease had died because of opium.

Ali Ashraf Khan, who was weak-limed and weak-minded when it comes to using opium, was upset with the itching for the first few days, but because his toothache subsided and he went to another world, he did not forget the effect of the bag, and the next day repeated his desire. He did it and increased the dose every day until he finally realized after a few months that the weight of that dangerous poison would not break his hangover.

Ali Ashraf Khan did not let go of opium easily. His face was getting yellower every day and he was getting thinner every hour, but because he was the head of the office in Isfahan ... and his subordinates knew very well that he had strong supporters in Tehran and the so-called back of the ace. Which showed that the work of his office was not coordinated. Coincidentally, one day Ali Ashraf Khan did not act as he should have acted on an issue in which a group of influential people and democrat clerics had an interest and opinion.

In the evening of the same day, a group of thugs from Isfahan attacked the office...

"Ah, this Tehran! See how we, the miserable people of the provinces, are tormented, and how, every day, an atheist rules over us, leaving all our honor and existence in the hands of those in their element."

People who did not dare to ask what happened and who's religion and honor were threatened and how, and out of fear, they blindly gathered around Mr. Sheikh and the number of rebellious people increased every moment. As soon as a large number of people approached the office, the said cleric went to the platform of the houses and first invited the people to remain silent and then ordered them:

'If any agent or gendarme wants to disperse you and prevent you from spreading your right words to the government officials, it is permissible to kill them and it is their fault that they have fallen in love with the true Muslims and have insulted our religion and Islam. Every Muslim must shed disbeliever blood."

Ignorant people who did not know the inside of the matter and did not know what vile motives and evil opinions were behind these words, assuming that they were insulted and that Islam, which if its orders are obeyed, would provide a very sweet and proud life for its followers, has been disrespected. And the principles of this great religion, which cares more than anything else about the equal rights of individuals, have been violated, without understanding and thinking that religion should not be a playground for traitors and thousands of catastrophes should not be committed in the name of it.

When the news reached the gendarmerie and they were informed of this outburst without any reason, they immediately sent some cavalry and infantry there to solve the problem. The gendarmes at first tried to disperse the crowd gently, but their efforts were unsuccessful, because the ignorant disciples of the ignorant clergy believed in the words of their leader and considered it so obligatory and obligatory to follow his orders that in no way they would refuse to give up their intention and insisted on the path that the mullahs had instilled in them, and they wanted the administration ... which they called the administration of the infidels, and which the government had established only to promote the principles of atheism.

The sheik was still standing on the platform, and while a group of Isfahan thugs, surrounded him with their machetes like a special guard, he repeatedly encouraged and incited the people to destroy the office... and what they should burn and not be afraid to kill the gendarmes and anyone who resists. Knuckleheads people also became more courageous every minute and tried to get closer to the office every moment.

The gendarmes, who were instructed not to use weapons when needed, and their chief ordered not to harm unfortunate people who had been manipulated. They draw a chain line in front of the office and repel the attackers, but because the sheik did not stop talking. The pressure on the people was increasing every moment, and finally, to threaten them, he removed the guns from his shoulders and held the pipes towards the insurgents. Suddenly one of the revelers attacked the gendarmes, and before the gendarmes could move and defend, he had taken the gun from him, then deftly grabbed the shawl from his waist and put it around the gendarme's neck, and then with the help of another group. The ignorant people, who had jumped up and down behind him, threw the gendarme to the ground and then dragged the unfortunate man, who was suffocating, into the crowd. The people, who saw the representative of the government as a gendarme, lamented over him, and each of them somehow got their heart out of the government.

Other gendarmes fired indiscriminately and fired into the air. Five minutes later, one of the ignorant people could not be seen around, except for a handful of white turbans, sugar milk, and the shoes and torn body of the unfortunate gendarme, who had been strangled.

Who are the real culprits of this event and these barbaric movements? The answer is very simple and easy:

Those who want ignorance, and ignorance for the nation and consider the promotion and dissemination of knowledge to be against their interests and prevent the ignorance of the people and the opening of their eyes and ears in the name of preserving the rituals of religion.

The tragedy did not end again. The Sheikh ran to Agha's house, and they were disappointed about not being successful enough to raid the office. The ignorant fans have been announced to gather to support the cause and some others went to the telegraph office and demand the immediate dismissal of Ali Ashraf Khan from the central government.

The central government, which had shown its weakness and incompetence in many cases, this time decided to summon Ali Ashraf Khan to solve the problem without any investigation, and was sent by the Ministry of Telegraphs under the name of Ashraf Khan:

Mr. Ali Ashraf Khan, head of the department...

For the sake of some clarification, your presence is needed in Tehran. It is necessary to hand over the office and leave as soon as possible.

Ali Ashraf Khan hastened his journey and left Isfahan the next evening, and of course, as a result of the news of his summoning, it was proved once again that he is his incompetent.

Three days later, Ali Ashraf Khan, who had not stopped anywhere, arrived in Tehran and went to see the minister. It seemed there was nothing important to say, and he was summoned just to calm the insurgents.
"Why should an experienced person like you not consider some points and not consider some people!"

In the end, he was promised that his efforts would not go unnoticed by the ministry and that he would be assigned a suitable job shortly.
But even though a month had passed since his arrival, he was still unem-

ployed, and not the slightest trace of all the minister's promises had appeared. Unfortunately for him, the former ministers, and his supporters, could not do anything, because one of them was in Europe and the other was unemployed, and no one would pay attention to his advice. The current minister was also famous for his theology and prayer. Therefore, the former did not work for him. In addition, Ali Ashraf Khan no longer had a wife, and it was not easy to obtain a woman like Effat who was both virtuous and obedient.

This incident naturally increased his interest in opium and reciprocated his nostalgia with the deadly poison. He would wear some old clothes every day and go to one of the opium dens.

Chapter Twenty Seven
Disturbed Psyche

Now, let's see how Farrokh came to this dirty place and for what purpose?
As we saw Farrokh that morning, he was completely reluctant and only to obey his beloved,
especially since he did not want to make a fuss due to an argument with F... Al-Saltnaneh,
and to create notoriety and disgrace, he had left Amoo Karim's house, but as said, he did
not move away from it. How could he go away from there, and how could he leave the
sweet memory of his lover in that humble rural home? Farrokh had left his soul in that
house.

The young man walked slowly a few steps north, but within a hundred paces he could no longer walk, so he climbed a short hill by a narrow road and sat down on a small boulder under a large mulberry tree. From there, the building of Amoo Karim's house could be seen, and Farrokh could see the father and daughter in the garden from afar, and he could understand their movements and conversations, and from there he was saddened to see that Mahin left the house. Farrokh realized that the gendarmes and Javad had stayed there. At first, he thought of going to Amoo Karim's house and, if necessary, he would fight with the gendarmes and free Javad from them, but could he hope for success? And could he, who did not have the slightest weapon, defeat the two armed gendarmes?

Farrokh never believed what he read in the books of Iskandarnameh and Hussein Kurd and which seems similar to the novels of some European writers. He knew very well that it was difficult for him to fight two armed men alone, and at the same time, he wondered if this was the case. Action on his part is necessary and was there any danger for Javad, who was not guilty, so he promised himself with complete simplicity:
'Certainly, he will be released soon. If they try to harass him, I will prevent it by all means.'

An hour after Mahin and his father left, the gendarmes took Javad away. Farrokh, who was still sitting on a rock, was thinking about his fate. Deeper in his thoughts was feeling that being away from his beloved was unbearable and that he was extremely sad that it did not take him more than a few hours to enjoy the pleasure of being with Mahin.

Farrokh got up and walked slowly towards Amoo Karim's house. His wife, who was standing near the door and realizing that Farrokh was saddened by his great sorrow, invited the young man in and showed empathy.

Farrokh went to the same room and for a while, he looked carefully at the corner of the nest of love as if he was looking for a memory of Mahin in every part of it. Screamed as he kicked the earth with his foot:
'Why has life been so unfavorable to him and why has it so easily taken away his beloved?'
Then, he squeezed his head hard between his hands as if he wanted to get the reason for this inconsistency of the time and this bitter event out of his brain.
'What do they want to do with her?'

Farrokh spent the whole day struggling with these thoughts and finally decided to go to the city, and by whatever means to find out all about Javad and how he was treated. At noon, Amoo Karim's wife brought him lunch, but Farrokh did not want to eat. He went to the river, next to the same stone they say the day before.
'What vile people and what ruthless creatures, why should they separate the soul from the body?'

He was lost in the world of imagination and thoughts, he saw Mahin sitting on the rock in front of him like the day before, he was replaying all the seconds in his head, and then came to his senses and remained disappointed. 'Where was Mahin at that time? What was Mahin doing at that time?'

Farrokh did not want to leave that place and that stone. He had not eaten for fifteen hours, he did not feel hungry, and his mental fatigue had weakened his body. The river water hitting the rocks repeatedly made a huge sound. Farrokh cursed the universe for giving power to people like F... Al-Saltanaeh, for giving them privileges such as money, jewelry, and properties. He was so outraged by the injustices committed by some human beings towards others that if he had the choice at that time, he would burn the whole world like a cotton ball and burn the wet and the dry together.

Finally, around midnight, Amoo Karim, came and convinced him to go inside, and went to bed without eating, but could he fall asleep?

He got up early in the morning and thought being there is useless and was worried about Javad's fate. He ate a little breakfast, then thanked Amoo Karim and his wife a lot and put a five Toman banknote in their hand and looked at that garden, and the room. He hurried out the door. Since the chariot could not be found in that village, he had to rent one of the village donkeys and after an hour he reached Tajrish and from there he went to the city in the carriage and came home and as soon as he arrived he went to his father and asked how he was doing. When he saw that the boy was stuck, he started crying and asked him insistently, where was he and how did he spend the night before?'

Farrokh, did not know that his father had seen him in a dream, in the middle of a big fire, and assured his father that he had spent the previous night with a close friend in Shemiran. He did not want to narrate the events, His father did not ask him any more questions. Farrokh went to his room. Suddenly, he remembered that he promised Effat and his father to visit them as soon as he returned from the trip. He immediately got dressed, got in a carriage, and gave the address of R... Al-Dawlah's house.

As soon as he got there, the servant who knew him bowed and invited him into the house without hesitation. Farrokh climbed the stairs of the mansion behind him and entered the same room where he had seen Effat's father for the first time a few days ago and sat on a chair. A few minutes later, Effat entered, she was wearing a blue silk dress, and silky socks, and shiny. The yellow color of her face had subsided in a few days and was replaced by a pleasant redness, and the traces of her beautiful and calm face had appeared.

"Sir, you forgot about us. You do not have a phone, so we sent people to your house more than three times, but no one knew where you went."

"As I said, I had a short trip ahead of me," Farrokh said.

Then, to change the subject, he asked modesty:

"Where are your parents, God willing, how are they?"

Effat felt Farrokh's sadness, and she felt that there was no simple and unintentional journey and realized that Farrokh had changed the subject so that he did not say anything personal, but was unaware that it's not that easy to get rid of women's curiosity.

"My father is in charge of real estate calculations, and my mother also had some work to do, so, they sent me to come on their behalf to give you company until they arrive."

Then he changed her tone and asked him like a close friend:

"Sir, do not hide anything from me, I understand from your face that great events have happened to you these days, don't you want me to know."

The warm and kind voice of Effat had a strange effect on Farrokh. He felt who better than Effat, she was a sister to him, and who could he find more prepared to hear the pain of a brother than a sister. So he recklessly expressed his love for his aunt's daughter and how much he is fascinated by her, how his parents withheld Mahin from her and want to forcefully give their daughter away, how they thought of running away, and finally, how their plans and their love nest was soon destroyed.

Effat listened carefully to Farrokh's story, and gradually, as she got to know his feeling, she look pale and was deep in thought.

What was going on in the heart of Effat? Of course, it can be easily guessed that the poor woman, who had faced Farrokh amid all the suffering and misery had gotten rid of that disgraceful life with his help, so had a special feeling for the young man. She had nurtured hopes, and now she once saw that everything she had imagined was in vain and that the so-called she had built a palace in Spain. Farrokh was in love with someone else, and she only was a sister to him.

The power of her intellect prevailed and she realized his situation. She blamed herself for why she should have thought like that. Because her life is over and after what had happened to her, happiness and dignified hope were a vain fantasy for her. She thought, 'He saved me from that disgraceful place, I must try to bring him to his beloved.'

She said in a soft and sad tone that made a great impression:

"It turns out that we are both miserable, but we should not be disappointed and the world will certainly not remain like this."

Farrokh thanked Effat, and added:

"First of all, I need to know what Mahin's father did to Javad and where that poor man is now, and after I need to know how Mahin is, unfortunately in the current situation, I can not go there myself and I can not send anyone."

"Ii is very easy to find out about Mahin, I will get the news, and I will inform you," Effat said.

Farrokh told her about asking around about Ali Ashraf Khan.

"I have sent a telegram to a friend in Isfahan and asked him to inform me about him."

Effat's face turned red, and was overwhelmed with grief and sorrow that he had remembered her history at that moment,

"It is better if you take care of Javad sooner!"

Farrokh, who did not realize the mental state of Effat, that she did not want to hear the name of the vile man or remember that wicked person. She did not want to hear his name from Farrokh's mouth. But he continued reassuring Effat,

"Taking care of Javad's situation does not prevent the other. We start both together."

Effat did not say anything and a moment of silence passed between them. It was near noon, and there was no news of the arrival of Effat's parents. Farrokh got up to go.

"Where are you going so soon? my parents have not come yet and have not seen you."

Farrokh sat down again. A few minutes later, R... Al-Dawlah entered with the help of a servant who was holding him in his arms, and immediately Effat's mother, who was wearing a white mottled prayer chador, came. Both of them were very happy to see Farrokh, and they talked for a while, and when Farrokh got up to say goodbye so that he could go, they all insisted so much on staying for lunch that he finally surrendered.

"If you think we are old and do not believe in the modern world, you are wrong. Here, you can have your lunch at a table and use cutlery, and talk between meals!" R... Al-Dawlah said with a smile.

Half an hour later, they went to the dining room, and after lunch, Farrokh said goodbye.

"I will be very grateful if that action is taken sooner," Farrokh said to Effat. Effat reassured him slowly: "You will be informed about Mahin's condition by tomorrow morning."

Farrokh wanted to visit Ahmad Ali Khan, he walked down Abbasi Street. After a quarter of an hour, he reached Borj Noosh Street and entered the courier house. He expressed his gratitude to his dear friend, and his valuable devotion, and narrated the events to Ahmad Ali Khan, how F... Al-Saltaneh found them in Evin and how he took Mahin from him, and finally, how poor Javad was brought to the city with his hands tied, then he added:

"Of course, I am deeply saddened that Mahin, whom I had had in my arm, was abducted, but since the unfortunate servant is also caught, I am more affected and I can not let this poor man suffer because of me."

Ahmad Ali Khan thought and said:

"F... Al-Saltaneh will not treat Javad except in two ways, either by keeping him at home, which does not seem practical, or by handing him over to Nazmieh Prison."

Hearing the word prison, Farrokh trembled on his fallen body and said slowly: "Poor Javad himself had guessed before!"

Then Ahmad Ali Khan followed his ideas:

"In any case, if he is taken to Nazmieh, we may investigate immediately."

He immediately called Nazmieh, and asked the head of the police officer, who asked his friends to investigate to see if a person named Javad had entered the prison office yesterday. Then he put the phone in its place and said to Farrokh: "If he is in there, we will be known right now."

A few minutes later, the phone rang, Ahmad Ali Khan picked up the phone and then after a short silence, said thank you, he put the phone in its place. "Well, I guessed correctly, Javad has been imprisoned and is currently in the number one cell in Nazmieh prison, but they have not interrogated him yet."

The word "imprisonment" and number one, made a strange sound in Farrokh's ear and he jumped up and shouted several times:

'Imprisonment number one, what has he done, what crime has this poor man committed, and who has he deprived of life?'

Then he thought to himself:
'In a country, where libertarians are imprisoned and subjected to thousands of tortures and hardships, the imprisonment of an impoverished person like Javad should no longer seem strange!'
Farrokh no longer wasted time and said goodbye to his friend. He immediately went home, and to find a way to save Javad.

Chapter Twenty Eight
Existence Of Evil

Farrokh could not find a way to save Javad. He was still thinking about finding a way to help Javad escape, when someone knocked on the door, followed by a woman in a black chador entering the yard. The elderly servant showed her in. She greeted Farrokh and said:

"Lady sent me to tell you that they have investigated that person, she is in their own house, but very sick."

Hearing the news of Mahin's illness, made him extremely worried, and Javad was also deprived, he was constantly blaming himself:

"Why should I take these two responsibilities and why should I create these problems for them and myself.'

He sent his greetings and thanks to Effat, and since he could no longer bear to stay at home, he left the house in a state of anxiety and spontaneously went to Nazmieh.

Tehran Nazmieh, which is supposed to be law enforcement, instead is one of the centers of disasters and what is not observed there is the law. It is located in the center of Tehran, on the western side of Toopkhaneh Square.

Farrokh, crossing the streets of Kent and Lalehzar, thinking that he would not be easily allowed to enter the prison yard. In front of Nazmieh, he accidentally caught sight of an agent, who was coming from the end of the corridor and had a prisoner in front of him. At first, he thought that the troubled young was going to be released and enjoy the freedom, but he soon realized his mistake. They surrounded the poor prisoner with guns and were taking him to the interrogation room. He saw closely and could not believe his eyes that the poor prisoner was Javad, and that unfortunate servant was taken to the interrogator of the judiciary for the first time that day by the agents. Farrokh, who saw his pursuit as fruitless, remained in his place for a while and was stunned; he returned home with regret, hoping to find a way to free him.

Several days later, most of these days, Javad was taken to the judiciary for questioning. Farrokh, who consulted Ahmad Ali Khan regularly, wondered who his interrogator was and what the accusations were against Javad so that he might secretly clarify the truth to the interrogator if he was a conscientious person. While he was investigating, he found out that Javad's case was to an interrogator of that branch called Alireza Khan who is the brother of Ali Ashraf Khan, and Javad may be sentenced to six months in prison and one hundred lashes for abducting a girl.

The idea of imprisoning and flogging Javad was unjust in Farrokh's eyes. He would try his best to establish its baselessness, and poor Javad will be released from this predicament. In the meantime, he received a detailed letter from his friend in Isfahan. His friend stated that Ali Ashraf Khan's excessive use of alcohol and opium, and also the recent events and losing his position.

Farrokh told all of these to Effat and asked her if he could go and see her ex-husband. If Ali Ashraf Khan was willing to force his brother to drop this baseless accusation. Effat, who wanted nothing more than Farrokh's happiness, willingly agreed. Farrokh kissed Effat's hand and was happy to carry out his plan. He went to Ali Ashraf Khan's house which was in Jalilabad Street, and when Effat's ex-husband finally left the house, Farrokh followed him until he entered the opium den.

Farrokh had thought that if he met Ali Ashraf Khan in such a place, he might reach his goal sooner, and out of fear of spreading the news of his addiction, he would inevitably accept his offer.
When the coffee-house keeper left the room, Farrokh reached out to him and handed him five white Qirans and said:
"I am familiar with this gentleman and I have an important conversation with him that will last a few minutes. Please do not come back in before I tell you."

And as we know, he entered that dirty room and started a conversation with the former head of the Isfahan office and made it clear that he had to listen to what Farrokh needed to say.

Then Farrokh, who had been standing until then, was sitting on the torn carpet with four knees and said:
"Mr. Ali Ashraf Khan, I know what you did to that poor woman, whose only flaw was ignorance and blind obedience to your will, and I am aware that by using her innocence, you reached a position in this country, the position that the young educated people can not even dream it, because of the people like you.

Fortunately, God did not want the miserable situation you had provided for her to continue, and now she is back in her parents' arms.
Ali Ashraf Khan laughed loudly when he heard the last sentence and said sarcastically:
"Sir, it turns out that you have forgotten where you live, but in this environ-

ment, these things are not new that you are threatening me with. If I have done something, I have followed the example of others and acted following this system, and in addition, what document do you have to prove your claim and slander?

Farrokh, in turn, answered him with a loud laugh:

"Of course, you have to be right to some extent, because in an environment where grace and merit have no value and ignorance, misunderstanding, ridicule, inaccuracy, inhumanity, and finally and most importantly illegitimate influences, resorting to illegitimate and disgusting means can not be criticized much and only the hand of nature should take revenge on those who like and encourage such traits and have such demands from subordinates, but you are very wrong to think that there is no document of your ugly and shameful deeds, because one of them is a letter that you sent to Effat through an old woman called Shahbaji in Isfahan, and I still have it."

Ali Ashraf Khan shook his head when he heard the word letter but he overcame it, so he said calmly:

"I advise you to look around, as if you have forgotten where you are and under what sky you live, sir, here is not Europe and America, do you think that with such a paper you can condemn me or hurt me! For your sake, I say not only this paper but thousands of more important documents in this work environment can not be against people like me!"

Although Farrokh knew inwardly that he was telling the truth, he did not change his appearance and said with intensity:

"No matter how ruined and chaotic the country is, it is not right you use a woman's ignorance to reach high positions, and then drive her out of your house with that shamelessness and cruelty, your wife had no relatives in that city. But you are well aware of who her parents are and what their status is in this city, and the degree of their relationship with the authorities."

Ali Ashraf Khan, who just wanted the door open and the coffee-house keepers to enter, asked tiredly and helplessly:

"Very well, after all this talk, what do you mean and what do you want from me right now?"

Farrokh pondered for a moment and then calmly replied:

"I have come to tell you that despite all the crimes and atrocities committed against the poor woman, her parents will not pursue you if you help one of my acquaintances."

Ali Ashraf Khan was interested in Farrokh's words, he was listening attentively, "Well, let me see what help you want from me?"

Farrokh replied:

"Of course, you did not think that my request was the same kind of work that you are used to. No, no. Rest assured, I do not have any illegitimate request, my only request is because one of my acquaintances has been arrested as a result of an unfounded complaint by an influential person and is currently being interrogated in detention...

Then Farrokh paused and asked the question:

"Surely now you guessed what I want from you?"

Ali Ashraf Khan thoughtfully replied:

"If you mean to ask my brother to drop all the charges, you are mistaken because he does not take my word for it and in addition, I am sure he did not do it without purpose!"

"I know these well and I know how your brother greets F... Al-Saltaneh and the orders he has received and the promises he has made that he is going to issue an innocent sentence, that is why I want you to talk to him. Talk and prevent the issuance of this agreement. Instead, I promise you that I will talk to Effat to forgive your sins."

Ali Ashraf Khan thought again for a moment, then raised his head and looked at Farrokh and asked:

"You did not say anything about yourself, what are you going to do, and in return for doing this, what else are you willing to commit to?"

Farrokh, who did not understand what he meant at first, answered simply:

"I don't have any position in government circles."

Ali Ashraf Khan also laughed out loud and said coldly in a bitter tone:

"In this case, do not hope for anything from me."

This time Farrokh read his evil thoughts and realized the extent of his ugliness, low nature, and bad humor. If there was money or a position to offer, he would talk to his brother and take a step to free Javad. Farrokh saw that talking to him was pointless. So he clenched his fist with a hard and evil look at Ali Ashraf Khan, and he growled in a threatening tone:

"Today, which is your era, you and people like you are in power, and our turn comes, you will see!" Farrokh left the room.

The coffee-house keeper who was waiting behind the door came, and brought a lamp, pillow as well as opium and put it in front of Ali Ashraf Khan. He lay down immediately and took several puffs from the opium pipe. Ali Ashraf Khan got high and felt relaxed, and laughed loudly,

"What stupid ideas does the stupid boy have and what nonsense does he say, he thinks empty hands and without a supporter can act and succeed in this country against the will of the wealthy!"

Farrokh hurried out of the yard and out of that dirty house. The poor young man was about to go crazy. He could not think of any way to save Javad, and he returned home exhausted.

***

Two months later, Farrokh's efforts to save Javad from the clutches of Nazmieh Prison did not yield any results. Mahin was feeling better but every time he had asked Shokoofeh to arrange a meeting with Mahin. Each time he was informed his beloved that this was not possible because Mahin's parents were suspicious of her and were closely monitoring her movements.

One day, when the young man was thinking about Javad's plight, he walked into the room and kept asking himself why he had not been released and why the poor man had been kept in prison until that moment. Then the door opened and Shokoofeh entered. She was happy seeing him:
"I was afraid that you would not be home and would not receive Mahin 's letter in time."

Farrokh was very worried about Shokoofeh's words and hurriedly took the letter from her and kissed it and held it in front of his eyes and read:

My dear Farrokh,

Even though I had made a vow to myself that I will not make you angry and I will not hurt you, but I need to explain what is happening to me in my parent's house, but what can I do if I have to? Maybe this is the last time I am holding a pen to inform you of a new thing that has increased my inner pain thousands of times.

Yesterday, my father came to me with the usual violence that you are aware of and an example of his behavior with poor Javad. He said: "Mahin, the doctor approved your health. And since there is no more reflection, I have ordered them to provide the means of engagement for the next three days, and God willing, our wedding will take place in a month or two and we will have a big celebration."
When I saw my father was aware of all the secrets and did not change his mind and all my moans and lamentations and finally my long period of illness did not affect him, I was astonished and closed my mouth and did not answer, thinking that my silence was the reason. Satisfied, he smiled and this time kindly added:
"Well done, well-done girl, it turns out that you have come to your senses. If I knew your illness will make you wiser, I would pray you became sick sooner."

My dear Farrokh, after those words, my father left the room and I was still astonished and stunned. A few minutes later, the people of the house came to me in their own time, and each of them expressed their joy and happiness:
"Praise be to God that the lady agreed to get married and a wedding will be held soon, and a reward will surely come to each of us." Of course, I did not answer any of them because I did not find it useful to discuss with them and I did not expect these misfortunes to understand me.

Farrokh, what can I do, unfortunately, I can not see you for a few minutes to explain my inner pain to you, although it may be better because when you know what I am feeling, it will be more painful for you.

Farrokh, I no longer think that there is any hope left for us, the pressure of getting married to another person is too much. Farrokh, it is no longer possible for us to meet in this world, but we may meet in the other world. Forget me, Farrokh, and take Mahin's memory away from your heart, be happy and live with other girls that nature will surely put in your way, but know and always remember that until the last hour of my life, I will be full of your love.

Indeed, what cruel, unjust, and injustice they have done to us. True happiness has not been considered for me. Although they are not to blame, I forgive them too, because they are ignorant of love, they have been deceived by appearances.

She who loves you to the end of her life and will not forget you in another one.
Mahin.

After reading her letter, he thought deeply about how nature had exposed him to the most severe trials. Farrokh's blood boiled hard in his veins. His face was very red and inflamed, then he hit his foot hard on the ground and shouted:
'Why should I live anymore, I will destroy myself.'
But at the same time a voice rose from the depths of his heart and heard a whisper:
'You have to stay and live and not give up.'

Baba Haidar came into the room and put the morning newspaper on the table. He looked inside the news and suddenly the news caught his eye and read aloud:

Javad ... was sentenced to 100 lashes and six months in solitary confinement for abducting a girl with the help of another person, and a new sentence will be imposed on him in the next three days in Toopkhaneh Square.

Farrokh remained silent and thoughtful for a few minutes, he did not know what to say, and when he turned back, he suddenly realized that Shokoofeh was still standing in the corner of the room, waiting for his answer, so he said:
"You see my mood, tell Mahin to not despair on my behalf, maybe God will

help from heaven. I will write my reply tomorrow and come in the morning to take it to her."

Shokoofeh said nothing more and left the room.

Farrokh became more and more frustrated as he thought, and soon he encountered obstacles and problems and realized his inability.

The room and the house seemed small to him. An hour later, he left the house, and without realizing where he was going, he reached the Mokhber-e Dowleh crossroads when it was about five o'clock in the afternoon, and while the young people were walking on Lalehzar Street, Farrokh wished to meet an acquaintance and get rid of his troubled thoughts at least for a moment, entered Islambul Street and turned left at the end. And under the old trees of Ala al-Dawleh Street, he slowly moved to the south of the city. 'Mahin will be engaged in three days. Poor Javad will be flogged in three days.'

He was disappointed with everything and his thoughts did not go anywhere. Suddenly he felt a hand on his shoulder and when he raised his head, he saw a well-dressed and stylish young man in front of him.

Chapter Twenty Nine
The Third Accident

If the readers allow, we can now recall the two people who played an important role in this story, and we have not talked about them in a while, let's see what happened to them during this period... These two people are Siavash Mirza and his servant Mohammad Taqi. We put them in a situation where Mohammad Taqi took his master, who had been injured by Hassan Rizeh's machete, and took him out of Nahid's house in the middle of the night and hurried home.

Mohammad Taqi's only concern was that the carriage would not be found at that time and he would have to carry the prince on his shoulders to the house. Toopkhaneh Square was empty and there was no sign of a carriage. He was short of breath and sweating when a carriage arrived on the corner of Marizkhaneh street. He put his master in and they arrived home shortly.

The old doorman opened the door and was waiting for them to enter, but as soon as he saw Siavash Mirza unconscious and injured in the carriage, he was scared and wanted to shout and wake the family. But Mohammad Taqi pointed silently and said into his ear:

"If you do not want to be kicked out tomorrow, be silent and ignore what you see!"

The doorman realized that Mohammad Taqi was telling the truth and that Siavash Mirza might make excuses and force his father to expel him, so remained silent. He brought water and laid it on the floor in the middle of the small room of the doorman, which was level with the garden floor and more like a peasant hut. They wrapped the wound with the white handkerchief that was in Siavash Mirza's pocket.

The prince, who had fainted from bleeding, recovered from the cold water and the gentle air of the garden, and opened his eyes. He asked Mohammad Taqi: "Where am I?"

Mohammad Taqi flattered the prince and assured him that he thought it would be better for the blood to be cleaned from his clothes and tied the minor wounds before going inside the mansion so that others would not say anything about it.

Siavash nodded his head and said in a weak voice:

"Well done, but now take me to my room."

Then, with the help of Mohammad Taqi, who was holding him in his arms, he slowly walked to his bedroom.

"In the morning, if there is a question about this wound, just say you had a minor boil which is infected!"

Then Mohammad Taqi went to his house, which was in the same neighborhood, a short distance away.

In the morning after, Siavash Mirza was still in the bed and his parents, who loved him very much and preferred him to his sister, were very worried as soon as they heard about the boy's illness and were very curious to know the cause of his sudden illness, but Siavash hid the truth as Mohammad Taqi taught him and answered their frequent questions that he had boil on his thigh, but it is getting better!

His mother has a complete belief in the ancients ways and prescribe medicine for any pain according to Kolsoom nanny, said:

"My child needs to have something cold, It's the hot temperament that caused the boil!"

She immediately ordered Khan Nazer to buy flixweed from the herbal store so that they could make a drink with lemons. Then she turned to her son, "If all this does not work, ten ounces of Cotoneaster will work and will completely cure my son's heat."

Siavash, who did not want to oppose his mother's opinion and did not consider such herbals harmful, ate flixweed with interest and as we know, Prince K... who also believed that his son was upset by the presence of a heart in his drift, the day he met F... Al-Saltaneh in the club, had pointed out the whole issue with his son.

A few days later, Siavash Mirza's minor wound healed and the evil thoughts fell on the prince again, and now he had all the desire to meet Effat again, so he summoned Mohammad Taqi and said:

"We have not been there for a long time and the truth is that I miss her very much, she was a good woman."

Mohammad Taqi was astonished by Prince's words and said in his heart that he was a young man who was thoughtless and did not have a head of fear. He promised Mirza to go to Nahid's house that day and make arrangements so that his master could once again spend the night in peace.

Mohammad Taqi fulfilled his promise, when returned to the mansion, saw the prince was sitting in a chair in the corner of the room, drinking Arak. He told him that Effat escaped the house, "As soon as I entered Nahid's house, she took my hand and shouted that I will not leave you anymore. You must tell me where you took my favorite, you must tell me soon because I bought her from the major bride for seventy Tomans.

Of course, I, who was not aware of it, was shocked, and when Nahid finally realized that I did nothing to do in that incident, she calmed down and explained to me with tears that after we left, the deputy police chief, came there with another agent, made promises about the pursuit of the Cossack, but Effat had disappeared, and since then, despite searching all the houses of her colleagues no one heard from her."

The prince was shocked and saddened by the news of Effat's escape and expressed his impression by drinking another glass of Arak.
Mohammad Taqi continued:
"For her to be sure that we didn't interfere in the disappearance of Effat, so she would not cause trouble, I said that His Highness wanted to come and visit your house again since he liked your hospitality. Nahid, who was very happy with you, showed me all the women of her house and said:
- Sir, if you do not like any of them, for sure, I will borrow from neighbors for the prince. I am very devoted to you and I always want to serve you"
Siavash Mirza said:
"Your promise to take me there when Effat is not there! Why should I do that?"
"As I said, I just wanted to calm her," Mohammad Taqi said.
Siavash was emotional, sighed, and said:
"Well, Mohammad Taqi, our arrow did not hit there, you have to think and find a new chick for me."

Mohammad Taqi bowed and promised that one night he would see an acquaintance in the neighborhood of the house that knew many respectable women and families, and asked him to bring a beautiful lady that would suit his taste.

The next day, Mohammad Taqi took the master's son to one of the houses on M.. Al-Saltaneh Street and threw him in the arms of one of the women who was pretty. The prince continued this kind of entertainment and often went to such houses once or twice a week, and several times he will feel discomfort, and he is referred to the doctor in ... street and underwent short treatments, and because he was young and thoughtless, he did not care much about these troubles, and he always assured himself that he would overcome all diseases with the force of youth.

It was his movements and deeds that his father interpreted as making medicine and making a laboratory and calling it service to the nation, and as good qualities and virtues son, the future father-in-law believes the prince intends to make medicine. He was the various bottles of medicine and love that his son collected all at home and used internally and externally. In Prince K...'s opinion, there was no doubt that Siavash Mirza was easing these sufferings to serve the nation.

One or two months passed, and during this period, Prince K ... talked to his son several times about the need for getting married, and each time he gave a detailed description of the wedding and other benefits of this union, but Siavash did not want to lose his freedom. Each time, under the pretext of freeing himself from his father, listening to his father's advice was suffering and he compensated for the pleasure of spending in the arms of promiscuous women.

Siavash Mirza was by no means willing to commit himself to love and to put an end to the happy and fun activities he had undertaken. One day, Prince K.. said that Mahin had been abducted on the way to Qom, and added with regret that if the girl was destroyed, all our plans would be wasted. It is no longer possible for her father's wealth to flow into our pocket. Then again after two or three days, his father announced that she was safe.

Siavash, who was busy with the women on M... Al-Saltaneh Street, Sandy Street, and Qajar alley, did not have the slightest place in his heart for Mahin, did not pay much attention to this news as he did not even ask his father how Mahin was kidnapped. By whom and with whose help was this done? Of course, Prince K .. was not happy with this behavior of the boy, he looked at him with concern. Finally, one day, he summoned him and said in a very serious and commanding tone:

"Son, it is time for you to get married and since Mahin has also completely recovered, we have made an appointment with the F...Al-Saltaneh. We will hold your engagementt ceremony in three days.

Although Siavash considered all this news this time with disregard and coldness because he had a lot of respect for his father, he did not dare to oppose and talk anymore and lowered his head as a sign of acceptance and with great reluctance said this short sentence for his father's satisfaction. said: "very good." Then, leaving the house with the thought of spending the last days of his freedom happily, he walked slowly to the Hassanabad intersection and reached the Toopkhaneh from Marizkhaneh Street. He saw two Armenian girls holding hands. They both wore skirts of crimson and white blouse and twisted their oak color hair behind their backs.

Siavash thought to himself, what is wrong with chasing the two and maybe he will get results, so he walked faster to them and as soon as he heard the two of them talking to each other in French, said something, but the girls did not pay the slightest attention to his appearance, and went on their way and walked slowly, so he said:

"It turns out that they do not know who I am, how can they reject me and not respond to me."

Siavash Mirza did not stop chasing the girls until the intersection of Qazaqkhaneh and the end of Borj-e-Noush Street. He said in frustration:

"What kind of bitter people are these Armenians. I thought coming to them will make it easier to be friends and get to know others, and now I see that it is quite the opposite. They did not say a single word."

When he reached Ala Al-Dawlah Street, he moved to the north. Then, a few steps away, he noticed a young man who was hard-thinking in his direction. He put his hand on her shoulder and said:
"Praise is to God, we saw each other after a while!"

Farrokh raised his head when he heard the sound and when he saw Siavash in front of him and knew him, he made a small sound of surprise Siavash made the usual compliments and expressed a special devotion to Farrokh, commenting on the news of the young man's health.
"You have completely forgotten me. Unfortunately, I did not know your address to come to say thank you, nor did I know your office."
Farrokh explained: "Fortunately, I do not have a job in any of these offices, the headquarters of some people who harassed, bribe-takers and trouble-makers, and I do not think that I will ever work in one and lose my freedom easily, but my house is across the street, which you are welcome to it."
"I do not remember giving my name and address that night, anyway our house is on Qazvin Gate Street and my father is Prince K... and if you ask anyone in that neighborhood, they will give you my address and you can come anytime." then Siavash shakes Farrokh's hand:
"I will not leave you easily, let's go to Lalehzar, sit in a cafe and talk a little."

Farrokh had a history with Siavash Mirza and did not want to be friends with people like him, but because he needed companionship and entertainment at that time so he might get rid of such a bad emotional moment, he accepted his invitation. They make their way to Lalehzar Street near Topkhaneh Square.

It was about five-thirty in the afternoon, the two young men, who had no similarities in terms of morality and thought, went down from Amin Al-Sultan alley into Lalehzar Street to the south and entered a cafe. The garden was relatively large, with several round tables and a large number of men sitting in the open-air eating ice cream. They sat and Siavash asked Farrokh what he wanted. Farrokh was not interested in anything so Siavash ordered two ice creams and started to smoke. Farrokh remained silent and sad, and although he listened to Siavash, his thoughts were elsewhere, Mahin's face did not disappear from his sight, and Javad's imprisonment and the punishment that lay ahead did not escape his imagination, and therefore the prince's words did not sink. He answered yes or no with short words. Siavash realized his grief and asked kindly the reason and insisted on knowing the reason, but Farrokh did not find it appropriate to open his heart to someone like him or reveal his secrets to a young man like him, said he is sleepless and remained silent. Therefore Siavash opened his mouth and, as is the custom of the children of the aristocrats and the wealthy, began to boast about the amount and crop and products of his father or his properties, and sometimes of the innumerable carriages and chariots and horses they had. He discussed some political, social, and economic issues, and suggested a simple and childish solution to each of the problems with his incomplete information, including the names of Lord Curzon, Karl Marx, and Bismarck. He had read in the newspapers, he also mispronounced them and attributed to them the words he did not understand. He criticized the musical drama that was shown several times in Tehran in those days. But he soon talked about his father wealth that he believed his father paid to a woman three thousand tomans just for three days but was nothing compared to one of the government officials in Mashhad, who earn a monthly salary of fewer than one hundred Tomans, had contracted another famous woman with fifty Tomans a night. He had used the money he took from the state treasury.

Farrokh, who did not want to hear this at all, often acknowledged his remarks by nodding, but the prince did not calm down. He kept on talking: Meanwhile, Farrokh asked him:

"As I understand it, you are not married yet?"

Siavash laughed:

"Why should I get married and why should I commit myself to a woman? I should probably get all the women of this city with this wealth that I have, and fortunately, I have succeeded to some extent so far ..."

Farrokh, hearing this baseless claim and this strange insolence, wanted to punch him in the mouth and get away from the shameless young man as soon as possible, but he refused and kept a contemptuous look on Siavash and kept his composure. He remained silent.

Siavash also continued his boasting:

"But my father insists on it and wants to force me to get married, and ironically, our engagement is three days away and you will surely attend."

Farrokh was shocked to hear that for another three days and was reminded that Mahin's engagement ceremony will be held in three days. So without changing his appearance, asked:

"God willing, but you did not mention with whom."

Siavash replied with a laugh:

"If I say I do not know, you will not believe me, because I have not been involved in this matter. This marriage will multiply our wealth, and of course, in this way, my field of entertainment will expand even more."

Farrokh could no longer bear it, his fist clenched and was close to land on the brain of that idiot that would take Mahin only for her wealth and breathed love with others. He said in his heart:

"What madness this is, I have to listen to what this idiot has to say right now and be aware of his inner thoughts." So he said in a ridiculous tone: "Congratulations. It is a good and graceful connection!"

Then Siavash Mirza, proud of himself, added with all arrogance: "Now that you know whose she is, I hope you come to celebrate the engagement with me."

"I am deprived of this happiness, because unfortunately I will not be in the city by chance that day, but God willing, I will serve you at the wedding celebration and I will offer my sincere congratulations," Farrokh replied.

Siavash did not insist anymore. The next moment, the topic of conversation changed and the prince started talking again. He speaks and calls himself a disciple of Socrates for a while and talks about the merits of his taste, and finally, he considered the change of taste more necessary than anything!

Farrokh, who looked at Siavash with open eyes and a steady gaze kept asking himself how they wanted to take Mahin from him and throw her in the arms of such a corrupt and filthy young man who has no interest in the girl. He suddenly stood up and said: "I have to go to a personal appointment at eight o'clock and please excuse me."

Siavash, who noticed Farrokh's disturbed condition and looked at his face with curiosity, did not insist on staying anymore and said with a smile: "But God willing, we will meet again soon. In any case, know that I will not forget that night. Thank you very much and I am always ready to fulfill your requests."

Farrokh thanked him for his compliments and hurried out of the cafe and hurried home.

Chapter Thirty
An Example Of Aristocracy Gratitude

When Farrokh reached the house, he went straight to his room and sat on a chair, and thought for a while about the person he met. Then he got up and stood behind his small desk in the corner of the same room, and put a piece of paper in front of him. He had thought of writing a letter to Siavash and reminding him that because he had saved him from certain death so he would accept the prince's promise that his request would be fulfilled.

The pen rotated on the paper for several minutes, and several times the blackened papers were torn and dumped into the basket. Finally, Farrokh wrote the following letter to Siavash Mirza,

Dear new friend:

Although I know that this is the beginning of our friendship, this request will seem very big, but because the issue is very important to me personally, my life and survival depend on it, and since you said if I need your help and assistance you will do it. I do not need to make an introduction, I will discuss the matter with you straight.
Mahin, the daughter of F... Al-Saltaneh, whom your father has considered to be your wife, is not only my cousin but also my beloved, and I am in love with her for many years, and she has reciprocated the love. This way, you might have to guess what my request is. Nevertheless, I would like to clarify, according to your confession, you have no special interest in Mahin and only insisted because of your father.

I hope that with your kindness and love, you will implement this decision as soon as possible and inform your father as well and I will be indebted to you.
Although this request of mine may seem very strange and bold, I am sure that if you search your heart you will see the greatness of love, and also do a little research about Mahin and me, you will find out my state of interest, and you would help, I will be looking forward to receiving your answer.

Sincerely, Farrokh

Farrokh enveloped the letter and put it on the table and said to himself: "I will send it in the morning. Then he remembered that he had to write Mahin's reply, and now that this accident had happened and a window of hope had been found, it would be better to inform his beloved as soon as possible, so he took the pen in his hand again and wrote the following letter:

Beloved darling,

I read your letter that emanated from the tips of those delicate fingers, but I must admit that I was very upset and disturbed by the reference you made to your decision. I did not understand how the strong heart I had for you easily succumbed to the pressure, and how it turned the strong will into weakness.
My darling. Of course, I give you the right with all the obstacles that we have both faced in the way to achieving a happy life, and with the injuries that you have suffered from the ignorance of your mother and the boundless greed of your father. But you should not forget that these kinds of troubles are common and affect the majority of people who, like you, are not deceived by appearances and are always looking for the truth.
But you must also keep in mind that no matter how dark the horizon is in front of one's eyes, a gentle breeze may rise at any moment, and a small light may appear through the dark clouds, promising a window of hope for success.

Mahin, I forgot to tell you about what happened a few months ago, the very night we sat on the garden wall and listened to your parents talking together.
That night, a young man from Tehran, in one of the famous houses on Sandy Street ... spends his night in the arms of a woman. A moment later, a drunk Cossack was pointing his pistol at the young man's head and his brain was about to shatter and be released from life, but suddenly another young man who was passing by, heard the scream, and at that critical moment, saved him. The young man who spent the night in the house and was threatened by a drunken Cossack was the one whom your father chose as your husband, Siavash Mirza, and the one who saved him was me.

Mahin, now you seem to have guessed what I mean. Siavash owes his life to me. Fortunately, yesterday I came across him when I was upset by reading your letter and went down to the street. I struggled to find a way to save ourselves from this trouble and helplessness. He was very friendly and grateful to me, and it was clear that he wanted to serve me at the first opportunity. After some thought, I dared to write letters to him and asked him to give up his marriage to you and inform his father of his decision.
I imagine that you now believe that the light of hope has appeared on the dark horizon of our destiny. If Siavash Mirza is willing to give up this marriage in exchange for what I did for him. It will take some time for your father to find another person to do his wishes.

My beloved darling. Hopefully, the goddess of love will never forget us and will not deprive us of attention.

The one who worships you - Farrokh

After writing these two letters, Farrokh felt and hoped the letter written to Siavash Mirza would bring a happy result and that the prince, whom he had saved from certain death, would be willing to renounce this connection and take this important step. He spent the night with all these thoughts, and this window of hope in which the dark horizon appeared for him, grew bigger in his thoughts and imaginations every moment, and he saw success and achievement almost certainly. Farrokh thought less of Javad while immersed in the intensity of happiness.

Early in the morning, after he drank tea, Shookoofeh came early. Farrokh gladly handed the letter he had written to the gardener's daughter to deliver and asked how Mahin was. Shokoofeh noticed the change in his appearance and happy face said:

"She is fine and nothing new has happened."

After Shokoofeh left, Farrokh called his old servant and handed him the letter he had written to Siavash Mirza, giving him the address of the prince's house and asking him to deliver it to him as soon as possible.

The servant was ready to go and promised his young master that he would walk much better and faster than the young, and he would deliver the letter to Siavash Mirza very soon. He left the house and hurried to the prince's house. Farrokh was left alone, he was excited and worried again. His heart was constantly squeezing and he was walking around the room asking himself: 'Will he agree? Will he be willing to give up?' He could not bear to wait, left the house and went to the city center. He was thinking if Siavash Mirza gives a favorable answer, he will be relieved about Mahin for a while and then he will try with all his might for the release of poor Javad. However, he did not ignore the family of the unfortunate servant and sent them money through Baba Haidar. But since it had been almost three months since that poor man had been caught and was suffering, every time he remembered that Javad had been imprisoned for ninety days and that he had not yet been able to save the unfortunate man from that prison. He would get upset and clench his fists and kick his feet on the ground as if he wanted to kill the unconscionability and injustice of the people and feed the soil to take revenge. The long prison time of Javad and the flogging came to his mind and imagined that his heartbeat would beat faster and his forehead veins would become more prominent he said:

"these cruel and unjust acts will turmoil a city and a country..."

Farrokh walks the northern streets of the city for about two hours. Because at that time, that part of the city was deserted and many people did not travel, few people noticed his distress, and the same silence and tranquility in the north of the city was a blessing for him as he did not cut his thoughts at any moment and was not like the south of Tehran a crowded neighborhood. He returned home around noon. But Baba Haidar had not come yet. Farrokh waited anxiously for another hour, and finally, the door was knocked, and Baba Haidar, sweaty and breathless, came forward and handed over the letter in his hand to the gentleman, telling Farrokh that he should no longer write for such people. And if he writes, he should not send him to deliver it!

Farrokh felt bad news about his expression because he wanted that window of hope and happy fantasies not to end so soon, so he calmly asked Baba Haidar how it went.

"As soon as I arrived at the house of Prince K. I called the servant who was standing in the middle of the garden and talking to another and asked him to deliver the official letter to Siavash Mirza and get an answer. The servant looked at me and it was clear that he did not pay attention to me because he was thinking that the letter was mine and I was asking for a job or help. He continued talking to his friend. I was also polite and hoped that he would finally finish his speech and take the envelope to him, I waited for a while and finally, my patience ran out and I said sharply to him that if he doesn't want to take it he should return it, I will return the letter to my master. Hearing this threat, he turned to me and asked, 'Did you bring the letter from someone?' I answered yes. My master sent the letter to Siavash Mirza. He hurriedly entered the mansion, fearing that the matter would be urgent, he came back and said his master is in the bathroom and if there is an answer, they will give it."

Baba Haidar was silent for a while and then sighed coldly and added: "They made me very upset, the old days were different, their peers would invite each other to at least a cup of tea. But these unjust people did not even think at all, about how far I had come. I cursed them in my heart to the constitutionalists who have made this day for us, and with the anger, I said to the prince's servant, 'Very well, so I will go and sit in a nearby coffee house and will come again in half an hour to take the answer to my master, and since he did not say a word, I went down the same street ... near Qazvin Gate Square. I sat for an hour and after drinking several cups of hot tea, I went back to the prince's house and ... the servant informed me that Siavash Mirza came out of the bathroom and read the letter and said he will reply. I sat on the step for another half an hour until finally, the servant called me, and when I reached the middle of the garden, he handed me a large envelope and said with a sneer: 'This is the written answer for your master!' At that moment, my eyes fell on Siavash Mirza, who was walking around the porch with a robe on his shoulders, like crazy people, he saw me, and

he laughed strangely, as if he especially wanted me to hear me, and said loudly..."
Baba Haidar remained silent for a moment and lowered his head. Farrokh, who wanted to know what the prince had said, asked him:
"Why are you silent, do not hide, tell me what he said."
Baba, while swallowing, said in a trembling and angry voice what the prince had said:
"What stupid expectations the stupid boy has!"
Farrokh, hearing Baba Haidar's words and especially the last sentence of another prince, found out the contents of Siavash Mirza's letter. So he opened the envelope and kept Siavash's letter in front of his eyes. The further he looked at the letter, the more cold sweat dripped down his forehead. "Shameless, shameless!"

Dear respectable man,

I received your letter. The truth is that I laughed at your simplicity and optimism for a while. I did not think that as I saw and knew you, you would be so naive and mindless and allow yourself to make such a misplaced request from me.
We express friendship to someone only for the benefit we have in mind, and if there is no interest and use, we will even turn farther away. If I thanked you, it was just to hold you in the future so that I might need your help at another time. But if you have taken another meaning from it and attached special value to my gratitude that it was nothing more than a compliment and thought that you could make such a request of me by relying on it, it is nothing more than a raw fantasy and a useless thought. I hope you don't regret it.

If Mahin is your cousin, and even if she is your beloved and secret friend, she will not turn me away for my intention and opinion. Of course, my father chose her for me for many reasons and calculations, and I chose to obey him for my interests. I do not know why I should act against my father's wishes and why I should act on your request, give up such a marriage, especially with a girl who, according to what I have heard, is beautiful and humorous, with her father's extraordinary wealth. Why would I deprive my bride and happiness to fulfill your expectation? And of course, as I said before, I am always happy to meet you, and if you want to marry someone else and need help to establish a relationship, tell me, and I will try to fulfill your request.

Dear friend, do not be too sad and discouraged by my answer and do not blame anyone, because there is not much truth and honesty that you expect in this world.

Yours Sincerely, Siavash Mirza
Farrokh was ridiculed and humiliated by Siavash Mirza's reply. A letter

that came from a stone heart, emotions-less, a hard and frozen brain, and the institution of an unjust and ignorant person, Farrokh had saved him from certain death, he could have crossed that street in disregard that night, ignoring the cries and pleas, allowing Hassan Rizeh to cleanse the world of such filth of such a fool.

Farrokh tied his fist in anger and said:

'Why did you force me to save him from death that night so that he would be my rival today and such a lowly person could talk about my dear Mahin's so ugly and also humiliate and ridicule me with such arrogance.'

But from the depths of his heart, he heard a voice saying:

'What are these words that you say, if you also resigned from your duty of conscience and did not fulfill your humanity that night, then what was the difference between you and Siavash?'

Following these internal conflicts, Farrokh felt very tired and could not stand still, so he fell into the bed with great sadness. What the young man went through over the last few months. An hour passed he had a severe fever and with every minute his condition got worse. He no longer knew those around him and was delusional. His maid was sitting by the bed, not taking her eyes off the boy with anxiety, and slowly weeping over the misfortune.

In the next two days, Mahin was getting engaged and Javad was getting flogged. Farrokh had the right to get sick because he had no hope left.

Chapter Thirty-One
Where The Tears Of The Poor And Miserable Fall?

During one of the autumn mornings. Due to the rain that fell the night before, the weather was very mild. Some woke up but some other residents of the capital were still asleep in their soft beds.

Those who have been up and running for hours are the same people who are called the third class. They have to get up early every morning and work hard to earn a living and they have to make a living with its meager benefits. In winter, they sell hot beetroot, and in summer, they sell vegetables, sometimes a bowl of buttermilk and curd, and another time baked beans and potatoes.

The other residents of the city who have more opportunity to sleep in bed are called the second or middle class, who, although they have a more colorful life than the previous group, are also suffering, especially from the government. Those who are suing the leadership administration of the country and are not safe. Among this class, there are all kinds of people with different tastes, as some are devoted to Westerners and some are devoted to Arabs. Some consider it necessary to use European words under the pretext of promoting a new civilization, and some consider Arabic words so it could help concentrate on the duties of religion, they gather people around them and deceive a group called the preservation and strengthening of the rites of religion. They spend time on a moonlit night by the blue-lighted creek, express their interest to their like-minded people and weave politics and discuss the day-to-day situation. Sometimes they weave politics and sometimes they seem to follow the path of research and study. They are journalists in the morning and publishers in the evening. Sometimes preachers are on the pulpit and sometimes they meet sitting around a table.

The other people of the capital who are still lying in bed are the ones who, according to the naive masses, have been condemned for embezzlement of great wealth and are called the first class. Their names are associated with parks, property, jewelry, and money, and in fact, they spend their captivity, which is called a luxurious life, in the bondage of these manifestations of wealth, and have no thought but to preserve and increase them. While they consider themselves naively, clever and intelligent, most of them drink cognac and whiskey, and pretend to be altruistic. They consider their wealth, position and status as a gift from God and humiliate others who have not succeeded in life despite many efforts. Those who rely on the power of money consider everything legitimate and permissible for themselves. If masses make a mistake out of extreme misery and misery, they will be considered poor, small, helpless and have no rights. They think that if the same small people got together, their reign will easily end. These nobles and aristocrats are constantly promoted to the position of minister and appointed to the cradle of government and command. Outwardly, they claim to guide and lead the nation, but inwardly they are the greatest enemy of knowledge and culture and the establishment of the people's rule over the people. They call young people inexperienced and, under this pretext, deprive them of important tasks. They rest most of the day until around noon next to a lover who has been forced into their arms by money, and when they wake up, they drink tea, coffee, chocolate, jams, and fruits, and then, engage in special affairs with the ministries, all of which only protect their interests.

On that day, as on other days, the sun had risen and the commotion of all the people of Tehran had begun. Someone rested in a small space that was perhaps no more than two square feet in size, on a rough, dirty cloth as a mattress. The sound of his breath resonating in that small dark space was a sign that he was still interested in life, he was still preparing to endure other sufferings.

The air was foul and unpleasant, and the smell of dampness rose from it, and only the sound of some animals such as mice and beetles occasionally disturbed its deadly silence and forced the weak creature into small movements for defending himself so that he might escape their bite.

This place was the prison number one of Tehran Nazmieh Prison, and that poor creature was Javad, Farrokh's servant for a few days, who had spent almost three months and dreaming of a hard but free time a few months ago. The thought of his mother, his sister-in-law and her little children did not leave his mind for a moment, he was skeptical that Farrokh would take care of his family. Poor Javad, who did not see a reason for his long imprisonment, was pessimistic about everything in the world and imagined all the people are the same as F... Al-Saltaneh, and believed that all human beings gathered to torture him.

What would he do if he did not find this belief? Had he killed a man or set fire to a city, or rebelled against the illegitimate influence and the utterances of all the nonsense and superstitions of the clergy, or had he paid tribute to the suffering and toiling people and made them aware of their rights? Had he disclosed the hypocrisy of a leader, or exposed an influential rich man? Did he speak of freedom or did he act against the interests of foreigners? Javad's only sin was that he served Farrokh by providing for his family, and he acted in

*complete honesty and faithfully on the orders of his master. But would silent obedience not
be considered a great sin in some cases?*

When F... Al-Saltaneh ordered the gendarmes to arrest Javad that day in
Evin, the poor servant did not pay attention to what happened at first and
thought to himself that the gentleman was very upset and had ordered his
arrest to alleviate his anger and he was sure that after a few hours, the gentleman's anger will subside and he will be released.

Poor Javad could never have imagined more punishment for himself because he had not sinned and it was unbelievable for him the existence of
violence and resentment in the human heart.

When he was brought in Nazmieh, he was still comforting himself:
'There must be nothing but threats and they have no intention other than
to show him that horrible place and scare him.' With these thoughts, Javad
entered Nazmieh, but as soon as he reached the guard on duty, he gradually realized that this was not the only threat because he saw that he was
talking about being handed over to the prison guard. In addition, he heard
the guard asking the agents if he was the same dangerous man that Mr. F...
Al-Saltaneh had ordered it to be kept?

Then one of the agents stepped forward and placed his hand on the side of
his forehead and answered in a serious tone:

"Yes, this is him."

Javad realized his apprehension and became even more anxious in the
office of the chief of the prison.

"What cell is vacant?" The chief asked.

The incumbent replied:

"In a public prison where there is nowhere, and the second prison is full.
There is just one space in prison number one."

The chief, without considering the difference between these three degrees
and the amount of the crime attributed to Javad, said:

"He seems very fraudulent, that imprisonment suits him!"

Javad no longer had any doubts about what lay ahead and realized that
he was being treated differently than he had imagined. A few minutes later, they searched his pockets and then placed him in a crypt called Prison
Number One. The crypt was very dark and the compressed and smelly air
was entering Javad's nose more and more. Even though he had arrived there
around noon, he could barely recognize his surroundings. The black eye of
the young man, who was not familiar with this darkness, was getting smaller
every minute, and finally, after a while, he was able to hardly realize the size
and quality of his prison.

He thought about it for a long time, but he had not yet lost the thought of getting rid of it. In that darkness, he lit his heart with a window of hope. He tried to sleep so at least relieve his physical fatigue until the iron door opened. He lay on a hard mattress that was in the corner, and closed his eyes but did not fall asleep easily. Eventually, fatigue overcame him, and his eyes, which had been crippled by mental and physical injuries, closed.

A few hours later, Javad opened his eyes and looked around. He went to sleep again, but the next hour, when he opened his eyes, he found his place still dark, and since he no longer felt the need to sleep, he yawned and sat down on the floor, then heard a sound from a thin crack of thick wood. He remembered where he had fallen asleep.

It was around noon that they were brought Javad to the prison and the prisoners were given lunch at that time, no one thought of feeding him, and he, who did not have any appetite, felt someone touching his big toe, and then he realized that the small teeth of a mouse were at work, so he reached out to his pocket to find something to kill the vermin, but was empty. Then the door's lock turned, he got up and the door opened the next moment.

The light of the prison corridor fell on Javad's head and face, and hit his eyes as he barely stood in front of the door. The guard hurriedly put a small copper bowl, a loaf of bread, and a jar of water in front of him, and before the young man could open his mouth and complain about what was happening to him, the sound of the key moving in the door lock was heard.

Javad was feeling hungry now, also was curious to know what was in that copper bowl, so he reached for the bowl and dipped his fingertip in the thick, cold liquid, taste it: 'the curd soup! this season?' but he soon realized where he was. Hunger overcame him, and his fingers helped eating the black bread of prison.

'Mr. Farrokh will not sit idle, he will help me, and if he does not succeed, he will go to my house from time to time and will not leave my family hungry.'

Javad struggled with these thoughts for hours, and finally fell asleep again, and when he woke up, there were a loaf of bread and a piece of cheese in front of him. He spent the next night until the door was unlocked, and he started to move. They were two prison guards standing in front of the door, then one of them said in a harsh voice:

"Get up and let's go..."

Javad thought that F... Al-Saltaneh had a soft heart after all or that Farrokh had finally provided the means of freeing him from this bitter and unfortunate life and that he had been sentenced to freedom, so in the hope that he would inhale the open air again and he got rid of those stubborn rats. He stood up happily, saying in his heart:

'May God not afflict anyone with this damp and stinking crypt!'

He hurried out of the cell. A flash of happiness appeared in his sunken eyes and a smile appeared on the corner of his mouth. But as soon as he came out of the cell, guns were held horizontally and pointed at him to move forward, and then they took Javad out of the prison building and brought him to Toopkhaneh square.

Javad eyes barely recognized the body of a young man coming toward him, and when he concentrated, he saw Farrokh and wanted to shout with joy, but Farrokh sadly put a finger on his lips. It was then Javad realized that there was no escape, so he lowered his head in despair, and without knowing where he was being taken, he went to the south of the city under the guidance of the agents, and passed Paradise CorridorStreet. They turned left at the crossroads and entered Palace Street, and after three hundred steps, they reached the large green door and then entered a large courtyard, around which there were old mansions with several doors.

During this time, Javad with great curiosity wanted to know where he was being taken, and recognized the mansion, and finally knew that he had been brought to the court. Numerous courtyards were full of mullahs, who wore dirty turbans, and some intellectuals, who wore black hats and glasses. They sat next to the walls, on small carpets behind short tables writing petitions and complaints to litigants who had turned to them because they were illiterate.

The two agents passed Javad among the people and took him to the end of a large courtyard in the northwest corner. They took him to a room and handed him over to the office manager, and a quarter of an hour later, the office manager interrogated Javad.

A short, brown skinned man sat behind a large table. He invited Javad to sit down, then took the pen from behind his ear and began to ask questions and wrote things on a piece of paper:
"What is your name?"
Then he interrogated Farrokh's servant for an hour, but the more the interrogator asked, the more he regretted that there was no difference in Javad's answers and that there was no excuse for issuing his punishment. Javad said that his house was in Chaleh Maidan and he had been unemployed for some time until one day Mr. Farrokh came and hired him...
Finally, the interrogation session ended, and when Javad was allowed to leave, the interrogator laughed and said in a mixed tone of ridicule and threats:
"If he answers the same thing next time and does not admit what he knows, many things will happen!"
Outside, the agents were waiting for him to take Javad back to prison.

Days passed. Twice a week, poor Javad was taken out of prison to the interrogation office. The interrogator repeated the same questions every time and heard the same answers from Javad's mouth. Neither dark imprisonment nor unpleasant life made him confess to the crime he did not commit. Finally, they said that his interrogation was over and his case would be referred to court soon.

For another month, Javad remained in that dark corner of the prison and became weaker and thinner every day, until one day he was taken again by two agents, and this time he was led to another corner of the mansion. Javad asked one of the agents why he had moved. The answer said sarcastically: "Do you not know that today is the day of your trial?"

Half an hour later, Javad stood in front of the court desk. The judge had a narrow-tip hat, looked at him with contempt, shrugged his shoulders like someone who wanted to get rid of tedious, announced the beginning of the trial in a dry tone, and as soon as the indictment was finished, questions were asked of Javad. He answered questions as though the court was the place of justice and hoped his innocence will be declared there.
The judge asked him if he had a defense. Javad, who did not understand any of these formalities, was able to say:
"Sir, I am not to blame."

The judge announced the end of the trial and immediately turned to the court clerk and calmly recited his entire detailed sentence, in which, after a long introduction, he found the attributed crime to be proven and sentenced Javad to six months in solitary confinement and one hundred lashes.

Javad, who had realized human injustice in prison due to his endless thoughts and had no other expectations, did not protest, and a few days later, when the verdict was announced, he was immediately taken back to prison.

Javad did not know who to attack and who to blame for this injustice, and from time to time he would say to himself:
'Certainly, Farrokh has forgotten me and surely the one that I thought is a gentleman has forgotten taking care of my mother, my sister-in-law and her children.'
This thought bothered him so much!

***

On that day when Javad helplessly was lying down on that dirty mattress, four armed agents came and lined up in front of the prison door. One of them violently invited him out. Javad, in which the troubled world had forgotten the court verdict, had imagined again that his innocence had finally been proven. He tried to get up but felt very dizzy and fell hard before his hand reached the wall.

The agents hurried to get him and first took each of his hands to lift him off the ground, but when they realized the degree of helplessness and weakness of the prisoner, they had to take him by the arms. They passed through the yard and the large door brought him out to the opposite of Nazmieh in Toopkhaneh square.

Javad's eyes, which were becoming accustomed to light despite his weaknesses, suddenly saw about twenty people standing around a stool, and two agents, each with a whip. He also saw a group of men and women waiting to watch him be whipped.

The young man's face was very inflamed as if the rest of his remaining blood was boiling in his arteries, and his yellow color had turned red. He did not expect such an injustice. His voice remained in his throat and did not moan for those stony hearts ...

Javad's foot did not move any further. The agents dragged him up to near the stool. The unfortunate prisoner was not able to offer the slightest resistance. They tied his arms and legs to a pedestal and took off his shirt.

Immediately two long and stringy whips moved into the air and landed on Javad's back.

Javad did not make a sound, he was passed out before the first lash.

When the 39th lash landed, suddenly a woman's voice was heard from the audience, and the people who turned to the sound, saw a veiled woman trying to get closer to the agents. She was crying:
"This is my son. I knew my son, Javad, had been imprisoned. I saw that in my dream..." Javad's mother struggled to reach the circle of bodyguards, and when she wanted to go to her innocent son, suddenly the bottom of a rifle hit her side, and the poor woman moaned violently and fell to the ground unconsciously.

Some of the spectators laughed when they saw this scene and applauded the guard's agility and ingenuity, which prevented them from disrupting the scene and interrupting the administration of justice, but others were very sorry for this savagery and shrugged off their embarrassment. Javad was now conscious and a weak moan came out of his throat every time he was whipped.

Finally, the last lash landed and then they opened his arms and legs and dragged the weak and injured body back into the Nazmieh. Blood was flowing from Javad's body. He was coughing. They took him to the prison's infirmary, the cough deepened with each passing moment, and the closer they got to each other, the harder it was to cough, and his whole body shook violently at once, and then a lot of blood flowed from his mouth in the corner of the room.

Law and justice were enforced on him!

Chapter Thirty-Two
How Come A Beautiful Word Sometimes Became Ugly?

In the evening, on the same day that Javad was flogged, the house of F... Al-Saltaneh was vibrant. A large number of men and women were moving around. Only Hassan Qoli and Reza Qoli were the available servants for Mahin's father.

In the great hall of the mansion and the two rooms around it, small tables were placed all around, and on each of them, all kinds of Iranian and European sweets and various fruits of the season were arranged in crystal and silver dishes. All the doors and windows were open but the smoke of hookah and cigarettes was all over the place.

A large number of women, young and old, were sitting on chairs next to each other, talking and enjoying themselves, and occasionally laughing out loud. All kinds of clothes and all colors of fabric could be seen as if everything from the world of "fashion" could be found there.

Each group of women was talking to their like-minded people. A young woman who had just gotten married was embarrassed to point out her husband's special desires and ironically had realized that her husband was paying more attention to his same-sex instead of expressing his interest in her, and then another woman pointed to that day's engagement party and said with compassion:
"God bless the end of this bride, I will be beaten whenever I complain about my husband."

A young girl was talking about the love letter she had exchanged with her beloved to her friend who was sitting next to her, saying:
"In the last letter, he wrote a phrase that embodied all my feelings!"

Meanwhile, Malek Taj, who wore a short blue veil around her waist and performed the duties of the bride's mother, left the room and asked servants for topping up the drinks and changed the coal of hookahs. She came into the hall again, trying to smile, and approached a different group of ladies to make sure they are enjoying their time.

A young lady who looked very angry was uncomfortable in her place and took her friend's arm helplessly several times, and each time she drew her attention to one of the attendees and objected to her dress or sitting. She once said to her friend with bitterness and full effect in a glorious tone:
"Look, Khanoom Bozorg does not leave us alone today. She is constantly

looking at us. Even on the wedding day, we are not comfortable with the mother-in-law. She thinks we have to be mute all the time "

A group of musicians, consisting of three people, was sitting on the ground in the middle of the hall, playing. One of them was playing a hand-organ, the other was playing the string and the third one was playing tombak. Two female dancers were entertaining the guests. The taller one had blond hair and raven eyes, wore a long dress, and raised and lowered her eyebrows. Another, who was shorter and a little fat, had tanned skin and wore a short waistcoat, and blue velvet pants. Guest ladies enjoyed watching them as they were deprived of any other entertainment in their daily life due to the selfishness of men.

Trays of tea, ice cream, and juices were brought to the guests one after the other, and the best hookahs were not forgotten for the old ladies either.

***

In the other room of the mansion, Mahin was looking at the white silk dress sewn for her according to the latest fashion. Her face was pale. her eyes were red. The effects of fatigue, insomnia, and crying were evident. Mahin was very thin as one could see the prominent veins with blue blood on her delicate hands.

On that day, they wanted to force Mahin to engage Siavash Mirza, who she knew nothing about. They wanted to determine the fate of the two beings, who were different from each other in every way.

But could Mahin do this, and could she accept such a spouse?

Was this called marriage? Forcing an unfortunate young girl to live with an unknown man was called marriage? Did the religious leaders prescribe this kind of union?

Mahin swore and insulted the whole world. She had resumed her nervous state. Towards evening, Mahin's mood worsened when the guests began to arrive in groups. The girl strangled the screams that were about to come out of her mouth at any moment. Her mother used to come to see her every few minutes, and because every time she saw Mahin in a nervous state, she would beg, and no matter what the girl said, she would talk about protecting her reputation, and she would repeatedly ask her with a trembling voice and tears in her eyes:

"Do not disgrace me and your father, do not embarrass us in front of so

many guests, I will give you whatever you want, our property and jewelry are all yours, and today we will give you everything we have."
Mahin did not give up in her opinion, Mahin did not count wealth...

However, the girl had personally issued her death sentence, and when her mother came again, and resumed moaning and groaning, Mahin, who had run out of strength, said with great tiredness and a voice of pain and sorrow:
"I will be ready soon."
Hearing this, her mother shouted happily and hugged Mahin. She pushed her mother back, and as her leg trembled violently, she sat down on a chair and looked at her mother silently for a while with motionless eyes. As soon as her mother eagerly left the room, Mahin was left alone and began to cry.

A few minutes later, a short old woman with a large chin and a fleshy red face, who wore a white kerchief came into the room.

Mahin was silent and did not answer the dry and tasteless expressions of tire-woman, who was artificially expressing joy and saying ordinary pleasures as if Mahin had killed any emotion in herself, and like a lifeless statue, permitted tire-woman and others to move her around.

An hour later, Mahin's make-up was finished. She was dressed and ready to get engaged. The girl's feet trembled as if she was walking towards the cemetery, this was no wedding for Mahin, she remained as if she was approaching the hangman, *and has anyone gone to the hangman with desire?*

Mahin did not see happiness in front of her and did not see a bright future for herself.

Mahin was seeing the monster of death and inexistence in front of her eyes.

Two women who were related to Mahin took her by her arms and helped her to sit on a pearl-embroidered cashmere shawl on the ground in front of a large mirror that was leaning against the wall.

***

In the courtyard of the garden near the outer mansion, male guests had also gathered, the colorful flowers on this day in early autumn were very refreshing, and the mild weather at five o'clock in the afternoon added to the beauty of the cypress trees. The gentlemen were sitting, among them were seen from all classes and of all ages. There was a group of young people and some wise men and groups of old people, most of the guests wore hats and there were some common people among them, the young people talked to their like-minded people and the wise people talked to their colleagues.

The youth talked more about new urban and political events. Some of them warmly expressed their feelings, criticized the cabinet at the time, and praised the work of the former cabinet. Some who were not interested in discussing political issues talked about the pastimes that he had in recent days. For example, a young man with big bloodshot eyes said:
"I have printed an invitation card, and I have given it to every woman who passes by Lalehzar Street near our house!"
His very curious friend asked for the details, so he immediately took a card from his purse and kept it in front of his friend:

"Your ladyship, you are invited on ... Saturday ... at ... in the afternoon, to our house located in the alley ... on the left side of Lalehzar street. It would be our honor to serve you with a glass of drink and a cigarette."
Signature ... Al-Dawleh.

Then he laughed out loud and explained:
"You do not know how useful this card has been and what ladies have been trapped with it. They were often deceived that this card was only printed for them and came in time thinking I have an excessive interest in them!"
His friend looked at him in surprise and said:
"Congratulations, comrade, for having such intelligence, you have really found a good way to deceive and mislead women!"

Another young man, wearing a military black hat, with part of his curly hair protruding from the corner of his forehead and had an inappropriate attitude. He described what had happened a few nights earlier in the cafe ... above Ala Al-Dawlah Street. He claimed that he had deceived and trapped one of the foreign women.
The other guest, who was addressed as a prince, had a flushed red face, a large crooked nose, and awkward eyes. He looked stupid, especially with his erotic thick lips. He was talking about a female actor to who he had made love. The description of the actor was written in one of the newspapers and he spoke and narrated his love games with that artist with all pomp and circumstance.
Another man, who looked a little older than his comrades and had a

mediocre body, a slender physique, and attractive eyes, was said to be the author of theater pieces. said:
"Except for an imperfect hall, there is no other theater hall in this city, and the owner of it does not rent it out unless paying sixty Tomans in advance, and people do not show interest in watching moral shows. How do you want this industry to develop and prosper?"

But the matured and so-called wise people were talking about their properties, and some expressed their opinion about the cotton and wool trade, and some spoke of the breakdown and disorder of government departments, one of them mentioned the new Minister of Finance:
"The new minister does not steal but takes bribes. In addition, the good thing is that at least for the money he wants, he does something."

Another described the former finance minister and said:
"He has heard that he was very bureaucratic and interested in his duties, and in his idle days, he wrote many regulations for various matters, which unfortunately are stored in the corner of his house and remain useless."
Then he sighed and added with sympathy:
"Of course, if it were not for the hardworking and caring people of the nation, who would not have written so many regulations!"

Another guest, who wore a slim-brimmed hat, a black coat, and white glasses, constantly dipping his hand into the pocket of his white and striped linen vest. He listened intently and said:
"Do not forget the former Minister of Finance, I have heard really unbelievable things. It was said that an educated young Iranian man who spent 12 years of his life researching in Germany and preparing to serve in his homeland was forced to resign because he did not want to agree with the wrongdoings of some Belgian advisers and was forced to take a long leave without pay. Consider whether other young Iranians are interested in studying science and art in this way?"

In the meantime, some of the guests, who were thinking about their children's future, led the conversation about the virtues of their sons and daughters, telling one of the boy's education levels and his final exam scores, and the other was a description of his daughter's skills and arts to prove his claim. He cites an example that was presented in Nasim Shomal newspaper and his daughter solved it and the same newspaper published her name among the other respondents, but of course, these statements, both of them provided the ground for the future connection of their children.

Trays full of juices, tea cups, and ice cream were rotated by servants in front of the guests at all times.
At that moment, a large black carriage stood in front of the door and a

servant hurried to open the carriage's door. Hazrat-e Agha... came to legalize the marriage vows.

All the guests respected the arrival of Hazrat-e Agha... They got up. F... Al-saltaneh offered him a seat.

A quarter of an hour later, after consuming tea and hookah, its head and jar were made of silver by the masters of Isfahan. Hazrat-e Agha.. and F... Al-Saltaneh went inside the mansion.

A few minutes later, a shiny black carriage, which was tied to two strong horses, stood in front of the garden and Siavash Mirza got it off.

The prince was wearing a black coat and a blackberry color tie, shiny black shoes, and holding a short whip. Mohammad Taqi, who was sitting next to the coachman, immediately jumped down while looking down at the other servants with contempt. He was proud of being Siavash Mirza's servant and stood behind his master. Siavash Mirza came among the guests and without greeting each of the attendees properly, with arrogance and pride that is specific to some princes, went to the assembly and sat where Hazrat-e Agha ... sat a quarter of an hour ago.

Hassan Qoli and Reza Qoli, who were competing with each other, now took trays from the kitchen and kept bringing juices, tea, and ice cream in front of the groom to flatter, and get a good gratuity.

Prince K ... who was sitting among a group of old men was ashamed of the boy's behavior. He got up and came to him, and rebuked him because of ignoring the guests. But Siavash ignored his father's warnings and shrugged. He called one of his comrades among the guests and talked to him loudly and the sound of his mad laughter rose in the garden courtyard.

The prince told his friend about the pleasure he had taken in one of the famous houses a few nights ago, and even though his friend reminded him that the time and place were not suitable for these words, he did not keep quiet and added with a smile:

"What's wrong, I have not committed myself to anyone, and neither can my father force me to stop doing these things!"

Siavash was busy with these boastings for a while and the guests were busy with their conversations.

A quarter of an hour later, Reza Qoli was running towards F .. Al-Saltaneh, and as soon as he saw Mahin's father, said a few words to his master's ear. F... Al-Saltaneh's face turned pale, jumped out of his chair, and went inside. The engagement room was crowded and the ladies were pushing each other, and everyone wanted to go inside, and they were all staring at one point. *What has happened?*

***

In a room, decorated for the ceremony, Mahin sat on the crown of a pearl-embroidered cashmere shawl in front of a large mirror.

Mahin's condition was getting worse minute by minute. Her complexion became yellow every moment. Gradually, the yellowish of her face reached a point where all the make-up that tire-woman used to decorate her face disappeared. Mahin wondered how she would live with a man other than Farrokh. If she was not successful in taking her life, how would she live with someone else? Thinking that the prince would embrace her, made her shake violently, and doubts about the success of her plan increased the girl's fear. Suddenly a voice arose and a woman said:

"Hazrat Agha came and he is in the side room."

After that, a short silence was established in that mansion, and Mahin was tormented by shouting, especially the dry and meaningless laughter of women. A moment later she heard two men representing her and the prince, were reading Arabic phrases and exchanging questions and answers: Then the voice of one of them came out loud and after saying a few Arabic words addressed Mahin and asked:

"Madam, is it acceptable?"

Mahin did not answer, the girl was unable to answer. The unfortunate Mahin was so unconscious and so anxious that it was as if she no longer had a tongue to speak.

The man repeated the question louder. This time Mahin heard a woman buzzing in her ear like a fly:

"Dear, A lady must sacrifice everything for her reputation. Even if the husband is a demon, she must not make Hazrat Agha... to wait."

Mahin did not see herself with the ability to turn back and see the speaker of these sentences. The girl seemed to have lost all her will and her senses and was completely disabled.

The man raised his voice again, asking her to accept. But the girl could not get rid of her drunkenness and lethargy like sleep, and with dull and motionless eyes she looked at her face in the mirror in front of her and continued to be silent.

Suddenly, her mother, who was in another room and had heard the news of Mahin refusing to say yes, rushed into the ceremony room and, seeing the mocking face of the guests, went to her daughter, pinched her, and said firmly:

"Why don't you answer?"

As if the effect of the pinch caused a strong flame in Mahin's senses, she screamed and unconsciously fell to the ground and hit everything around her with her hands and her feet.

The women who were standing in the room immediately gathered around her, and when they saw the girl being severely attacked, each of them tried to prevent her from making difficult movements. People around her could not stop her. She kicked hard with her feet and hands, and hit everyone. Mahin was shaking.

Hazrat-e Agha... and his friend, who heard these sounds in the other room, guessed the matter, but because they had seen such frequent events, they calmly waited... *This incident was not new to them, and what effect could these events have on both of them? Most of them would not pay attention to the satisfaction of both man and woman, which is the first condition of marriage. They were after twenty-five Tomans fees. They did not consider themselves responsible for this vital matter.*

The handkerchiefs soaked in cold water, the vinegar and thatch kept close to the girl's nose but did not work. Mahin's attack intensified every moment, and her screams grew louder every time. Eventually, as there was no way out, several young maids lifted Mahin from the room with great difficulty and took her to her room, and placed her on the bed.

The engagement ceremony was in disarray. The guests were all standing in the corridor, each in a corner of the room, commenting on the incident, and meaningful glances were exchanged between them.
Malek Taj was sitting on the floor in her daughter's room and was crying.

F... Al-Saltaneh, who had been informed of this by Reza Qoli, came in with anxieties and saw the guests in the corridor of the complex. He went to his daughter's room and once his wife saw him, raised her voice and cried loudly. He went straight to the doctor, who was a close friend and one of the guests, took his hand and brought him in, and on the way, he briefly recounted what had happened, and then they went to Mahin's bedside.

F... Al-Saltaneh, despite all his worries, did not refrain from watching beautiful women who, as a result of this incident, no longer thought of covering themselves.

The doctor first asked the guests to leave the room and leave him alone with Mahin, then ordered them to strike Mahin in the face with a cold water towel.

Little by little, Mahin calmed down, and once his delicate body, which was tired and incapacitated by all the movements, because the inanimate statue lay on the bed. He turned around and said:
"The attack was severe. Fortunately, it calmed down. Today's ceremony is no longer possible, and the guests should leave. In addition, there is something else ..."

F... Al-Saltaneh was very sad that the engagement was broken and at the same time, he was more worried about what the doctor would say.

The doctor said a few words slowly in the F... Al-Saltaneh's ear.

F .. Al-Saltanah's face was pale, turned red and he asked in shock: "Are you sure that you are not wrong?"

The doctor looked around and when he saw that the room was empty, he answered in a soft voice:

"No, No. Be sure, your daughter is pregnant!"

Chapter Thirty-Three
How Farrokh Finds A Way To Save Javad From Prison

Farrokh, who had run out of energy, had a high fever as he did not know those around him and was delirium. His maid was overwhelmed by the plight of the boy. She stayed by his bed for a while and tears welled up in her eyes, asked Baba Haidar to go bring their family doctor who had come to treat Effat in the past.

The doctor, who was one of Farrokh's friends, came an hour later and when he arrived, he was surprised, especially his high fever and delirium, and asked the maid what happened:

The maid, who did not understand anything from the recent events, had no answer and did not know what reason to give for Farrokh's illness then Baba Haidar said:

"The truth is that in the last one or two months, the gentleman was very thoughtful and sad, and last night he wrote several letters and one of them was sent today, and he was extremely disappointed after reading the answer to the letter I brought."

The maid acknowledged Baba's explanations, then she said in a thin voice: "Yes, yes, he is right, sir, he has been very sad for the last two or three months, but he has not told us anything about it.

The doctor knew what he needed to know, and after examining the patient's heartbeat, he was convinced that the fever was temporary, resulting in fatigue and mental weakness, so he instructed them not to allow anyone to come or visit him, because the slightest will aggravate his illness. Then he prescribed some painkillers and gave the necessary instructions and promised to come again early in the morning to examine the patient.

That night Farrokh was feeling better, just had a fever and occasionally was moaning. The next morning, the doctor came to see him. This time, Farrokh was better, and as he knew the doctor, and in response to a question from the doctor about his condition, he was able to answer: "My head still hurts a little but nothing." The doctor urged him to rest and advised him to continue taking the medication he had given him. The next day, the doctor came to see Farrokh again. This time, the young man had recovered more and his fever had stopped. The doctor sat on Farrokh's bed for a while and talked to him. He added that such fevers often occur due to mental fatigue and hearing bad news, I know both have happened to you!

Farrokh took a deep and sad look at the doctor's face and answered in a weak and impressive voice:
"Doctor, you guessed it right, my illness is the result of the incompatibility of the times and people!"

And since he did not want to narrate all his inner pains, he raised the issue of Javad and said:
"I had a young servant who was arrested, and he has been imprisoned for over three months due to the unjust accusations made against him. He was also sentenced to one hundred lashes, which will be executed in two days."

Although the doctor realized that such a thing should not be the only reason for Farrokh's distress, he did not insist and uttered a few words about his surprise at this incident and called such events disgraceful.
"Farrokh, if the only reason for your sorrow and mental fatigue is that I know a way to save him, a friend of mine was dealing with the same matter a while ago, I hope it will be useful in this case as well."
Farrokh was happy and did not notice the doctor's sarcasm and asked:
"What that way is, and what are the means?"

The doctor explained that a few months ago, a robbery took place in the neighbor's house of one of his friends, Mohammad Hassan Khan, whom Farrokh also knew, and a precious rug was lost. He claimed the importance of that rug as an old and expensive, that an American doctor had even offered him three hundred Tomans but he was not willing to sell it. Nazmieh summoned his servant and he did not confess since was innocent. But they were stubborn and was thinking the poor servant was to be blamed for stealing it. They put him in prison so that he would finally have to confess to a crime he did not commit!

Mohammad Hassan Khan, who was very interested in his servant, could not get him out of prison, until the servant's mother, who was Mohammad Hassan Khan's maid, was crying days and nights. One day she went to see a clergy and told her story in despair. The influential mullahs who felt sorry for his unfortunate mother, wrote a letter to the head of Nazmieh, and to point out that the imprisonment and harassment of that servant caused a severe impact on his family but also the defeat of Hazrat-e Agha.
Muharrar Agha also prepared a hard paper from Hazrat-e Agha..., the head of Nazmieh, and Hazrat-e Agha... sealed it, and a few lines went along the edge of his blessed line, and by composing his own words and using a few Arabic words, Baris Nazmieh understood the matter correctly!

The head of Nazmieh, who feared that if he did not do what Hazrat-e Agha... wanted, his position would be shaken. So he wrote back that the innocence of the servant has been proven and he was released.
Then the doctor paused and after a moment added:

"In my opinion, if you want, you may use this way to help your servant."
But Farrokh, who was listening carefully to the whole story, shook his head
and said in a mocking tone:
"Do you think that I am the maid of Mohammad Hassan Khan and I am
also willing to sit in the house of Hazrat-e Agha... or I am one of those people who would change religion in the blink of an eye?
"My friend, you do not need to go there yourself, you can ask his amanuensis, but Hazrat-e Agha... has to send such a letter with his signature, and
communicate with them in their language!.."

Farrokh was convinced by the doctor's explanation and a smile appeared
on the corner of his mouth. Then Farrokh called Haidar Baba and asked
him to go to Hazrat Agha's house and ask the amanuensis to come to see
him the same day in the early evening for an important task. Baba Haidar
went to deliver Farrokh's request The doctor also said goodbye and took
Farrokh's hand when he left and wished him success.

An hour later, Baba Haidar returned and reported that Hazrat Agha's
amanuensis had promised that he would come in the evening, and about
two hours into the evening, Sheikh Mohammad Karim fulfilled his vow.

Mr. Sheikh had a tall body, a tawny face, gray beard hairs, and a bunch
of hair under his chin. Farrokh welcomed him in a room without a chair or
a table. Haidar Baba brought some tea and hookah,
"The purpose of meeting you was because Javad, my servant, who was devoted to Hazrat-e Agha..., has been held by the irreligious agents for some
time and he is suffering. I wanted to see if Hazrat-e Agha... would kindly
take action to save Javad as he did for Mohammad Hassan Khan's servant?"
Then he added:
"Of course, I know this is a lot to ask and you have to convince Hazrat-e
Agha ... to send a hand-written letter to Nazmieh. This is why I especially
ask you to help me put an end to this injustice and finally release my servant
from the clutches of executioners."

Mr. Sheikh Mohammad Karim, who listened carefully to him, first
straightened his chest, coughed, asked God for forgiveness several times,
and then said:
"I did not know that such a problem had happened to you. Of course, action
must be taken for this oppressed person as soon as possible, but you know
better than anyone that writing such a letter is beyond the scope of me, and
when necessary, Hazrat-e Agha... would write with his blessed handwriting,
but the only action that comes out of this humble claimant is to convey the
content to the holy Hazrat-e Agha... I am aware of the course of the orders,
injuries, and persecutions that these government officials have inflicted on
these miserable and helpless Muslims without any reason, so I will do my

best to convince them of his blessed existence."

Farrokh confirmed what Mr. Sheikh had said and asked him to inform Hazrat-e Agha... of the case of Javad. Mr. Sheikh Mohammad Karim stayed for a few more minutes and drank the third cup of tea and then got up and said with a laugh:

"However, I must say that if this oppression had not been committed with such heinous acts, I would not have the honor of meeting you!"

***

Farrokh spent the night with disturbing thoughts that Mahin's engagement ceremony had taken place. This thought fills his heart with sorrow. But he consoled himself:

"Even if she marries, I will not give up on her and she will finally return to me, but for now, I must use all my strength to save and release Javad."

Although he had hoped to hear the news from Hazrat-e Agha... but was skeptical, considering his recent series of failures, he became more disappointed and often asked himself:

'Will Hazrat-e Agha... be willing to write the necessary advice to Nazmieh and finally, this unfortunate servant will be freed.'

The next morning, at about two o'clock in the afternoon, they knocked on the door of the house. Baba Haidar, who opened the door, saw Sheikh Mohammad Karim in the alley. He entered the house without asking any more questions and while he was saying Ya Allah, Halloo! He was hitting the ground hard with his long cane and walked straight towards the living room. Farrokh, who was reading a book, put the book aside at the sound of Mr. Sheikh's footsteps.

Mr. Sheikh Mohammad Karim greeted loudly and like someone who has not seen his old acquaintance for many years, first asked about Farrokh's mood several times and then inquired about the health of his father and other relatives. Farrokh, who wanted to know the result of Mr. Sheikh's actions as soon as possible, gave short answers and hardly hid his impatience with these inappropriate questions. Finally, the compliments of Mr. Sheikh Mohammad Karim ended and Farrokh was able to ask:

"Well, God willing, you persuaded Hazrat-e Agha... to write to the head of Nazmieh?"

Mr. Sheikh Mohammad Karim coughed and counted with all his might like a child who is returning the lesson he has just learned:

"Of course, so that you can rest, I knew last night that we would succeed. Because of the level of benevolence and altruism of Hazrat-e Agha... who is the manifestation of the sun and there is no room for doubt and it was certain that he will never be willing to see any Muslims at the hands of these Godless agents of Nazmieh, let alone the servant of Your Excellency. I have to say, when Hazrat Agha... heard this, he was so moved that tears welled up in his eyes, and he expressed their desire to fulfill the request of Your Excellency, which I must say was, in fact, the soul of the pious and following his holy intentions. There were talks about your father and Hazrat-e Agha... said in his blessed wording that 'he is my son' whatever he asks of me, it is as if my son asked for it. It is my duty to fulfill this request and to say why they left us unaware that servant has been caught in the clutches of these atheists, for so long."

Farrokh was very happy with the words of Mr. Sheikh and in his heart was complementing Hazrat-e Agha... and his good intentions, and he even blamed himself for the ideas and theories that he had in his heart about this class, and for rebuking them for their beliefs.

Sheikh Mohammad Karim continued:

"You do not know, Hazrat Agha... has a good heart and endures the hardships and especially the expenses of the many children he has around them. God willing, he has five married and concubine wives, and fourteen children, from infants to adult men in their thirties. It costs a lot of money to maintain the household, although the income of real estate, shops, and religious transactions of Hazrat-e Agha is good, it is still not enough to cover everything, as I am often the mediator of Agha's debts, and especially these days when more expenses have been incurred. You may have heard that one of his sons is going to get married and also there are a lot of expenses to provide for his daughter's dowry!"

Farrokh, who did not see the connection between these events and the issue of Javad's release, became impatient.

"Although Hazrat-e Agha... as soon as he moves the pen on the paper and writes a few lines of advice, it is possible for any of the nobles, even if they are not literate, to take any position at the will of the commander, as one of them did some time ago. The head of the State Customs Translation Office of Azerbaijan was appointed and another gentleman was appointed as the deputy director of ... in Kerman just a few days ago..."

Farrokh could not bear it any longer and interrupted the amanuensis and said:

"Sir, these words have nothing to do with my work."

Mr. Sheikh gave a meaningful look to Farrokh and when he realized that the young man did not understand what he meant, this time he said more bluntly:

"Well, Hazrat-e Agha... thought that you, who is like his son, might be able

to alleviate the troubles that have naturally been caused by his son's marriage, and take some burden off of his shoulders."
Farrokh who he did not understand fully what he meant, promised warmly:
"Of course, I will not refuse any help that comes from me, Hazrat Agha... rest assured, I will do my best."

Mr. Sheikh Mohammad Karim smiled to his lips and said:
"I knew and I was sure that I would hear the same answer from your mouth, you are truly great. Fortunately, the expenses of Hazrat-e Agha's son's engagement ceremony are not much."
F arrokh was shocked to hear about the engagement expenses, but soon calmed down and asked calmly:
"Did you say that the expenses of Hazrat-e Agha...'s son or I did not hear correctly?"

Mr. Sheikh Mohammad Karim touched his beard with one hand, then with his other hand brought his turban up and down on his forehead, and finally explained:
"Yes, it is not too much, do not be confused, to buy a diamond ring, at least one hundred tomans is needed, and to prepare a dignified cashmere scarf that is worthy of the position of Hazrat-e Agha... eighty tomans should be calculated, the price of a mirror is forty to fifty tomans. The sweets and fruits of the ceremony also cost at least twenty-five tomans." He started to collect these amounts with his finger and said under his breath: "One hundred tomans and eighty tomans. Hundreds eighty. Plus fifty tomans. Two hundred and thirty tomans, and two hundred and fifty, yes... A total of three hundred tomans should be considered."
Then he paused and added:
"Of course, the effort of the caller to come and go will not be forgotten."

Then Mr. Sheikh, as if he had thrown everything in his bag, remained silent.
Farrokh, who was staring at him, asked after a moment:
"Excuse me, I'm not very familiar with these conversations, if you can clarify, let me see what you want from me?"
Mr. Sheikh Mohammad Karim scratched his beard again and answered with his head bowed:
"It's nothing, I do not expect much, some money for henna. The mother of my children and I would be grateful."
Farrokh, who had heard that henna money usually did not cost more than seven hundred dinars or a Qirans, did not understand the proportion of this small amount to Mr. Sheikh and his family. So to clarify the exact amount of the amanuensis demanded, he asked:
"Sir, I said that I am not familiar with such compliments and words, so

please tell me without hesitation what is the price of henna that I should be offered."

This time, it was the turn of Mr. Sheikh Mohammad Karim to be surprised by Farrokh's simplicity. Because assumed everyone would know that mediating such a matter, costs fifty to a hundred Tomans. But since there was no way out, and this time Mr. Sheikh had come across a newcomer, so he touched his beard with his hand, and replaced the turban a little. Then he played for a few seconds with the rosary of large seed in his hand and recited a few words of the prayer of forgiveness, and turned his eyes to the sky for a while and finally said as if he had found the necessary courage and boldness: "Your Excellency, you know better than anyone, I said, just a price of henna."

Farrokh was bored and was about to start talking and swearing when he heard Mr. Sheikh say:

"Yes. Henna's money is nothing. May your soul be healthy, one hundred tomans."

Farrokh jumped up and said in surprise:

"Four Hundred Tomans! Where can I get this money, paying the amount that you want for Hazrat-e Agha... and you want to provide me with the means to save my unfortunate servant is beyond my power and I can not make such an obligation and deal."

Hearing the word of the deal, Mr. Sheikh turned away and then said in a reprimanding tone:

"Dear sir, this is a good deed, please do not call it a transaction. If you want to say a transaction, at least do not forget its religious adjective! In this matter, only good intention is involved, Hazrat-e Agha... they have no interest in money, they spend their days and nights thinking about the hereafter, and all their prayers are only for this purpose, which may save a pavilion in heaven for himself!"

Farrokh was worried about the expression of Mr. Sheikh Mohammad Karim and tried to appease him:

"I did not mean that, but as I said, the problem is that I do not have such a large amount of money."

Mr. Sheikh Mohammad Karim played with his beard again, lowered his head for a while, and then looked at his nails, which were painted with henna, and finally said in a sympathetic tone:

"Young man, I feel you and I want to serve you anyway. Let me see how much you want to spend on this matter and how much you are willing to contribute to Hazrat-e Agha...'s son's wedding, and finally, what kind of henna do you want to give me?"

Farrokh did not know what to answer, he did not have much money for himself and he could hardly prepare fifty Tomans and turn it into five thousand golden coins and offer a bowl of rock candy to Hazrat-e Agha... so he had to say with embarrassment:

"What I can offer, of course, will not be worthy of Hazrat-e Agha... But if you allow me, I will prepare and offer fifty of five thousand golden coins."

Hearing fifty tomans, Mr. Sheikh took his cane, pressed the tip of it on the ground, and said 'God willing', took it high by the throat, and then, leaning on the stick of his hand, said it with protest:

"Very well, dear sir, I did not know that you are so unaware of everything. Hazrat-e Agha... is a religious man and would not desire to be involved with Nazmieh. I am also skeptical about the officials of Namzieh are atheists, and perhaps because they imprison and punish the unbelievers, their enemies give them these relations. Otherwise, they are up to bring security."

Farrokh was astonished by Mr. Sheikh's statements and thought how the humiliation of fifty Tomans people had caused such an immediate change in the opinion of Mr. Sheikh Mohammad Karim and how he, who spoke badly about Nazmieh's oppression, now stood up for that system and Supports operations against the humanity. Poor Farrokh did not believe that Agha did not have a belief at all!

Mr. Sheikh was on his way, and although Farrokh did not regret his departure and the deprivation of seeing that ugly look, he saw that with the departure of the amanuensis, Javad's imprisonment would continue. So he had to change his tone and appearance and shouted:

"Sir, where are you going; please, why did you offend?"

Farrokh knew that a glass of drinks and a hookah would relieve the bitterness, he called Baba Haidar and ordered both of them. Mr. Sheikh sat down and then complained:

"Sir, do yourself justice, you say do not make people angry and do not change, you have no place left to not be angry, the way you talk about four hundred Tomans as if you are dealing with these market traders. They swear falsely and in the end, they take the real price from the poor customer. This is how you bargain with me. Sir, I am not a businessman and I do not want to sell you ten tomans for fifty Tomans!"

Farrokh said:

"It is true, your words are accurate, but in the end, what can I do?"

Mr. Sheikh shook his head and said:

"This is the word of a person who has seen the world, and Mashallah, God willing, you are educated. Dear sir, if you go to any broker, he will immediately give you to ten thousand Tomans for you."

"Of course, you are right, but at least a guarantee is necessary and I do not have such a guarantee!"

Mr. Sheikh Baz shook his head and after a moment of thinking, he looked at the courtyard and the mansion and said with a smile:

"You act like you have a house in the Chaleh Maidan neighborhood or near Agha's grave, as if your whole house is not worth more than fifty tomans, God willing, you have such a big and beautiful house!"

This time, Farrokh soon realized that Sheikh was suggesting to pledge his house for these arrangements, but he was not willing to do so and was afraid that he would not be able to pay back on time. And his father was in his old age, but what can he do otherwise, Javad was still in prison, and if no action was taken, he might remain in that dark crypt for a long time."

So he made his decision and asked Mr. Sheikh:

"Tell me what I have to offer."

Mr. Sheikh thought for another moment as if he was making calculations in his head, then he said, "I do not want to be delayed in this matter. Hundred and fifty to present to Hazrat-e Agha... and fifty Tomans of mercy, and the work will be done, but do not say anything else which has no result."

Farrokh understood from the tone of the speech that this was his last offer, he did not say another word and with his silence, he promised to pay this amount.

"Honestly, I have not forgotten to say that if you want to make a deal with the government of Ark, come in the presence of Hazrat-e Agha... and be sure that we will arrange the right of notarization and writing a deed."

Farrokh accepted his offer and brought a humiliating bitter smile to the corner of his mouth.

When leaving Mr. Sheikh Mohammad Karim reminded Farrokh with all his might that the letter of Hazrat-e Agha... would not be sent until the amount was paid!

Well, it was thankful that the amanuensis demanded half of the amount, and it was clear such people would not be willing to fulfill their commitment before receiving the full amount. It seemed they were worried if Agha's letter reached its destination first and after the result was achieved, Farrokh would refuse to pay the rest of the money.
But would Farrokh do the same?

Chapter Thirty-Four
Where Deception Is More prevalent

After Mr. Sheikh Mohammad Karim left, Farrokh was puzzled for a while. He wanted to save Javad but could not pledge his father's house for it.

Farrokh had not been involved in this sort of arrangement before, he did not know who to talk to about it. His life was governed by the meager income of his father's retirement, and because they had lived a life of contentment, they had never needed such transactions before. Fortunately, he was not worried about owning a house because his father had given him property, the one they were living in. He asked Baba Haidar if he knew a broker.

An hour later Baba Haidar returned with someone called Mirza Reza. He was tall and slender, with a yellow face and small, sunken eyes, and was holding a large rosary. As soon as he arrived, raised his voice and sat down in a corner at Farrokh's invitation.

Farrokh said the following after a moment of silence:

"I need some money and I am willing to pledge a part of this house as collateral."

The broker, who was interested in the house, asked:

"You said a part of it, how did I not understand the purpose?"

Farrokh explained:

"Yes, because I do not need a lot of money, only two hundred Tomans are needed."

The broker did not like the number two hundred because he wanted Farrokh to need much more than that amount, so the chance of paying back could be lessened, said softly:

"Of course, many people in this city make such transactions, but the truth is that most of them do not want partial transactions. Two hundred Tomans of money is little. If I had the money myself, I would not wait for a second to solve your problem but for those who I am dealing with, this will not work. I would say that if you do not want to trade the entire property, you should benefit more for the party to the transaction."

Farrokh thanked him for his kind gesture and warned him to put aside the idea of pledging the entire house, but he did not say anything about the benefit which could be fair.

The dealer, in his explanation, said with complete pomp:

"It is in the transactions of customs and rules that is around from the time of

Adam and will remain in the world until the world ends! For example, from one hundred to five hundred Tomans, three hundred Dinars, and from five hundred to one thousand Tomans, one Abbasi, and from one thousand to ten thousand Tomans, three Shahis."

"With your explanation, I have to pay 300 dinars per month, this is too much," Farrokh said.

The broker immediately assured with flattery:

"Sir, I did not say anything against the norms. You might ask anyone, but because I have the will, I do not want anyone else to enter into this deal, otherwise, I should have said two Abbasi."

Farrokh was shocked to hear the word of the two Abbasis because he could not believe that such greed was common. And now that he is in need and deals with these people, he realizes how unjust traders benefit from the poor people. Now he understands why those who do not have a steady job and a regular income, and who are fired and unemployed every day due to the lust and ostentation of some ministers, are shouting at the tyranny of tax collectors, especially mortgage institutions, with which the permission of the Ministry of Public Works, It is made for the poor but in fact to tarnish the reputation of the people!

But because by comparing what he had heard, he saw that the broker was telling the truth and that others were even more demanding, he had to give his consent:

"Very well, I do not want to talk too much about this, please try to finish the deal in five Shahis."

Mirza Reza also rolled the rosary in his hand and once put it in his fist and said:

"I obey, I will serve you, but are you pledging all the six portions of the property?"

"You are an expert. This house costs more than three thousand Tomans, so, I think if we consider the loan for the money, it will be enough to pledge one portion of it," Farrokh said.

The broker moved his head in despair and said:

"No, no, no one is willing to take a portion as collateral."

Farrokh was convinced of his reasons but emphasized:

"I do not want more money, but if a deal less such is not possible, I do not see any obstacle for two portions to be traded."

The next morning, the broker came to him early and announced that Haji Agha, a resident of the same neighborhood who trades sheep skin and intestines, and is a theologian, had agreed with the deal and could go to Farrokh the same evening.

At the appointed time, along with the broker and Haji Agha, who was waiting outside, they went to Hazrat-e Agha…'s house, and as soon as they entered Hazrat Agha's house, the amanuensis came forward and flattered him without familiarizing himself with the subject. He acted as if they were old friends, and because the young man replied coldly that he had come to execute a deal. Sheikh took them to Hazrat-e Agha… and introduced Farrokh warmly and gently.

Agha was very happy to see Farrokh and showed that he knew him well and said to prove his special interest:

"Your late father was very familiar with me and came to see me in this room many times!"

Farrokh hardly refused to laugh, saying in his heart:

'The fact that Hazrat-e Agha… is very interested in me, poor thing, he still does not know if my father is alive or dead, and it is as a result of this kindness and mercy to my father that he asks his imaginary friend's son for two hundred Tomans to write a piece of letter. And without realizing why Farrokh needed money and decided to pledge his house.'

Hazrat-e Agha… said with apparent compassion:

" Indeed, when I heard from Mr. Sheikh Mohammad Karim that Godless agents unknowingly arrested your servant, who is devoted to me, I was so saddened that I asked Sheikh Mohammad Karim to write to the head of Nazmieh a few lines on my behalf, but what can I do that the accursed devil intervened again and did not allow and caused this poor Muslim so much pain in his hand that he could not even write a few words."

Then Hazrat-e Agha… exchanged a look with Sheikh Mohammad Karim and followed his statements:

"But be sure that tomorrow morning, whatever it is, he will write, and of course, I will add one or two words below it, and know for sure that if they fail to do what we want, I will immediately order the believers to destroy the whole mansion of that center of corruption, and burn it down!"

Sheikh Mohammad Karim, who was silent all the time, as if to alleviate the anger of Hazrat-e Agha… and change the subject:

"Sir, Mr. Farrokh is here for a deal."

This time it was Mirza Reza's turn to enter the battle. He also said in completing the statements: "Yes sir, he wants to make a brief deal with Haji Agha. He is going to collateral the two portions of his house for two hundred Tomans."

Hazrat-e Agha… fixed his eyes on Haji Agha's face and then Mirza Reza's face, turned to Farrokh and asked in a sarcastic tone: "Child, what do you want to do? Why do you need this money? Hope it's not the evil fantasies, do not trap yourself both in this world and in the Hereafter!"

Farrokh, who did not expect so much sarcasm and hypocrisy, was about to

lose consciousness and say what he had in his heart, but he thought again about Javad being imprisoned in a dark prison, so he answered gently:
"No Agha... there is no extravagance, rest assured, I need this money for the necessary matter"

Hazrat-e Agha ... showed no more curiosity and invited all to sit, and sat at the top of the assembly and the others sat around him on a faded carpet on their knees.

It was a large hall with three sash-shaped windows in the courtyard. The doors were all dark and old carvings were visible on them, and lines of fine plastering were visible around the ceiling. At the top of the hall, the skin of a brown lamb was spread out, and the rosary and prayer turbah, which belonged to Agha..., were in the corner of it. There was a small table with a black leather notebook, especially for taking notes of the deals.

Farrokh and Haji, the parties to the transaction, were sitting at the foot of the table next to the wall. Both parties agreed to the terms. Then Hazrat-e Agha... smiled and called Jafar Qoli, the servant, and ordered him to bring tea and hookah. And asked Haji to pay the fee.

Haji, viewed this deal with contempt, because he used to repeatedly trade several thousand Tomans, and of course, such a small and inShahis, did not turn into much in his pocket. He took out a back silky cloth from his cloak's pocket containing an old bundle of banknotes and broken and soldered money, and then counted every five Qirans and set them aside. It reached twenty. The voice of twenty-two, twenty-three rose, Farrokh wanted to protest and not accept the broken and soldered money, but the amanuensis, who saw his disgust, expressed:
"Sir, do not be upset, but you will also give them to someone else, how do you know that person does not accept these Qirans!"

Farrokh understood what he was saying and knew that Hazrat-e Agha... was used to taking such money, so he did not say anything anymore.

Eventually, the package was emptied, and since its contents were not more than forty-four Tomans, eight silver Qirans, and seven Shahis, Haji Agha first took thirty-three more Shahis from his dirty suede bag and completed the number forty-five Tomans. Counting the batch of torn banknotes that it turned out that he had saved for these transactions, he paid, but those banknotes that were all dirty and torn and most of them were stuck together with this cigarette paper did not cost more than one hundred and six Tomans, and finally, Haji calmly took out a small bag of cashmere with a tassel on its head from his the other pocket, and added ten or fifteen Ottoman lira and announced loudly: "The Ottoman Lira is less than five Tomans and two Qirans in the market today!" Then he made some calculations with himself and finally put eleven Lira on the banknotes and instead took a few silver coins, and completed the amount of two hundred Tomans in his account and the sum of the different currencies combined was in front of Farrokh.

At this time, Jafar Qoli brought tea. After drinking the tea, Hazrat-e Agha… turned his face and said:
"Very well, I will ask to write your deed for and will be ready by tomorrow."

Then everyone got up and Haji Agha said goodbye in front of the others under the pretext that he should go back to his shop as soon as possible.

Farrokh asked Hazrat-e Agha… for permission to leave, and outside the hall, he took out a relatively new three Toman note and put it in Mirza Reza's hand, but to his surprise, Mirza Reza pushed his hand back and said:
"Have!"

Farrokh, who was not familiar with these transactions and these words, and why the broker refused to accept the money.
"I did not understand what you meant?"
Mirz Reza, who looked at Farrokh with a mysterious look, replied:
"Sir, it seems that you have not made a deal yet, if you want to pay me, it is much more than that."

The young man was astonished and did not know what his demand was, and said to himself that this man only put two hours on work and that he was still not satisfied, even though he received fifteen Qirans per hour.
Then he asked loudly:
"Let me know what your rights are."
At this time, Sheikh Mohammad Karim approached Farrokh and whispered in his ear:
"Would you pay for the introductory part now?"
Farrokh pointed out that it would be better if they went to a small room.
Then he turned his face back to Mirza Reza and waited for his answer. The broker also said with great arrogance:
"This small deal is not worth these words. Everyone knows that the brokerage fee is ten Shahis, but since it has been traded for only two hundred Tomans, you have to pay ten Tomans."

Farrokh, who was tired of everything and was not ready to talk, even though he saw the broker's claim too much, wanted to surrender. But the amanuensis came between them'
"Comrade, you are being unfair. Customers like Mr. Farrokh should not be treated this way. Of course, ten Tomans are your right, but the parties to this transaction should play fair." Then told Farrokh,
"Please pay five Tomans, he will pray for you."

Farrokh obeyed and put five Tomans in Mirza Reza's hand, then in a small room he handed over one hundred Tomans of Haji Agha's money and asked the amanuensis to prepare the letter as soon as possible and deliver it with Hazrat-e Agha...'s signature, and especially reminded him to add a few extra lines of his handwriting!

Sheikh Mohammad Karim, who seemed his hand has completely recovered from last night's pain, warmly promised that the paper would be ready in two hours and that he would bring it to Farrokh himself before sending it to Nazmieh.

Farrokh went straight home and was very happy that at least he had succeeded in this task and he was sure that he had finally got the way and means of rescuing Javad from the clutches of the law enforcement officers.

Two hours later, Sheikh Mohammad Karim, as he had promised, came in person and presented the envelope containing the letter that he had prepared by Hazrat-e Agha... to the head of Nazmieh:

The Great Office of Nazmieh,

A young man of our relatives has been imprisoned for three months and according to the information received, relying on baseless and untrue statements from one of the people who is ignorant and denies the Hereafter, one of those who commit all kinds of sins and transgressions. They considered it an act of pride and arrogance for themselves to commit any heinous act and attribute it to an innocent young man. You have beaten that infallible miserable person in public with a hundred lashes, if of course you should have known and realized that in the Islamic country, the punishment and flogging of a Muslim should only be issued by the scholars and the religious, after the referendum from this respected class. And we are amazed how an unknown theologian and the known judge have committed such an unjust sentence and caused this great disrespect to our religion, and how you, too, should do your part to preserve the rites of the religion. You have blindly considered it necessary to obey such an oppressive and unlawful ruling.

Therefore, it is necessary to use this letter to compensate for the mistakes of the past, and to release the prisoner as soon as possible and provide him with satisfaction, and do not allow a moment to reflect on this act. Do not ignite our anger more than this, that its fire will take an infidel and a believer and burn the wet and the dry together.

It is not necessary to mention that if you are negligent in carrying out our order and delaying the release of the prisoner, we will report your office to the government that they should not allow the skirt of the Islamic world and Islamists to be tarnished anymore and they should not allow the humiliation the Muslim people more in front of the eyes of foreign nations.

...

Farrokh saw a few lines in the footnote written in very bad handwriting, which he could hardly read:

We also write these few words, especially in our handwriting, so you know the degree of our impression and our interest in this case. Of course, freeing the prisoner will happen in less than a minute, Do not reflect that our satisfaction has priority over everything else.

Farrokh liked the theme of the letter and thanked Sheikh Mohammad Karim. He also promised that if it was effective and Javad got out, he would pay another hundred tomans immediately.
The amanuensis assured that the letter will be sent immediately in a special envelope directly to the head of Nazmieh and Javad may be released by the evening of the same day.

After the departure of Sheikh, Farrokh felt relief as if a heavy burden had been lifted from his heart because he was sure that the slanders of F... Al-Saltaneh were suddenly against the threatening letter of Hazrat-e Agha...would collapse like cardboard palace, and the head of Nazmieh will immediately release Javad.
He remembered Mahin,
'How is she and has her engagement ceremony taken place and has she become fiance of the scoundrel Siavash or not?'

Farrokh wanted to be informed of Mahin's condition as soon as possible, but how?

Eventually, after thinking for a while, he thought of a way and went to the gardener of F... Al-Saltaneh, and if Shokoofeh was at home, to inquire about Mahin.

There was a lot of activity in the street at that time, men and women were moving from all sides, and private carriages and the rented ones with their beautiful horses and colorful glitter took the adorned passengers here and there. The people were taking advantage of the good autumn weather in Tehran and going around the city for fun and entertainment.
Farrokh waited for a while for a carriage that was empty of passengers, but there was no hope, so he became frustrated and decided to walk there. It was sunset, the air was getting darker. Farrokh did not realize that Reza Qoli, the servant of F... Al-Saltaneh was a hundred steps behind him.

Half an hour later, he arrived at the gardener's house and knocked on the door. The young man asked slowly:

"May I come to the hall?"

And when shokoofeh had lowered her head in agreement, he entered the house and stood in the small covered head that was behind the door, and then, with complete anxiety, asked her about Mahin.

But Shokoofeh, unlike in the past, who always mediated messages with a sweet smile and joy, had a sad look on her face and was shocked to hear Mahin's name.

Farrokh was more worried and asked with great concern:

"What happened, why are you hiding it from me?"

Shokoofeh responded:

"engagement ceremony did not take place"

Farrokh wanted to hug Shokoofeh out of happiness, but he heard the gardener's daughter say the following words:

"But Mahin became seriously ill again and was taken away to Shemiran."

Farrokh's heart collapsed at the news of Mahin's illness.

Chapter Thirty-Five
No matter how bold the traitor may appear in appearance, is shaken inwardly

If you remember, that day when Farrokh was disappointed and left the opium den, Ali Ashraf Khan had said with an evil laugh,

"What stupid ideas does the stupid boy have and what nonsense does he say, he thinks empty hands and without a supporter can act and succeed in this country against the will of the wealthy!"

Ali Ashraf Khan laughed for a while after Farrokh left and the threats of the young people were ridiculed. Of course, these words were new to him because he did not know anything about fairness and conscience, he had seen young people like him around and had not talked to them except for obscenities and illegitimate uses, and now suddenly for once At first, he knew an unknown young man who, although he thought a handful of empty words were coming out of his mouth, at the same time his words had caused him some discomfort.

The first ball of opium was brought to him, and was close to completion. Ali Ashraf Khan got high, called the coffee-house keeper, and ordered him to bring tea.

Effat's ex-husband who had a relatively luxurious life and slept on a mattress in his house under a satin quilt, now due to his addictions, without paying attention, with all interest was lying on the torn and dirty carpet of a smelly room He leaned his head on the stinking lice-filled pillow instead of the sturdy pillow he had in the house. He was imagining that the pipe looked like a precious jewel, and kept bringing his lips closer to it, and every time a thick smoke came out of his mouth and nostrils.

The coffee-house keeper soon returned and placed the black tea in front of his special customer. Ali Ashraf Khan drank the tea with great pleasure. Half an hour later, two half-mithqal balls of opium were burnt into his body and soul, and after a few cups of tea he drank in a row, his bitterness had disappeared. Then he got up and paid full with two Qirans extra, and went out of the room and passed through the yard. He put black money in a boy's hand and asked him to go out and inform him as soon as the alley was empty. Coincidentally, the alley was deserted at that time and Ali Ashraf's waiting period did not last long.

On that day, the Tehran irregular carriages movement was very compatible with Ali Ashraf Khan's mental and physical condition. An hour ago, he had shown composure and disregard for Farrokh's words, and the threats of the hero of our story had dealt with that humiliation and arrogance. Now, in the depths of his heart, he felt great anxiety and worry.

Ali Ashraf Khan, although he was sure that any complaint from ordinary people and any kind of trial that might be held against him, will end in the plaintiff's unrighteousness, he still thought that he could not get rid of Farrokh easily. 'If people hear what I have done to my wife's Effat and how shamefully I have kicked the daughter of a respectable family out of the house, everyone will surely turn away from me and no one will be willing to marry me." Of course, this situation hindered his plans because although he did not consider marriage and having a family necessary, but to gain an opportunity to occupy other important positions in the ministries. He was planning to get a new wife. He was not too worried about Farrokh because he knew that society would pay less attention to unknown young people like him, but since Farrokh talked about Effat's parents, that was alarming.

That night and a few days later, Ali Ashraf Khan spent it with great anxiety, and like a criminal who was waiting for the police to arrive and arrest him, he listened carefully to what was being said around him and watched the slightest movement of people in the bazaar with suspicion.
Finally, he decided to talk to his brother, Ali Reza Khan. He called him,
"I need to see you, it is important!"
His brother, worried about the way he spoke, replied:
"I have a group of guests, you can join us, come whenever you want."

Ali Ashraf Khan washed his face and wore a clean gray shirt, a blue tie, and black pants which had an ironed line very straight and sharp like a knife.

***

Ali Ashraf Khan got off a carriage and entered an alley in the middle of the bazaar. He walked a few steps, then knocked on the blue door, a servant opened the door, recognized him, bowed, and let him in.

Effat's ex-husband entered the yard and on the large and wide porch in front of the mansion hall, he saw several people sitting next to each other. Alireza Khan, who had got up, first introduced him to the guests and since most of them did not know his brother, described him: "Ali Ashraf Khan is acquainted with many officials and can do important things for us in time!"

Hearing this sentence, the guests looked at Ali Ashraf Khan with more curiosity, and he sat in a quiet corner without guessing the purpose of the gathering, and at the same time noticed one of the guests who was sitting next to his brother, whispered a few words to his brother, but he replied loudly:
"No, there is no problem, be sure that he is one of us, so we can follow all our negotiations freely."

When this assurance was given, a young man with a thick beard, in his early twenties, got up and first cleared his throat and then said in a loud voice: As I said, we are not here just for drinking tea and eating sweets, which shows the generosity of the home-owner, but we pursue a very high purpose and we have very high goals."

Hearing the sweets, Ali Ashraf Khan had not eaten anything except a few cups of strong tea in an opium den. A servant put a cup of tea and a container of sweets in front of him. He ate some sweets and listened more attentively to the young bearded man, who heard him say with warmth:
"The meaning and purpose of us, the youth of this country, who are the reserve force of this system and form the so-called intellectual class of this land, is to find a way for fundamental reforms in the country and not let this chaos continue any longer. And I am going to bring this issue to the attention of the public!"

The young man was very hot-tempered at the time of uttering these sentences, and he paused and pondered over each word so much that it was clear that the fire of his love and interest in reaching a position in the government would not be easily extinguished and he would be happy with a small job in one of the government departments with a monthly salary of thirty or forty Tomans, that will not satisfy his appetite.

Ali Ashraf Khan remembered his mission in Isfahan and was nostalgic and got lost in his thoughts and missed the last speech of the speaker. He heard a new voice, turned his head, the speaker looked like a thirty-five years man,
"I no longer need to introduce myself. What services I have done in the world of journalism, and enlightening the thoughts of the people that are evident to all gentlemen. Everyone knows how hard it is to include sweet anecdotes that also contain very delicate and meaningful points, that I have been preparing every week for the paper... and now I wanted to say a few words to the presence of the esteemed gentlemen. In confirmation of the words of our dear comrade Mr. B... I would like to convey to the esteemed guests that in the end there should be a way to reform. But it has to be fundamental and also practical. I must say plainly and simply that I have never agreed with

some inexperienced young people who are constantly breathing modernity and desiring to change our culture, customs, and traditions. They consider such a procedure as the best way to achieve progress and excellence in the country but I believe that modernity is a kind of revolutionary, and a wise man should avoid any revolution that may cause many troubles. One thing I do not believe in is modernity's ideas in regards to having one mistress, of course, according to the law and the Sharia, a man can have a new woman at any time, I too agree in this regard, and if I can afford, I will nor deprived myself, but we should not allow spreading of some other culture and habits that comes with modernity. The customs and habits of our ancestors can not be changed. How can we let such revolutionary and evil thoughts spread, and beat the pure souls of our ancestors and forefathers?

The speaker, who was called Mr. H..., showed a lot of fervor when expressing his thoughts and ideas, and made very ridiculous gestures with his hands and head. He continued his statements in this regard for a while, and at the end, he added:

"Finally, gentlemen, be fair. How can a person endure when seeing a group of men, presenting themselves as women in broad daylight in an Islamic country? We must prevent this. In my opinion, the reform of the country starts from here, and I am sure that if those who do these ugly things are stopped in time, the situation of the people will improve and the food will be plentiful, and as they say -bread will reach the people!"

Then, like a clockwork that has been opened to the end of its tuning, as if it had already poured out what it had in its pocket, sat down tired and helpless, and with the curious glances around him, it seemed as if he wanted to see the effect of eloquence and important points of its speech in the face of the audiences! But the sheik, who was among the guests and wore a small turban and was said to be the son of one of the Hazrat-e Aghas of Tehran, and was famous for imitating some voices, did not give many opportunities for Mr. H...'s curiosity. He immediately got up and with his loud voice broke the silence:

"I do not need to introduce myself anymore. All gentlemen are aware of my services in guiding the people, but above all, I must say to my esteemed friends that we should all be proud of an enlightened and righteous member, like Mr. H..., those precise points that he expressed, show nothing but his natural talent and his divine grace. We should not allow the slightest violation of our rights as men for the rest of our lives. I think we should run a secret ballot in this session, the minutes of the meeting should be recorded and left for the future and history, and the memories should never be forgotten, so I am asking permission from Mr. Alireza Khan, the esteemed chairman, to put this matter to vote."

Alireza Khan looked at the faces of the members, and when he saw every-one was silent and satisfied, he said:
"It turns out that all the gentlemen agree with this proposal, so the vote will be taken."
Then one of the younger spectators stood up and distributed small pieces of paper that had already been prepared. A quarter of an hour later, the votes were collected in a container on the table in front of Alireza Khan. Unanimous votes have been approved except in the case of marriage.
Then Alireza Khan got up and said:
"Tonight, when the assembly took an important step fairly and resolved a vital and great issue, there is not much to be said in this regard, but since the gentlemen declared their strong opinion and faith with their votes, I would like to say something about this important issue. Comrades, let me mention one more issue, which is to say a few words about the intimacy that prevails among the members of this community and is the best promise of our great progress and success in the future."
The audience listened carefully to the last sentence of the chief's statements. Ali Reza Khan followed his speech:
"I was a member of many assemblies that have been formed in Tehran since the beginning of the constitution, although all those communities had good faith and kindness towards me and did what they could to help, as I was appointed by the Qom Judiciary due to the pressure of the first popu-lation leaders. It was through membership in the Second Assembly that I was given a special mission as an auditor and earned large sums of money, but I must admit that unfortunately in all those assemblies there was a kind of constant fragmentation of opinions and ideas that hindered progress and often the suggestions of young members.

My opinions at that time were not taken into consideration and some older people objected to it, and the reason was that some awkward elements had penetrated between us and there were secret hands involved. A few young people were claiming that education and the information from Eu-rope and America, is good for the nation, but they would not consider that will cause a deadly poison in the minds of the workers, so they called all the young people inexperienced.

But today that we are expressing our interest in the life of our ancestors, I say those young people should not be allowed to put their new ideas into practice because those who went to school for a few days and claim to be lit-erate and educated, often have learned nothing but atheism, while illiterate people, if they have none, at least have a religion, and now, fortunately, I see in this assembly that none of these differences are between us. And those delusive ideas do not exist, that is, with the experience, we had from the beginning, we blocked the entrance to such people whose brains and minds were corrupted by reading stray books and seeing just the glamor of Europe and America, and a horizon of consensus and enlightenment among us prevents any disagreement and dialogues. Yes, and thank God none of us claim the new education!"

Then Alireza Khan turned to Sheikh to testify about this recent matter and said:
"Sir, except for a few days at St. Louis School, you did not go there except for a special occasion!
Then he turned to Mr. H... that storyteller with a thick beard:
"Your Excellency, it seems that your education horizon has not risen above the Mullabaji school!"
And finally, he turned his head towards that young bearded man:
"And you are the youngest, and frosh between us, I know that you were going to school every other day, and now that you are printing evening papers?"
The audience laughed at the word frosh.
After a moment, Ali Reza Khan continued his speech and this time turning his face to one of the audiences, who was wearing a yellowish-white turban and was said to be called the Cabinet shaker, said in an encouraging tone:
"Praise is to God, you no longer have any claims about literacy and education, and it is better that sometimes you are part of the market and sometimes the leader of the parties!"
Hearing this description, the yellowish-white-turban man shook his eyelids several times and added in completing the titles given by Ali Reza Khan:
"But do not forget that after my recent exile to Iraq, since I was with the former ministers, I also became one of the aristocrats!"

At the end of his speech, Ali Reza Khan once again mentioned the issue of consensus, and consensus of the members of the community and considered the same consensus that was reached a few minutes ago on this important issue as the best sign of the spirit of cooperation and intimacy between the members of the community. Suggested the end of the meeting.

For a while, the audience shook hands and everyone congratulated each other on joining such a united community.

Then Sheik, who was in charge of the meeting, stood up and announced:
"The next meeting will be held on Wednesday at two hours to the evening, in Mr. B...'s house, located at the end of the shoemakers market, and the

gentlemen please arrive on time."

The members got up and said goodbye one by one, and when the two brothers were finally left alone, Ali Reza Khan, who was the elder, said to his brother:

"I was very worried about what you said on the phone and I did not understand what you meant. What is the matter?"

Ali Ashraf Khan, who used to make the case of his separation with Effat a simple and normal thing for his brother and attributed the ugly slanders to her, now gave him more details and facts, and in the end, he was anxious. He added that the unknown young man came to see him and threatened him with severe punishment and infamy from his ex-wife's parents.

Ali Reza Khan, who listened carefully to his brother's words, did not show much surprise on his face, and it was clear from his composure that he had more or less done such things himself, so he asked his brother for an explanation:

"Very well, but you did not say how the young man threatened you and what tactic he used to scare you?"

Ali Ashraf Khan replied:

"Of course, his threats were general, but he firmly said that if I must ask you to release someone called Javad who is a prisoner in your branch, otherwise, Effat's parents will complain and disgrace me."

Ali Reza Khan shook his head and said:

"Javad's court has ended, he was sentenced to six months in prison and one hundred lashes. This person who threatened you. I think he is the accomplice!"

Then he pondered and said:

"Very well and I know what to do with him."

Ali Ashraf Khan, who had gained strength from his brother's expression, said: "But despite his name, I did not know him."

Ali Reza Khan asked:

"What did he say his name is?"

"Farrokh"

Then the interrogator added to calm his brother:

"Be calm, he can not take action against you and me, and he will not be able to do anything, he will not get the slightest result from this, because he has a bigger and stronger enemy than us, and that is F... Al-Saltaneh."

Although Ali Ashraf Khan knew who F... Al-Saltaneh is, but he did not understand what his brother had said and asked for more explanation.

"Well F... Al-Saltaneh was very interested in Javad's punishment and had forced a prominent member of the Ministry of Justice to issue Javad's sentence; he was the one who ordered Javad's conviction in court."

After a moment of reflection, said:

"In any case, it is necessary for us both to meet F... Al-Saltaneh as soon as possible to inform him of Farrokh's actions and endeavors for the salvation and liberation of Javad, so that he may give Farrokh another piece of advice if necessary put him in prison and let this bold and daring young man get rid of these empty thoughts and fantasies in those dark corners of the prison."

Ali Ashraf Khan liked his brother's suggestion and asked:

"When do you think we will meet F... Al-Saltaneh!"

Ali Reza Khan replied:

"We have to wait for now, because I need to go tomorrow for a local investigation about a crime and it may take a few days."

Ali Ashraf Khan did not say anything about this anymore, then they talked about family matters for a while. Then Ali Ashraf Khan asked his brother:

"Honestly, I did not understand this assembly's purpose!"

Ali Reza Khan replied with a smile:

"How can you not understand? Of course, there is no other purpose other than to make a profit. These people who you see have a position in this city and are useful, one is a journalist and supports me in time and curses the opponents. One comes from a politician family and he is the leader of the party during the elections, they garnered votes for me. The other is a salesman and comes from Bazaar, and when it is necessary, he would mess up the market to advance my work. And Mr. Sheikh is from the pulpit and is responsible for the necessary propaganda among the common people. But the funny and interesting part is that these people themselves have gathered around me to use me!"

Ali Ashraf Khan, who was unprecedented in these matters and provided the means for his success from other sources, remained in a state of confusion for a while, and then raised his head and congratulated his brother on having such a useful and valuable skill and accomplice, and then he added with full belief:

"Really, we do not have anything less from others to reach the high positions in this country?"

Chapter Thirty-Six
Where Farrokh's Madness Was Proven

As we have said, Siavash Mirza was talking to one of his comrades on the engagement day in the garden courtyard of F... Al-Saltaneh's house. He was talking about his habits when his friend mentioned that there is not a right place to talk about this stuff, Siavash Mirza said boldly and arbitrarily:
"I have not committed myself to anyone and I am not."
As we know, F... Al-Saltaneh, due to a few words that Reza Qoli had said to him, got up and went inside and after a few minutes, he returned and took the doctor with him.
The guests, except for one or two people who were sitting near Mahin's father. The others did not notice the commotion. The groom was talking loudly with his friend and wanted to explain how one of the sex-worker of Tehran had fallen in love with him.

Reza Qoli came out of the house for the second time, and this time he approached Prince K... and said a few words in his ear, prince's mood changed, and asked him curiously:
"Are you telling the truth?"
Reza Qoli lowered his head, Prince K... wanted to go inside and inquire about the bride, but thinking that the guests would notice and would make a scene, he remained in his chair. He was impatiently waiting for news, but gradually there was a whisper among the guests: "The bride is sick. Her uncontrollable jerking and shaking have been severe. The inner reception has been disrupted and no engagement has taken place."
Finally, whispers got to Siavash Mirza. He called Reza Qoli to know what was going on.
"Yes, sir, unfortunately, the lady had an attack and according to the doctor, it is no longer possible to carry on the ceremony today."
But Siavash Mirza calmly considered the news and shrugged his shoulders and said softly under his breath:
'It's too bad, today fell between two stools!'
Then he dismissed Reza Qoli, then without showing any interest in staying there anymore and waiting for the result of the doctor's treatment, he got up and said goodbye to the guest who was nearby and went to his father and said:
"There is nothing to do here today."

Prince K... was deeply saddened by the delay in performing the ceremony and also astonished at the strange behavior of his son, said firmly:
"Of course, you can not do anything to treat the bride, but your departure is not appropriate at this time, at least wait for some time until you hear the news of your future wife's recovery."

But Siavash Mirza smiled while shrugging his shoulders like consoling his father:
"Do not be anxious, there is nothing wrong with her, it must be the cold temperament, she will be fine, I have a lot of work to do and I can not waste any more time here!"

His father was familiar with the boy's morals and knew that more discussions with him would cause more noise and disgrace.
"Very well, so if you go, go quietly so that at least no one notices your departure."

Siavash went straight to the garden and got into a private carriage while Mohammad Taqi jumped up and sat next to the coachman.
"Mohammad Taqi, we can not waste the day, so far we missed the air, it is good to visit one of those houses."
"But going with this carriage will not end well, because they will ask for 30 Tomans instead of ten Tomans." Mohammad Taqi replied.
"You're right, we are going to walk when we get nearby."

The carriage guided by Mohammad Taqi passed through Marizkhaneh Street and Toopkhaneh Square, passed Cheragh Bargh Street, and finally stopped at Qajar street.

They walked and entered a house. The courtyard was small. It had short, long, and ugly walls, the arches of which had been whitewashed with plaster, but most of the plaster crust had collapsed and stains like baldness appeared on the walls and was mixed with the mud on the roof due to the rain.

The prince who was sitting in the lush garden half an hour ago, with was shocked to see the dirty condition of that house and said to Mohammad Taqi in a reprimanding tone:
"It's so messy here!"
Mohammad Taqi overlook and show Siavash Mirza a picture of a beautiful woman and said in a convincing tone:
"Sometimes sacrifice is necessary for something like this!"
The prince did not say another word and spent the drunkard night in a woman's arm there.

When they went back home the next morning, his father was walking outside the mansion. Prince K... was very upset and worried about the cancellation of the engagement ceremony, which he had prepared with all his might, and also because his son had not come home last night. He kept asking himself:

'Why did this happen? Where is this boy? Why did he not come home last night?'

As soon as he saw Siavash, although he was happy to see the boy, he asked him in anger: "Where were you? You did not know that your mother and I would be worried?"

This time, Siavash seemed to have lost his courage. He could not answer, then Mohammad Taqi bowed and said,

"Sir, yesterday, when we left F... Al-Saltaneh's house, Siavash Mirza was so upset so I suggested going to one of the gardens outside the city to cheer him up."

Prince K..., who knew that Mohammad Taqi was lying, interrupted him and said violently:

"I did not ask you anything."

Then he pointed to Siavash to follow him and as soon as he moved closer, he said gently to him: " I want to go and greet Mahin right now, I think you should come with me."

Siavash rejected his father due to tiredness but promised he would go in the evening, and then he turned his back on his father and went to his room, fell on the bed immediately to relieve last night's fatigue.

It was noon, when Prince K... had returned from F... Al-Saltaneh's house, he said to his son, who had just woken up, that Mahin's condition had not changed yet and the doctor had stated she would not recover soon. Siavash did not say a word.

His father continued:

"In any case, you are the groom, and visit your father-in-law's house as soon as possible to greet the bride,"

Siavash promised that would go that evening or tomorrow.

About two hours before sunset, Siavash went to F... Al-Saltaneh's house, his father-in-law was walking around the mansion, smiled when he saw Siavash, and said kindly:

"What a delight you come here?"

Siavash greeted and remained silent, then came to his senses after a few moments and inquired about Mahin with a few broken words.

F... Al-Saltaneh replied with a false calmness to reassure the grieving groom: "There is nothing major, but because the doctor had prescribed fresh air, I sent her to Shemiran in our private garden in Jafarabad. My Mrs has gone with her so as not to be alone. And of course, I will inform her that you came, and I am sure she will be very happy."

Then he changed the subject and spoke of the mild weather, but as if he could not get rid of his inner discomfort, in the meantime he attacked the servant and cursed him for delaying in bringing the tea, then to keep himself busy, suggested to Siavash that if he wanted, they should go to the room and play backgammon.

Siavash did not notice much about his fiancé's father's distress, but since he liked gambling, accepted the offer with great interest. The servant had not yet brought the backgammon when Reza Qoli brought two name cards on a small tray and presented them to his master.

F... Al-Saltaneh picked up the cards and read to both of them aloud. Ali Ashraf Khan and Ali Reza Khan. He knew Ali Ashraf Khan but at that time he was not in a mood to meet a person like him, asked:

"Did you say that I am home?"

And when Reza Qoli lowered his head F... Al-Saltaneh frowned, "There is no choice, tell them to come in."

A few seconds later, Ali Reza Khan and Ali Ashraf Khan came in. F... Al-Saltaneh got up and shook hands with them and introduced Siavash Mirza, "It seems these gentlemen do not know each other, Siavash Mirza, the son of Prince K... and my future son-in-law."

Hearing the names of Siavash and his father and that he is the future son-in-law, the voice of Mashallah and bless rose from the mouths of Ali Reza Khan and Ali Ashraf Khan. Then F... Al-Saltaneh told Siavash, "Mr. Ali Ashraf Khan is an old friend and I am very devoted to him."

Then referring to Ali Reza Khan, he added:

"This gentleman must be his brother since they are lookalike."

This time it was Ali Ashraf Khan's turn to introduce his brother, so he said in a husky voice:

"Your Excellency's guess is completely correct. Mr. Ali Reza Khan is my brother and the interrogator of the sixth branch of the justice department."

Then Alireza Khan completed the introduction, he explained:

"I have not had the honor of meeting Your Excellency, I have always been among your sincere and indirect servants, and I think Mr. M... who is in the Ministry of Justice has spoken about me to you, and of course, it has reached you that that man was also sentenced to six months in prison and one hundred lashes in court, and this punishment was to be carried within two days."

F... Al-Saltaneh heard Ali Reza Khan's flattering statements and seemed to have forgotten the moment of inner anxiety and worry he had about Mahin. He look at Khan and said warmly:

"You are very, very welcome. You do not know how happy I am to meet you and how much I thank you. Yes, yes, Mr. M... talked to me many times about you. Yesterday, the punishment of that bastard, about whom, in my opinion, the court was very merciful and gave a low sentence, was carried out in Toopkhaneh square, but unfortunately, due to my daughter's engagement ceremony, which was also unfortunately disrupted, was not able to see the punishment of the bastard. I could not find time to at least pass through there in the carriage and watch it from afar."

Ali Ashraf Khan realized the great interest of F... Al-Saltaneh on monitoring Javad's punishment, so interrupted him, and said flatteringly:

"Fortunately, I was blessed with this. Yesterday, when I went to the bazaar, I saw a large crowd in Toopkhaneh Square in front of Nazmieh Mansion, and heard someone was being flogged!"

Then he pondered and, like someone who wants to visualize, added in a husky voice:

"It was spectacular, especially when a woman came out of the audience and ran towards the convict and was crying while shouting, -He is my son, he is my son, It turns out that last week my dream was true."

Ali Ashraf thought for a moment again, then continued his story:

"But sir, the cleverness and agility of one of the agents who astonished all the spectators, he silenced her voice with a rifle by hitting the old woman's side in time and did not allow the assembly to be disturbed."

F... Al-Saltaneh listened to Ali Ashraf Khan's words with all his heart, he was so happy and smiling that he had forgotten the pure sorrow and grief he had in his heart due to Mahin's illness!

Ali Ashraf Khan, who needed the help of F... Al-Saltaneh to get rid of Farrokh's threats, now by knowing his desire to know about how Javad was flogged, continued:

"But the most ridiculous and spectacular of all was when a hundred lashes were over and the hands and feet of this wicked man were untied from the stool as a cloth or rug hung on a wall with nails, and once his nails were cut, he fell hard to the ground and all the people laughed. It turned out to me that it is completely unfair to say that the people of Tehran are tasteless and do not like to watch shows!"

F... Al-Saltaneh, who was still staring at Ali Ashraf Khan, asked:

"I did not understand what you meant, but how was Javad?"

"No, the victim was completely unconscious and more like a dead body."

F... Al-Saltaneh, who had been laughing put on a serious look, and said philosophically:

"We see how strong the hand of God's revenge is. Some say the deeds of human beings are not punishable in this world, while in my opinion, punishments of sins all happen in this world, and soon!"

Ali Ashraf Khan, who still did not want to give up poor Javad, continued to follow the case to the delight of Mahin's father: "As I saw him, he is sure to be sent to the infirmary for a while, and unfortunately, not to a dark prison."

F... Al-Saltaneh was not happy with that part of the story, "It is late now but tomorrow I will ask the head of Nazmieh to transfer him back to a dark prison again."
Then a few minutes passed in silence and finally Ali Reza Khan asked:
"You said that the ceremony was not done yesterday, what happened?"

F... Al-Saltaneh looked sad, "Yes, yes, yesterday, was the engagement of my dear daughter and Prince Siavash Mirza, but unfortunately, an attack was carried out on my daughter and she needed complete rest so the ceremony is delayed for a while."

Ali Reza Khan stood up and moved closer to F... Al-Saltaneh said in his ear: "Well we came here to discuss a matter with you about someone who has caused all of these."
Then Ali Reza Khan pondered.

F... Al-Saltaneh understood the reason for his actions and said loudly to re-assure them: "There is no problem, please, Siavash Mirza is my son-in-law and like my son."

At this time, Ali Ashraf Khan stepped forward and explained:
"Some time ago, a young man came to my house and started saying a se-ries of strange things without any introduction, including my recent job in Isfahan and other details of my life. Of course, I did not know the person but he was serious about the threat. I could not understand, so I asked him for an explanation, and he, without the slightest empathy, like a person who says the truth and the facts, and breathes in the obvious, said rude things, and then threatened me, and finally, he added that he would disgrace me."

F... Al-Saltaneh was very interested in the words of Ali Ashraf Khan, and commented with full conviction:
"He must be crazy?"

Ali Ashraf Khan also confirmed Mahin's father's theory and continued his statements:
"Certainly, such a person must be crazy, otherwise how can he come to peo-ple's homes without knowing them and make accusations; At first, I wanted to call the servants to take him and hand him over to the authorities, but the truth is that he was ridiculous and audible because of what he was say-ing, and importantly he was giving those strange proportions to me with a strange courage. I was so interested and with great curiosity, I wanted to understand his ultimate purpose. He said if I do not want to be ashamed and disgraced, I must accept his offer. Then, when I was laughing in my

heart, I asked him what he wanted. I noticed that despite all his threats, he was insane, I showed composure again and asked him: 'Well, what will you do if I do not do this?' This time, instead of him telling me what he wanted, he attributed it to the servant and started shouting, he kept saying that he would announce what he knew about me in all the newspapers so that the whole city could read it, and would let the public know about it."

F... Al-Saltaneh listened attentively and asked:
"And despite all these ugly words and proportions, you remained silent and listened to and tolerated everything he said?"

Ali Ashraf Khan replied:
"As I said, I intended to understand his main purpose, so while I was mocking him in my heart, I expressed some concern falsely and then I said to him, 'With all these, don't you know that it is not possible to prove these slanders without having a document, and on the contrary, repeating these baseless words will cause you trouble!' Hearing this remark, he laughed strangely, which was a definite sign of his madness, and then he brought a sloppy paper out of his pocket and read it to me with complete confidence: 'This is your line and you will be condemned with the same paper.' I was frightened and trembling while acknowledging what he had said: 'What do you want me to do?' This time he came to the position of explanation and stated: 'He means what he said, which means that I have to force my brother to free the innocent Javad whose case came under his control.' -"

Hearing the name of Javad, F... Al-Saltaneh, who had guessed that the person must be Farrokh, said in his heart, and when he was sure that the young man who had referred to Ali Ashraf Khan and looked crazy was Farrokh, he sighed and had a moment of silence.

At this time, Siavash Mirza, who remained silent for a few minutes and listened carefully to Ali Ashraf Khan's remarks, joined the conversation and turned to his father-in-law and said in a low and trembling voice:
"If you allow me, I will tell you a story about this person."
F... Al-Saltaneh turned his head towards the prince and said with all his interest: "Of course. Of course, my dear groom, tell me what else this madman has done?"
Then Siavash, with a lot of stuttering and confusing sloppy sentences, narrated his own story: "This person was introduced to me about a week ago by a friend, and we sat together in a cafe for an hour and ate ice cream. Half an hour later we got up, said goodbye to each other outside the cafe,

and each of us went home. Now imagine the unbelievable. To my surprise and astonishment, a young man who met me for a few hours had such an imaginary story and such a strange request."
Then Siavash Mirza reached into his pocket and took out a piece of paper from an envelope and handed it to F... Al-Saltaneh.
"This is the letter he wrote to me."

F... Al-Saltaneh hurriedly took Farrokh's paper from her son-in-law and read it quickly, and without paying much attention to the part that Farrokh explained about saving Siavash from Nahid's house, he paid more attention to the last part of the letter and understood Farrokh's request. And laughed out loud. He passed the letter to Ali Reza Khan but advised him to read the last part, which was more interesting.
Ali Reza Khan quickly reviewed the letter and then gave it to his brother Ali Ashraf Khan, then they all laughed at Farrokh for a while and at the end, Ali Ashraf Khan asked Siavash:
"Well, what was your reply?"
Siavash replied:
"Could I write anything other than telling him he is crazy?"
Everyone praised the intelligence and taste of His Highness and unanimously liked the answer, and all three of them, while hiding their inner concern laughed!

Maybe if Farrokh himself was between them at that moment and heard those crazy laughs, he would have given them the right to make such a judgment about him because he believed that he has gone crazy; he has never known such hypocrisy and would not imagine this degree of lies and hypocrisy among human beings.

Chapter Thirty-Seven
The Last Meetings

"Mahin became seriously ill again and was taken away to Shemiran."

Farrokh was very distressed and worried after hearing the news of Mahin's illness. And because he did not consider it appropriate to stay there for a long time, he wanted to leave sooner.
"Is Mahin alone in Shemiran?"
Shokoofeh replied:
"No, her mother is there too, but she occasionally comes to the city to shop."

Farrokh, who had been deprived of Mahin's visit for almost three months, was thought as soon as Javad got released, he would go to Shemiran to visit her. He was thinking to rent a place in Jafarabad, near the garden of F... al-Saltaneh, and when the Malek Taj goes out, by whatever means possible; If it is for a breath, it will be worth it to see Mahin's beautiful face.
Farrokh, amid these thoughts and plans, was walking towards his house at the Hassanabad crossroads. Several gendarmes were walking around a group of rags, and the officer on horseback was walking in front of them. Farrokh became curious about those miserable people and asked one of the passersby:
"Who are these people, what have they done and where are they going?"
The passerby happened to know more about those poor people than Farrokh, replied in surprise:
"Sir, if you have not read the newspapers, these are some of the prisoners in the north who are going to Kalat."
Farrokh was heartbroken by their mourning and his heart was pressed hard by seeing their torn and dirty clothes and their suffering faces and he said to himself: 'Certainly, the ambitious and rebellious person has used these misfortune people as a tool in his hand and wanted to achieve his ill intentions with the help of these poor people.' He cursed the laws and customs for giving power and property of people to one person and allowing a selfish and tyrannical person to sacrifice the life and existence of the people to alleviate his low and material desires.

Farrokh arrived home. His maid ran to him and threw her arms around him and hugged the young man and while the tears of happiness were falling from her eyes, he said:
"Praise is to God, sir, I was scared you will be harmed."
Farrokh laughed at the maid's thoughts and said to reassure her:
"Well, now you see that nothing has happened, you will not think about it again!"
But the maid lowered her head in amazement and whispered:
"I did not understand the meaning of my anxiety!"

The next morning when Farrokh was eating breakfast and thinking about how he was going to meet Mahin, the door was slammed open. Baba Haidar went to open the door, and Mr. Sheikh Mohammad Karim, as someone familiar with the family, walked towards Farrokh's room.
Farrokh saw him through the glass door, he guessed that he had come to get the remaining 100 Tomans, but thought it was too soon to hear news about Javad.

A minute later, Sheikh Mohammad Karim, without getting permission, went to Farrokh's room and after a short greeting, he addressed the issue with a cheerful and happy face:
"Praise be to God that the prisoner was saved from the unbelievers."
Farrokh, who did not believe, asked happily:
"How, but I have not seen him yet?"
Mr. Sheikh Mohammad Karim explained to reassure him:
"No, no. Rest assured, yesterday evening, I took the letter myself. Fortunately, the head of Nazmieh was in the office, and after learning about the content of the letter, he became very anxious, and he repeatedly asked why he had not yet been informed about this case, why we did not tell him the prisoner is a relative of Hazrat-e Agha... and he immediately summoned the head of the prison and became very violent. The head of the prison, who defended himself said that the prisoner was the one as Mr. F... Al-Saltaneh had personally recommended to the head of Nazmieh and demanded his severe punishment. But the head of Nazmieh was not satisfied with his explanations and his anger did not subside so he ordered angrily: 'Go and release him immediately.' Then we went together with the head of the prison to the infirmary where Javad was, but because Javad was still very ill after the lashes he had received, it was not possible to take him out of there last night but they were supposed to send him home this morning."
Mr. Sheikh continued his statements,
"This morning, I went to the prison infirmary again. He was a little better,

I told him how Hazrat-e Agha... found out about his suituation by you and acted on it. We put the poor young man in a carriage, which was provided to us by the head of Nazmieh. The poor young man was not feeling well, however, I took him to his house.
Farrokh asked:
"Can I be completely sure that Javad is with his mother and sister now?"
Mr. Sheikh looked at him reproachfully and replied warmly:
"Sir, you have the right, if you still do not believe, I swear."
But Farrokh stopped him and confidently told Mr. Sheikh that Javad had finally been freed, and paid him another hundred Tomans.

Mr. Sheikh Mohammad Karim counted the money one by one with greed and craving, and when he was sure of the amount, he placed it in the side pocket of his robe and then drank a cup of tea, and after a moment, got up and said a warm goodbye to Farrokh then repeat several times:
"Sir, do not forget us anymore, we are always ready to serve, and whenever something happens, of course, please let us know."

Farrokh made the promise and because he was happy with the success of Javad's freedom, he thought about Mahin and said to himself with great hope:
'Javad was saved. Mahin's engagement was disrupted. God is with me and has not taken the grace away from me!'
Then he thought of going to see Javad as soon as possible. He passed through the bazaar and several long and short alleys and turned several times. Finally, he reached Javad's house, the address that Javad had previously given to him, and knocked on the door. After a while, Javad's brother's wife opened the door, Farrokh said his name and asked her to tell Javad that he had come to see him, a few minutes later the woman returned and invited Farrokh to enter the house.
It was a very small courtyard, the only building on the north side, and like other houses in the neighborhood, it did not have more than two rooms, which were built at a height of one and a half meters above the ground on two damp basements, which were considered kitchens and water storage. On a part of the roof, two smaller rooms were in the form of an attic, and Javad and his family lived in the attic. There was a round basin in the middle of the yard, which was half empty and the rest was filled with green water, most of which was covered with soap scum and other debris that gave off a foul odor.
Farrokh lowered his head, following Javad's brother's wife, and at the corner of the corridor, they climbed a narrow staircase with crooked stairs and broken bricks to the roof. There was a pack of beds wrapped in a filthy

night tent leaned against the wall, exposing the uneven floor of the rest of the room. Farrokh's eyes spot a thin, lifeless man who was lying and moaning on a torn quilt. He barely recognizes Javad. Three months ago, when he met him, Javad was helpless but healthy. But now his eyes were sunken and the bones of his face were prominent. The unfortunate servant could barely open his eyes and could hardly move. During his imprisonment, the humid atmosphere of the prison and the lack of light made him suffer from rheumatism and deafness, and worst of all, his body was severely injured due to lashes.

Farrokh called his name several times. Eventually, the young man shook his head and turned his head towards Farrokh.
"Did you hire me to endure these sufferings and pains?"
At that moment, Javad's mother came in through the door and brought a bowl of medicine that she had prepared for Javad. She said with a tone full of sorrow of accusers:
"Sir, this is how you took good care of my son?"

The voice of the poor mother who uttered this small sentence had a painful effect on Farrokh. The young heart suddenly caught fire, as if it wanted to split. Tears welled up in his eyes and without being able to answer, he came to Javad's quilt and gently lifted his head from the piece of cloth whose cotton had come out of its many holes and placed it on his knees, then with great regret, and with great difficulty said to him:
"I'm not to blame, I did what I could. But the enemy was strong."

Javad's mother, who realizes Farrokh's innocence, misery, and helplessness, deeply affected by it, no longer hurts his heart with more reproachful words.

Farrokh stayed there for an hour and asked Javad questions about what he had left during his stay in prison and the hardships he endured in that dark prison. Javad gave short as answers as he could. Farrokh wanted to turn to the other side, but this time Farrokh's eyes fell on his back and he was upset because he saw his whole body was injured and was bloody.
Farrokh saw a great change in his spirit as if he were no longer the former man, and at once all his altruistic feelings were extinguished and were roaring, said in his heart:
'If human beings are so cruel to their kind, why should I and others like me not follow them? We must follow the same procedure and punish them.'

A strange lightning flashed from the young man's eyes at that moment, and that bright light and the angry voice that was muffled in his throat were like lightning and thunder, which promised a vengeance.
Eventually, Farrokh got up and said goodbye to Javad and his family and promised that they will pay back soon.

Along the way, Javad's miserable condition did not go away from Farrokh's mind. He remembered his weak and lifeless eyes and injured body, which made him angrier, and the thought of revenge became stronger in his mind. But the more he thought about it, the less he saw the means to accomplish that.

When he got home, he asked his maid for his travel bags and what he needed, such as a comb, a towel, and a toothbrush, and prepared himself for the departure that evening.

It was not the best time to go to Shemiran, its popular season was over. Most of the people of Tehran would spend the summer in that beautiful scenery on the slopes of Alborz Mountain. Before heading there, Farrokh thought of visiting Ahmad Ali Khan and Effat, both of whom he had not seen for some time. After lunch, he took a carriage and went to the courier-house and narrated the recent events to Ahmad Ali Khan, and gave the good news of Javad's release. Ahmad Ali Khan, who listened to him carefully, was very sorry when he heard that his friend had to pledge his house for two hundred Tomans. Then he thought for a moment, then said:

"Well, what can I say? That is the only way, in this country, it is not possible for anyone to succeed, except through pressure, orders or money. Only with these means can everything be achieved and the path of progress and development will be easier. Unfortunately, everything revolves around money here, and without money no success!"

Then Farrokh said goodbye to Ahmad Ali Khan by informing him that he is going to visit Mahin in Shemiran.

***

The servant who was close to the door guided him to the building. Farrokh sat on a chair for a few minutes, Effat hurriedly came and happily greet him. She was staring at Farrokh, and noticed his tired and pale face and sunken eyes and asked with concern but Farrokh used his brief illness as an excuse. But of course, she did not believe it and she dared to ask about Mahin. Farrokh gave a short answer:

"To be honest, I do not have any good news."

Then he added:

"I am going to Shemiran to rest for some time, but did not want to leave you without saying goodbye to you."

Effat did not show any more curiosity and thanked Farrokh and changed the subject and asked about Javad.

In response, Farrokh said:

"Unfortunately, that person refused to help and despite all the dishonesty and unscrupulousness he had done to you, he did not want to at least compensate with such a brief help. Maybe that would have been better, though, because if he had not withheld this little help from me, he would not have been prosecuted and punished. Such a person deserves severe revenge!"

Effat asked:

"Do you manage to free him in another way?"

Farrokh shook his head impressively and said:

"Yes, he was finally released after three months of imprisonment and one hundred lashes."

Effat was very affected and tears welled up in her eyes. Farrokh was silent for a few moments, then he got up and while sending many greetings to Effat's parents, he said goodbye and went home. Effat accompanied him to the threshold of the room, and felt a strange state as soon as Farrokh left. She remained thoughtful and silent for a moment. It was as if an inner feeling was telling her that she would not see him again soon. She wanted to make a noise and prevent Farrokh from leaving, but she realized that it was in vain. Eventually, the young man left the big garden door, and as he disappeared, the heart of Effat squeezed hard, and tears fell from his squinting eyes, and she thought to herself:

'What is happening to me, what are these thoughts and fantasies?'

Farrokh went home. The rays of the autumn sun were fading every moment. He thought to himself that the later he gets to Shemiran, the better. No one would see him in the middle of the road. So as soon as he entered the house, he took his handbag. He hurried out of the house.

It was getting dark. There were not many passersby on Shemiran Road. Farrokh was deeply immersed in his thoughts and did not notice Reza Qoli, who was following him. He had now reached Shemiran Street, and was still slowly waiting for the empty carriage, and he passed the three-lane road of Shemiran. But he had not yet walked a few steps on the main road when he heard the footsteps of horses behind him. Then he turned and saw two gendarmes hitting hard on the side of their horses with their feet, and advancing rapidly, and as soon as they approached him, they both said commandingly:

"Stop."

Farrokh looked up without any anxiety and asked with complete confidence:

"Did you have anything to do with me?" Then one of the two gendarmes said dryly:

"Yes, sir, we have been on duty since this morning and we have an order to

arrest someone with the description that matches you."
This time Farrokh sighed in surprise and asked angrily:
"I do not understand what you mean?"
Immediately, the gendarme jumped down from the horse and, while pulling his pistol from his waist and holding it towards Farrokh, explained calmly:
"We intend that you, without making a fuss, follow us to the chief, he will tell you more details himself."
Farrokh did not lose himself and asked:
"Who is the chief and why should I come, you must have made a mistake."
But the gendarmes laughed together and said:
"No, no, no mistake, the addresses are correct and you are the person we are arresting."

Immediately, the other gendarme got off the horse and both of them surrounded Farrokh while holding their pistols. No one was in the neighborhood. It was quiet. The slightest footsteps could be heard. Farrokh was astonished and did not understand what they meant, moreover, he saw that the resistance with two armed gendarmes was ineffective. Suddenly, in the darkness, he felt the gendarme standing behind him hold him from behind and took off his hat and put a light object on his head instead, and at the same time the other gendarme stripped him and put on a shirt made of coarse cloth that they had untied from their horse.

Farrokh was not surprised by the gendarmes, but he was delighted, because he was convinced that the two gendarmes were hungry agents who, instead of catching the thief, they are seeking money. So was assuming that the gendarmes had not been paid for several months. He said nothing and did not protest, waiting to be released after that. But he soon realized that this was not true. Because the gendarmes tied his hands behind his head, and then one of them ordered:
"Go ahead and move silently."
The gendarmes jumped on the backs of their horses and pointed their pistols at Farrokh. There was no more talk. Farrokh did not understand this at all and had to walk toward the city with them. But at the intersection, instead of going to Darvazeh Dawlat, they went to the Shemiran's ditch, which was deserted. There was no point in shouting. Farrokh was thinking that it would be better to reach their chief and ask him for an explanation.

Chapter Thirty-Eight
The Four Villains Exploration

At the house of F... Al-Saltaneh, four people discussed Farrokh's madness. "I think you all agree with me that no matter how a madman seems harmless, there is no guarantee that he will stay away from causing danger. So I think you should try to repeal it and not let it repeat such ugly jokes with others!" F... Al-Saltaneh said.

All of them understood the purpose of F... Al-Saltaneh said that he wanted to harm Farrokh severely, and that was the truth. Because of F... Al-Saltaneh, after learning of Mahin's condition, his resentment against Farrokh has been multiplied. He wanted to remove the young man from the face of the earth.

Except for Ali Reza Khan, he did not have a special and direct interest in this work. The others liked his theory and showed their great enthusiasm and desire to accomplish such a goal. Of course, F... Al-Saltaneh imagined that he would avenge her daughter from Farrokh, and Ali Ashraf Khan considered it necessary to deprive Farrokh of his peace of mind. What did he hope for in this way? Siavash Mirza used the letter he received a few days from his savior as an excuse and unknowingly signed Farrokh's death sentence. He also was one of those people who enjoyed seeing the suffering and humiliation of others.

The three of them thought for a few minutes and each of them set out to destroy Farrokh. The public execution on the gallows came up, but they feared its consequence, they discarded the thoughts. So each sought to find a way that would not pose such a danger to them. The prison sentence and an exile order were not punishments that quenched the wrath of F... Al-Saltaneh. He wanted to find a means to destroy Farrokh completely, or at least not give him another opportunity to express himself in Tehran and Iran. Suddenly Siavash Mirza raised his head and said:

"I think there is a way and if it is done, we can easily and quietly eliminate this voyeuristic and pretentious young man and he will not cause us any trouble."

Others pay attention to the prince's plan. Siavash Mirza, seeing their attention explained his whole plan in detail:

"Coincidentally, yesterday, a friend with whom I have known since child-hood wrote me a card from Qazvin, saying that he was going to Tehran and that he had a mission to take some of the northern insurgents, who had been entrusted to him, to Mashhad and hand them over to local agents, so they will be sent to Kalat. I think if we can arrest Farrokh and send him with the insurgents, we can carry out this plan, it will be the best way to get rid of him in this way. Either he dies of the intensity of suffering and discomfort in the middle of the road or if he reaches Kalat, he will have a hard time in the infamous castle without being able to make a statement and no one will pay attention to what he says."

Everyone found the prince's offer remarkable and agreed with a nod and smiles on the corners of their lips.

Siavash also said:

"But, of course, the implementation of this plan is subject to the fact that I have to see my friend, and share the matter with him, and get his words to help and accompany us."

F... Al-Saltaneh was a hurry to implement this plan, he said:

"He must have arrived in Tehran now."

Siavash confirmed with a nod.

"According to what he wrote, they should arrive in Tehran tonight, and he will definitely see me in the morning, and of course, I will discuss the matter with him as soon as he comes."

Then Ali Ashraf Khan suggested:

"In this case, Farrokh should be monitored as soon as possible, if we are de-termined to carry out this plan, there will be no more problems and we can easily kidnap him and throw him among the prisoners."

F... Al-Saltaneh liked this theory, so he immediately called Reza Qoli and ordered him:

"Now you go near Farrokh's house without him and the family realizing that you are investigating whether he is at home or not. If he is at home, you will stay around, and whenever he comes out of the house, you will follow him and see where he is going, and only at the end of the night, when you are sure that he has gone home to sleep and rest, you go home too. But you have to go there again early in the morning and watch his movements until I instruct you again."

Reza Qoli bowed and went out the door.

The next moment, Ali Ashraf Khan and Ali Reza Khan, followed by Sia-vash Mirza, got up and said goodbye. They decided to gather again tomor-row after Siavash's friend agreed to accompany and help them so they could study the details of the plan and how to complete and silently implement it.

F... Al-Saltaneh kept thinking for a while, then got up and walked in the room several times, and occasionally smiled and whispered to himself:

'What evil has the bad boy done to my daughter? By doing so, he can take possession of her. What an inept idea. He does not know that I am not one of those people who have such feelings!'

He spent the beginning of the night with disturbing thoughts, and at about four o'clock in the morning, when he was ready to go to bed, Reza Qoli went inside the building and sent a message to him by a maid that he had an important message. F... Al-Saltaneh had not yet gone to bed, summoned him, and asked him about his mission.

"When I got close to Farrokh's house, I realized he had been home for more than a few hours and never seen him leaving the house, so I sat in the shoe store next to the grocery store and looked at the house from a distance. First, a sheik left the house, and half an hour later, Farrokh, who had a smile on the corner of his mouth, came out of the house and searched for the carriage for a while. Without realizing it, I was walking a hundred steps behind him until we finally reached the crossroads of Agha Sheikh Hadi and Farrokh stood in front of your gardener's house ...

F... Al-Saltaneh interrupted Reza Qoli and asked in surprise:

"In my gardener's house!"

Reza Qoli replied:

"Yes, sir."

F... Al-Saltaneh shook his head:

"Of course, I guess, it must have Shokoofeh."

Reza Qoli nodded and followed up with his explanations:

"My lord, because I was far away, I could not hear what they were saying to each other, but I saw that Farrokh entered the yard and came out after some minutes."

F... Al-Saltaneh thought for a moment, then raised his head and said to himself:

'Now I understand who leaked the news of Mahin's trip to Qom!'

Then, while screaming with anger and rage, he ordered Reza Qoli:

"Very well, you go to sleep for now, but early in the morning, go around Farrokh's house again and carefully consider all of his movements."

F... Al-Saltaneh spent the whole night with horrible dreams. Early in the morning, he sent one of the servants to bring Shokoofeh. The gardener's daughter, who knew that Mahin and Malek Taj were in Shemiran, was very surprised that the gentleman had summoned her and asked herself with concern:

'What happened that he wants to see me!'

Inevitably, she went there with fear and trembling, and as soon as she entered the mansion, went to F... Al-Saltaneh office, bowed and stood silently in a corner.

F... Al-Saltaneh raised his head and looked at the gardener's daughter with a fixed gaze for a while. Then, like a bomb exploding, he suddenly asked:

"What was this bastard act you were doing during this time?"

Shokoofeh became very anxious and stammered so much that she was unable to answer:

"What ... what ... you say ..."

F... Al-Saltaneh again said with full intensity:

"Tell me, what does Farrokh have to do with you when he comes to your house?"

Shokoofeh wanted to deny it, but she realized from the tone and appearance of F... Al-Saltaneh that his words were not just speculation and he was convinced that they had seen Farrokh coming to their house, lowered her head, and remained silent.

F... Al-Saltaneh was getting angrier at every moment, this time asked with intensity:

"Why did Farrokh come to your house yesterday and what did he want from you?"

Shokoofeh, who was very scared thought to herself that there was no denying it and that it would be better if she told the truth, so she answered again with a stutter and a trembling voice:

"He did not ask me for anything, he only asked about Mahin."

F... Al-Saltaneh mockingly said:

"Of course, you have to tell me how many times you have been feeding him information?"

Shokoofeh thought that Mahin's father knew nothing about their meetings, just wanted to try to see if there is anything more.

"I had not seen him except yesterday. I did not want to let him enter the house. Because it is a blemish for a girl, he insisted so much that I had to accept but they left after a few minutes."

The calm tone of the girl seemed to ignite the fire and wrath of F... Al-Saltaneh, "Bastard, are you lying to me now?"

And immediately a hard slap hit the poor girl:

"I know you informed Farrokh about Mahin's trip to Qom and you, your father, caused my daughter's misfortune, now you deny it."

The girl could not stand it any longer, and because she had trembled so much from the fear, she suddenly fell to the ground and explained all she knew.

*What is this law in nature that man sees the suffering and misery of others with indiffer-
ence but the slightest pain and boredom of his children with sorrow? We are the same in
form and structure but why do human beings not consider happiness for each other and do
not pay attention to one of the secrets of creation.*

The girl remained under the feet of F... Al-Saltaneh for two or three minutes, and showered her with the rain of insults and curses. They tried to save
that unfortunate girl from the clutches of that ruthless master. But he did not
give up and continued to punch and kick her body as she continue to shout:
"I must send your father to Nazmieh so that he dies in their prison."

Finally, the maids dragged the girl out of the room and the girl was free
from his fists and kicks. Someone would say, 'Why did you pry and why did
you answer, sir?' Another rebuked him for interfering in what the master
did not want. The third was reminded with all his might and warmth unless
you did not know that the gentleman is right even if he kills us too! Because
we are servants of this house and in the end, we should not go against him!

The poor ignorant girl did not know that the little money and bread that
F... Al-Saltaneh gives in return for the hard work and suffering that he im-
poses on them, and why he does not give a Toman to others.

Meanwhile, one of the older women said to the joy and relief of the girl:
"Do not cry, no matter how much he hits us, he is still a gentleman. I was
beaten several times by his hands, in return, you will receive a good gratuity
and I want to be in your place!"

Shokoofeh was still crying and moaning in pain, and the promise of a
reward from F... Al-Saltaneh did not make her happy. Her only consolation
was that she went through this because of Mahin, that good-hearted girl.

The anger and wrath of F... Al-Saltaneh did not subside only to punish
the girl. He had found the savage animal trapped in an iron cage. He used
to harass and because he could not easily find a suitable victim, he kept kicking and cursing the earth, the sky, and all the people of the world, calling
the whole city ignorant and stupid and calling his servants bastards and his
maids prostitutes.

No one dared approach him. Finally, at about two o'clock in the afternoon, one of the servants, who knows his master's reputation, entered the
mansion and entered the room with fear and trembling, and bowed and
announced that the gentlemen had arrived

Hearing this news, and especially in the hope that Farrokh's severe punishment would be ordered soon, the anger of F... Al-Saltaneh subsided to some
extent, and order his servant:

"All right, go, take the gentlemen to the reception room so that I can come
to join him."

A few minutes later, Mahin's father hurried to the room. Ali Reza Khan and Ali Ashraf Khan were sitting in the room and waiting for him, short compliments were exchanged, then F... Al-Saltaneh said:
"Siavash Mirza has not come yet and has not called and I do not know if he has concluded or not?"
At that moment, the sound of a carriage wheel was heard, which stopped in front of the mansion, and immediately Siavash Mirza and the gendarmerie officer sitting next to him came down from it and headed towards the mansion.

The official had a large black face and a turned nose and military ranks on his collar. Siavash Mirza introduced him as Nayeb Jalal Khan, one of his old friends who came from Qazvin.
All three guessed that the deputy was the same official who was in charge of taking the prisoners to Kalat.
Then Siavash Mirzar explained to F... Al-Saltaneh:
"Last night, I talked to the Deputy Chief of Staff about this issue, and he is willing to fulfill our request."

F... Al-Saltaneh smiled and said:
"Thank you very much, surely Siavash Mirza has told you what we want, we are serving the community and we want to eliminate the dangerous element, what else can I say about the great crimes this person has committed. Each of his crimes is enough to sentence him to life imprisonment, even his execution!"
Then he pointed to Ali Ashraf Khan and said:
"What accusations did he not give to this honorable man? The language is incapable of repeating them. He sent a letter to me about the future son-in-law, Siavash Mirza, whom you know well, and the unreasonable requests about my daughter, which is shameful, and I am sure it is not possible for an honorable person to even think about it, let alone write it."

Nayeb Jalal Khan was considered one of the top names and had a high hand in this work of flattery and service so this was not new to him. Although he was thinking that if this case worked out the way F... Al-Saltaneh wanted to benefit from his blessings later in the year, or when necessary, he would help him to raise his rank.
"Your Excellency. all of this has been narrated to me, and before you say anything, I have promised to do what I can to repel such a dangerous and harmful person, but of course, now that I am in your service and with what I heard from you I became more determined than before, and at this very moment, I have ordered my two gendarmes to monitor him and, if possible, to arrest him tonight, if the opportunity arises."

F... Al-Saltaneh was extremely pleased with the compliments and flattery, and especially the explicit promise of the deputy gendarme,
"Are those insurgents in Tehran now?"
Deputy Jalal Khan replied:
"No, they got moved to Mashhad earlier today, and since I had some work to do and a family visit, I will be going after them with four gendarmes later."
Then he described the order in which he thought of arresting Farrokh.
F... Al-Saltaneh liked that way and it was as if he had suddenly forgotten the bitter times of a few hours ago. Then he called a servant to bring sweets and watermelons.

An hour later, they brought a tray full of various fruits, all of which were arranged in beautiful dishes in the best style, and among them were slices of rosy watermelon with green and yellow melons.
Ali Ashraf Khan took a slice of sweet melon and ate it with the desire to eliminate the bitterness in his mouth then asked F... Al-Saltaneh:
"It is a great melon, can you tell me where it was bought from?"
F... Al-Saltaneh looked at the fruits with complete disregard then looked at him in surprise and then said with a broken breath:
"It was not purchased in the bazaar, it belongs to our private garden in Malekabad located southwest of Tehran."
Ali Reza Khan, followed his brother and put a piece of melon in his mouth,
"A few years ago, when the same property belonged to Mr. S... a famous businessman, there was an opportunity. I ate their melon, but I swear to you that it had no taste and I can not compare it to this melon, this is without a doubt it must be believed that the name also has an effect, note that since the day the name of His Excellency was placed on this property, everything has changed and even its melons has become sweeter! I did not believe in this sort of thing until now, but I must say that now I have a strong faith in it."
F... Al-Saltaneh was more pleased with these words of Ali Reza Khan, and he was very proud of himself.

Chapter Thirty-Nine
How did Farrokh find out that Hazrat-e Agha... was not so unjust in calling government officials Godless!

It was about five o'clock in the morning; it was still dark. Close to a humble village building on the side of the road, similar to the service coffee houses, and under the vast sky while the stars disappeared one by one, a group of people was lying next to each other like a flock of sheep. One of them held a stone under his head like a soft pillow, and the other chose a relatively flat, barren ground instead of a mattress. Two gendarmes, each with a gun, were walking around to prevent them from escaping.
"The deputy has not arrived yet, he was supposed to be here at this hour."
The other gendarme imitated him and replied loudly to his comrade:
"He will come and until then we can not move from here."
It was cold, and as the morning approached, a gusty breeze began to blow. These miserable and poor people were exposed to such cold weather without an overcoat, and they were subjected to all kinds of hardships, humiliations, and suffering.

Why? Because a law passed by a powerful group had imposed such a punishment on them. Why? Because these unfortunates were not fortunate enough to be born with a silver spoon in their mouth and in a blessed environment. One day they opened their mouths and complained about their miserable life, and protested against the interests of influential and wealthy people.

In the daylight of early morning, the sound of wheels came from afar, and a quarter of an hour later a carriage stopped in front of the insurgents. Four gendarmes were riding around the carriage, and one of them was pulling a horse. The detainees had woken up. Then, four gendarmes got off the horses and one of them opened the carriage and a young official came down. The two gendarmes who were in charge of the prisoners saw the officer shouting and hitting the bottom of the gun, and ordered the prisoners to pay their respects to Jalal Khan! The official, without stopping the two gendarmes from committing these barbaric gestures, first greeted them and turned his face towards the prisoners, rebuking them in a harsh tone and saying ugly, things and then mocking them all,

"I have brought a happy madman as a gift for you to make you laugh a little from time to time, he speaks very well and makes strange claims!"

He then pointed to the gendarmes who were still standing next to the carriage. The prisoners, out of curiosity, wanted to find out what the official intended to do. They saw a twenty-two to a twenty-three-year-old man who came out of the carriage with a very sad face and stood among the gendarmes. His face was pale and there were many traces of sadness on his face. Like the other prisoners, he wore coarse cloth. As soon as he saw his future comrades, he was stunned for a moment and looked at their situation, and then he shook his head as if he understood the quality of life that lies ahead, and he was there to endure any suffering and hardship.

***

Farrokh hoped that the gendarmes would not only realize their mistake once he spoke to their chief but would also try to appease and apologize to him. He did not know that he was arrested because of their chief Nayeb Jalal Khan's order. When they arrived at Shemiran gate, Farrokh paused but heard two gendarmes unanimously ordering him:
"Go behind the ditch!"

It was so dark, Farrokh could barely see his feet. At that moment, in this part of the city, which was mostly desert, there was no pedestrians at the gate of Dushan Tappeh. He had to walk behind the ditch towards Dolab Gate. Farrokh was getting tired, but because he still hoped that they would eventually reach the house of the official, and when he talked to him, it would be clear that the gendarmes were wrong, he endured this difficult situation.

In front of the Dolab gate, the gendarmes reminded him that he should continue to go to the Khorasan gate. Farrokh, who had no choice but to obey, continued to go, in the darkness of the night and on that rugged road.

Eventually, they reached the gate, which was at the southeastern tip of Tehran. The horses' whinny was heard, Farrokh was happy and said in his heart: 'I will shout as soon as I get close to the carriage, and with the help of their passengers, I will get rid of these two ignorant gendarmes.' But as they got closer, he saw a carriage with two gendarmes on horseback standing around it.
"Why are you so late? I was about to despair and move on, so did you finally arrest him?" Someone shouted from inside the carriage.
Then one of the gendarmes, who had gotten off the horse, replied:

"Chief, we arrested him earlier in the night on Shemiran Street and brought him from behind the gates without anyone noticing"
Then that came out of the carriage and approached Farrokh, and said in a mocking tone:
"You must have been very confused by this; But I will tell you the reason, according to the order of the director general, you have been considered a fugitive and I had an order to arrest you!"
Farrokh was shocked to hear the word fugitive and said softly:
"You have made a mistake, I have never dealt with the gendarmerie. My name is Farrokh, I was neither a tax collector, nor a thief, and never had worked in the governmental offices. I am young and unemployed."
The official laughed out loud in response.
"That Farrokh should be arrested and go to Kalat."
Hearing the name of Kalat, he jumped up and this time protested loudly:
"Sir, what have I done that you are imprisoning me in Kalat? How can you bother people like this?"

He remembered the captives he had seen the other day on the street among the gendarmes. His eyes were gradually becoming accustomed to the darkness. And heard the deputy say dryly:
"I no longer have time to answer your questions, you must go to Kalat without making any noise and protest, and you should be very happy that you will go from here to Khatunabad in a carriage, but of course for the rest of the way you should not make these comfort promises to yourself because you have to walk after that."

Farrokh thought that he was dreaming, that the official was talking to him with complete composure, as he was dealing with thieves and criminals. He suddenly felt the gendarme's wire whip on his back and heard someone violently ordering:
"Be quick, go in the carriage."
And when he could not move, two gendarmes pick him up and threw him in the middle of the carriage. The carriage immediately set off on the road to Khorasan. It was four o'clock in the morning.

The carriage was moving fast. Farrokh had been silent for a while, he knew that he could not get rid of the gendarmes and their hard-hearted chief, so thought maybe using a soft tongue would work. He started talking in an effective tone that his old father would surely perish waiting for him and that some people's lives would disturb distressed by this incident. But Nayeb Jalal Khan, who had not yet forgotten the promises of F... Al-Sultaneh who would help his promotion to be secured soon, listened calmly and hard-heartedly to all the young man's statements and reasoning. In the end, he alleviated Farrokh's troubled mind, and revealed the reason for his arrest:

"It seems that you have done some curiosities during your life and bothered some important people who are considered to be the pillars of our lives, so-called aristocrats and nobles. According to the verdict issued by one of them, you are going to go to Kalat for a while to get rid of these useless thoughts, but I hope that they will soon forgive you and issue the verdict of innocence again. But, of course, this case depends on you to stop your madness from now on, and in the first stage, join your future comrades and go to Kalat without any objection and with gentleness, and do not say words that you were used to!"

Farrokh did not argue with him anymore, he understood that there is no hope for that deputy who is a petty eater of influential people and nothing would affect his stone heart, so he decided to endure with courage and patience what F... Al-Saltaneh and his accomplices have put him into, and to wait for the day of his salvation.

They arrived in Khatunabad, and the official got off the carriage and introduced him as a delicious madman so that Farrokh's true words would not be accepted by the prisoners and sedition would arise. But those prisoners, seeing Farrokh's face and his innocent demeanor, soon realized the baselessness of the official's statements and made sure that he was as miserable as they were.

Farrokh, as he had decided, not object to the statements of the gendarme, looked down at him with contempt and then went to a corner, but at once his physical and mental strength was exhausted, fell and his cheek faced the ground. Some prisoners, who were crying, were deeply moved to see him, and crowds gathered around him, each speaking in consolation. But Farrokh did not answer and cried slowly.

An hour later, the officer ordered them to move, and the gendarmes surrounded the prisoners. Farrokh, while lowering his head, walked slowly among the other prisoners, who were now considered his comrades.

Occasionally, along the way, they came across a mail coach or a rental carriage. Farrokh was hoping that he might be an acquaintance among their passengers and hid among the prisoners out of embarrassment. Every step that he got farther than Tehran and the residence of his father, his hope of salvation turned to despair. The unfortunate young man, who was not used to walking, now has to walk for days.

Farrokh did not understand the reason for this unbearable oppression they were facing, and he kept asking himself what sin he had committed and who he had killed, and what feeble he had trampled on, that such punishment has been inflicted, and finally, after much thought, he found a reason to this problem:

'It seems that my only mistake was that I went the wrong way in my life because if I were a thief and a hypocrite, a deceiver, and a selfish person, I would certainly not have such difficulties!'

Farrokh saw himself on the path of nothingness. He had no hope of returning, he had to forget seeing his beloved Mahin again...In the meantime, he remembered the last word of Shokoofeh, and he asked himself: 'Mahin is pregnant, will we have a son or a daughter?'

Chapter Forty
When Tears Flowed From F… Sultaneh's Eyes

Six months have passed.

It was an early spring night, and the cold breeze that had left the winter's army was blowing. The branches of the trees, which were still devoid of beautiful green leaves, showed their naked limbs like poor men who had no clothes in winter and trembled from the cold wind.

The river water was abundant that season, flowed rapidly in its rugged path, and every time it hit the rocks, made a frightening sound in that silence of the night. There was another sound as if it had just risen to the tune of the roaring water of the river, but it sounded more like a groan, rising from the room of a mansion built in a large garden.

The garden overlooked the river, and this was the lament of the young woman who was giving birth to a human being to endure suffering and hardship in the world.

There were two other women in that room next to the young woman. One of them, who seemed older and in a higher position, kept giving the pregnant woman evil glances, and instead of being kind to the young woman who was suffering from pain. The young woman had twisted, moaned, and screamed.

"You are going to give birth to a bastard, what are your sighs and groans for?" The older unkind woman shouted.

Then the third woman, who could not bear such cruelty and injustice, stood up and gently reminded:

"Ma'am, it is not the time for this talk!"

The young woman was in severe pain and did not pay attention to what the two had said.

"Firoozeh, where is the midwife? Why has she not come yet?" The old lady asked the other woman.

"She will arrive at any minute. They left after her as soon as Mahin's Pain started."

A quarter of an hour later, the door opened and a woman hurried in. Malek Taj took a breath when she saw her and asked:

"Tavoos, why are you so late?"

Tavoos was a short lady with a large oblique nose, round eyes, and brown

hair took off his black chador and threw it aside. She wanted to get close to Mahin as soon as possible to deliver the baby, but Mahin Taj whispered in her ear:
"Tavoos, see no evil, hear no evil! You will do the job, get your money and stay silent!"
Tavoos seemed familiar with this sort of situation and had reassured her. Malek Taj was relieved and convinced. Then the Tavoos went to Mahin's bedside and said that they still have time. The girl's moans grew louder and louder by the minute, the intensifying wind blowing in that night.

It was more than six months that Mahin has been living in that Jafara-bad garden due to her father's order. She had not seen Farrokh for several months. Her mother used to go there three days a week, and the girl spent the rest of the day under the care of one or two servants and Firoozeh.
His father came to see her from time to time. Her only constant companion was Firoozeh, who, despite the compassion and grief felt for his little lady, did not dare to take the slightest action to relieve her concern towards Far-rokh. There was no news about Farrokh.

Finally, that night came to the moment when the loudest moan was heard, then Tavoos voice rose, while holding the baby up into the air with his bony hands, "Praise is to God, she gave birth to a boy."
Mahin was searching for her son's eyes.

Mahin became feverish, and her mood worsened every moment. She was suffering from severe mental fatigue and exhaustion throughout her stay in Shemiran as if she had asked nature and God to only let her live until she gave birth to a baby. As soon as the baby was delivered, she became more and more miserable. It seemed that Mahin's forces were gone all at once and her weak body and tired soul had done their last duty. Mahin was burning with fever, sometimes cried, and sometimes uttered Farrokh's name slowly. Then, with great difficulty, she turned to the little creature who was the fruit of her love and looked at the baby with a gaze that only they two felt the meaning of.

Mahin did not know why nature should cause her suffering so much and why it condemned her to endure those sufferings.

The next day, her father, who had learned the news, arrived there, but he did not stop the violent behavior and mockingly asked how she was. Mahin was severely inflamed by the fever, and turned her face towards the wall so that her eyes could not catch her father's eyes as she replied to him.
"Thank you, I'm very well."

Her father, who could not refrain from taunting and reprimanding the girl, rebuke her again:

"God willing, now that you are a mother, you will become wise, in any case, I have brought the doctor with me to see you."

The doctor looked at Mahin, congregated her while examining her, checked her pulse, and smiled, then left the room.

Outside the room, pulled aside her father, and in a trembling voice said: "You are a man, you can handle everything, do not rush to go to the city. It would be better if you do not leave your daughter and your wife alone."

F... Al-Saltaneh, who had hitherto withstood the gentle feelings of his daughter like a hard stone, lost his train of thoughts and words. He shivered and asked the doctor, stuttering with great worry and fear:

"What happened? What do you say? But ... what will happen to my daughter Mahin?"

The doctor saw his condition, and consoled him for fear that he might cause a stroke:

"There is nothing, God willing, she will get better, but of course, you have to be careful and not leave her alone."

The doctor's loud voice pounded into his iron heart like a hammer, as if each of his words lifted a thick veil from his eyes.

F... Al-Saltaneh did not stand there anymore and went straight to his wife, who was still sitting in the side room with Firoozeh.

"Did you see what happened to us?" F... Al-Saltaneh helplessly said.

Minutes later, everyone gathered around Mahin. The girl, who had suffered for more than nine months, had suffered a lot from her father's tyranny and her mother's ignorance, seemed to be no longer able to tolerate life. Mahin realized her plight, and felt that soon she would give up all the joys and pleasures of this world. Her thoughts were with Farrokh. Her fever got worse. She did not know where he is. She whispered her last thought:

"Who knows, maybe I too gave birth to another misfortunate?"

Then her delicate shoulders shook violently and her eyes were fixed on the ceiling of the room.

Morteza Moshfeq Kazemi
Tehran, 1922